Worlds Collide

A World So Cold Universe, Volume 2

Jordan Simpson

Published by Jordan Simpson, 2024.

WORLDS COLLIDE

First edition. December 13, 2024.

Copyright © 2024 Jordan Simpson.

ISBN: 979-8230689683

Written by Jordan Simpson.

To My loving Mother And Father, Thank you For Following Me On This Journey

Worlds Collide

Author: Jordan Simpson

Prologue

1 - 2

The pungent smell of damp earth and asphalt rose in the still evening as Drake Miller's black sedan snaked along the wet road. Streetlights cast an eerie sheen on the surface, making the lane markers shimmer like ghostly ribbons. Without warning, the peace was shattered; a screech echoed through the night, a banshee wail of rubber against pavement. Drake's grip tightened around the steering wheel, instincts kicking in too late as the car spun out of control, a sleek projectile launched into the void.

His world became a maelstrom of sound and motion—metal groaned and glass shattered, punctuating the symphony of destruction. The vehicle, once a testament to luxury and status, was now a tumbling coffin, descending with reckless abandon down the hillside. Each revolution, a tempest of confusion and fear, flung Drake against the confines of his seatbelt's embrace.

When stillness finally claimed the wreckage, Drake swam back to consciousness through a haze of pain and disorientation. His head throbbed in protest, and he could feel the warm trickle of blood where his temple had met resistance. His hands fumbled, patting down the fabric of his suit, no longer pristine but torn asunder, betraying the violence of their descent.

"Li-Linda?" His voice was a ragged whisper, the sound foreign even to his own ears. No answer came but the soft patter of rain beginning to fall, nature weeping for the tragedy it witnessed.

He turned, agony lancing through him as he sought his wife. Linda, his pillar of reason, lay slumped, her chest rising and falling with a rhythm agonizingly too shallow. Her blonde hair, usually so carefully styled, was a halo of disarray around her pallid face.

"Harrison," Drake gasped, twisting to see their son. The boy, a mirror to his ambition, with dreams that soared as high as the skyscrapers of his father's cases, was motionless in his seat, a fragile doll in the hands of fate. In the dimness, Drake could make out the Spider-Man tie Harrison had insisted on wearing, now spotted with droplets that weren't from rain.

"Stay with me," Drake urged, though his words seemed to dissolve into the oppressive silence that had reclaimed the scene. His family, his entire world, reduced to whispered prayers amongst the carnage.

Drake's mind reeled, trying to piece together the fragments of what had led them here—the arguments about time never spent, the cases that took precedence over bedtime stories, the promises of 'one day' that may have perished in this very car. As the sirens wailed in the distance, a mournful counterpoint to his own despair, Drake made a silent vow. If they survived this, if destiny granted him that grace, he would change. They would not be a footnote in the ledger of his life; they would be the very narrative itself.

But as the darkness encroached and the first responders' lights pierced the night, Drake could only cling to the hope that there would be a chance for redemption.

3 - 4

The sound of Dr. Evans' voice was like a lifeline, distant but distinct through the haze of Drake's shock-addled mind. "So, tell me how it works."

Drake blinked, and the present moment seemed to slip away, enveloped by the fog of his recollections. There he was, standing in the grand foyer of Miller & Co., the polished marble floors reflecting the gleam of ambition in his eyes. The air was thick with the musk of leather-bound books and the sharp tang of ink—a scent that was as invigorating to him as the aroma of dark-roast coffee.

His hands felt the weight of case files, thick with the promise of victory and prestige. Each one was a stepping stone to greater heights, a chance to outshine the luminaries of legal lore that lined the oak shelves of his spacious office. He had been relentless in his pursuit, a hunter stalking success through the dense jungle of legislation and legal precedent.

Around him, the office buzzed like a hive of industrious bees. Phones rang incessantly, a cacophony of negotiations and litigious strategies. His colleagues, dressed in suits as sharp as their wits, moved with deliberate urgency. They were allies in battle, yet rivals in the silent war where only the most cunning and resilient could claim triumph.

In this world of perpetual motion, he had thrived, feeding off the challenge, the adrenaline, the thrill of a well-earned win. But at what cost? Memories of missed anniversaries, cold dinners, and empty seats at school plays began to creep into the edges of his consciousness, painting a stark contrast to the glossy image of success.

"Tell me how it works," Dr. Evans had said, and in that question lay the unspoken reality. How did the mechanism of his life operate, with its gears greased by sacrifice and its cogs turning ever away from the simple joys that made existence meaningful?

"Drake?" The voice called again, tethering him to the here and now, pulling him back from the precipice of his past.

5 - 6

Drake pushed through the glass doors, the gentle chime above signaling his entry into a world far removed from the courtroom's harsh lights and the sterile chill of the hospital room he had woken up in. The overhead lights here bathed him in warmth, softening the lines of worry that had etched themselves across his forehead. He paused, allowing the calmness of the reception area to envelop him.

The walls, painted in tones of cream and beige, seemed to absorb the buzz of anxiety that had followed him like a shadow. His eyes wandered over the artwork—a landscape serene, a portrait contemplative—each piece chosen with care to inspire ease rather than provoke thought. For a moment, Drake let himself admire their simplicity, a stark contrast to the complexities of his own life which Dr. Evans so keenly dissected.

Behind the desk, a receptionist with a smile as inviting as the atmosphere looked up from her monitor. "Mr. Miller," she greeted, voice melodic against the backdrop of the instrumental music whispering through the air. She was the gatekeeper of this tranquil domain, her polished wooden desk a testament to order amid chaos. Files stood sentinel in neat stacks, and the computer screen flickered with names and times, each slot an appointment filled with hopes for healing.

"Good morning," Drake replied, his voice steadier than he felt. Here, in this pocket of tranquility, the relentless drive that fueled his days at Miller & Co. seemed distant, almost foreign. He approached, drawn by the promise of understanding that waited beyond the veneer of professionalism.

"Is it still pouring outside?" the receptionist asked, her concern genuine as she took note of the droplets clinging to his overcoat.

"Coming down in sheets," Drake confirmed, offering a half-smile that did not quite reach his eyes. The storm outside mirrored the turmoil within—a tempest of regret and ambition that no amount of success could quell. But inside these walls, the chaos was held at bay, if only for the length of a consultation.

"Dr. Evans will see you shortly," she assured him, her fingers dancing across the keyboard to check him in. "You can take a moment to relax."

"Thank you," he said, appreciating the normalcy of the interaction. It grounded him, a lifeline thrown across the turbulent sea of his thoughts. As he moved aside, allowing another soul seeking solace to approach the desk, Drake wondered if the doctor's office could offer the peace that the accolades and accomplishments adorning his office walls never could.

7 - 8

Drake slumped into one of the comfortable chairs that lined the waiting area, the plush fabric a welcome cradle to his weary form. His fingers traced the edge of the coffee table before him, mindlessly flipping through the stack of magazines and informational brochures without really seeing them. The chair seemed to envelope him in its embrace, offering solace from the weight of the world outside.

Through the large windows, the grey light of the stormy morning diffused into the room, casting soft shadows across the floor. Drake's gaze wandered between the droplets streaming down the glass and the contrasting view they framed—a slice of a serene garden with rain-speckled flowers bowing under the downpour, and beyond, the relentless energy of the cityscape, where cars streaked by, indifferent to the tempest.

He found his attention drawn back inside as another patient reached for a cup beside the water dispenser near the reception desk. The gentle burble of the water coupled with the rustle of paper cups was oddly soothing. A potted plant perched on the corner of the nook, its leaves a vibrant green that stood out against the neutral palette of the office decor. For a moment, Drake allowed himself to fixate on the simplicity of the plant's existence, envious of its stillness amidst the human complexities that filled the room.

The tranquility was a stark contrast to the cacophony of a life spent in courtrooms and board meetings. Here, there were no deadlines, no ringing phones demanding immediate answers, no clients with insatiable needs. Just the quiet hum of an office serving as a refuge from the chaos, the steady beat of rain against window panes, and the chance, perhaps, to untangle the knots in his soul.

9 - 10

Drake followed the nurse down the corridor, the soft soles of his shoes silent against the polished tile. The hallway stretched ahead like a pristine artery of the clinic, its cleanliness projecting an air of meticulous care. He glanced at the doors they passed, each bearing a nameplate with the promise of expert attention: Dr. L. Ramirez - Cardiologist, Dr. J. Cho - Neurologist, and so forth.

They stopped before a door marked simply with his own doctor's name. The nurse gestured for him to enter, her smile as bright as the light spilling from the open doorway. Inside, the examination room was a blend of clinical precision and human touch. An examination table stood at the center, its paper cover crisp and unwrinkled, surrounded by instruments that gleamed with the sterility of unblemished metal. A blood pressure cuff hung neatly on the wall beside a chart detailing the intricacies of the human heart, its pathways colored in vivid reds and blues.

Drake eased into a chair designed more for comfort than he would have expected in such a place. The cushioning embraced his weary frame while he eyed the diagrams that adorned the walls—a visual education. They told stories of the body's complexities, illustrated in a way that made the invisible workings within him seem less daunting, more understandable.

A scale model of the spine sat on a small table, vertebrae aligned with textbook perfection, and Drake found his fingers tracing the curve of his own back, contemplating the invisible architecture that held him upright. Here, in the quietude of the examination room, the professional facade he presented to the world outside could be shed. He was not Attorney Miller with the sharp mind and sharper tongue; he was simply a man, fallible and fragile, seeking answers or perhaps solace in the hands of medicine.

The soft lighting seemed to hush the voices in his head—the constant strategizing, the mental rehearsals of courtroom battles—and in their stead, a rare peace settled over him. This was a space where vulnerabilities were not weaknesses, but keys to healing. And as he waited for the doctor to arrive, Drake allowed himself to embrace the strange comfort found in the sterile scents and the soothing geometry of health charts, finding in their certainties a temporary respite from the uncertainties that waited beyond these walls.

11 - 12

Dr. Evans' fingers danced lightly over the keys, each tap punctuating the silence that filled the room between the soft hum of the computer and the gentle whir of medical equipment from the hallway outside. The doctor's gaze remained fixed on the screen, his expression unreadable behind wire-rimmed glasses that caught the glow of the monitor.

Drake shifted in the chair, the white upholstery cool against his skin despite the warmth radiating from his body. His hand instinctively went to his neck, thumb rubbing at the knot that seemed perpetually lodged there since the accident. He could feel the weight of Dr. Evans' attention shift towards him, though the doctor's eyes did not leave the keypad.

"I don't know," Drake began, voice a low murmur filled with the weariness of long days and longer nights. "I'd close my eyes. I open them. Just like you." His words hung in the air, a confession stripped of pretense, revealing the raw edges beneath his polished exterior.

There was a pause, a cessation of keystrokes, as if the admission had disrupted some unspoken rhythm between patient and healer. And in that quiet space, Drake wrestled with the vulnerability that came with laying one's psyche bare, even in the pursuit of understanding.

13 - 14

Dr. Evans finally halted his typing, the cessation of clicks bringing a stillness that seemed to amplify the distant echo of footfalls in the corridor outside. He peered over the rim of his glasses at Drake, who sat slumped slightly forward, his hands clasped as if he were about to unravel the very fabric of his thoughts.

"Very well. You're back to work?" Dr. Evans' voice was tinged with a professional curiosity, his head tilted slightly as he studied his patient, assessing the weight of his words against the shadows beneath his eyes.

Drake blinked slowly, the question dragging him from the murky depths of introspection. "Yes," he answered, and there was a heaviness to the word, like an anchor tethered to his soul. The office around him seemed alien, a stark contrast to the familiar battleground of litigation and legal strategy. "Though it feels like a lifetime ago."

The statement lingered between them, laden with an unspoken truth that Drake had yet to face fully. In those four walls, time was both enemy and ally, and every second spent recounting the past was a step away from the remnants of the life he once knew.

15 - 16

Drake's gaze locked onto the wreckage, the twisted metal a stark reminder of how quickly life could unravel. The crash site swarmed with the hurried movements of first responders and the murmurs of onlookers formed a low, incessant drone. He threaded his way through the crowd, each step steadying his resolve. The future of Miller & Co. hinged on his ability to compartmentalize, to focus not on the personal calamity but on the empire he had built.

"Drake," a voice cut through the clamor, charged with urgency. Vega, his silhouette sharp against the blur of flashing lights, closed the distance between them in swift strides. His eyes, usually calm and calculating, now bore an intensity that matched the gravity of the night.

"We need to talk. The Chaisson deposition, what's your strategy?" Vega's words tumbled out, barely above a whisper, yet they landed with the weight of the concrete blocks that lay scattered around the hillside.

Drake's mind, momentarily derailed by the scent of burnt rubber and gasoline, snapped back to the legal battlefield. He knew the Chaisson case was a linchpin for the firm's reputation, and Vega's timely reminder served as a rallying cry amidst the chaos.

17 - 18

Drake's fingers traced the edge of his sleeve, the fabric fraying where it had brushed against the stark reality of asphalt and broken dreams. The sterile scent of the doctor's office was a stark contrast to the acrid smoke still clinging to his senses, a lingering ghost from the crash site. He was here but not present, his thoughts ensnared in the tumultuous events that led to this moment.

"Drake?" Dr. Evans' voice coaxed him back, its gentle inflection grounding him to the now — the ticking clock on the wall, the soft whir of the air conditioning, the comforting certainty of four walls and a roof. "And they've got you working with a partner?"

He blinked slowly, matching the rhythm of the rain tapping against the window pane. "Yes, Vega. He's new, but he's eager to prove himself." Drake's words emerged detached, as if spoken by someone else — someone watching his life unfold from a distance.

Vega's face flashed in his mind, sharp and earnest, a stark reminder of ambition. That same ambition now seemed like a distant echo in the hollow chamber of Drake's chest. His new partner's zeal felt like a relic from a past life, one where the scent of rain meant nothing more than a change in weather, not a harbinger of personal cataclysm.

"New," he muttered again, almost to himself, "and eager." It was an affirmation of sorts, a lifeline thrown into the sea of uncertainty that churned within him. Vega, with all his hunger for success, might just be the beacon that Miller & Co. needed — that Drake needed — to navigate the stormy waters ahead.

19 - 20

Drake's fingers drummed an absent rhythm on the mahogany surface of his desk, a stark contrast to the organized chaos of legal briefs and court documents that surrounded him. Each stack was a monument to his victories, yet their shadows cast long doubts across the gleaming nameplate: Drake Miller, Esq. The office buzzed with the energy of phones ringing and keyboards clacking, a symphony of success that played on loop from nine to five.

But behind the door marked 'Private,' in this sanctuary of leather-bound books and diplomas framed in gold, the air felt heavier, charged with unspoken truths. Here, where deals were made and alliances forged, the line between right and wrong often blurred like ink on damp paper. Drake's gaze swept over the accolades decorating his walls — each one a story, a secret, a silent compromise.

"Miller!" The voice cut through the din outside, sharp and insistent, but it might as well have been miles away. He leaned back in his chair, the leather creaking under his weight, and closed his eyes for a moment, allowing himself a brief escape from the relentless march of ambition.

"Drake?" Dr. Evans' voice probed once more, softer this time, pulling him out of the darkness that threatened to swallow him whole at his own desk. "And are you okay?"

A simple question, yet it hung in the air like a verdict waiting to be passed. Drake opened his eyes, the accolades coming back into focus, each one a reminder of what he had built and what it had cost. The corners of his mouth lifted in a practiced facsimile of reassurance as he met the doctor's gaze.

"Okay?" he echoed, weighing the word, testing its substance. It was a suit tailored to fit any occasion, versatile enough for courtroom battles and hospital visits alike. But now, it hung off him awkwardly, the seams straining against the truth.

"Okay is a relative term, isn't it, Doctor?" His response skirted the edges of the question, leaving room for interpretation, much like the closing arguments he so skillfully crafted in court.

"Indeed," Dr. Evans agreed, noting the evasion with a small nod, understanding that some questions take more than words to answer.

21 - 21

Drake's fingers drummed a staccato rhythm on the mahogany surface of his desk, betraying an undercurrent of tension that belied his calm exterior. The office around him hummed with the energy of legal minds at work, each absorbed in their own intricate dance of persuasion and power. Yet, the symphony of clicking keyboards and muted conversations seemed to recede as he contemplated Dr. Evans' question.

It was a momentary divergence—a brief lift of the veil that shrouded his thoughts when the walls of his fortress-like office felt less like protection and more like a prison. His gaze swept over the cityscape outside his window, the skyline jagged with the teeth of skyscrapers biting into the gray veil of dusk. They stood as monuments to ambition, yet now they appeared as something else—silent sentinels to a reality only partially perceived.

"Drake?" The doctor's voice pulled him back from the precipice of introspection, and Drake turned his chair slowly to face him.

He leaned forward, elbows resting on the desk, hands clasped together as if to anchor himself to the present. "I'm fine," he said, the words measured and deliberate. However, it was the pause that followed, a breath held too long, that carried the weight of unspoken truths.

"But this world..." A flicker of something indefinable crossed his face—was it doubt, fear, or perhaps the glimmer of revelation? "...is not what it seems."

In those words, Drake Miller, the prominent attorney known for his tenacity and unwavering logic, allowed a crack to form in the façade of certainty that he presented to the courtrooms and boardrooms alike. It was an acknowledgment of the invisible threads that wove through the tapestry of his life, hinting at a pattern that escaped easy comprehension.

Dr. Evans regarded him quietly, the silence stretching between them not as an absence of sound but as a space for contemplation. In that office, where every inch spoke of victories hard-won and a reputation meticulously crafted, Drake had voiced an uncertainty that resonated with the echo of something deeper—a sense that the fabric of his existence was interwoven with strands of enigma and paradox.

The clock ticked on, indifferent to the gravity of the moment, as Drake sat there, the master of argument and articulation, suddenly finding himself at the edge of an uncharted expanse that lay beyond the familiar battlegrounds of law and order.

Awakening in Darkness

1 – 2

The Green World - 2024

Her eyelids fluttered, heavy as if glued shut, and when they cracked open, there was nothing—no light, no shapes, just an all-consuming blackness that threatened to swallow her whole.

A sharp intake of breath meant to scream, but it ended in a choked gasp, her lungs rebelling against the weight crushing her chest. She lay still for a moment, trying to will away the panic clawing at her insides, her heart thrashing wildly like a caged bird against ribs that felt as though they were bound by iron.

Her hands, trembling, sought the boundaries of her dark prison. Fingertips skated over what felt like cold earth inches from her face—a confining dome that allowed no room for movement. The reality of her situation sank in with the dirt that began to slip through her frantic fingers: she was buried alive.

3 - 4

Linda's chest heaved, each breath a battle against the invisible weight that threatened to crush her. Fear, thick and visceral, pulsed through her veins, filling the cramped space with its bitter taste. The air was stale, heavy, and every inhalation felt like breathing through a wet cloth. Her heart hammered against her sternum, a drumbeat of terror that resonated through the void that held her captive.

In the pitch-black cocoon, her mind churned with chaotic speed. Thoughts ricocheted off the walls of her consciousness, disjointed and wild. They were whispers of dread, fragmented sentences that spoke of despair, yet she grappled with them, trying to forge them into a ladder of reason that might lead her out of this abyss.

Amidst the turmoil, memories flickered to life—ethereal and taunting. She saw the sun-drenched kitchen of her home, felt the warm embrace of sunlight on her skin as she watched her son chase soap bubbles across the lawn, his laughter a melody that once filled her days. She could almost feel the solid presence of her husband beside her, his hand finding hers, fingers intertwining in silent communion.

But these flashes of a life so cherished, so full of color and warmth, now seemed like phantoms from another world. Each recollection was a spectral image that faded as quickly as it appeared, leaving her colder, more alone. The oppressive silence of her earthen cell swallowed the echoes of her past, leaving only the stark reality of her present—a reality where those moments of joy and love felt as remote as stars in a sky she could no longer see.

5 - 6

Linda's fingers, caked with earth, clawed at the compact soil above her. Each breath was a battle against the weight that pressed like a silent behemoth upon her chest. The darkness wrapped around her like a shroud, and the cold embrace of the grave seeped into her bones. Yet in this constricted space, where each movement was an agony, her hands moved with desperate purpose. They scraped and dug, fingernails breaking against the unyielding dirt that threatened to become her eternal bed.

Panic threatened to overwhelm her, a beast gnashing at the edges of her resolve. It whispered of surrender, of the ease of slipping into the void that beckoned with a siren's call. But as her mind teetered on the brink of madness, she felt something within her stir—an ember of defiance that refused to be smothered. Her body, though pinned and powerless, burned with a furious need to survive.

Muscles strained against the prison of earth, her limbs fueled by an instinctive terror of the abyss. But it was more than mere fear that drove her now; it was an awakening, a reborn will that glimmered faintly in the dark. Linda seized upon it, fanning the flame with every indrawn breath, with every heartbeat that pounded a frenetic rhythm against her ribcage.

"Survive," she whispered to herself, the word a mantra that carved through the dread. "Survive for them." In her mind's eye, the faces of her family emerged, their smiles a distant promise. She imagined her son's laughter, a sound that once filled her world with light. It was this thought, this piercing shard of hope, that lent her a strength she had not known she possessed.

Her arms worked with renewed vigor, pushing against the crushing despair. Small clods of dirt began to give way, loosening under her frantic efforts. With each small victory, the determination within her grew bolder, eclipsing the shadows that sought to claim her.

"Survive," she urged herself again, the word echoing in the hollow chamber of her makeshift tomb. And with each repetition, the darkness seemed a fraction less absolute, the walls of her confinement a measure less constricting. Linda, buried but unbowed, continued her struggle, rallying against the very earth that sought to claim her.

7 - 8

Linda's fingers scraped against the jagged edges of her earthen cell, her breaths shallow and ragged. Mud caked beneath her nails, a testament to her refusal to succumb to the grave's embrace. Each gasp for air was a whisper of resistance, and with it, her thoughts crystallized around the images of her husband and son. They shone like twin stars in the murky oblivion, their love piercing through the veil of fear and darkness.

"Drake... Harrison..." she mouthed silently, the names instilling a surge of warmth that coursed through her chilled veins. She imagined Drake's steady gaze, the one that had always anchored her in life's tumultuous seas. Harrison's youthful exuberance, a beacon that now guided her through this abyss. It was for them, for the future they deserved, that she mustered the will to endure, to claw her way back to the realm of the living.

Her resolve hardened like the earth that entrapped her, every memory of her loved ones fortifying her spirit. Linda's heart pounded with a rhythm that defied the silence, each beat a drum call to battle the dark. She could not, would not, let this be her end. Not while the faintest hope of reunion flickered in the distance.

The rawness in her throat ebbed as she focused on the fragments of recollection, piecing together the puzzle of her predicament. There was a glint of metal, the screech of tires—a symphony of chaos that had crescendoed into silence. The echoes of those final conscious moments danced before her, elusive specters that she chased with desperate need for understanding.

"Remember," she coaxed herself, the word a lifeline thrown into the churning sea of her mind. She grasped at the flashes of light, the snatches of sound, weaving them into a lifeline back to the world she knew. A world where sunlight kissed her face, where the wind whispered through the trees, where her family awaited her return.

With renewed fervor, Linda pushed against the compacted soil, her body screaming in protest, yet unyielding. Each inch of progress was a step towards the life that called to her, a life she was determined to reclaim. The darkness would not have her—not today, not ever. For amidst the terror, nestled within the confines of her own resolute heart, Linda held an unwavering conviction: she would emerge from this nightmarish chrysalis.

9 - 10

Gritting her teeth, Linda scraped at the earth above her, each handful of soil a small victory against her premature burial. Her fingers, raw and bleeding, became conduits for the memories that assaulted her—each one a shard of glass in the mosaic of her life's tapestry.

And there it was, vivid against the black: Drake's presence enveloped her, his blood—a warm, viscous lifeline—mingled with hers in an intimate tableau of survival. The memory surged with startling clarity. She could almost feel the heat radiating from his skin, the tremor of his hands as they pressed against the wound on her arm, staunching the flow. His eyes, wide with terror and determination, locked onto hers, conveying a silent but urgent message. "Stay with me," they seemed to plead, even as chaos roared around them—a conflagration of noise and fear that had led to this dark silence.

"Mom?"

The voice jolted her, ethereal and yet so achingly real. Harrison. Her heart clenched with the rawness of maternal love, pulsing like a beacon through the oppressive shadows. "Harrison?" she whispered, her voice hoarse, breaths coming in ragged gasps. Was it possible? Could he be here, reaching out to her through the suffocating layers of earth and despair?

"Mom, you need to wake up."

His words were a whisper across time and space, yet they resonated with the power of a tempest. For a moment, the darkness receded, replaced by the image of her son's face—his eyes reflecting the same fierce resolve that burned within her own. Linda seized upon his voice, let it guide her, tethering her to the world she so desperately sought to rejoin.

"Fight, Mom."

The soft command spurred her onward, igniting a spark deep within her chest. Yes, she would fight. For her son, for her husband, for the touch of sunlight and the breath of wind. For life itself. Clawing through the heavy earth, Linda embraced the pain, the fatigue, the fear—all transformed into fuel for her ascent. She would not succumb to the dark embrace of the grave. Not while her son's voice called her home.

11 - 12

Linda's fingertips grazed the locket, its cold metal a sharp contrast to the warmth of her son's voice that still lingered in her mind. Her breath hitched as she tried to hold onto the sensation, to keep him near. But just as her heart swelled with the possibility of his closeness, light erupted behind her closed eyelids—a searing explosion that banished the shadows.

"Harri—" The name died on her lips as the light receded as quickly as it had appeared, taking with it the presence of her boy. Her arms reached out, grasping at the empty space where his voice had been, her fingers clenching nothing but emptiness. The silence that followed was deafening, the darkness once again absolute.

A sob caught in her throat. She longed for his embrace, to see his smile, to hear his laughter—one more time. But reality was a cruel master, and she remained alone, entombed beneath the earth. Linda pressed her palm against the cool earth above her, each grain of soil a testament to the distance between her and the world she yearned to return to.

Yet, even as despair threatened to overtake her, something flickered within. It was more than the instinct to survive; it was a mother's love, unyielding and fierce. The memory of her family, of their last embrace, their final words, became a lifeline in the consuming void. Linda closed her eyes, not to succumb to the blackness, but to visualize their faces—her husband's encouraging nod, Harrison's impish grin. They were her strength, her reason, her everything.

The locket against her chest seemed to pulse with her heartbeat, a beacon of hope against the crushing dark. Linda drew a deep, steadying breath. She would not let this be her end. For them, she would claw through the night, battle the suffocation, and fight her way back to the light.

"Remember," she whispered to herself, the word a vow etched into her very soul. "Remember love, remember life." Every memory, every shared moment, was a spark that ignited the will she needed to push forward, to resist the grave's embrace.

And so, with the love for her family lighting her way, Linda began once more the arduous journey, inch by painstaking inch, toward the distant promise of the surface. Each movement was a declaration, each breath a challenge to the dark: she would return. She must return. For Harrison. For all of them.

Beneath the Lillies

The Red World – 2024

1 - 2

Drake stood motionless amidst the sea of black suits and dresses, his eyes fixed on the twin mahogany caskets before him. The scent of lilies hung heavy in the air, mingling with the damp earthiness of freshly turned soil.

He felt a hand on his shoulder and turned to see his best friend John, eyes rimmed with red. "I'm so sorry, Drake. Linda and Harrison...they were such bright lights. This isn't right."

Drake nodded numbly, John's words washing over him like white noise. Nothing felt real anymore. Three weeks ago he'd been in a coma, lost in the hazy realm between life and death. When he finally clawed his way back to consciousness, it was to a waking nightmare - his beloved family ripped away forever.

The memories came unbidden then, flashes of happier times superimposed over the bleak present. Harrison's gap-toothed grin as Drake pushed him on the swing. Linda's musical laugh, her hair gleaming under the summer sun. All of it gone now, consigned to dust and fading photographs.

Drake's fingers curled into fists at his sides. It wasn't supposed to be this way. He was always the risk-taker, tempting fate with his daredevil antics. Linda was his anchor, his port in the storm. And Harrison...that boy had been his entire world.

What cruel trick of destiny allowed him to survive while they perished? He squeezed his eyes shut against the hot sting of tears.

"Drake? It's time." John's voice, gentle yet insistent, drew him back. Drake forced his eyes open to see the mourners beginning to file towards the grave site in a solemn procession.

He fell into step robotically, hands balled in the pockets of his black suit. Linda's parents stepped up beside him.

"Son, are you hanging in there?" Linda's father asked, voice gruff with emotion. "You know Linda...she adored you. Thought you hung the moon."

"I should have been with them, should have protected them. I failed them," Drake choked out, each word scraping his throat raw.

"Now you listen to me," Linda's mother interjected fiercely. "This is not your fault. Linda and Harrison loved you more than anything. They wouldn't want you blaming yourself."

Drake nodded wordlessly, afraid to speak lest the howl of anguish building in his chest rip free. As they approached the gaping mouths of the graves, he felt a wave of vertigo, as if the earth beneath his feet had given way.

He wanted to rail against the unfairness of it all, to bargain with the fates or whatever cruel gods had authored this sick cosmic joke. But he remained silent, face carved from stone, as the first shovelful of dirt thudded dully onto the coffin lids.

3 - 4

As the final prayers were uttered and the mourners began to disperse, Drake remained rooted in place, his gaze fixed upon the mounds of freshly turned earth that now entombed his heart. The sun dipped below the horizon, casting long shadows across the cemetery, but Drake paid no heed to the encroaching darkness.

"Linda, Harrison," he whispered, his voice barely audible above the wind's mournful howl. "I'm so sorry. I should have been there for you, should have protected you."

Tears streamed down his face, mingling with the dirt and grime that clung to his skin. He sank to his knees, his fingers digging into the damp soil, as if by sheer force of will he could claw his way back to them.

But even as despair threatened to consume him, a small, insistent voice whispered in the back of his mind. It was Linda's voice, the same gentle, loving tone she had always used when soothing his fears and doubts.

"Drake, my love," she seemed to say, "you mustn't blame yourself. You must be strong now, for us, for the life we shared."

And then, like a flicker of light amidst the gloom, Harrison's laughter echoed through his memories, a sound so pure and joyful that it pierced the veil of his grief.

In that moment, Drake felt a spark of something ignite within him, a tiny ember of hope that refused to be extinguished. He rose to his feet, brushing the dirt from his hands, and gazed out over the cemetery, his eyes shining with a newfound resolve.

"I won't let you down," he vowed, his voice steady and strong. "I'll carry on, for both of you. I'll make you proud."

With a final, lingering look at the graves of his beloved wife and son, Drake turned and strode out of the cemetery, his heart heavy with sorrow, but his spirit buoyed by the love and memories that would forever bind them together.

5 - 6

As Drake stepped through the iron gates of the cemetery, the weight of his grief seemed to lift ever so slightly, replaced by a sense of purpose that had been absent in the weeks since the accident. He knew that the road ahead would be long and difficult, but he also knew that he owed it to Linda and Harrison to keep going, to find a way to honor their memory and make their sacrifices mean something.

He walked slowly to his car, his mind churning with thoughts and memories. He remembered the day he and Linda had first brought Harrison home from the hospital, the way the tiny bundle had felt in his arms, so fragile and precious. He remembered the pride in Linda's eyes as they watched their son take his first steps, the joy in her laughter as they chased him through the park on sunny afternoons.

Those moments were gone now, lost to the cruel twists of fate, but Drake knew that he would carry them with him always, a testament to the love and happiness that had once filled his life.

As he reached for the car door, a sudden gust of wind rustled through the trees, carrying with it the faint scent of Linda's perfume. For a moment, Drake could almost feel her presence beside him, her hand on his shoulder, her voice in his ear.

"I'm with you," she seemed to whisper. "Always."

Drake closed his eyes, letting the sensation wash over him, a balm to his aching soul. When he opened them again, the world seemed a little brighter, the colors a little sharper. He knew that the darkness would come again, that the pain would never truly fade, but for now, he would hold onto this feeling, this glimmer of hope in the midst of his despair.

With a deep breath, Drake climbed into the car and turned the key in the ignition. As the engine roared to life, he felt a sense of determination settle over him, a resolve to face whatever challenges lay ahead. He would do it for Linda, for Harrison, for the love that had once burned so brightly between them.

And as he pulled out of the parking lot and onto the open road, Drake knew that he was not alone, that even in death, his beloved wife and son would always be with him, guiding him forward, towards a future that he could not yet see, but that he knew he must embrace with all the strength and courage he could muster.

7 - 8

The drive home was a blur, a haze of grief and memory that threatened to consume him. Drake gripped the steering wheel tightly, his knuckles turning white as he navigated the familiar streets, each turn and landmark a painful reminder of the life he had once shared with his family.

As he pulled into the driveway, the sight of the empty house loomed before him, a stark contrast to the warmth and laughter that had once filled its walls. Drake sat in the car for a long moment, his heart heavy with the weight of his loss, his mind reeling with the enormity of the task that lay ahead.

"I don't know if I can do this," he whispered, his voice barely audible over the hum of the engine. "How am I supposed to go on without them?"

But even as the words left his lips, Drake knew that he had no choice. He had to be strong, to carry on in the face of unimaginable grief, to honor the memory of his beloved wife and son in the only way he knew how.

With a deep breath, he stepped out of the car and made his way up the front steps, his hand trembling as he unlocked the door and stepped inside. The silence that greeted him was deafening, a stark reminder of the emptiness that now pervaded his once vibrant home.

Drake moved through the house like a ghost, his footsteps echoing hollowly on the hardwood floors. Everywhere he looked, he saw reminders of the life he had once shared with Linda and Harrison - a framed photograph on the mantel, a forgotten toy on the living room floor, a half-empty cup of coffee on the kitchen counter.

He paused in the doorway of their bedroom, his heart clenching at the sight of the unmade bed, the rumpled sheets still bearing the imprint of their bodies. For a moment, he could almost imagine that they were still there, that if he just closed his eyes and wished hard enough, he would wake up from this nightmare and find them beside him once again.

But the illusion was fleeting, and as the reality of his loss crashed over him once more, Drake felt the tears begin to fall, hot and bitter on his cheeks. He sank to the floor, his back against the wall, and let the grief consume him, his body shaking with the force of his sobs.

"I'm sorry," he choked out, his voice raw and broken. "I'm so sorry. I should have been there, I should have protected you. I failed you both, and now I don't know how to go on without you."

But even as the words left his lips, Drake knew that he had to find a way. He had to be strong, to carry on in the face of unimaginable grief, to honor the memory of his beloved wife and son in the only way he knew how.

And so, with a shaky breath and a trembling hand, he pushed himself to his feet and began the long, painful process of putting the pieces of his life back together, one shattered fragment at a time.

9 - 10

As the days turned into weeks, Drake found himself drawn deeper into the labyrinth of his memories, searching for solace in the echoes of happier times. He spent hours poring over old photo albums, his fingers tracing the smiling faces of Linda and Harrison, as if he could somehow reach through the glossy pages and touch them once again.

With each passing day, he felt a growing sense of unease, a nagging feeling that there was something he was missing, some crucial piece of the puzzle that remained just out of reach. He began to question the events that had led him to this moment, the choices he had made, the paths he had taken.

Late one night, as he sat in the darkened living room, nursing a glass of whiskey, a sudden realization struck him like a bolt of lightning. He set the glass down with a trembling hand, his mind racing with the implications of his discovery.

"It can't be," he whispered, his voice hoarse with emotion. "It's not possible."

But even as he spoke the words, he knew in his heart that it was true. The life he had been living, the world he had come to accept as reality, was nothing more than a façade, a carefully constructed illusion designed to keep him from the truth.

With a sense of growing urgency, Drake began to search for answers, pouring through old journals and letters, seeking out any scrap of information that might shed light on the mystery that surrounded him. And as he delved deeper into the shadows of his past, he began to uncover a web of secrets and lies that threatened to unravel everything he thought he knew.

But even as the truth began to take shape, Drake knew that he could not turn back now. He had to press on, to follow the trail wherever it might lead, no matter the cost. For somewhere out there, in the tangled threads of his fractured existence, lay the key to his redemption, the answer to the questions that had haunted him for so long.

And so, with a heavy heart and a determined spirit, Drake stepped out into the unknown, ready to face whatever challenges lay ahead, armed only with the strength of his convictions and the memory of those he loved.

11 - 12

Drake's eyes snapped open, the remnants of a half-remembered dream still clinging to the edges of his consciousness. He sat up in bed, his heart pounding, his mind racing with a thousand unanswered questions. The room around him was shrouded in darkness, the only sound the gentle ticking of the clock on the nightstand.

He reached for the lamp, his fingers fumbling in the shadows until they found the switch. The soft glow of the bulb illuminated the room, casting long shadows across the walls. Drake's gaze fell upon the pile of papers and photographs scattered across his desk, the fruits of his labors over the past few weeks.

Since the funeral, he had thrown himself into the task of unraveling the mystery of his past, searching for any clue that might help him make sense of the fragmented memories that haunted his every waking moment. But the more he searched, the more questions he seemed to uncover, each one leading him deeper into a labyrinth of secrets and lies.

Drake swung his legs over the side of the bed, his bare feet touching the cold hardwood floor. He stood up, stretching his arms above his head, feeling the kinks and knots in his muscles slowly unwind. He padded over to the desk, his eyes scanning the chaos of papers and pictures, searching for something, anything that might help him make sense of it all.

13 - 14

As the first rays of dawn pierced through the veil of night, Drake found himself standing at the edge of a precipice, both literal and metaphorical. The cool morning breeze caressed his face, carrying with it the faint scent of promise and possibility. He gazed out over the sprawling cityscape below, the twinkling lights of a world slowly awakening to a new day.

"I know you're out there somewhere," he whispered, his voice carried away on the wind. "I can feel it in my bones, like a half-remembered dream that refuses to fade."

With each passing moment, the weight of his grief seemed to lift, replaced by a newfound sense of purpose and resolve. Though the road ahead was fraught with peril and uncertainty, Drake knew that he had no choice but to press on, to confront the demons of his past and embrace the promise of a brighter tomorrow.

He reached into his pocket, his fingers brushing against the worn edges of the photograph he always carried with him. It was a picture of Linda and Harrison, taken on a sunny afternoon in the park, their faces alight with joy and laughter. Drake felt a pang of longing in his heart, a bittersweet ache that threatened to overwhelm him.

"I miss you both so much," he murmured, his eyes glistening with unshed tears. "But I know that you're still with me, guiding me forward, even in death."

With a deep breath, Drake squared his shoulders and took a step forward, his feet carrying him towards the unknown. He knew that the path ahead was shrouded in darkness, that he would be forced to confront truths that had long been hidden from him. But he also knew that with each step he took, he was drawing closer to the answers he sought, closer to the redemption he so desperately craved.

As the sun rose higher in the sky, bathing the world in a warm, golden glow, Drake felt a flicker of hope ignite within his heart. Though the journey ahead would be long and arduous, he knew that he was not alone, that he carried with him the love and strength of those he had lost.

And so, with a newfound sense of purpose and determination, Drake strode forward into the dawn, ready to face whatever challenges lay ahead, armed with the knowledge that he was one step closer to the truth, one step closer to the redemption he had been seeking for so long.

Neon Nightmares

Red World – 2024

1 - 2

The night pulsed with an electric tension, a symphony of chaos orchestrated by flashing police lights and the low hum of voices. Detective Franklin Bird stood at the edge of the yellow tape, his weathered face illuminated by the garish neon of the nearby bar. The crashed cab before him was a stark reminder of the fragility of life, its crumpled metal a silent witness to the night's tragic events.

Beside him, Holly Kierstead's presence was a counterpoint to his stoic demeanor. Her fingers trembled slightly as she flipped through her notes, the pages whispering secrets only she could decipher. Bird glanced at her, noting the determined set of her jaw.

"First big case, Kierstead?" he asked, his voice gruff but not unkind.

Holly's eyes snapped up from her notebook. "Yes, sir. I mean, not my first case, but... the first one like this."

Bird nodded, his gaze sweeping across the scene. The milling crowd behind the police line seemed to pulse with a morbid curiosity. He'd seen it all before, but it never got easier.

"What's your read so far?" he prompted, curious to see how his new partner would handle the pressure.

Holly took a deep breath, steeling herself. "Well, the impact suggests the cab was traveling at high speed when it crashed. But why? And where's the driver?"

Her brow furrowed deeper as she spoke, and Bird could almost see the gears turning in her mind. He felt a flicker of approval; she was asking the right questions.

"Good observations," he said. "What else?"

As Holly opened her mouth to respond, a gust of wind rustled through the crime scene, carrying with it the acrid scent of burning rubber and something else – something metallic and unsettling. Bird's instincts, honed by years on the force, prickled with unease.

This is more than just a simple crash, he thought grimly. There's something else going on here, something we're not seeing yet.

3 - 4

Holly Kierstead leaned into the cab, her gloved hand carefully tracing the edge of the GPS display. The screen's blue glow cast eerie shadows across her face as she turned to Detective Bird.

"So... the driver picked up a fare downtown, registered this address with dispatch." She pointed to the device, its last known location frozen in time. Holly's eyes darted to the backseat, her analytical mind piecing together the puzzle. "Um, he's still got his wallet, and there's a twenty on the seat beside him, so I think not only was it not a robbery, it looks like the fare was actually paid."

She stepped back, brushing a stray hair from her face. This doesn't add up, Holly thought. Why would someone pay for a ride and then... what? Attack the driver? Her stomach churned with a mix of excitement and apprehension. This was her chance to prove herself, to show Bird she deserved this promotion.

Detective Bird's weathered face remained impassive, but his eyes narrowed slightly. "Witnesses?" he asked, his gravelly voice cutting through the ambient noise of the crime scene.

The single word held weight, and Holly felt the pressure of Bird's expectations. She knew her response could set the tone for their entire investigation.

5 - 6

Holly nodded, her eyes scanning the area for any potential leads. The chaotic scene before her was a jumble of flashing lights and milling onlookers, but her trained gaze picked out a uniformed officer approaching with a witness in tow. The man was thin, wearing a knit cap pulled low over his ears, his face etched with concern.

She's been waiting for this, Holly thought, her heart racing with a mix of nerves and determination. This could be the break they needed.

Turning to Detective Bird, Holly squared her shoulders and reported, "Okay, so I've interviewed about thirty. Basically, everybody came out of the bar when it happened." She gestured towards the neon-lit establishment; its door still ajar as curious patrons peered out. "But this guy lives in the apartment building above it, saw from his window."

As she spoke, Holly's mind raced. This witness could be crucial. Did he see something the others missed? Why didn't he come forward earlier? She fought to keep her expression neutral, not wanting to betray her excitement to Bird.

I can't mess this up, she thought. This is my chance to show I deserve to be here.

7 - 8

The witness shuffled forward, his shoulders hunched, and hands shoved deep in his pockets. Holly noticed his eyes darting nervously between her and Detective Bird. She softened her expression, hoping to put him at ease.

"It's okay," Holly said gently. "Just tell us what you saw."

The man swallowed hard, Adam's apple bobbing visibly. When he spoke, his voice quavered, barely audible above the surrounding commotion.

"After I heard the commotion," he began, pausing to lick his lips, "I looked out, saw a man in a mask jump in a car and take off that way?" He pointed a trembling finger down the street.

Holly's heart raced. A masked man fleeing the scene? That had to be significant. She glanced at Bird, trying to gauge his reaction. His face remained impassive, but she could almost see the gears turning in his mind.

This could be it, Holly thought. The lead we need to crack this case wide open. But why did he phrase it like a question? Is he unsure about what he saw?

She opened her mouth to ask for more details, her mind already formulating follow-up questions. But before she could speak, Bird stepped forward, his presence commanding the witness's attention.

9 - 10

Holly watched as the witness shuffled away, his hunched form disappearing into the crowd. A chill ran down her spine, the man's uncertainty leaving behind a lingering sense of unease. She turned back to Detective Bird, her expression grim.

"Well, that was..." she began, searching for the right words.

Bird's piercing gaze met hers. "Go on, Kierstead. What are you thinking?"

Holly swallowed hard, acutely aware of the weight of this moment. She couldn't mess this up. "Sir, it's exactly the same report we got from the bar witnesses. Just a little more chaos on the ground, you know?" She gestured towards the nearby establishment, its neon sign casting an eerie glow over the scene. "Guy in a mask running away, but no one close and no one who claims to have seen what actually happened."

As she spoke, Holly's mind raced. Why was everyone's story so vague? Was there more to this than met the eye? She longed to share her theories with Bird, but hesitated, not wanting to overstep.

"Interesting," Bird muttered, his brow furrowing. "And frustrating."

Holly nodded, relief washing over her. At least he seemed to share her concerns. "It's like we're missing a crucial piece of the puzzle," she ventured, emboldened by his response.

11 - 12

Bird absorbed the information, his mind racing as he tried to piece together the puzzle before him. His sharp eyes scanned the scene, searching for any detail they might have overlooked. Suddenly, his gaze flickered to the nearby building, its facade illuminated by the flickering streetlights.

"Kierstead," he said, his voice low and thoughtful. "What do you make of that building?"

Holly followed his line of sight, studying the structure. "It's an apartment complex, sir. Looks fairly modern."

Bird nodded, a glimmer of something - hope, perhaps - in his eyes. "Look closer. What do you notice about the entrance?"

Holly squinted, then her eyes widened with realization. "The front door... it's secured!"

"Exactly," Bird replied, a hint of approval in his tone. "And where there's a secured door..."

"There's usually a camera!" Holly finished, excitement bubbling up inside her.

Bird's lips quirked into the ghost of a smile. "The building looks like it's got a secured front door. Let's see if they've got a camera on it. Might have caught something we can use."

Holly's heart raced. This could be the break they needed. As she prepared to investigate, she couldn't help but feel a surge of admiration for Bird's sharp instincts. Maybe, just maybe, they were one step closer to unraveling this mystery.

13 - 14

Holly nodded, a flicker of admiration dancing in her eyes as she watched Detective Bird take charge of the situation. His keen observation skills and quick thinking never ceased to impress her. She felt a surge of determination coursing through her veins, ready to follow his lead and prove her worth.

"I'm on it, Detective," she said, her voice steady despite the adrenaline pumping through her system. Holly took a deep breath, steeling herself for the task ahead. As she moved towards the building, her senses were on high alert, taking in every detail of the crime scene around her.

The neon lights from the nearby bar cast an eerie glow on the wet pavement, creating shimmering puddles of color. Holly's mind raced, piecing together the fragments of information they had gathered so far. Who was the masked man? What was his motive? These questions swirled in her thoughts as she approached the apartment complex.

Detective Bird's voice cut through her musings. "Kierstead, stay sharp. This could be our best lead yet."

Holly turned back to face him, her expression softening. A mixture of gratitude and determination evident in her eyes as she absorbed Bird's words. She nodded slowly, acknowledging the weight of the situation and the trust he was placing in her.

"Understood, sir," she replied, her voice quiet but firm. "I won't let you down."

15 - 16

Holly hesitated for a moment, her fingers fidgeting with the edges of her notepad. The cool night air nipped at her cheeks, but she barely noticed, caught up in the whirlwind of emotions surging through her. Taking a deep breath, she turned to face Detective Bird, her eyes meeting his with a mix of nervousness and sincerity.

"Well, I-I-I been meaning to thank you, sir," Holly stammered, her usual confidence wavering slightly. "I been passed over for detective, twice, before this assignment, so I'm pretty sure I'd still be in uniform if you hadn't requested me."

She felt vulnerable admitting this, but the weight of her gratitude compelled her to speak. Holly's mind flashed back to the disappointment of those rejections, the sting of being overlooked despite her dedication and hard work. Now, standing here at an active crime scene, she felt a surge of pride at how far she'd come.

Detective Bird's expression remained impassive, his piercing gaze fixed on Holly. His voice was gruff but not unkind when he replied, "I didn't request anyone. If you got promoted, it has nothing to do with me."

Holly felt a sudden rush of heat to her cheeks, embarrassment mingling with a renewed sense of determination. She straightened her shoulders, processing Bird's words. If he hadn't requested her, then her promotion was based solely on her own merits. The realization both thrilled and terrified her, reinforcing the pressure to prove herself worthy of this position.

17 - 18

Holly's posture shifted, her spine straightening as she squared her shoulders. A newfound resolve gleamed in her eyes, replacing the momentary vulnerability. She might not have Bird's endorsement, but she had her own skills and determination to rely on. The weight of the badge on her hip seemed to ground her, a tangible reminder of her hard-earned position.

Detective Bird's steely gaze swept over her, noting the change in her demeanor. His voice cut through the night air, crisp and authoritative. "Now, go check the camera."

The words were simple, but to Holly, they felt like a test. She nodded sharply, her mind already racing through the steps she'd need to take. As she turned to carry out the order, a mixture of excitement and nerves churned in her stomach. This was her chance to show Bird—and herself—that she deserved to be here, solving cases and making a difference.

'I won't let him down,' Holly thought, her jaw set with determination as she strode towards the building's entrance. 'More importantly, I won't let myself down.'

19 - 19

Holly's footsteps echoed against the pavement, each step purposeful and determined as she made her way towards the building. The rhythmic sound seemed to match the pounding of her heart, a steady beat of anticipation and resolve.

As she approached the entrance, Holly's mind raced through potential scenarios. "If the camera caught anything useful, it could break this case wide open," she murmured to herself, reaching for the door handle.

Behind her, Detective Bird watched her retreating form, his expression inscrutable. A faint crease appeared between his brows as he considered the weight of responsibility now resting on his rookie partner's shoulders. He hadn't requested her, true, but now that she was here, it was his job to guide her, to shape her into the detective she could become.

"Don't screw this up, Kierstead," Bird muttered under his breath, more out of habit than actual concern. Despite his gruff exterior, a part of him hoped she'd succeed. The department needed good detectives, and Kierstead had potential – if she could learn to trust her instincts.

As Holly disappeared into the building, Bird turned back to the crime scene, his mind already piecing together the puzzle before them. The challenges ahead loomed large, but for now, all he could do was wait and see what his partner would uncover.

Courtroom Tension

Red World – 2024

1 - 2

The fluorescent lights of the courtroom cast a harsh glow on Drake Miller's face as he stood, his posture rigid and unwavering. His dark eyes scanned the room, taking in every detail - from the nervous twitches of the jury to the beads of sweat forming on the prosecutor's brow. Across the aisle, Raymond Vega leaned forward, his gaze fixed on Drake with an intensity that bordered on obsession.

Drake's mind raced, analyzing every angle of the case. He couldn't afford to lose focus, not when so much was at stake. The memory of his wife and son flashed through his thoughts, fueling his determination. He pushed the grief aside, channeling it into a laser-sharp focus on the task at hand.

"Your Honor," Drake began, his voice steady and measured, "I'd like to call attention to Exhibit C, which clearly demonstrates the inconsistencies in the prosecution's timeline."

As he spoke, Drake could feel Vega's eyes boring into him. He resisted the urge to glance in his direction, knowing that any sign of weakness could be exploited.

The prosecutor jumped to his feet. "Objection, Your Honor! This evidence has already been reviewed and deemed admissible."

Drake allowed himself a small smile. "With all due respect, Your Honor, the prosecution's interpretation of this evidence is fundamentally flawed. If I may elaborate..."

As he launched into his argument, Drake's mind continued to work overtime. He thought, 'Every word counts. One misstep and this whole case could unravel.' He gestured towards the exhibit, his movements precise and controlled.

"As you can see, the timestamp on this security footage directly contradicts the witness statement provided by Mr. Johnson. This discrepancy isn't just a minor oversight - it's a gaping hole in the prosecution's entire narrative."

Drake paused, letting his words sink in. He could almost hear the gears turning in the jurors' minds. Out of the corner of his eye, he caught a glimpse of Vega, who was now scribbling furiously in his notepad.

'What are you up to, Vega?' Drake wondered, a flicker of unease passing through him. He pushed the thought aside, refocusing on his argument.

"Furthermore, Your Honor, I'd like to draw attention to the inconsistencies in the forensic report. The prosecution's expert witness failed to account for..."

As Drake continued to dismantle the prosecution's case, piece by piece, he felt a familiar surge of adrenaline. This was what he lived for - the intellectual chess match, the high-stakes battle of wits. Yet beneath it all, a nagging doubt persisted. In this crimson-tinged world of shadowy alleyways and flickering neon, nothing was ever quite as it seemed.

3 - 4

Drake's train of thought was suddenly interrupted as the prosecutor launched into a new line of questioning, his voice dripping with smug confidence.

"Mr. Roberts, isn't it true that on the night in question, you were seen entering the victim's apartment building at approximately 11:45 PM?"

Drake's eyes narrowed, his mind racing. 'This is it,' he thought, 'the moment they've been building towards. But I won't let them manipulate the facts.'

Without missing a beat, Drake rose from his seat, his voice cutting through the tense atmosphere of the courtroom like a knife.

"Objection, Your Honor. The prosecution's line of questioning is leading and speculative, designed to confuse the jury and cast doubt on my client's innocence."

Drake's heart pounded in his chest as he awaited the judge's response. In the brief moment of silence, he could almost hear the faint echo of sirens from the bustling city beyond the courthouse walls, a stark reminder of the crimson reality they inhabited.

The judge's gavel came down with a resounding crack. "Sustained. Please rephrase the question, Counselor."

As Drake settled back into his seat, a small smile of satisfaction played at the corners of his mouth. 'One battle won,' he thought, 'but the war is far from over.' He glanced at his client, offering a reassuring nod, all the while acutely aware of the weight of responsibility resting on his shoulders.

5 - 6

The prosecutor's eyes flashed with barely concealed frustration. He adjusted his tie, a nervous tic Drake had observed throughout the trial, before launching into his next salvo.

"Mr. Miller, isn't it true that your client has a history of violent behavior? How can you possibly defend someone with such a checkered past?"

Drake felt a surge of indignation rise within him. 'So predictable,' he thought, 'resorting to character assassination when the facts aren't in your favor.' He rose swiftly, his tall frame casting a shadow across the polished courtroom floor.

"Your Honor, I object," Drake declared, his voice resonating with conviction. "The prosecution is attempting to introduce prejudicial evidence that is not relevant to the case at hand. My client's past has no bearing on the charges against him."

As he spoke, Drake's mind raced, analyzing the courtroom's atmosphere. The jurors' faces were a mix of curiosity and uncertainty. He could almost feel the tension crackling in the air, reminiscent of the constant undercurrent of unease that permeated this crimson reality.

'Stay focused,' Drake reminded himself. 'Every word, every gesture matters. Linda would want you to fight with everything you've got.' The memory of his wife's gentle encouragement steeled his resolve, even as the ache of her absence threatened to overwhelm him.

7 - 8

The judge's gavel cracked through the air, sharp and decisive. "Objection sustained. Move on, Counselor."

Drake allowed himself a brief moment of satisfaction, his lips curving into a subtle smile. He returned to his seat, fingers drumming a silent rhythm on the polished oak table. The prosecutor's face flushed with frustration, a sight that only fueled Drake's growing confidence.

'They're floundering,' Drake mused, his dark eyes scanning the courtroom. 'Time to press the advantage.'

As the trial progressed, Drake's arguments flowed with increasing fluidity and persuasion. He rose again, addressing the jury with measured tones that carried an undercurrent of authority.

"Ladies and gentlemen, let's examine the evidence objectively," Drake began, his gaze intense. "The prosecution's case rests on circumstantial evidence and conjecture. But the law demands more. It demands certainty beyond reasonable doubt."

He paced before the jury box, each step calculated. The courtroom's tension seemed to pulse in time with the flickering neon signs visible through the windows, casting an eerie red glow across the proceedings.

'This world may be unfamiliar,' Drake thought, 'but the pursuit of justice remains constant across all realities.'

"Consider the timeline presented," Drake continued, gesturing to a display board. "My client's alibi is corroborated by multiple witnesses. The prosecution would have you believe in an impossible scenario, defying both logic and physics."

As he spoke, Drake's mind raced ahead, anticipating counterarguments and formulating rebuttals. The familiar thrill of legal combat coursed through him, temporarily drowning out the ever-present grief that had become his constant companion.

9 - 10

The judge's gavel cracked through the air, signaling a recess. Drake exhaled slowly, his shoulders relaxing as the tension of the courtroom battle momentarily eased. He gathered his notes, mind already racing with strategies for the next round.

As he turned to exit, a familiar figure materialized from the crowd. Vega approached, his face a carefully constructed mask of neutrality. Drake's muscles instinctively tensed, sensing the undercurrent of something unspoken between them.

'What's his angle?' Drake wondered, studying Vega's guarded expression. 'There's always an ulterior motive with him.'

Vega stopped a few feet away, his voice low and measured as he spoke. "Impressive work in there, Miller. You've got quite the knack for this."

Drake's eyes narrowed slightly, searching for any hint of sarcasm or hidden meaning in Vega's words. The compliment seemed genuine, but experience had taught him to be wary.

"Thanks," Drake replied cautiously, his tone professional but cool. He shifted his weight, unconsciously adopting a more defensive stance. "It's a complex case, but the truth has a way of revealing itself."

As he spoke, Drake's gaze drifted momentarily to the window, where the pulsing neon of the Red World's cityscape cast an otherworldly glow across Vega's features. For a fleeting instant, he was struck by a sense of déjà vu, as if he'd seen this scene play out before in another life, another reality.

11 - 12

Drake shook off the unsettling feeling and refocused on Vega, his jaw tightening as he spoke. "Save your praise, Vega. We both know you're only here because you see an opportunity to advance your own agenda."

The words came out sharper than he'd intended, laced with the frustration and distrust that had been simmering beneath the surface. Drake's hand clenched involuntarily at his side, his knuckles whitening around the leather briefcase handle.

Vega's eyebrows raised slightly, a flicker of surprise—or was it amusement?—crossing his face. He leaned in closer, his voice dropping to a conspiratorial whisper. "Is that any way to treat an old friend?"

The question hung in the air between them, heavy with unspoken history. Drake felt a surge of conflicting emotions: anger, nostalgia, and a nagging sense of unease. His mind raced, parsing through memories of their shared past, searching for clues to Vega's true intentions.

'Friend?' Drake thought bitterly. 'After everything that's happened, how dare he use that word?' He opened his mouth to retort, but hesitated, aware of the eyes watching them from across the bustling courthouse corridor.

13 - 14

Drake's eyes narrowed, his voice dropping to a low, controlled tone that barely masked his simmering anger. "We were never friends, Vega. And I have no intention of letting you worm your way into my life again."

As he spoke, Drake's mind flashed to fragments of memories—shadowy deals, broken promises, and the bitter taste of betrayal. He could almost smell the metallic tang that seemed to permeate the air of this crimson-tinged world, a constant reminder that nothing here was quite as it seemed.

Vega's expression hardened, the facade of camaraderie slipping away to reveal something colder, more calculating. He straightened his tie, a gesture that seemed both casual and threatening at once. "Suit yourself, Miller," he said, his voice eerily calm. "But mark my words, you'll come to regret this decision."

Drake felt a chill run down his spine, not from fear, but from a strange sense of inevitability. He'd heard those words before, hadn't he? In another life, another version of reality? The courthouse corridor seemed to blur around him, the red-tinted world threatening to dissolve into another.

'Focus,' Drake told himself, forcing his attention back to the present moment. He couldn't afford to let his guard down, not with Vega circling like a shark scenting blood in the water. Whatever game Vega was playing, whatever angle he was working on, Drake knew he had to stay one step ahead.

15 - 16

Drake turned his back on Vega, his footsteps echoing in the marble hallway as he strode back into the courtroom. The heavy doors swung shut behind him, muffling the persistent hum of the city beyond. Inside, the air felt charged with tension, thick with the weight of justice hanging in the balance.

As he took his place at the defense table, Drake's eyes swept across the room, taking in the jury's wary expressions, the judge's stoic demeanor, and the prosecution's barely concealed frustration. His client, a nervous man with darting eyes, leaned in close.

"Mr. Miller, are we... are we going to win this?" he whispered, his voice trembling.

Drake's jaw tightened. "We're going to fight," he replied, his tone low and determined. "Every step of the way."

As the trial resumed, Drake threw himself into his arguments with renewed vigor. Each objection, each cross-examination felt like a battle against not just the prosecution, but against the very fabric of this crimson-tinted reality. The world around him seemed to pulse with an otherworldly energy, reminding him of the greater mysteries at play.

'Focus on the case,' Drake chided himself, pushing away thoughts of parallel worlds and lost families. 'One fight at a time.'

Hours passed in a blur of legal jargon and heated debates. When the verdict finally came—not guilty—Drake felt a mixture of triumph and exhaustion wash over him. As the courtroom began to empty, he caught sight of two familiar faces approaching: Holly Keirstead and Franklin Bird.

The sight of Holly sent a jolt through Drake's system. Her features, so eerily similar to the Keirstead from his dreams, caused reality to waver around him. For a moment, he wasn't sure which world he was in—the red one, or one of the others that haunted his memories.

"Quite a performance, counselor," Franklin's gruff voice cut through Drake's disorientation. "You haven't lost your touch."

Drake forced a smile, his mind racing. "Bird, Keirstead," he acknowledged, his gaze lingering on Holly. "I didn't expect to see you here."

17 - 18

Holly Keirstead's piercing gaze met Drake's, her lips curving into a sardonic smile. "Well, well, if it isn't Drake Miller. Looks like you haven't lost your touch."

The fluorescent lights of the courtroom corridor cast an eerie red glow on her face, accentuating the resemblance to her otherworldly counterparts. Drake suppressed a shudder, his mind reeling with the implications of her presence in this crimson reality.

"Keirstead. Bird. What brings you two here?" Drake asked, his voice steady despite the turmoil churning inside him. He clasped his hands behind his back, a gesture that helped ground him in the present moment.

As he awaited their response, Drake's thoughts raced. 'Are they here about the accident? Or is there something more sinister at play?' The weight of his briefcase seemed to grow heavier, filled with the ghosts of his past and the uncertainties of his future across multiple realities.

19 - 20

Franklin Bird's weathered face crinkled with a mixture of admiration and curiosity. "We heard about the trial and thought we'd come see the master in action. Looks like you haven't lost your edge."

Drake's mind whirred, parsing the detective's words for hidden meaning. Was this a simple social call, or something more? The pulsing neon of the city beyond the courthouse windows cast an otherworldly glow on Bird's face, reminding Drake of the surreal nature of his current reality.

"Just doing my job, Bird," Drake replied, his tone measured. He allowed a faint smile to touch his lips, a calculated gesture of familiarity. "Though I must admit, it's nice to have some familiar faces in the crowd."

As he spoke, Drake's gaze darted between Bird and Keirstead, searching for any sign of recognition beyond this world - any hint that they, too, were aware of the multiversal tapestry he found himself entangled in. The weight of unasked questions hung heavy in the air, mingling with the metallic scent that seemed to permeate every corner of this crimson-tinged reality.

'How much do they know?' Drake wondered, his outward composure belying the storm of thoughts within. 'And more importantly, how much should I reveal?'

21 - 21

Drake's eyes lingered on Holly Keirstead, her striking resemblance to the Keirstead from his dreams—from the other worlds—sending a shiver down his spine. He fought to keep his expression neutral, even as his mind raced with possibilities.

"It's been a while since we've caught up," Drake said, his voice carefully modulated. "How have things been at the precinct?"

As Bird launched into a response about recent cases, Drake found his attention split. Part of him listened attentively, noting details that might prove useful later, while another part of his consciousness grappled with the surreal nature of his situation.

'I'm making a difference here,' he thought, a warm sense of satisfaction blooming in his chest. 'But at what cost? And for how long?'

The bustling courthouse corridor seemed to fade away, leaving Drake hyper-aware of the subtle wrongness of this world. The too-bright neon, the ever-present metallic tang, the undercurrent of tension that thrummed through the air—all served as constant reminders that this wasn't his original reality.

"You know, Miller," Keirstead interjected, her eyes sharp and searching, "your performance in there was impressive. It almost makes me wonder if you've picked up some new tricks since we last worked together."

Drake's heart rate spiked, but he kept his face impassive. "Just honing my skills, Keirstead. This job doesn't allow for complacency."

As he spoke, he couldn't help but reflect on the cruel irony of his situation. Here he was, still fighting for justice, still making a difference—but in a world that wasn't truly his own, separated from the family he'd lost.

Tidal Wave of Grief

Red World – 2024

1 - 2

The world tilted on its axis, colors bleeding together as Drake gripped the edge of his desk. Kierstead's words echoed in his ears, each syllable a dagger to his already shattered heart. The loss of his wife and son crashed over him anew, a tidal wave of grief threatening to drag him under.

Focus, he commanded himself, forcing air into his lungs. He couldn't afford to fall apart now, not when answers might finally be within reach. Drake's jaw clenched, muscles tightening as he fought to maintain composure. He'd spent weeks adrift in a fog of despair, but now a spark of determination ignited within him.

Kierstead watched him carefully, her keen detective's eyes no doubt cataloging every micro-expression that flitted across his face. Drake straightened, squaring his shoulders as he met her gaze.

"You found the car?" he asked, his voice rough with emotion he couldn't quite conceal.

As he waited for her response, Drake's mind raced. Could this be the breakthrough they'd been waiting for? Or would it lead to another dead end, another crushed hope? He clung to that fragile thread of possibility, desperate for anything that might bring him closer to understanding what had happened that terrible night.

3 - 4

Kierstead nodded, her expression a mix of professional detachment and genuine sympathy. "Yes, we received a tip from an anonymous source. We traced the vehicle to a salvage yard on the outskirts of town."

Drake's heart hammered in his chest. The car. The instrument of his family's destruction now found. He pictured it, twisted metal and shattered glass, a grotesque monument to his loss. His hands clenched involuntarily at his sides.

Before he could voice the questions swirling in his mind, Bird stepped forward, his weathered face etched with concern. "We haven't been able to find the owner yet, but we're hoping you might be able to shed some light on the situation. Anything you remember about the car, or the driver could be crucial to our investigation."

Drake closed his eyes, willing his memory to cooperate. Fragments of that night flashed behind his eyelids—headlights, the sound of screeching tires—but nothing concrete about the vehicle, or its driver materialized. Frustration burned in his chest, mingling with the ever-present ache of grief.

"I..." he began, his voice faltering. He wanted desperately to help, to offer something—anything—that might move the investigation forward. But the details remained stubbornly out of reach, locked away in some dark corner of his mind.

5 - 6

Drake's mind raced, memories of that fateful night flooding back with painful clarity. He could see the headlights bearing down on them, bright and merciless. The screech of tires echoed in his ears, a haunting prelude to the sickening crunch of metal that followed. His breath caught in his throat as he relived those terrible moments, his body tensing as if bracing for impact once again.

But try as he might, Drake couldn't summon any details about the car or its driver. The specifics slipped away like smoke, leaving only the raw emotions of fear and loss behind. He ran a hand through his hair, frustration evident in the tightness of his jaw.

"I'm sorry," Drake said, his voice thick with regret. He met Kierstead's gaze, then Bird's, seeing the hope in their eyes dim slightly. "I wish I could help. It all happened so fast... I barely had time to react."

He paused, swallowing hard against the lump in his throat. "One moment we were driving, talking about our plans for the weekend, and the next..." Drake trailed off, unable to finish the sentence. The weight of his inability to provide useful information pressed down on him, adding to the burden of grief he already carried.

7 - 8

Kierstead's face softened, her brown eyes filled with understanding as she nodded. The tension in her shoulders eased, and she leaned forward slightly, her voice gentle when she spoke.

"It's okay, Drake," she said, her tone carrying a warmth that seemed to wrap around him like a comforting blanket. "We know how difficult this is for you. Trauma has a way of clouding our memories, especially in such intense moments."

Drake felt a small measure of relief at her words, though the frustration still simmered beneath the surface. He watched as Kierstead exchanged a quick glance with Bird, a silent communication passing between the two detectives.

"We'll keep digging," Kierstead continued, her determination evident in the set of her jaw. "This isn't a dead end, just a bump in the road. Maybe we'll get lucky and find some evidence that leads us to whoever was behind the wheel."

As she spoke, Drake's mind raced. He wanted to believe her, to have faith that justice would prevail. But a nagging doubt gnawed at him. What if they never found the person responsible? What if his family's killer walked free? The thought made his stomach churn, and he clenched his fists, trying to push away the dark thoughts threatening to overwhelm him.

9 - 10

Drake forced a small smile, the corners of his mouth tightening with the effort. His eyes, tinged with a mixture of gratitude and barely concealed pain, met those of Kierstead and Bird. The weight of their unwavering support settled on him like a warm, comforting blanket in the midst of his grief.

"Thanks, both of you," he managed, his voice rough with emotion. "I appreciate everything you're doing." Drake's gaze flickered between the two detectives, taking in Kierstead's compassionate expression and Bird's steady, reassuring presence.

As he spoke, Drake's hand unconsciously moved to his chest, fingers brushing against the outline of his wife's locket hidden beneath his shirt. The cool metal against his skin grounded him, a tangible reminder of what he had lost and what he was fighting for.

Swallowing hard, Drake added, "It means more than you know, having you both in my corner." He paused, wrestling with the tumult of emotions threatening to spill over. "I just... I need to find out what happened. For them."

11 - 12

Bird's eyes softened, a mix of compassion and determination flickering across his weathered features. "Of course, Drake. We're here for you," he said, his gravelly voice cutting through the heavy silence that had settled in the room.

Drake nodded, unable to find words as he watched Kierstead and Bird gather their things and make their way to the door. As they left, a palpable shift occurred within him. The weight of grief that had been crushing him for weeks began to transmute into something else – a steely resolve that straightened his spine and set his jaw.

He may not have all the answers now, but he wouldn't rest until he found justice for his wife and son. Their faces flashed in his mind – his wife's radiant smile, his son's mischievous grin – fueling the fire of determination burning in his chest.

Suddenly, like a bolt of lightning cutting through fog, fragments of memory began to surface. Drake's breath caught in his throat as details he'd thought lost forever came into focus. The screech of tires, the glint of metal in the darkness, a fleeting glimpse of...something. His heart raced as he tried to grasp at these elusive threads of recollection.

"Wait," he whispered to himself, his mind reeling. "I remember..."

13 - 14

Drake's voice rose, urgency threading through his words. "I do recall something, it's very faint in my memory but it's there."

Kierstead and Bird, who had just reached the doorway, froze mid-step. They exchanged a quick, hopeful glance before turning back to face Drake. The tension in the room ratcheted up several notches as they waited for him to continue.

Bird took a step forward, his weathered face etched with anticipation. "What do you recall?" he asked, his gravelly voice barely above a whisper.

Drake's brow furrowed in concentration; his eyes unfocused as he strained to grasp the elusive memory. His hands clenched and unclenched at his sides, knuckles white with effort. The silence stretched, broken only by the sound of his ragged breathing.

In his mind's eye, fragmented images flashed by in rapid succession. The glint of headlights, a flash of metal, a fleeting shape in the darkness. Drake's heart pounded in his chest, each beat seeming to echo in the quiet room. He could feel Kierstead and Bird's eyes on him, their anticipation palpable.

'Come on,' he thought desperately. 'Remember. For them. For justice.' The faces of his wife and son swam before him, spurring him on. He knew this could be the breakthrough they'd been waiting for, the key to unlocking the mystery that had shattered his world.

15 - 16

Drake's eyes snapped open, his gaze intense as he locked eyes with Bird and Kierstead. His voice came out in a hoarse whisper, laden with a mix of shock and dawning realization.

"I remember a figure coming down over the embankment. His face was disfigured, he had a limp." Drake's words tumbled out faster now, the memory crystallizing as he spoke. "He looked into the driver's side window and stared at me. He was staring at me; he was wearing a white robe with a symbol on it."

Drake's hands trembled slightly as he brought them up to his temples, pressing hard as if he could physically extract more details from his mind. His eyes squeezed shut, brow furrowed in deep concentration.

'What else?' he thought frantically. 'There has to be more. Come on, remember!'

The silence in the room was electric. Bird and Kierstead stood stock-still, hardly daring to breathe as they watched Drake struggle with his memories. The weight of potential breakthrough hung heavy in the air.

Suddenly, Kierstead's eyes widened. She glanced at Bird, a spark of recognition passing between them. Without a word, Holly pulled out her phone, her fingers flying over the screen. Drake's eyes opened at the sound, focusing on Kierstead as she stepped forward, holding out her device.

"Drake," she said softly, her voice tinged with a mix of excitement and trepidation. "I need you to look at this."

17 - 18

Drake's eyes locked onto the phone screen, and the world around him seemed to fade away. There, zoomed in on the driver's seat of a car, was a white robe with a symbol emblazoned on it. The image hit him like a physical blow, and suddenly he was drowning in a flood of memories.

"Do you recall if this was the symbol?" Kierstead's voice sounded distant, as if coming from underwater.

Drake couldn't respond. His mind reeled, overwhelmed by visions of two distinct worlds - one green, one blue. Worlds he had inhabited during his coma, realms he hadn't revisited since the explosion that jolted him back to consciousness. They had felt like dreams, but now...

His gaze fixed on the symbol: a vibrant green dragon intertwined with a tree, surrounded by ancient, mystical runes. It was exactly as he remembered, exactly as it had appeared in those other worlds. Worlds where his wife and son were still alive.

A jolt of determination surged through Drake. 'They're real,' he thought, his heart racing. 'Those places, those versions of reality - they exist. And if they exist, there must be a way back.'

His throat tight with emotion, Drake managed to croak out, "That's... that's the symbol." He swallowed hard, fighting to keep his voice steady as he added, "My son drew it."

19 - 20

Kierstead's eyebrows shot up, her gaze darting to Bird. "Your son?" she asked, her voice a mixture of confusion and concern. The two detectives exchanged a puzzled look, clearly caught off guard by Drake's statement.

Drake's mind raced, realizing he'd revealed more than he'd intended. He needed to redirect their focus, to buy time to process this revelation himself. His fingers twitched nervously at his side as he formulated his next move.

"There's something I need to ask," Drake said, his voice steadier now. He locked eyes with Kierstead, trying to project a calm he didn't feel. "Did you by chance find any DNA at the scene? Any possible connection to who could have been behind the wheel?"

As he spoke, Drake's heart pounded in his chest. He silently prayed for a lead, any lead, that might help him unravel the mystery of the crash and its connection to the worlds he'd glimpsed. At the same time, a part of him feared what the answer might reveal. What if the evidence pointed to something impossible, something that further blurred the lines between reality and his coma-induced visions?

21 - 22

Drake's question hung in the air; the tension palpable. As he awaited their response, a name flashed through his mind: Gabriel. The pieces of the puzzle were slowly falling into place, and Drake felt a surge of anger mixed with grim satisfaction. Of course, it was Gabriel behind the wheel – the man who had orchestrated this entire nightmare.

Keeping his face neutral, Drake studied the detectives' reactions. He couldn't reveal his knowledge of Gabriel, not yet. Not until he understood more about the connections between the worlds he'd experienced and this harsh reality.

Bird cleared his throat, his weathered face creasing with a mix of frustration and empathy. "There's nothing conclusive yet," he said, his gravelly voice tinged with disappointment. "But forensic experts are still examining the car. We'll inform you if anything turns up."

Drake nodded, his jaw clenching involuntarily. He'd hoped for more, but this was hardly surprising. Gabriel was clever – he wouldn't leave obvious traces behind. As Drake processed this information, his mind raced, considering his next move. How could he pursue Gabriel without arousing suspicion? And more importantly, how could he find a way back to those other worlds, where hope still lived?

23 - 24

As Kierstead and Bird turned to leave, their footsteps echoing in the quiet room, Drake felt a sudden jolt of intuition. A memory surfaced, fragmented but insistent, from one of his coma-induced visions. He couldn't let them go, not yet.

"Wait," Drake called out, his voice hoarse with urgency. The detectives paused, turning back to face him with questioning looks.

Drake's heart raced as he formulated his words carefully. He knew he was treading a fine line between helpful witness and suspicious person of interest. But he had to know.

"Did you find the cab driver?" he asked, trying to keep his tone casual despite the weight of the question.

Kierstead's eyebrows shot up, a flicker of surprise crossing her face. Bird's hand instinctively moved towards his notepad.

As Drake awaited their response, his mind whirled with possibilities. Had the cab driver from his vision been real? And if so, what did it mean for the connection between his dream worlds and this reality? He held his breath, hoping their answer might provide another piece to this maddening puzzle.

25 - 26

Kierstead turned, her expression a mixture of curiosity and concern. "What cab driver?" she asked, her tone careful and measured.

Drake's throat tightened. He was stepping onto thin ice, but he couldn't back down now. Taking a deep breath, he pressed on, choosing his words with painstaking precision.

"The one the car belongs to," he explained, his voice steady despite the tremor in his hands. "It belongs to a cab driver." He paused, steeling himself for the next question. "Did you find one dead down an alley recently?"

As the words left his mouth, Drake's mind raced. How much should he reveal? How much did he truly understand about the connections between his visions and reality? He watched Kierstead and Bird carefully, searching their faces for any sign of recognition or suspicion.

Internally, Drake grappled with the implications of his own question. If they had found a dead cab driver, it would confirm the eerie accuracy of his visions. But it would also raise questions about how he knew—questions he wasn't prepared to answer. Yet, he needed to know. This could be the key to unraveling the mystery, to finding a way back to the world where his family still lived.

27 - 28

The silence that followed Drake's question was deafening. Bird and Kierstead exchanged a quick, bewildered glance, their professional composure momentarily cracking. Drake could almost see the gears turning in their minds as they struggled to process this unexpected turn of events.

Kierstead's brow furrowed deeply, her usual calm demeanor giving way to visible confusion. Bird's hand instinctively moved towards his notepad, as if preparing to jot down some crucial piece of information.

After what felt like an eternity, but was likely only a few seconds, both detectives spoke in near-perfect unison, their voices a mixture of surprise and suspicion:

"Now how did you possibly know about that?"

Drake's heart raced. He hadn't anticipated their reaction, and now he found himself at a crossroads. Should he reveal more about his visions, risking their disbelief or worse, their suspicion? Or should he backpedal, claim it was just a hunch?

As he weighed his options, Drake couldn't help but notice the intensity in Bird's eyes, the detective's gaze boring into him as if trying to unearth the truth through sheer willpower. Kierstead, on the other hand, had an air of cautious curiosity about her, as if she was open to possibilities beyond the usual scope of their investigations.

Drake took a deep breath, buying himself a moment to think. The truth was stranger than fiction, but maybe, just maybe, it was time to start sharing it.

29 - 30

A knowing smirk played across Drake's lips, his eyes glinting with a mix of triumph and bewilderment. The puzzle pieces were falling into place, forming a picture that spanned across realities he'd only glimpsed in his coma-induced visions. The Blue world, vibrant and alive with possibility. The Green world, lush and mysterious. And now, the Red world - their world - all interconnected in ways he was only beginning to comprehend.

"It's a long story," Drake said, his voice low and tinged with a hint of excitement. He glanced between Bird and Kierstead, noting their confused expressions. "And I'm not sure you'll believe me if I tell you."

Bird's hand twitched towards his notepad again, clearly itching to document whatever revelation was coming. Kierstead's posture shifted, her professional detachment giving way to genuine curiosity.

Drake took a deep breath, steeling himself for what he was about to propose. The weight of his experiences - both in this world and the others - pressed upon him, urging him to share the truth, no matter how fantastical it might sound.

"I think," he began, his tone measured but tinged with urgency, "we're going to need to discuss this over coffee."

Virus Chase

Blue World – 2024

Detective Holly Sharp

1 - 2

The antiseptic smell of the hospital assaulted Holly Sharp's senses as she strode purposefully through the crowded hallways. Her detective's badge cleared a path through the sea of anxious faces, each one a reminder of the deadly virus ravaging their city. Holly's heart raced, her mind a whirlwind of theories and questions. She needed answers, and she needed them now.

"Excuse me," she muttered, sidestepping a gurney. The chaos around her was a stark contrast to the calm determination she forced herself to maintain. Dr. Lee's office was just ahead, a beacon of hope in this storm of uncertainty.

Holly burst through the door without knocking, her eyes immediately locking onto the hunched figure behind the desk. Dr. Lee, renowned virologist and possibly their last hope, sat surrounded by a fortress of papers and lab reports. His salt-and-pepper hair was disheveled, dark circles under his eyes betraying countless sleepless nights.

"Dr. Lee," Holly began, her voice cutting through the silence. She didn't wait for pleasantries; there was no time. "I need to know everything you've found."

The doctor's head snapped up, startled by her sudden appearance. Recognition flickered in his tired eyes. "Detective Sharp," he acknowledged, gesturing to a chair. "I was just reviewing the latest data. It's... not good."

Holly remained standing, her fingers drumming against her thigh. How many lives hung in the balance? How many more would be lost if they couldn't crack this case? She took a deep breath, centering herself. Focus, Sharp. One question at a time.

"Tell me about the virus," she demanded, her tone brooking no argument. "How is it spreading? What are we dealing with here?"

Dr. Lee sighed, pushing aside a stack of papers. "It's unlike anything we've seen before, Detective. The rate of mutation is unprecedented. We're struggling to keep up with—"

"Cut to the chase, Doctor," Holly interrupted, her patience wearing thin. "Can you stop it?"

The heavy silence that followed was all the answer she needed. Holly's stomach dropped, but she forced herself to push forward. There had to be something, some lead they hadn't explored yet.

"What about patient zero?" she pressed, leaning forward. "Have you made any progress identifying the source?"

Dr. Lee's brow furrowed deeper, if that was possible. "We have a theory, but it's... complicated. There's a patient, Drake Miller. His blood work showed some anomalies that could be significant. If we could just—"

Holly's sharp intake of breath cut him off. Drake Miller. The name sparked a connection in her mind, pieces of the puzzle starting to fall into place. "Tell me everything about Drake Miller," she demanded, her detective instincts kicking into high gear. "His blood work, his background, everything."

As Dr. Lee began to speak, Holly's mind raced. Whatever the connection, she was determined to uncover it. The city was counting on them, and failure was not an option.

3 - 4

Holly's voice cut through the tense silence of the office, her words clipped and urgent. "Dr. Lee, we need to talk. The virus is spreading faster than we anticipated, and we're running out of time. What do you know about Drake Miller's blood samples?"

The detective's piercing gaze bore into the researcher, her stance rigid with barely contained anxiety. She could feel her heart pounding, each beat a reminder of the lives at stake.

Dr. Lee looked up from his papers, his expression grave. The lines on his face seemed to have deepened since Holly last saw him, testament to the sleepless nights and relentless pressure. With a weary sigh, he motioned for Holly to take a seat.

As Holly sank into the chair, her mind raced. What could the doctor have discovered? Was there hope, or were they truly at the end of their rope? She leaned forward, her fingers gripping the armrests, ready to spring into action at a moment's notice.

The weight of the city's fate hung heavy in the air between them as Dr. Lee gathered his thoughts, clearly choosing his words with care. Holly's impatience threatened to bubble over, but she forced herself to remain still, knowing that rushing the doctor wouldn't yield answers any faster.

5 - 6

Dr. Lee clasped his hands together, his knuckles whitening under the pressure. "Detective Sharp, I've been studying Drake Miller's blood samples since the explosion. There was something remarkable about them, something that could have potentially led to a cure for this virus. But now..."

His voice trailed off, and Holly felt her stomach drop. The hesitation in Dr. Lee's tone set off alarm bells in her mind. Whatever he was about to say, it wasn't good news.

Holly leaned forward, her eyes narrowing. "What do you mean 'now'? What happened to the blood samples?" Her voice was sharp, tinged with a mix of frustration and fear. She couldn't shake the feeling that they were on the precipice of a breakthrough, only to have it slip away.

As she waited for Dr. Lee's response, Holly's mind raced through possibilities. Had the samples been contaminated? Destroyed in an accident? Or worse, stolen by someone who understood their value? The implications of each scenario sent a chill down her spine. Time was running out, and with it, their chances of finding a cure.

7 - 8

Dr. Lee's eyes darted away from Holly's intense gaze, his fingers drumming a nervous rhythm on his desk. The usually composed researcher seemed to be wrestling with his words, each second of silence amplifying the tension in the room.

Holly's heart pounded in her chest, her detective instincts screaming that something was terribly wrong. She leaned forward, her voice barely above a whisper, "Dr. Lee, please. Whatever it is, I need to know."

Finally, Dr. Lee met her eyes, his face a mask of defeat and bewilderment. "They're gone," he said, his voice cracking slightly. "Vanished without a trace. I don't understand it, Detective. One moment they were here, and the next... poof, they're gone."

The words hit Holly like a physical blow. She gripped the arms of her chair, her knuckles turning white. Gone? How could something so crucial just disappear? Her mind raced through possibilities - theft, sabotage, or something even more sinister.

"That's impossible," she muttered, more to herself than to Dr. Lee. But even as she said it, she knew that in this new world of deadly viruses and desperate measures, nothing was truly impossible anymore.

9 - 10

Holly felt the weight of despair settle over her like a suffocating blanket. Her gaze drifted to the window, where the city skyline loomed ominously through a haze of smog. Each of those buildings housed countless lives, all now hanging in the balance.

"This can't be happening," she whispered, her voice barely audible. The implications hit her like a freight train. Drake's blood - their one beacon of hope in this nightmare - was gone. With it vanished the possibility of a cure, the chance to save thousands, maybe millions.

She turned back to Dr. Lee, noting the deep lines of worry etched on his face. He looked as defeated as she felt. But Holly knew she couldn't afford to wallow in despair. She was a detective, damn it, and it was time to act like one.

Straightening her shoulders, Holly locked eyes with Dr. Lee. "We can't afford to lose any more time, Dr. Lee," she said, her voice regaining its usual steel. "We need to find out what happened to those samples and fast."

As she spoke, her mind was already racing, formulating plans and strategies. Who had access to the lab? What security measures were in place? Every second counted now, and Holly was determined not to waste a single one.

11 - 12

Dr. Lee's eyes flashed with renewed determination as he pushed himself up from his chair. The weariness that had hung over him moments ago seemed to evaporate, replaced by a sense of urgent purpose. Holly watched as he straightened his lab coat, a habit she'd noticed he employed when steeling himself for action.

"Agreed, Detective," he said, his voice low but resolute. "I'll pull up the security footage from the lab and see if we can find any clues."

As Dr. Lee moved towards his computer, Holly felt a flicker of hope ignite in her chest. Maybe they weren't too late after all. Maybe there was still a chance to recover Drake's blood samples and save countless lives.

But Dr. Lee's next words doused that spark of optimism. "But I'm afraid it may already be too late," he added, his fingers hovering over the keyboard.

Holly's jaw clenched. Time. It always came down to time. The ticking clock that haunted her every move since this virus outbreak began. She could almost hear it now, counting down the precious seconds they had left to solve this mystery and find a cure.

"Let's focus on what we can do right now," Holly said, as much to herself as to Dr. Lee. She moved closer to the computer screen, ready to scrutinize every frame of the security footage. Whatever answers they needed, she was determined to find them.

13 - 14

As Dr. Lee's fingers flew across the keyboard, Holly's phone buzzed insistently in her pocket. She pulled it out, her heart rate quickening when she saw the caller ID. Franklin Bird, her trusted colleague and Captain. If he was calling now, it couldn't be good news.

Holly hesitated for a split second, torn between watching Dr. Lee's progress and answering the call. The virus was spreading rapidly, and every moment counted. But Bird wouldn't interrupt unless it was critical.

With a deep breath, she swiped to answer. "Bird, what do you have for me?" Holly asked, her voice taut with tension. She turned slightly away from Dr. Lee, trying to focus on Bird's words while still keeping an eye on the computer screen. Whatever Bird had to say, she knew it would only add to the mounting pressure of their race against time.

15 - 16

The line crackled with static, and Holly could hear the chaos of sirens and shouting in the background. Bird's voice came through, strained and urgent, cutting through the noise.

"Sharp, where are you?" Bird demanded, his usually calm demeanor replaced by barely contained panic. "The city is in a mass panic, and I need all officers on deck."

Holly's stomach tightened as she processed Bird's words. She glanced at Dr. Lee, still engrossed in the security footage, then back at the office door. The weight of her responsibilities as a detective conflicted with her desperate need to find answers about the missing blood samples.

She clenched her jaw, mind racing. If the situation in the city was deteriorating this quickly, how much time did they really have left? And yet, if Drake's blood truly held the key to stopping this virus, leaving now could mean losing their only chance at salvation.

"Bird, I'm..." Holly began, her voice trailing off as she struggled to make a decision that could impact countless lives.

17 - 18

Holly's mind raced with possibilities, each more dire than the last. Could the vanishing blood really hold the key to a possible antidote? If so, every second spent away from this lead could cost lives. Yet the city needed her too. She closed her eyes briefly, steeling herself for the difficult balancing act ahead.

"Thanks, Bird," Holly finally responded, her voice tight with tension. She kept her eyes on Dr. Lee, who was still frantically searching through security footage. "I'm following up on a lead right now about a missing colleague. I'll meet you at the station."

She could almost hear Bird's frustration through the phone, but she pressed on before he could object. "This could be crucial to stopping the virus. Give me an hour, tops. I promise I'll be there as soon as I can."

As she ended the call, Holly's stomach churned with a mix of determination and doubt. She'd made her choice - now she just had to hope it was the right one.

19 - 20

Holly pocketed her phone and turned back to Dr. Lee, her jaw set with fierce resolve. The fluorescent lights cast harsh shadows across her face, highlighting the intensity in her eyes.

"Dr. Lee," she said, her voice low and urgent. "I need your help." She leaned forward, placing her palms flat on his cluttered desk. "We're going to find out what happened to Drake Miller, and we're going to stop this virus before it's too late."

Dr. Lee looked up from his computer screen, his eyes wide behind his wire-rimmed glasses. Holly could see the fatigue etched in the lines of his face, but there was a spark of determination there too.

As she waited for his response, Holly's mind raced. We're running out of time, she thought. Every minute we waste is another life at risk. But if anyone can crack this, it's Dr. Lee.

"Detective Sharp," Dr. Lee began, his voice steady despite the tension in the room. "I'm with you. But I must warn you, we're dealing with forces beyond our understanding. The disappearance of those blood samples... it's not natural."

Holly nodded, her fingers drumming on the desk. "Natural or not, we don't have a choice. We need to track down those samples and figure out what makes them special. It's our only shot at developing a cure."

She straightened up, her eyes scanning the chaotic office. "Where do we start?"

21 - 21

Dr. Lee rose from his chair, his lab coat rustling as he moved. He nodded, his expression resolute. "You're right, Detective. We can't afford to waste any more time."

Holly felt a surge of relief. Having Dr. Lee's expertise on her side could make all the difference. She watched as he strode to a large whiteboard on the wall, grabbing a marker.

"First," Dr. Lee said, scribbling furiously, "we need to retrace Drake Miller's steps before the explosion. His blood samples didn't just vanish into thin air."

Holly's mind raced, piecing together the puzzle. "Could someone have stolen them?" she wondered aloud. "Someone who knows their value?"

Dr. Lee turned to her, his eyes gleaming with a mix of fear and excitement. "It's possible. But who would have that kind of knowledge? And more importantly, why?"

As they brainstormed, Holly felt the weight of responsibility settling on her shoulders. Lives are at stake, she reminded herself. We can't fail.

"We should start by reviewing the security footage," Holly suggested, moving towards the computer. "Maybe we missed something the first time around."

Dr. Lee nodded in agreement, joining her at the screen. As they prepared to dive into their investigation, Holly couldn't shake the feeling that they were embarking on a journey that would change everything.

Echoes of Desolation

Apocalypse world – year 2044

1 - 2

Harrison's footsteps echoed through the desolate streets, each crunch of debris under his feet a stark reminder of the world he'd stumbled into. The acrid smell of ash and decay assaulted his nostrils, making him wince as he surveyed the apocalyptic landscape before him.

"What happened here?" he whispered, his voice barely audible above the eerie silence.

Towering skyscrapers, once symbols of progress and prosperity, now stood as skeletal remnants of a bygone era. Their shattered windows gaped like hollow eye sockets, staring blindly at the ash-choked sky. Harrison's gaze swept over the rusted husks of abandoned vehicles littering the streets, each one a silent testament to the chaos that had engulfed this world.

He approached a nearby car, its door hanging off its hinges. Peering inside, Harrison's mind raced with questions. How long ago did this happen? Where are all the people?

"Hello?" he called out, immediately regretting the decision as his voice echoed off the decaying buildings. The silence that followed was deafening.

Harrison's heart pounded in his chest as he continued down the barren street. His eyes darted from one crumbling structure to another, searching for any sign of life. The weight of isolation pressed down on him, threatening to crush his spirit.

"Focus, Harrison," he muttered to himself, clenching his fists. "There has to be a reason you're here. Dad wouldn't have sent you to an empty world."

As he rounded a corner, a gust of wind kicked up a swirl of ash and debris. Harrison shielded his eyes, coughing as the acrid particles invaded his lungs. When the miniature storm subsided, he found himself face-to-face with a massive billboard, its faded message barely legible: "WELCOME TO BridgeWater - THE CITY THAT ENDED TOMORROW."

Harrison's breath caught in his throat. "Bridgewater? This can't be..."

He stumbled backward, overwhelmed by the realization. This wasteland, this apocalyptic nightmare – it was his home. Or at least, a version of it. The familiar skyline, now broken and battered, confirmed his worst fears.

"What could have caused this?" Harrison wondered aloud, his mind racing through possibilities. "A war? A natural disaster? Or something... worse?"

As he contemplated the devastation around him, a flicker of movement caught his eye. Harrison's heart leaped, a mix of hope and apprehension flooding his veins. He wasn't alone after all.

"Hey!" he shouted, breaking into a run towards the source of the movement. "Wait! I need help!"

But as he rounded another corner, Harrison skidded to a halt. The street before him was empty, save for more abandoned vehicles and swirling ash. Had he imagined it? Or was someone – or something – watching him from the shadows?

Harrison's hand instinctively reached for a weapon he didn't possess, his body tensing for a threat he couldn't see. The silence pressed in around him once more, broken only by the racing of his own heart.

"Dad," he whispered, a plea to the ashen sky. "I don't know if you can hear me, but I could really use some guidance right about now."

3 - 4

Harrison's eyes darted nervously as he pressed on, his footsteps crunching on debris. Rounding a corner, he froze at the sight before him. A makeshift shelter constructed from corrugated metal and tattered tarps huddled against a crumbling wall. Scrawled across the concrete in angry red letters was a message: "THE END IS HERE. REPENT OR PERISH."

"Charming," Harrison muttered, suppressing a shudder. He approached cautiously, curiosity warring with caution. "Hello? Is anyone there?"

A sudden burst of gunfire in the distance made him flinch. The sound echoed off the empty buildings, followed by an ominous rumble as part of a nearby structure collapsed.

"Okay, definitely not going that way," Harrison said to himself, heart pounding. He peered into the shelter, finding only discarded food wrappers and a ratty blanket. "Someone was here recently. Maybe they're still close by."

As he ventured deeper into the city's heart, Harrison's keen eyes took in every detail. A child's teddy bear, grimy and one-eyed, lay abandoned in a doorway. Faded posters advertised movies that would never premiere. The eerie silence was broken only by the whisper of wind through empty streets.

Rounding another corner, Harrison stumbled upon a small group huddled around a burning trash can. Their gaunt faces turned towards him, a mix of wariness and desperation in their eyes.

"Um, hi," Harrison said, raising his hands to show he was unarmed. "I'm looking for information. My name's Harrison, and I'm trying to find my father, Drake Miller."

An older woman with steel-gray hair fixed him with a piercing stare. "Another lost soul," she said, her voice raspy. "Ain't we all looking for someone?"

5 - 6

Harrison hesitated, then stepped closer to the group, drawn by the warmth of their fire and the flicker of humanity in their eyes. "I know it's a long shot, but have any of you heard of Drake Miller? He was... is... a lawyer."

A man with a scarred face chuckled bitterly. "Lawyers. What use are they now? The only law here is survival."

The gray-haired woman shushed him. "Now, Jem, don't be rude. Boy's just looking for his pa." She turned to Harrison, her expression softening. "Can't say I've heard of him, love, but you're welcome to share our fire for a bit."

Gratitude washed over Harrison as he settled near the group. "Thank you. I... I don't really know my way around here."

As they shared meager rations - a can of beans and some stale crackers - Harrison found himself struck by the camaraderie of these survivors. Despite their hardships, they exchanged quiet jokes and shared stories of better days.

"It's not much," a young woman said, offering Harrison a sip from a battered water bottle, "but we look out for each other. It's the only way to stay human in all this."

Harrison nodded, a lump in his throat. "I can see that. It's... inspiring, actually."

As the group talked, Harrison's mind raced. These people have adapted to this harsh reality. Maybe I can learn from them. But I can't stay long. I need to find Dad and figure out what happened here.

The sky darkened, and with it, the atmosphere changed. The survivors grew tense, glancing nervously at the deepening shadows.

"You should find shelter for the night, boy," the older woman warned. "It's not safe to be out after dark."

Harrison stood, brushing off his clothes. "What's out there?"

Jem's scarred face twisted into a grimace. "Things that used to be human. And worse."

A chill ran down Harrison's spine. "Right. Thank you all for your kindness. I'll be careful."

As he walked away, the young woman called out, "If you need help, look for the blue lanterns. There are safe houses."

Harrison nodded gratefully, then set off into the gathering gloom. The city seemed to loom larger now, its broken silhouette menacing against the night sky. Every shadow could hide a threat, every sound a potential danger.

Stick to the plan, Harrison. Find shelter, then keep searching tomorrow. He clenched his fists, determination warring with fear. Whatever's out there, I'll face it. I have to find Dad and get some answers.

7 - 8

Harrison's footsteps echoed off the crumbling facades as he navigated through the desolate streets. The air grew thick with an oppressive silence, broken only by the occasional skitter of unseen creatures in the darkness. His eyes darted from shadow to shadow, searching for any sign of the blue lanterns the woman had mentioned.

"Come on, there has to be something," he muttered, his voice barely above a whisper. The weight of the unknown pressed down on him, each step taking him deeper into the mystery of this apocalyptic world.

A flicker of movement caught his eye. Harrison froze, heart pounding. "Hello?" he called out cautiously.

From behind a rusted car emerged a figure – a man with weathered features and eyes that spoke of hard-won survival. "You're out late, kid," the man said, his voice gravelly. "Name's Todd. What brings you to this lovely neighborhood?"

Harrison hesitated, weighing his options. This could be the lead I've been searching for, he thought. But can I trust him? Aloud, he replied, "I'm looking for someone. My father, Drake Miller. Have you heard of him?"

Todd's eyebrows shot up. "Drake Miller? Now there's a name I haven't heard in a while. You're his boy?"

Hope surged through Harrison. "Yes! Do you know where he is?"

"Maybe," Todd said, a hint of caution in his voice. "But it's not safe to talk here. I can guide you, if you're willing to trust me."

Harrison's mind raced. This is it. The chance I've been waiting for. But what if it's a trap? He took a deep breath, decision made. "Lead the way, Todd. I need to find my father."

As they set off, Harrison couldn't shake the feeling that with each step, he was walking deeper into the heart of this world's mysteries – and perhaps, closer to the truth about his own sudden appearance here.

9 - 10

Harrison's heart raced as he approached Todd, the weight of his quest pressing upon him. The desolate landscape of crumbling buildings and ash-filled air seemed to close in around them. He swallowed hard, steeling his nerves before speaking.

"Excuse me, I was wondering if you could help me? I'm looking for someone. Actually I'm not even sure he's alive. His name is Drake Miller, he's a detective ◆ ◆ was a detective." Harrison's voice wavered slightly, betraying his anxiety.

Todd's yellow-stained teeth flashed in a grimace as he coughed, a harsh, smoker's rasp. His eyes narrowed, studying Harrison with a mix of suspicion and interest. "Ah yes, Drake Miller. You mean the Lawyer. Tell me, what do you want with Mr. Miller?"

Harrison's mind reeled. Lawyer? But Dad was a detective... Unless things have changed in this world. He fought to keep his expression neutral, not wanting to reveal his confusion. "I... I need to find him. It's important."

As Todd considered his response, Harrison's gaze darted around the desolate street, half-expecting danger to emerge from the shadows at any moment. The eerie silence of the abandoned city pressed in on him, making every small sound – the crunch of debris underfoot, the whisper of wind through empty buildings – seem amplified and ominous.

11 - 12

Harrison took a deep breath, his heart pounding. The weight of his mission, the strangeness of this world, and the urgency of finding his father all converged in this moment. He extended his hand towards Todd, hoping to bridge the gap of mistrust between them.

"He's my father. I'm Harrison. Harrison Miller," he said, his voice steady despite the tremor in his chest.

Todd's eyes widened, a flicker of recognition quickly replaced by doubt. He glanced at Harrison's outstretched hand but made no move to take it. Harrison let his arm fall awkwardly to his side, trying not to let the rejection sting.

"Names Todd Weatherby," the older man growled, his voice rough as gravel. His gaze raked over Harrison, scrutinizing every detail. "But you're not Harrison. Harrison Miller is older. You can't be more than 16 years old."

Harrison's mind raced. Older? How much time has passed here? He fought to keep his expression neutral, even as confusion and alarm battled within him. Should I tell him the truth? Would he even believe me if I did?

"I know it's hard to believe," Harrison began cautiously, "but I am who I say I am. Things are... complicated." He glanced around the desolate street, painfully aware of how exposed they were. "Look, I just need to find my father. Can you help me or not?"

Todd's eyes narrowed further, suspicion etched deep in the lines of his weathered face. Harrison could almost see the gears turning in the man's head, weighing whether to trust this strange young man or not.

13 - 14

Harrison's heart thundered in his chest, the shock of Todd's words reverberating through him. Older? The implications sent his mind reeling. He swallowed hard, trying to maintain his composure as he formulated his next question.

"What... what exact year is it?" Harrison asked, his voice barely above a whisper. He braced himself for the answer, knowing it could shatter his understanding of this world entirely.

Todd's eyebrows shot up, disbelief etched across his face. He let out a harsh, barking laugh that echoed off the crumbling buildings around them. "Do you really not know?" he asked, shaking his head in bewilderment. "It's 2044, or 20 A.C as we call it."

Harrison felt the blood drain from his face. 2044. Twenty years into the future. His legs suddenly felt weak, and he had to fight the urge to sit down right there in the debris-strewn street. How is this possible? he thought, his mind racing. Did I jump forward in time, or has this world's timeline somehow accelerated?

"You alright there, kid?" Todd asked, a hint of concern creeping into his gruff voice. "You're looking a bit green around the gills."

Harrison nodded mechanically, still processing the information. "I'm fine," he lied, forcing himself to focus on the present moment. "It's just... a lot to take in."

15 - 16

Harrison's brow furrowed, his mind struggling to process the torrent of information. He latched onto the unfamiliar term, hoping it might provide some clarity.

"A.C.?" he echoed, the question hanging in the ash-laden air between them.

Todd's weathered face twisted into a mix of disbelief and amusement. He spat on the ground, a habit that seemed ingrained after years of living in this desolate world.

"Do you really not know anything, boy?" Todd scoffed, shaking his head. "A.C. After Collision. Or After Collapse as some call it."

Harrison's heart raced, each beat echoing in his ears. Collision? Collapse? The words felt heavy, laden with untold horrors. He clenched his fists, trying to ground himself in this unfamiliar reality.

What happened here? he wondered, his gaze sweeping across the ruined cityscape. The weight of twenty lost years pressed down on him, suffocating in its intensity. How much had changed? And where was his father in all of this?

Harrison opened his mouth to ask for more details, but hesitated. Todd's earlier suspicion gnawed at him. If he revealed too much ignorance, would it put him in danger? In this harsh world, knowledge was clearly power – and its lack could be a death sentence.

17 - 18

Harrison's mind reeled, struggling to process the implications of Todd's words. The crumbling buildings around him seemed to loom closer, a stark reminder of how much had changed. His eyes darted from the rusted shells of abandoned cars to the ash-coated streets, desperately searching for any familiar landmark that might anchor him to his lost past.

"Collision? Collapse?" Harrison finally managed, his voice barely above a whisper. He swallowed hard, trying to mask his confusion. "What are you talking about?"

Todd narrowed his eyes, studying Harrison with renewed suspicion. The younger man's heart pounded, afraid he'd revealed too much. He tried to keep his face neutral, but his fingers twitched nervously at his sides.

"You're really not from around here, are you?" Todd growled, taking a step closer. The acrid smell of smoke clung to his tattered clothes. "How can you not know about the Event that tore our world apart?"

Harrison's mind raced. Should he admit his ignorance or bluff his way through? The weight of the situation pressed down on him, threatening to crush what little composure he had left. He needed answers, but every instinct screamed that revealing his true nature could be dangerous.

"I... I've been isolated," Harrison stammered, grasping for a plausible explanation. "Please, I just need to find my father. Can you help me or not?"

19 - 20

Todd's expression shifted from suspicion to outright shock, his weathered face contorting as he processed Harrison's words. The sudden change in demeanor made Harrison's stomach lurch with apprehension.

"You really don't know?" Todd breathed, his voice a mixture of disbelief and something else—was that pity? "After the timelines collided, after the collapse of civilization..." He trailed off, shaking his head in bewilderment. "Who did you say you were again?"

Harrison's heart hammered in his chest. The words 'timelines collided' echoed in his mind, conjuring images of parallel worlds crashing together like tectonic plates. He'd suspected he'd traveled through time, but this... this was beyond anything he'd imagined. His throat felt dry as he answered, each word carefully measured.

"Harrison Miller," he said, fighting to keep his voice steady. "I'm Drake Miller's son."

As the words left his mouth, Harrison watched Todd's face intently, searching for any flicker of recognition. Would his father's name be a lifeline in this desolate world, or had the collapse erased all traces of the life he once knew?

21 - 22

Todd's eyes widened, a spark of recognition igniting in their depths. His weathered face transformed, years seeming to melt away as understanding dawned upon him.

"You're one of them," Todd breathed, his voice a mix of awe and trepidation. "The Temporal Guardians. You're a traveler. That's why you don't know anything. You're not from this time."

Harrison's breath caught in his throat. The Temporal Guardians. The name hit him like a physical blow, memories flooding back of Gabriel's cryptic warnings to his father. He struggled to maintain his composure, his mind racing.

"What do you know about the Temporal Guardians?" Harrison asked, trying to keep his voice steady despite the tremor in his hands.

Todd glanced nervously around the desolate street before leaning in closer. "They're the stuff of legends, kid. Guardians of the multiverse, they say. But if you're really Drake Miller's son... well, that changes everything."

Harrison's thoughts whirled. Gabriel had vanished the moment he'd arrived in this world, leaving him stranded and clueless. And now Todd was calling him a traveler, as if it were common knowledge. Had his father's abilities become public in this timeline?

He remembered Gabriel's words, the claim that Drake had forged the Temporal Guardians. A chill ran down Harrison's spine as he considered the implications. Had his father ignored the warnings from the future? Had he chosen not to alter history, leading to this apocalyptic world?

"My father," Harrison began, his voice barely above a whisper, "is he still... is he alive in this time?"

23 - 24

Harrison's heart raced as he locked eyes with Todd, desperate for answers. "What do you know about traveling? What do you know about my father?"

Todd took a step back, his hands raised in mock surrender. The gesture seemed almost playful, but Harrison detected a flicker of wariness in the man's eyes. "Listen kid," Todd said, his voice gruff and tinged with impatience, "I don't got time for a history lesson. How about I just take you to see the man himself. Follow me."

Harrison hesitated, his mind churning with conflicting thoughts. Could he trust this stranger in a world that seemed so hostile? But the promise of seeing his father, of finally getting answers, was too tempting to resist. He clenched his fists, steeling himself for whatever might come next.

"You know where my father is?" Harrison asked, unable to keep the hope from creeping into his voice. He studied Todd's face, searching for any sign of deception.

Todd merely shrugged, already turning away. "Like I said, kid. No time for questions. You coming or not?"

Harrison took a deep breath, the acrid air of this ruined world burning his lungs. He knew following Todd could be dangerous, but staying put in this desolate landscape seemed equally perilous. With a silent prayer that he wasn't making a terrible mistake, Harrison nodded.

"Lead the way," he said, falling into step behind Todd as they ventured deeper into the unknown.

25 - 26

Harrison's footsteps echoed off the crumbling walls as he followed Todd through a maze of narrow alleys. The skeletal remains of fire escapes creaked ominously above them, and shards of broken glass crunched beneath their feet. Every twist and turn felt both alien and hauntingly familiar to Harrison.

"This used to be Murphy Street," he murmured, more to himself than to Todd. "There was a bakery on the corner that made the best cinnamon rolls..."

Todd grunted, not slowing his pace. "Lot's changed since then, kid. Best not to dwell on ghosts."

As they ventured deeper into the heart of the ruined city, an unsettling quiet descended. The distant sounds of scavenging and survival that had filled the air near the outskirts faded away, replaced by an eerie stillness that set Harrison's nerves on edge.

"It's so quiet," Harrison whispered, his hand unconsciously tightening on the strap of his backpack. "Where is everyone?"

Todd's response was terse. "Smart folks steer clear of this part of town. Too many... unpredictable elements."

Harrison's unease grew with each step. The air felt thick with danger, an invisible weight pressing down on him. Despite his apprehension, he pressed on, clinging to the hope of reuniting with his father.

Dad has to have answers, Harrison thought desperately. *About the timelines, about why I'm here... about everything.*

As they rounded another corner, Harrison's foot caught on something. He looked down and froze, his blood running cold. Half-buried in the rubble was a child's teddy bear, its once-soft fur matted and stained a dark, rusty brown.

"Todd," Harrison called out, his voice tight with tension. "Maybe we should turn back. This doesn't feel right."

27 - 28

Todd turned, his eyes narrowing. "Too late for that, kid."

Before Harrison could process those ominous words, they rounded another corner and his world exploded into chaos. The acrid stench of burning flesh hit him first, followed by the horrifying sight of a human leg roasting over a makeshift fire. Surrounding it were a group of emaciated figures, their eyes gleaming with a feral hunger that made Harrison's stomach lurch.

"No," he breathed, stumbling backward. But it was too late. More shadowy forms emerged from the ruins, cutting off any chance of escape. Harrison's mind raced, searching desperately for a way out. "Todd, we have to run!"

But when he turned to his guide, the betrayal in Todd's eyes struck like a physical blow.

"Sorry, kid," Todd said, his voice devoid of emotion. "Nothing personal. Just survival."

As the cannibals closed in, Harrison's thoughts whirled in panic. *This can't be happening. I came all this way, survived so much... it can't end like this!*

He lashed out, his fist connecting with the nearest attacker's jaw. But he was outnumbered and outmatched. Rough hands seized him, pinning his arms behind his back.

"Let me go!" Harrison shouted, struggling against his captors. "My father—Drake Miller—he'll come for me! He'll make you pay for this!"

A guttural laugh rose from the group. "Drake Miller?" one of them sneered. "That name don't mean nothing no more, boy."

As they bound his wrists with cruel efficiency, Harrison's hope crumbled. The world spun, reality blurring at the edges as shock set in. *Dad... where are you?* he thought desperately as they dragged him into the shadows, away from the light, away from any chance of rescue.

29 - 30

Todd's raspy laughter cut through the air as he gestured towards Harrison. "Look what I have here, fellows. The great savior's son himself. Let's see you travel out of this one."

Harrison's heart pounded in his chest as he glared at his captor, struggling against the tight bonds that bit into his wrists. "You don't know what you're doing," he spat, his voice trembling with a mix of fear and defiance.

The leader of the cannibals, a towering man with a scarred face, leaned in close, his fetid breath making Harrison recoil. "Oh, but we do, boy. Your daddy might've been something once, but now? You're just meat to us."

Harrison's mind raced, searching for a way out. *There has to be a way. Dad wouldn't give up, and neither will I.* He scanned the ruined landscape around him, looking for anything that might aid his escape.

"You're wrong," Harrison said, meeting the leader's gaze. "My father is still out there, and when he finds out what you've done—"

A harsh slap silenced him, his cheek stinging from the impact. "Shut it, kid. Your fairy tales won't save you now."

As they shoved him towards a makeshift cage, Harrison's resolve hardened. *I can't let it end like this. I have to find Dad, to understand what happened here.* He stumbled forward, his mind working furiously to piece together a plan.

"Twenty years," he muttered to himself. "What could have changed so much in twenty years?"

The cage door slammed shut behind him, the sound echoing with a terrible finality. But as Harrison sank to his knees, a familiar warmth began to pulse in his veins—the same sensation he'd felt when he'd first traveled between worlds.

Maybe, he thought, a glimmer of hope kindling within him, *just maybe, I'm not as trapped as they think I am.*

Neon Secrets in a Grimy Diner

Red World – 2024

1 - 2

The flickering neon sign outside cast an eerie glow through the grimy diner window, painting shadows across Drake Miller's face as he slid into the worn leather booth. The air hung heavy with the scent of stale coffee and decades-old grease. Across from him, Detective Franklin Bird's weathered features were etched with skepticism, while Officer Kierstead's sharp eyes darted between them, assessing.

Drake's fingers drummed a nervous rhythm on the chipped Formica tabletop. How could he possibly make them understand? The weight of multiple realities pressed down on his shoulders, threatening to crush him. He drew in a deep breath, tasting the metallic tang of fear on his tongue.

"I appreciate you both meeting me here," Drake began, his lawyer's instincts kicking in as he carefully chose his words. "What I'm about to tell you... it's going to sound impossible."

Bird leaned back, crossing his muscular arms. "We've heard some pretty wild stories in our time, Miller. Try us."

Drake nodded, a wry smile tugging at the corner of his mouth. If only it were that simple. He glanced at the empty coffee mugs before them, wishing for something stronger to steady his nerves.

"I know this may sound unbelievable," he continued, his voice steady despite the turmoil roiling within, "but it's the truth. After the accident, I found myself waking up in two different worlds."

The words hung in the air between them, heavy with implication. Drake braced himself for their reactions, studying their faces. Bird's eyebrows furrowed, his jaw clenching as he processed the information. Kierstead's eyes widened slightly, a flicker of curiosity breaking through her professional mask.

I sound like a madman, Drake thought, fighting the urge to backpedal. But I have to make them understand. Everything depends on it.

"Two worlds," Bird repeated, his tone carefully neutral. "Care to elaborate on that, counselor?"

Drake leaned forward, his voice low and intense. "Imagine waking up one day, and everything you know has changed. The sky, the air, even the people around you. Then you blink, and suddenly you're back in a world that's familiar, but not quite right. That's what I've been experiencing."

He paused, memories of green-tinged shadows and crimson-hued cityscapes flashing through his mind. The weight of loss – of Linda, of Harrison – threatened to overwhelm him. But he pushed on, knowing that his story was their only hope of unraveling the mystery that had engulfed them all.

3 - 4

Kierstead and Bird exchanged glances, their expressions a mix of skepticism and intrigue. Drake could almost see the gears turning in their minds, trying to reconcile his outlandish tale with their grounded worldviews.

Drake took a deep breath, steeling himself for the most painful part of his story. "In one world, my son Harrison was alive," he continued, his gaze becoming distant as he recalled the memories that haunted him. "He was the same vibrant, energetic kid I've always known. But in the other world, it was my wife Linda who was alive."

He paused, his throat tightening with emotion. The fluorescent lights of the diner seemed to flicker, momentarily casting shadows that reminded him of the eerie green world. Drake's fingers tightened around his coffee mug, anchoring himself to the present.

"Each time I crossed over," Drake said, his voice barely above a whisper, "I had to come to terms with the fact that I was leaving one of them behind."

The weight of his words settled over the table. Bird leaned back, his weathered face etched with concern. Kierstead's sharp eyes narrowed, studying Drake intently.

How can I make them understand? Drake thought desperately. The pain of loss, the disorientation, the sheer impossibility of it all?

"I know how this sounds," Drake added, meeting their gazes. "But I swear to you, every word is true. And it's only the beginning of what we're facing."

5 - 6

Bird leaned forward, his stocky frame casting a shadow across the table. His eyes, sharp and observant, locked onto Drake's. "And this symbol you mentioned," he said, his voice gruff with curiosity, "the one Gabriel stole from your son's drawings. What significance does it hold?"

Drake's jaw tightened, a muscle twitching beneath his skin. He could almost see Harrison's small hands clutching the crayon, tongue poking out in concentration as he created the symbol. The memory sent a pang through his chest.

"It's a drawing that Harrison created," Drake replied, his voice low and tinged with emotion. "A symbol of hope and resilience." He paused, his mind racing through the implications. How could a child's drawing become so pivotal? "Somehow, Gabriel got his hands on it."

As he spoke, Drake's fingers unconsciously traced the shape on the tabletop. A circle, bisected by a jagged line – simple, yet somehow profound. He could feel its importance, like a tangible weight in the air around them.

What does Gabriel want with it? Drake wondered, a chill running down his spine. And how did he even know about it in the first place?

The diner's muted chatter seemed to fade away as the gravity of the situation settled over their small group. Drake looked from Bird to Kierstead, searching their faces for any sign of belief or understanding.

7 - 8

Kierstead leaned forward, her brow furrowed, eyes glinting with a mix of skepticism and intrigue. "And your blood, Drake," she said, her voice low and measured. "How does it fit into all of this?"

Drake's hand stilled on the table, the phantom symbol fading beneath his fingertips. He inhaled deeply, the scent of stale coffee and grease filling his nostrils. How could he explain something he barely understood himself?

"My blood," he began, then paused, searching for the right words. The weight of their gazes pressed upon him, expectant and wary. "It's... different."

He closed his eyes briefly, recalling the moment of discovery in that sterile lab, surrounded by beeping machines and stunned scientists. The memory felt both vivid and dreamlike, as if viewed through a haze.

"In one of the worlds," Drake continued, his voice steadier now, "I discovered it has the ability to connect me between both realities." He met Kierstead's gaze, then Bird's, willing them to understand. "It's as if my very existence is a bridge between these parallel universes."

As he spoke, Drake could almost feel the pull of the other world, a subtle tug at the edges of his consciousness. He resisted the urge to look over his shoulder, half-expecting to see a shimmering portal materializing in the dingy diner.

What am I? he wondered, not for the first time. A cosmic accident? Or something deliberately engineered?

The silence that followed his words was deafening, broken only by the distant clatter of dishes from the kitchen. Drake waited, his heart pounding, for their reaction to this impossible truth.

9 - 10

The fluorescent lights flickered overhead, casting an eerie glow on the worn formica tabletop. Drake's fingers traced the rim of his untouched coffee mug, the ceramic cool against his skin. The weight of his revelations seemed to press down on all of them, making the air thick and heavy.

Kierstead's brow furrowed deeply, her eyes darting between Drake and Bird as if searching for some sign that this was all an elaborate joke. Bird, on the other hand, leaned back in his seat, his weathered face a mask of careful neutrality.

Drake's mind raced, grasping for some way to make them understand. How could he convey the vertigo of waking up in different realities, the heart-wrenching choice between his wife and son? The words felt inadequate, pale shadows of the experiences that had reshaped his entire understanding of existence.

Finally, Bird broke the tense silence. "But why you, Drake?" he asked, his gruff voice tinged with a reluctant awe that surprised Drake. "If what you're saying is true, and I highly doubt this is nothing more than a coma dream... Why were you chosen to traverse these worlds?"

Drake met Bird's piercing gaze, recognizing the mixture of skepticism and curiosity in the detective's eyes. He took a deep breath, considering his response carefully.

"I wish I knew, Franklin," he admitted, his voice low and intense. "God knows I've asked myself that question a thousand times. Why me? Why my family? I don't have an answer. All I know is that it's happening, and I can't ignore it or wish it away."

He paused, glancing down at his hands, half-expecting to see them flickering between realities. "Maybe it's random chance. Maybe there's some greater purpose I can't see yet. But whatever the reason, I'm caught in the middle of something bigger than any of us can imagine."

11 - 12

Drake's fingers tightened around his coffee mug, the warmth grounding him in this reality. He looked up, meeting Bird's gaze with renewed determination.

"What I do know is that I won't rest until I uncover the truth behind it all," Drake declared, his voice steady despite the turmoil churning inside him. "For Harrison. For Linda. For everyone who's been affected by this madness."

Kierstead leaned forward, her skepticism evident in the slight furrow of her brow. "So tell us more," she pressed, her tone a mixture of disbelief and growing intrigue. "You say in these worlds the cab driver was killed. That the person who killed him – this Gabriel Angel person – is the same one who caused your accident. You say he stole this symbol from your son, that your blood is a bridge between alternate realities."

Drake nodded, grateful for her willingness to listen, even if she didn't believe him yet. He could see the gears turning in her analytical mind, trying to make sense of his fantastical story.

"So what happens?" Kierstead continued, her eyes narrowing. "How did you stop the killer?"

"It wasn't easy," he began, his voice low. "Gabriel... he's not just a killer. He's something more. Something that doesn't obey the laws of our reality."

As he spoke, Drake's fingers unconsciously traced the outline of Harrison's symbol on the table's surface, the memory of his son's drawing vivid in his mind. "But in the end, it came down to a choice. A terrible choice that no one should have to make."

13 - 14

Drake leaned forward, his eyes locked on Kierstead's face. The dim light of the diner cast deep shadows across his features, emphasizing the gravity of his words.

"When I was a detective in the Green World, me and you, we worked together after I was shot and we caught Gabriel after he surrendered."

The words hung in the air, heavy with implications. Drake could see the skepticism in Kierstead's eyes warring with his inherent trust in her old partner. The detective's brow furrowed, her mind clearly grappling with the impossible scenario Drake had laid out.

Bird's voice was gruff when he finally spoke, a mix of disbelief and curiosity coloring his tone. "You were shot?"

Drake nodded, his hand unconsciously moving to his hip where the phantom pain still lingered. He could almost smell the damp, mossy air of the Green World, feel the eerie silence that had enveloped them as they'd cornered Gabriel in that abandoned funhouse.

"I can still remember every detail," Drake said softly, his gaze distant. "The way the green-tinged twilight filtered through the broken windows, the echo of our footsteps in the empty halls. And then the searing pain as the bullet tore through me."

He paused, watching Bird's reaction carefully. The older detective's face remained impassive, but Drake could see a flicker of something – concern, perhaps, or the first stirrings of belief – in his eyes.

15 - 16

Drake leaned forward, his voice low and intense. "Yes, in the hip. And in both worlds the wound traveled over. What happened in one world carried over into the other."

He watched Bird's face, searching for a sign of understanding, of acceptance. But instead, a wry smile crept across the older detective's weathered features. Bird chuckled, the sound both familiar and jarring in the tense atmosphere of the diner.

"You see, there's your proof it was a dream," Bird said, his tone a mixture of triumph and sympathy. "Do you have a bullet wound in this world?"

Drake felt a surge of frustration. He'd known Bird for years, respected his no-nonsense approach and keen intellect. But now, faced with something that defied conventional logic, his old partner was retreating into skepticism.

"It's not that simple, Frank," Drake replied, his mind racing. How could he make Bird understand? The memories of both worlds felt equally real, equally vivid. The pain, the fear, the desperate race against time – none of it felt like a dream.

As Bird waited for an answer, Drake's hand unconsciously moved to his hip again. He could almost feel the rough texture of scar tissue that should have been there. But he knew that in this reality, his skin would be smooth, unmarked. The absence of physical evidence was a chasm between his experiences and what others could perceive.

17 - 18

Drake's fingers traced the unmarked skin beneath his shirt, a stark reminder of the disconnect between his memories and reality. He met Bird's skeptical gaze, determination etched into his features.

"You're right, Frank," Drake admitted, his voice low and intense. "There's no wound here. But that doesn't negate everything else."

He leaned forward, hands clasped tightly on the table. "When I woke up, the first thing I did was check for that bullet wound. It wasn't there, and for a moment, I thought maybe it had all been a dream."

Drake's mind raced, recalling the vivid details that couldn't be explained away. The cab driver's lifeless eyes, the intricate symbol from Harrison's drawings, the weight of the gun in his hand as he faced Gabriel. How could his subconscious have fabricated it all?

"But here's the thing," Drake continued, his tone urgent. "How could I have dreamed about the cab driver's death? Or the symbol? There are too many specific details that I couldn't have known."

Bird's expression softened slightly, a flicker of doubt crossing his face. Drake seized the moment, knowing it might be his only chance to convince his old partners.

"Listen," he said, leaning in even closer. "You want to know if I'm right on this? Check the DNA sample."

Drake's heart pounded as he waited for Bird's response, hoping against hope that his words would be enough to spark an investigation. The truth was out there, waiting to be uncovered. He just needed someone to believe him enough to start looking.

19 - 20

Kierstead's brow furrowed, her skepticism palpable. "We don't have a DNA sample," she said, her voice tinged with exasperation.

Drake felt a surge of adrenaline course through him. This was it - the moment that could change everything. He leaned forward, his eyes intense and focused.

"You'll find one," he said, his voice low and urgent. "And when you do, you'll notice it has three DNA profiles. It'll be my son Harrison's and the other two are mine."

The words tumbled out of him, each revelation feeling like a weight lifted from his shoulders. As he spoke, he could see the confusion and disbelief warring on Kierstead's face.

"Don't ask me how that's possible," Drake continued, raising a hand to forestall her questions. "Somehow Gabriel shares similar DNA to me and Harrison."

He paused, taking a deep breath. The next part was crucial. "If I'm right, the Harrison DNA will contain a protein that allows people to be around high levels of radiation. If I'm right, then mine should as well."

Drake's mind raced, imagining the implications of what he was saying. How could he make them understand the gravity of the situation? The lives at stake?

"Then you'll need to find Megan Johnson," he added, his voice dropping to a whisper. "She's the next victim."

As the words left his mouth, Drake felt a chill run down his spine. He knew how it sounded - crazy, impossible. But he also knew it was true. And if they didn't act soon, more lives would be lost.

21 - 22

Detective Bird leaned in, his weathered face etched with a mixture of skepticism and intrigue. His sharp eyes bore into Drake's, searching for any sign of deception or madness. The diner's dim lighting cast long shadows across the table, mirroring the darkness of the subject at hand.

"Let's say you're correct, then what?" Bird's gravelly voice cut through the tense silence. "What happened to Gabriel after he was arrested?"

Drake's throat tightened as memories from both timelines flooded his mind. He could still see Gabriel's disfigured face, that eerie calmness that sent chills down his spine. Taking a deep breath, he steadied himself before responding.

"He confessed to planting a biological bomb," Drake said, his voice barely above a whisper. "In both timelines. One was at the hospital and one was in an old abandoned building on the outskirts of the city."

As he spoke, Drake's mind raced. How could he make them understand the magnitude of the threat they were facing? The image of the hospital, teeming with innocent lives, flashed before his eyes. Simultaneously, he recalled the desolate landscape surrounding the abandoned building, a perfect cover for Gabriel's sinister plans.

Bird's eyebrows shot up, his skepticism giving way to alarm. "Two bombs? In different locations?"

Drake nodded grimly, his hands clenching into fists on the table. The weight of responsibility pressed down on him, knowing that the fate of countless lives hung in the balance. He couldn't shake the feeling that time was running out, that somewhere in this reality, Gabriel was already setting his plan in motion.

23 - 24

Holly Kierstead leaned forward, her sharp eyes boring into Drake's. The fluorescent lights of the diner cast harsh shadows across her face, accentuating the intensity of her gaze. "What did you do about the bomb?" she demanded, her voice tight with urgency.

Drake's mind raced, flashing between memories of both timelines. He could almost smell the antiseptic of the hospital corridors, feel the crumbling concrete beneath his feet in the abandoned building. His heart pounded as he recalled the frantic search, the ticking clock, the lives at stake.

"We stopped one," Drake replied, his voice hoarse with the weight of the memory. He ran a hand through his hair, trying to shake off the phantom sensation of adrenaline coursing through his veins.

As he spoke, Drake's eyes darted between Kierstead and Bird, searching for any sign of belief or understanding. The diner around them seemed to fade away, leaving only the three of them suspended in this moment of revelation.

I need them to believe me, Drake thought desperately. If they don't, how many more lives will be lost? His mind raced with possibilities, strategies to convince them, ways to prevent the impending disaster he knew was coming.

25 - 26

Kierstead's brow furrowed, her fingers tightening around her coffee mug. "And the other?" she pressed, her voice barely above a whisper.

Drake's heart clenched, the memory of his desperate act flooding back. He could almost feel the heat of the bomb against his skin, hear the frantic shouts of his colleagues. His eyes locked with Kierstead's, seeing not the skeptical detective before him, but the terrified partner he'd saved in that other world.

"I threw myself on top of it to protect you from the explosion," Drake said, his voice steady despite the tremor in his hands. He swallowed hard, the phantom pain of the blast echoing through his body. "Then I woke up here, back to reality."

As the words left his mouth, Drake felt a wave of exhaustion wash over him. How could he make them understand the weight of two worlds, the impossible choices he'd faced? He watched Kierstead's face, searching for any flicker of recognition or belief.

I sacrificed everything, Drake thought, his mind reeling. For Linda, for Harrison, for a world I'm not even sure exists anymore. But I'd do it again in a heartbeat.

The diner around them seemed to hold its breath, waiting for a response that could shatter or validate Drake's entire existence.

27 - 28

The sudden crash of Bird's hands slamming against the table shattered the tense silence. Coffee cups rattled, their untouched contents sloshing dangerously close to the rims. Drake flinched, his heart racing as he watched the stocky detective rise to his feet, his weathered face a mask of barely contained frustration.

"Let's settle this once and for all," Bird growled, his voice carrying the weight of years spent chasing down leads and separating fact from fiction. "Let's go to the hospital and do a blood test. See if you really are telling the truth."

Drake felt a surge of hope mingled with apprehension. This was his chance to prove himself, to validate the impossible experiences that had become his reality. He stood slowly, his legs unsteady beneath him.

"I'm ready," Drake said, meeting Bird's piercing gaze. "Whatever the results show, I need you to believe that I'm not lying. Not about any of this."

As they moved towards the diner's exit, Drake's mind raced. What if the test showed nothing? What if all traces of his journey through the multiverse had vanished when he woke up in this world? The thought chilled him to his core.

Bird's hand landed heavily on Drake's shoulder, steering him towards the door. "I want to believe you, Drake," he muttered, his voice gruff but not unkind. "God help me, but I do. But we need more than just your word on this."

Stepping out into the night air, Drake took a deep breath. The familiar cityscape around him suddenly felt alien, as if it could shift and change at any moment. He glanced at Bird and Kierstead, these alternate versions of his partners, and wondered if they could ever truly understand the weight he carried.

"Let's go," Drake said, his resolve strengthening. "It's time to face the truth – whatever it might be."

29 - 30

The shrill ring of Kierstead's phone cut through the tense atmosphere like a knife. Drake watched as she fumbled to answer it, her usually composed demeanor faltering. As she listened, the color drained from her face, her eyes widening with a mix of shock and disbelief.

Drake's heart began to race. Could this be it? The confirmation he'd been waiting for? He glanced at Bird, who was watching Kierstead intently, his brow furrowed with concern.

The call ended abruptly, and Kierstead lowered the phone, her hand trembling slightly. The silence stretched between them, heavy with unspoken questions.

Bird was the first to break it. "What is it?" he demanded, his voice sharp with urgency.

Drake held his breath, his mind whirling with possibilities. Whatever news Kierstead had received, it was clear it had shaken her to her core. He braced himself for the revelation, knowing that whatever came next would irrevocably change the course of their investigation – and possibly their understanding of reality itself.

31 - 32

Kierstead's voice was barely above a whisper as she relayed the news. "That was the major crimes unit. They found some blood in the car."

Drake felt a wave of relief wash over him, his tense muscles relaxing as he leaned back in his chair. A small, knowing smile played at the corners of his mouth. He'd been right. Of course he'd been right. The pieces were finally falling into place.

"Told you they would," Drake said, his tone calm and assured. He met Kierstead's bewildered gaze, noting the conflict in her eyes. She was struggling to reconcile her skepticism with this new evidence.

Bird leaned forward, his hands clasped tightly on the table. "What does this mean, Drake? How could you have known?"

Drake took a deep breath, considering his words carefully. How much should he reveal? How much would they believe? "It means," he began slowly, "that everything I've told you is true. The multiverse, the alternate realities, all of it."

As he spoke, Drake's mind raced through the implications. The blood in the car was just the beginning. Soon, they'd discover the truth about the DNA, about Harrison's unique protein, about the connection between worlds. And then, they'd have to face the looming threat – the biological bomb, Megan Johnson's impending danger, the race against time to prevent catastrophe.

"We need to move quickly," Drake urged, his lawyer's instincts kicking in. "There's still so much at stake, and time is running out in every reality."

Trapped in Darkness

Green World – 2024

1 - 2

Darkness. Absolute and unyielding.

Linda's breath came in short, ragged gasps, each inhale a struggle against the weight pressing down on her chest. The air was thick, musty, laden with the scent of damp earth. She tried to move, but her limbs met solid resistance on all sides.

"Stay calm," she whispered, her voice trembling. "You have to stay calm."

But the words did little to quell the rising tide of panic threatening to engulf her. Linda's mind raced, grasping for any shred of understanding, any explanation for how she'd ended up in this nightmarish situation.

She squeezed her eyes shut, willing herself to remember. Images flashed behind her eyelids, disjointed and hazy. A flash of green light. The sensation of falling. And then...

"Oh God," Linda whimpered, the memory hitting her like a physical blow. "I woke up here. In the dark. In the cold."

She remembered the moment of terrifying realization, the way her heart had thundered in her chest as her fingers scrabbled against unyielding earth. The suffocating pressure of soil all around her, threatening to crush the very breath from her lungs.

"This can't be happening," Linda murmured, her gentle voice cracking with fear. "This has to be a dream. Please, let this be a dream."

But the biting chill seeping into her bones, the gritty texture of dirt beneath her fingernails – it was all too visceral, too real to be a figment of her imagination. Linda's breath quickened, her chest constricting as the full weight of her situation bore down upon her.

"No," she gasped, fighting against the rising tide of claustrophobia. "I can't... I can't give in to this. I have to be strong."

Linda closed her eyes, forcing herself to take slow, measured breaths. She thought of her family, of the warmth and love that had always been her anchor in times of trouble. Even now, trapped in this hellish darkness, she clung to that memory like a lifeline.

"I will survive this," Linda whispered, her voice gaining strength despite the tremor that still ran through it. "I have to. For them."

With trembling fingers, she reached out, feeling the confines of her prison. Cold, unyielding earth met her touch on all sides. But as her hand brushed against something smooth and metallic, a flicker of hope ignited in her chest.

"What is this?" Linda murmured, her fingers tracing the object's contours. "Maybe... maybe it's a way out."

She clung to that tiny spark of possibility, refusing to let the overwhelming darkness extinguish it. Whatever cruel twist of fate had brought her to this nightmarish world, Linda was determined to find her way back to the light – back to the ones she loved.

3 - 4

As Linda's fingers traced the metallic object, a sudden jolt of realization struck her. Her mind flashed to Drake, her beloved husband, and the gunshot wound he had sustained in that other world. The memory hit her like a surge of electricity, igniting a spark of determination within her.

"Drake," she whispered, her voice barely audible in the oppressive silence. "Our connection... it's still there."

Linda's heart raced as she recalled the bizarre phenomenon they had discovered – injuries transcending realities, defying all logic and reason. It was as if the universe itself had woven an unbreakable thread between them, binding their fates across the vast expanse of the multiverse.

"If he could feel my pain," Linda mused, her thoughts swirling with a mix of hope and desperation, "maybe he can sense where I am. Maybe he's already looking for me."

She pressed her palm against the cold earth, imagining she could feel Drake's presence on the other side. "Drake," she called out, her voice stronger now. "If you can hear me, if you can feel me, please... find me. I'm here, waiting for you."

Linda's resolve hardened, her fear giving way to a steely determination. She focused on the memory of Drake's unwavering love and courage, drawing strength from the image of his piercing eyes and the sound of his reassuring voice.

"I won't give up," she declared, her words a defiant challenge to the darkness surrounding her. "You've never failed me, Drake. And I won't fail you now. We'll find our way back to each other, no matter what it takes."

With newfound purpose, Linda began to explore her confined space more methodically, her fingers probing every inch for any clue or potential escape. She refused to surrender to despair, clinging to the hope that Drake would heed her silent plea and come to her rescue.

5 - 6

Linda's fingernails scraped against the unyielding earth, her heart pounding as she steeled herself for what she was about to do. The darkness pressed in around her, but she pushed it back with sheer force of will.

"I have to do this," she whispered, her voice trembling. "For Drake. For us."

Gritting her teeth, Linda dug her nails into the soft flesh of her forearm. A sharp gasp escaped her lips as pain lanced through her, but she didn't stop. With agonizing precision, she began to carve.

"B... U... R..."

Each letter was a testament to her determination, a beacon cutting through the multiverse. As she worked, Linda's mind raced with thoughts of Drake.

"He'll understand," she murmured, her voice strained. "He always understands."

The metallic scent of blood filled her nostrils, mingling with the earthy smell of her prison. Linda paused, catching her breath.

"Drake," she called out, as if he could hear her across the dimensions. "I'm leaving you a message. Follow it. Find me."

She resumed her grisly task, etching the final letters into her skin.

"...A... L... I... V... E."

Linda slumped back, exhausted. "Buried alive," she whispered, tracing the words with trembling fingers. "Please, Drake. Decipher this. Save me."

7 - 8

Linda's ragged breathing filled the tight space as she stared into the impenetrable darkness, her arm throbbing with each heartbeat. The pain was a constant reminder of her desperate act, but it also anchored her to reality—to hope.

"I won't give up," she whispered fiercely, clenching her fists. "Drake wouldn't give up on me, and I won't give up on him."

She thought of their life together, of the challenges they'd faced and overcome. A small, determined smile tugged at her lips.

"Remember when we first met, Drake?" Linda's voice was soft, almost dreamy. "You said we were destined for great things. I didn't know then it would mean fighting across universes to find each other."

She shifted slightly, wincing as her bloodied arm brushed against the earthen wall. The motion sent a fresh wave of pain through her, but it also sparked a memory.

"The Nexus," Linda breathed, her eyes widening in the darkness. "Drake, if you're there, if you can hear me somehow—remember the Nexus. It's the key."

Her fingers traced the carved message on her arm once more, each letter a promise.

"I believe in you, Drake," she murmured, her voice gaining strength. "I believe in us. Distance, dimensions, death itself—none of it can keep us apart. Find me. I'll be waiting."

Prison Shadows

Apocolypse World – 20 A.C.

1 - 2

Harrison's eyes strained in the gloom, the acrid stench of unwashed bodies and stale fear permeating the air. Shadows danced across rusted bars, cast by the flickering torchlight beyond their prison. His gaze settled on Jonathan, a gaunt figure huddled in the corner, eyes sunken with weeks of captivity.

"Jonathan," Harrison whispered, his voice barely audible. "We need to get out of here."

The words hung in the stifling air as Harrison's mind raced. How long before they came for us? The cannibals' appetites were insatiable, and he'd seen too many prisoners dragged away, never to return. A shudder ran through him at the memory of agonized screams echoing through the night.

Jonathan stirred, his hollow eyes meeting Harrison's. "And how do you propose we do that, kid?" he rasped, a bitter laugh escaping his cracked lips.

Harrison leaned closer, urgency coloring his words. "There has to be a way. Have you noticed anything, any weakness in their defenses?"

As Jonathan considered, Harrison's thoughts drifted to his father, to the mystery of the Temporal Guardians. Would he find answers if he escaped, or just more questions? The weight of his family's legacy pressed down on him, fueling his determination.

"They're not as careful during the night shift," Jonathan finally muttered. "But even if we got past the guards, where would we go? This world... it's not like it used to be."

Harrison nodded, a grim smile tugging at his lips. "I know. But I can't give up. There are truths I need to uncover, about my father, about what's happening to reality itself. Will you help me?"

Jonathan's eyes narrowed, studying Harrison intently. "You're different, aren't you? There's something... I can't quite place it."

Harrison hesitated, wondering how much to reveal. "Let's just say I have a unique perspective on things," he said carefully. "Now, about those night guards..."

3 - 4

Jonathan's eyes widened, a spark of hope igniting in their depths. He leaned in, voice barely above a whisper. "Alright, kid. You've got my attention. Maybe there's a chance after all."

Harrison felt a surge of relief, his curiosity piqued by Jonathan's sudden change in demeanor. "What do you mean?" he asked, trying to keep his voice low.

Jonathan glanced furtively around before continuing. "I've been working on something. See those bolts on the door?" He jerked his chin towards the cell entrance. "I've managed to loosen a few. It's not much, but it might be our ticket out of here."

Harrison's heart raced as he processed this information. Could it really be this simple? No, he reminded himself. Nothing in this fractured multiverse was ever simple.

"That's brilliant," Harrison whispered, his mind already racing with possibilities. "But we'll need more than just a loose door. Have you thought about what comes after?"

As they huddled closer, Harrison couldn't help but wonder about the strange twists of fate that had brought him here. Was this part of some greater design, or just another cruel joke of the multiverse?

"We'll need to time it right," Jonathan murmured, interrupting Harrison's thoughts. "The guard change at midnight might be our best shot. But after that..." He trailed off, uncertainty clouding his features.

Harrison nodded, a plan already forming in his mind. "We'll figure it out together. For now, let's focus on getting past that door. Tell me everything you know about the guards, the layout, anything that might help."

As Jonathan began to whisper details of their prison, Harrison felt a mix of excitement and dread. Whatever lay beyond those cell walls, he knew it would bring him one step closer to unraveling the mysteries that had defined his life. The weight of his family's legacy, the enigma of the Temporal Guardians, the looming threat of collapsing realities – it all hinged on this moment, on this desperate bid for freedom.

5 - 6

The dim cell grew darker as night fell, shadows deepening in every corner. Harrison's heart pounded, each beat a reminder of the risk they were about to take. He glanced at Jonathan, barely able to make out his companion's tense features in the gloom.

"Almost time," Harrison whispered, his voice barely audible.

Jonathan nodded, his eyes fixed on the cell door. The faint glow of torchlight flickered in the distance, growing steadily brighter. Harrison's muscles tensed, ready to spring into action.

As the light drew nearer, Harrison's mind raced. What if this failed? What if they were caught? The consequences would be dire, but the alternative – remaining captive – was unthinkable. He had to find his father, had to uncover the truth about the Temporal Guardians and the collapsing realities.

The torchlight passed their cell, illuminating it briefly before plunging them back into darkness. Harrison held his breath, counting the fading footsteps. One... two... three...

"Now," Jonathan hissed.

They moved as one, surging towards the door. Harrison's fingers found the loosened bolts, his muscles straining as he pulled. The metal groaned in protest, seeming to resist their every effort.

"Come on," Harrison muttered through gritted teeth, willing the door to give way. Sweat beaded on his forehead, his arms burning with exertion. For a heart-stopping moment, he feared they'd failed.

Then, with a sudden jerk, the door shifted. Hope surged through Harrison as he redoubled his efforts, Jonathan pushing from the other side. The gap widened, inch by excruciating inch.

"We're doing it," Harrison breathed, a mixture of disbelief and triumph in his voice. "Just a little more..."

7 - 8

With a final creak of protest, the cell door swung open. Harrison and Jonathan exchanged a triumphant glance, their eyes gleaming with a mixture of relief and apprehension in the dim light.

"We did it," Harrison whispered, his heart pounding so loudly he feared it might give them away.

Jonathan nodded, a grim smile on his face. "Now comes the hard part."

They slipped out into the corridor, the cool air a stark contrast to the stuffy confines of their cell. Harrison's senses were on high alert, every shadow seeming to conceal a potential threat.

"Which way?" he murmured, eyeing the labyrinthine passages stretching out before them.

Jonathan pointed left. "Guards came from that direction. We go right."

As they crept along the dimly lit passageway, Harrison's mind raced. How many more obstacles lay between them and freedom? And what awaited them beyond these walls?

Suddenly, the echo of approaching footsteps reached their ears. Harrison's blood ran cold.

"Quick," he hissed, pulling Jonathan into a shadowy alcove.

They pressed themselves against the wall, hardly daring to breathe as a pair of guards passed by, their casual conversation a stark contrast to the fugitives' terror.

"That was close," Harrison breathed once the danger had passed. "We need to move faster."

Jonathan nodded grimly. "Agreed. But remember, one wrong move and we're cannibal chow."

The reminder sent a shiver down Harrison's spine. He pushed the gruesome thought aside, focusing instead on their next move. Freedom was close – he could almost taste it.

9 - 10

The dilapidated fence loomed before them, a rusted barrier between captivity and freedom. Harrison's heart raced as he surveyed the final obstacle, searching for a weak point.

"There," Jonathan whispered, pointing to a section where the metal had corroded away. "We can squeeze through."

Harrison nodded, his muscles tense with anticipation. "On three. One... two..."

"Three!" They bolted from the shadows, sprinting across the open ground.

The fence rattled as they pushed through the gap, jagged edges tearing at their clothes. Harrison winced as a sharp point grazed his arm, but the pain barely registered through the surge of adrenaline.

"Keep going!" he gasped, plunging into the darkness beyond.

They ran, branches whipping at their faces as they crashed through the underbrush. Harrison's lungs burned, but he didn't dare slow down. Behind them, an alarm began to wail.

"They've noticed," Jonathan panted.

Harrison's mind raced. "We need to find cover, throw them off our trail."

As they burst into a small clearing, the enormity of their situation hit Harrison. They were free, but lost in a hostile world. He turned to Jonathan, seeing his own mix of elation and fear mirrored in the other man's eyes.

"What now?" Harrison asked, his breath coming in ragged gasps.

Jonathan scanned the horizon. "We keep moving. Put as much distance between us and them as possible."

As they set off again, Harrison's thoughts turned to his father. "I will find you," he vowed silently. "And I'll get the answers I need, no matter what it takes."

11 - 12

Harrison's chest heaved as he leaned against a gnarled tree trunk, his muscles burning from the frantic escape. The eerie silence of the forest pressed in around them, broken only by their labored breathing. He turned to Jonathan, who was hunched over, hands on his knees.

"Jonathan," Harrison panted, his voice barely above a whisper, "thanks man. Couldn't have done that alone."

Jonathan straightened up, a wry smile playing across his weathered face. His calloused hands flexed unconsciously as he replied, "Honestly man, I'm just glad they didn't take my hands. Without them, I never would have gotten those bolts loose."

Harrison's gaze dropped to Jonathan's scarred hands, a shudder running through him as he imagined the fate they'd narrowly avoided. The cannibals' camp loomed large in his mind, a nightmarish tableau of blood and despair. He pushed the thoughts away, focusing instead on their next move.

"We should keep moving," Harrison muttered, more to himself than to Jonathan. "They'll be searching for us."

As they set off again, picking their way through the shadowy undergrowth, Harrison's mind raced. The virus, the collapsing realities, his father's role in it all – the pieces swirled in his head, refusing to form a coherent picture. He glanced at Jonathan, wondering just how much the man knew about the chaos engulfing their world.

13 - 14

Harrison's curiosity got the better of him. He turned to Jonathan, his voice low but urgent. "So where are you heading?"

Jonathan's pace slowed, his shoulders sagging visibly. The man's eyes, once bright with the thrill of escape, now dulled with a haunted look. "Honestly, nowhere," he replied, his voice cracking slightly. "They ate my wife and before that it was just the two of us surviving on our own."

The brutality of Jonathan's words hit Harrison like a physical blow. He stumbled slightly, his mind reeling as he tried to process the horror of what his companion had endured. The forest seemed to close in around them, the shadows deepening, as if reflecting the darkness of Jonathan's revelation.

Harrison swallowed hard, trying to find the right words. What could he possibly say in the face of such loss? He settled for a simple, "I'm sorry," knowing it was woefully inadequate.

Jonathan nodded, his gaze fixed on the path ahead. After a moment of heavy silence, he turned to Harrison. "What about you?"

The question hung in the air, forcing Harrison to confront his own uncertain future. He hesitated, weighing how much to reveal. Trust was a precious commodity in this world, but something about Jonathan's raw honesty compelled him to open up.

15 - 16

Harrison took a deep breath, his fingers unconsciously tracing the outline of the worn photo in his pocket. "I'm trying to find my father, Drake Miller," he said, his voice barely above a whisper. "Do you know him?"

The words hung in the air, heavy with unspoken tension. Harrison's eyes darted to Jonathan's face, searching for any sign of recognition or threat. His muscles tensed, ready to bolt at the slightest provocation. The last time he'd asked a stranger about his father, he'd nearly ended up as the main course in a cannibal feast.

Jonathan's reaction was immediate and visceral. His eyes widened, a mix of surprise and something darker flashing across his face. "The Temporal Guardians' messiah," he spat, his voice dripping with disdain. "Sure, I know him. If you're asking if I like him, the answer's an astounding NO!" He paused, his gaze boring into Harrison. "He's your father, eh?"

Harrison's mind raced, trying to process Jonathan's words. Temporal Guardians? Messiah? His father had always been secretive about his work, but this was beyond anything he'd imagined. He felt a familiar ache in his chest, the weight of unanswered questions threatening to crush him.

"Yes," Harrison replied cautiously, his hand instinctively moving towards the hidden knife at his belt. "What exactly do you know about him?"

17 - 18

Harrison's fingers tightened around the knife's hilt, a cold sweat breaking out on his forehead. "Yeah," he said, his voice low and tense. "Why don't you like him?"

Jonathan's eyes flashed with a mix of anger and grief. He paced in a tight circle, his wiry frame coiled with barely contained emotion. "He's the one who started all this," he snarled, gesturing wildly at the desolate landscape around them. "After the pandemic and the virus outbreak, Drake Miller stepped forward with his band of Guardians by his side."

Harrison's breath caught in his throat. His father, responsible for this devastation? It couldn't be true. Yet Jonathan's pain seemed all too real.

"Offered a cure to those willing to take it," Jonathan continued, his voice cracking. "Only thing is, the cure only worked on selected people. Those it didn't work on? They came down with the virus. We dubbed it Xenith-9."

A chill ran down Harrison's spine. He remembered his mother's tears, his father's haunted eyes in the days before... before everything changed.

"It was like Drake and his ragged tag team of guardians, led by Dr. Rachel Summers, had only given the cure to a selected few." Jonathan's fists clenched at his sides. "My son... my son wasn't one of them."

The weight of Jonathan's words settled over Harrison like a shroud. He struggled to reconcile this version of his father with the man he knew - or thought he knew. "I... I'm sorry," he managed, though the words felt hollow even to his own ears.

19 - 20

Harrison's mind reeled, grappling with the implications of Jonathan's revelation. The desolate landscape around them seemed to close in, a stark testament to the devastation wrought by this mysterious virus. He swallowed hard, his throat dry as he forced out the question burning in his mind.

"What did this virus do?" Harrison asked, his voice barely above a whisper.

Jonathan's eyes clouded over, lost in painful recollection. "It all started with patient zero, some detective. From there, it spread like wildfire." He paused, running a hand through his matted hair. "The virus... it was unlike anything we'd ever seen before."

As Jonathan began to detail the virus's structure and effects, Harrison found himself picturing the invisible threat. He imagined microscopic invaders with complex protein coats, slipping past the body's defenses with terrifying ease.

"Highly contagious," Jonathan continued, his words painting a grim picture. "You could be spreading it without even knowing. And when the symptoms hit..."

Harrison's stomach churned as he visualized the cascade of effects: fever, cough, fatigue - all escalating rapidly into something far more sinister. He couldn't help but wonder if he'd unknowingly encountered the virus in his journey across realities.

"The lungs," Jonathan said, tapping his own chest. "That's where it really dug in its claws. People gasping for air, their bodies turning against them..."

Harrison's hand unconsciously moved to his throat, as if to reassure himself he could still breathe freely. The thought of entire populations struggling for oxygen, of hospitals overwhelmed and powerless, sent a shudder through his body.

"And it didn't stop there," Jonathan pressed on, his voice growing hoarse. "It invaded the brain, shut down organs... healthy people dropping like flies alongside the vulnerable."

As Jonathan's grim litany came to an end, Harrison stood in stunned silence, the full weight of the catastrophe settling on his shoulders. His father's role in all this, the Guardians, the selective cure - it was almost too much to process.

"I... I had no idea," Harrison finally managed, his voice thick with emotion. "How could anyone create something so... devastating?"

21 - 22

Harrison swallowed hard, his mind racing with the implications of what he'd just learned. The apocalyptic landscape around them suddenly felt more ominous, as if the very air could be teeming with invisible danger. He turned to Jonathan, his eyes reflecting a mix of fear and determination.

"This is serious," Harrison said, his voice barely above a whisper. He hesitated, then asked the question that had been nagging at him since Jonathan's explanation. "What happened to those that weren't treated or the vaccine didn't work on?"

Jonathan's face darkened, his eyes taking on a haunted look. He ran a hand through his disheveled hair before answering, "They simply died. Unless you're referring to the collision."

Harrison's brow furrowed, his curiosity piqued despite the grim subject matter. He opened his mouth to inquire further about this 'collision,' but something in Jonathan's expression made him hold back. Instead, he focused on processing the information at hand.

As they continued walking through the desolate landscape, Harrison's mind whirled with possibilities. Could he be immune due to his unique heritage? Or was he unwittingly carrying the virus between realities? The weight of responsibility settled heavily on his shoulders, adding to the already overwhelming burden of his quest.

"We need to be careful," Harrison muttered, more to himself than to Jonathan. "There's so much at stake here, more than I ever realized."

23 - 24

Harrison's heart raced as he processed Jonathan's words. The implications were staggering. He took a deep breath, steeling himself before asking, "What's the collision?"

Jonathan's eyes took on a distant, haunted look. He stopped walking, turning to face Harrison fully. "Your father spewed nonsense about other worlds and how the realities were crashing in on one another. No one took him seriously until..."

He trailed off, swallowing hard. Harrison noticed Jonathan's hands trembling slightly.

"Until what?" Harrison pressed, his voice barely above a whisper.

Jonathan's gaze snapped back to Harrison, his expression grim. "Until people around the world started imploding. Poof, one second you're talking to your friend and the next you're covered in a cloak of blood and guts."

Harrison recoiled, his mind reeling at the horrific image. He could almost smell the metallic scent of blood, feel the sticky warmth of it on his skin. His stomach churned.

"That's when people started panicking," Jonathan continued, his voice hollow. "The virus was bad enough, but when people start imploding? That's when all hell broke loose."

Harrison's thoughts raced. Dad was right about the multiverse? But how? Why? He struggled to reconcile the loving father he knew with this harbinger of apocalyptic truths.

"There was mass chaos and destruction," Jonathan said, his eyes unfocused as if reliving the nightmare. "People scrambled to get ahold of the vaccine. And those it didn't work on? If the virus didn't kill them, the crushing weight of reality did."

Harrison felt the weight of Jonathan's words pressing down on him, suffocating. He stumbled slightly, overwhelmed by the enormity of what he was hearing. His father's warnings, once dismissed as paranoid ramblings, now took on a terrifying new significance.

"My God," Harrison whispered, his voice cracking. "What have we done?"

25 - 26

Harrison's mind raced, grappling with the horrific revelations. He turned to Jonathan, his eyes searching for answers.

"Did dad explain why reality was collapsing in on itself?" Harrison asked, his voice barely above a whisper. The weight of countless lives lost pressed heavily on his conscience.

Jonathan's eyes narrowed, a flicker of something—recognition, perhaps—crossing his weathered face. Without a word, he turned and began walking, his footsteps crunching on the debris-strewn ground.

Harrison hesitated, rooted to the spot. His heart pounded, torn between the desire for answers and the fear of what those answers might reveal. Dad, what were you really up to?

After a few paces, Jonathan stopped and turned, gesturing impatiently for Harrison to follow. The older man's face was a mask of grim determination.

Harrison's legs moved of their own accord, propelling him forward. As he fell into step beside Jonathan, he couldn't shake the feeling that he was walking towards a truth that would shatter his world even further. The silence between them was heavy with unspoken questions and the echoes of a dying multiverse.

27 - 28

Jonathan's eyes glinted with a mix of determination and apprehension as he spoke. "I know the answer, but it's better I show you."

Harrison's breath caught in his throat. His father's secrets, the truth about the collapsing realities—it was all within reach. Yet a part of him recoiled at the prospect of uncovering knowledge that had brought such devastation.

"Where are we going?" Harrison asked, his voice barely above a whisper. He fell into step beside Jonathan, their footsteps echoing in the eerie silence of the ravaged landscape.

As they walked, Harrison's mind raced. What could be so critical that it needed to be seen rather than explained? And how did Jonathan, a stranger until mere hours ago, know so much about his father's work?

The desolate terrain seemed to stretch endlessly before them, a grim reminder of the apocalypse they'd narrowly escaped. Harrison's muscles ached from their earlier flight, but the promise of answers drove him forward.

"Jonathan," Harrison ventured, breaking the tense silence. "How do you know all this? About my father, about the collapse?"

Jonathan's pace didn't falter, but his jaw tightened visibly. "Let's just say I had a front-row seat to the end of the world. Your father's actions affected us all, whether we wanted to be involved or not."

Harrison absorbed this, a knot forming in his stomach. What horrors would he uncover about Drake Miller, the man he'd idolized for so long?

29 - 29

Jonathan's eyes narrowed as he glanced at Harrison, his voice dropping to a near growl. "Why to the Temporal Guardians Headquarters. The very place where your father created the vaccine that destroyed humanity."

Harrison stumbled, his breath catching in his throat. The Temporal Guardians - he'd heard whispers of them before, but always as mythical protectors, not harbingers of doom. His father's face flashed in his mind, kind eyes and reassuring smile at odds with the destruction Jonathan described.

"That's impossible," Harrison muttered, more to himself than his companion. "My father was trying to save people, not destroy them."

As they crested a hill, a gleaming structure came into view, its golden spires piercing the ashen sky. Harrison's heart raced, a mix of awe and dread coursing through him.

"Looks can be deceiving," Jonathan said bitterly. "Just like your father's vaccine."

Harrison's fists clenched involuntarily. He wanted to defend Drake, to argue against these accusations, but doubt gnawed at him. What if Jonathan was right? What if the man he thought he knew was capable of such horrors?

"I need to see for myself," Harrison said, his voice steadier than he felt. "Whatever the truth is, I have to know."

They approached the shimmering barrier surrounding the building, the air crackling with otherworldly energy. Harrison steeled himself, knowing that beyond this threshold lay answers that could shatter everything he believed about his father and himself.

Anxiety in White Walls

Red World – 2024

1 - 2

The antiseptic scent of the hospital room assaulted Drake's nostrils as he sat rigidly in the chair, his knuckles white from gripping the armrests. The rhythmic beeping of distant machines and the soft shuffling of nurses' shoes in the hallway only heightened his anxiety.

Drake's gaze darted between Kierstead and Bird, who flanked him on either side. Their stoic presence offered a modicum of comfort, but it did little to quell the storm raging in his mind.

"What if the results confirm my worst fears?" Drake thought, his heart pounding. "Without my connection to the other worlds, how can I possibly save Harrison and Linda?"

He took a deep breath, trying to center himself. "No, I can't think like that. There has to be a way, even if..."

The sudden creaking of the door jolted Drake from his thoughts. A nurse entered, her pristine white uniform a stark contrast to the tumultuous emotions churning within him. She held a folder close to her chest, her expression unreadable.

"Mr. Miller," she said, nodding at Drake as she approached.

Drake's throat tightened. "That's me," he managed to croak out, his lawyer's articulation deserting him in this crucial moment.

The nurse extended the folder towards him. "Your test results, sir."

Drake's hand trembled slightly as he reached for the folder. He could feel Kierstead and Bird's eyes on him, their silent support palpable in the tense atmosphere.

"Thank you," Drake said, his voice barely above a whisper. He held the folder in his lap, suddenly afraid to open it.

Bird leaned in, his gruff voice tinged with concern. "You've faced tougher challenges than this, Drake. Whatever those results say, we're here for you."

Drake nodded, drawing strength from his friend's words. "You're right, Chief. It's just... this could change everything."

Kierstead placed a reassuring hand on Drake's shoulder. "We'll face it together, no matter what."

Taking another deep breath, Drake steeled himself. "Alright," he said, his resolve returning. "Let's see what we're dealing with."

3 - 4

With a practiced flick of his wrist, Drake opened the folder. His eyes darted across the page, scanning the medical jargon and complex charts. As a lawyer, he was used to dissecting dense documents, but this was different. This was personal.

His heart plummeted as he reached the conclusion section. The words seemed to blur before his eyes, but their meaning was unmistakable. Drake felt a cold numbness spreading through his body, starting from his core and radiating outward.

"No," he whispered, barely audible. His mind raced, desperately searching for an alternative explanation, a loophole, anything. But the evidence was there in black and white.

The nurse's voice cut through his spiraling thoughts. "I'm sorry, Drake," she said softly, her voice filled with sympathy. Her eyes met his, conveying a depth of understanding that went beyond professional detachment.

Drake's throat constricted, making it difficult to speak. He wanted to ask questions, to demand answers, but the words wouldn't come. Instead, he found himself staring at the folder in his hands, as if willing the results to change through sheer force of will.

"Is there... is there any chance of a mistake?" he finally managed to ask, clinging to a last shred of hope.

The nurse shook her head gently. "I'm afraid not, Mr. Miller. We ran the tests multiple times to be certain."

Drake closed his eyes, feeling the weight of the revelation settling heavily upon him. How could he face what lay ahead without his unique abilities? How could he hope to save Harrison and Linda now?

5 - 6

Drake lifted his gaze, meeting the concerned eyes of Kierstead and Bird. The room seemed to shrink around him, the harsh hospital lighting accentuating the worry etched on their faces. He swallowed hard, his voice barely above a whisper.

"It's gone," he murmured, the words tasting bitter on his tongue. "My connection to the other worlds... it's gone."

The admission hung in the air, heavy and suffocating. Drake's mind raced, memories of his journeys through the multiverse flashing before his eyes – the eerie green world, the pulsing red metropolis, the desolate blue reality. All of it, now beyond his reach.

Kierstead stepped forward, her normally stoic demeanor softening. She placed a comforting hand on Drake's shoulder, the warmth of the touch a stark contrast to the cold dread spreading through Drake's body.

"We'll figure this out, Drake," Kierstead said, her voice firm and reassuring.

Drake wanted to believe her, desperately needed to. But how could they possibly navigate the complexities of the multiverse without his unique ability? The faces of Harrison and Linda floated in his mind, their fates now seeming more uncertain than ever.

"I don't know how," Drake admitted, his voice cracking slightly. He clenched his fists, frustration and fear battling within him. "Without this connection, I'm just... just a lawyer from Maine. How can I possibly hope to—"

He cut himself off, unable to voice the enormity of the challenge ahead. The room fell silent, the weight of the moment palpable.

7 - 8

Drake's gaze darted between Kierstead and Bird, his dark eyes filled with a mix of anguish and desperation. He took a shaky breath, his normally composed demeanor crumbling.

"But how?" Drake asked, his voice tinged with frustration and desperation. His fingers gripped the edge of the hospital bed, knuckles turning white. "Without that connection, I'm powerless to help Harrison, to save Linda..."

The words hung in the air, each syllable a painful reminder of what was at stake. Drake's mind raced, trying to grasp at any possible solution, but coming up empty. The loss of his ability felt like a physical wound, leaving him exposed and vulnerable.

Bird stepped forward, his weathered face set in a determined expression. His sharp eyes locked onto Drake's, conveying a strength that seemed to push back against the waves of despair threatening to overwhelm the room.

"We'll find another way, Drake," Bird said, his voice gruff but filled with unwavering conviction. "You've faced impossible odds before, and the good guys always come out on top."

Drake wanted to believe him, to draw strength from Bird's resolute demeanor. But doubt gnawed at him, whispering of failure and loss. He closed his eyes, trying to steady himself.

'How can we possibly navigate the multiverse without my connection?' Drake thought, his inner voice tinged with panic. 'Every second we waste, Harrison and Linda could be...'

He couldn't finish the thought. The weight of responsibility, of love and fear intertwined, pressed down on him like a physical force.

9 - 10

Drake took a deep breath, his eyes snapping open with sudden clarity. The fog of despair lifted, replaced by a sharp focus that energized his weary body.

"You're right," he said, nodding to Bird and Kierstead. A flicker of hope ignited in his chest, growing stronger with each passing second. "I know how we can solve this."

Drake leaned forward, his voice low and urgent. "Check the security cameras. Gabriel was a janitor here at the hospital."

Kierstead's eyebrows shot up. "Here? Are you certain?"

"Positive," Drake confirmed, his mind racing with the implications. "You'll see he's badly disfigured and walks with a limp. It's unmistakable."

Bird's eyes narrowed. "Clever bastard. Hiding in plain sight."

"We'll look into it," Kierstead said, already moving towards the door. She turned back, her expression determined. "Kierstead, go see if you can't get a copy of the surveillance cameras for the past year."

As Kierstead nodded and left the room, Drake felt a surge of renewed purpose. 'This is it,' he thought. 'Our first real lead. We might not need my connection after all.'

"It's not much," Drake admitted aloud, "but it's a start. And right now, that's all we need."

11 - 12

As they exited the hospital room, the sterile fluorescent lights cast long shadows in the hallway. Drake's mind raced, the gears turning as he processed the new information. The loss of his connection to other worlds still stung, but a glimmer of hope ignited within him.

"You know," Drake said, his voice low and contemplative, "even without my ability to traverse between worlds, we're not out of options." He paused, his brow furrowing as he considered their next move. "Gabriel may have taken that from me, but he can't erase all the knowledge we've gained."

Bird nodded, keeping pace beside him. "What are you thinking, Drake?"

Drake's eyes narrowed, focused on some distant point as they walked. "We need to approach this methodically. Like peeling back layers of an onion." He turned to face his companions, his expression hardening with resolve. "We need to gather all the information we have on Gabriel. Every lead, every connection."

"Sounds like a plan," Bird agreed. "Where do we start?"

Drake's mind flashed to Linda and Harrison, their faces etched with fear in his memory. He swallowed hard, pushing down the wave of emotion threatening to overwhelm him. 'I will find you,' he promised silently. 'Whatever it takes.'

Aloud, he said, "We need to leave no stone unturned. His time as a janitor here is just the beginning. We need to dig deeper, look at his past, his associates, any trace he might have left behind in any world we've encountered."

As they reached the hospital exit, Drake paused, his hand on the door. The weight of their task settled on his shoulders, but instead of crushing him, it fueled his determination. 'This is how we bring them home,' he thought. 'This is how we make things right.'

13 - 14

Kierstead nodded, his eyes gleaming with determination. "Agreed. I'll reach out to our contacts in the intelligence community, see if they've come across any new intel on Gabriel's whereabouts." She pulled out her phone, fingers already flying across the screen. "I've got a few favors I can call in. Maybe someone's picked up a whisper we haven't heard yet."

Drake felt a surge of gratitude for his friend's swift action. 'We're not starting from scratch,' he reminded himself. 'We've got resources, connections. We can do this.'

"Good thinking," Drake said aloud, his voice tight with anticipation. He turned to Bird, noting the chief's furrowed brow and clenched jaw. "What about you, Chief? Any ideas?"

Bird's weathered face set in a look of grim determination. "And I'll dig into our case files," he added, his gravelly voice carrying the weight of years spent pursuing justice. "There might be something we missed, some detail that could lead us to him." He paused, his sharp eyes scanning their surroundings before continuing. "Gabriel's disfigurement, his limp - those are distinctive features. If he's been moving between worlds, he might have left a trail we can follow."

Drake nodded, feeling a spark of hope ignite in his chest. 'This is how we start,' he thought. 'Piece by piece, clue by clue. We'll build the puzzle that leads us to Gabriel, to Harrison and Linda.'

"Let's reconvene in an hour," Drake suggested, his mind already racing ahead to the next steps. "We'll pool what we've found and decide our next move from there."

15 - 16

The sudden vibration in Drake's pocket startled him, cutting through the tense atmosphere like a knife. He fumbled for his phone, heart racing as he pulled it out. The screen lit up, revealing the caller ID: T. Guardians.

Drake's breath caught in his throat. 'T for Temporal,' he thought, a surge of adrenaline coursing through his veins. 'Could this be it? The breakthrough we've been waiting for?'

His fingers trembled slightly as he swiped to answer, bringing the phone to his ear. The weight of possibility, of hope, hung heavy in the air.

"Hello?" Drake said, his voice a mix of trepidation and eagerness. He could feel Kierstead and Bird's eyes on him, their expressions a mirror of his own anticipation.

As he waited for a response, Drake's mind whirled with possibilities. 'The Temporal Guardians,' he mused, 'keepers of the multiverse. What could they want with me? And why now, when we're at our lowest point?'

The silence on the other end stretched for what felt like an eternity, each second amplifying Drake's anxiety and hope in equal measure.

17 - 18

A crisp, authoritative voice finally broke the silence, each word deliberate and precise. "Is this Drake Miller, the lawyer from Bridgewater, Maine?"

Drake's grip on the phone tightened, his knuckles whitening. He glanced at Kierstead and Bird, their faces etched with concern and curiosity. A myriad of thoughts raced through his mind. 'How do they know who I am? What do they want?' He took a deep breath, steeling himself.

"Yes... speaking," Drake replied, his lawyer's instincts kicking in, cautious yet controlled. He paused, weighing his next words carefully. The loss of his connection to other worlds still stung, a raw wound that left him feeling vulnerable. But here was a potential lifeline, a thread of hope he couldn't ignore. "Who may I ask is calling?"

As he waited for the response, Drake's free hand absently reached for the hospital bed railing, seeking stability. The sterile room seemed to close in around him, the beeping of nearby machines a distant echo. He felt poised on the edge of a precipice, about to plunge into unknown depths.

'This could change everything,' he thought, his heart racing. 'But at what cost?'

19 - 19

"This is Dr. Rachel Summers. I'm a lead expert with the Temporal Guardians. I think we need to talk."

Drake's breath caught in his throat, his mind reeling at the implications. The Temporal Guardians - a name whispered in legends, spoken of in hushed tones among those who knew of the multiverse's intricacies. He had always doubted their existence, dismissing them as myths ever since Gabriel revealed their existence to him..

"The Temporal Guardians?" Drake echoed, his voice barely above a whisper. He noticed Kierstead and Bird exchange puzzled glances. 'They're real,' he thought, a mixture of awe and trepidation washing over him.

Dr. Summers' voice cut through his thoughts, crisp and authoritative. "I understand you've recently experienced a... disconnection from your multiversal abilities, Mr. Miller. We believe we can help."

Drake's free hand clenched into a fist, hope surging through him like an electric current. He turned away from his friends, lowering his voice. "How do you know about that? And how can you possibly help?"

"We have our ways of monitoring temporal and dimensional anomalies," Dr. Summers replied, a hint of amusement in her tone. "As for help, well, that's why we need to talk. In person."

Drake's mind raced, weighing the potential risks against the desperate need to regain his abilities. 'This could be our only chance to save Harrison and Linda,' he thought, his resolve solidifying.

"Alright," Drake said, his voice firm. "Where and when?"

Dimensions of Discovery

Red World – 2024

1 - 2

The Temporal Research Institute loomed before Dr. Rachel Summers, its sleek glass panels reflecting the vibrant cityscape of New Haven. As she approached the entrance, her mind raced with possibilities for the day ahead.

"Another day, another dimension to explore," she mused, swiping her access card.

The lobby bustled with activity as scientists from various corners of the globe converged, their excited chatter filling the air. Rachel nodded to a few colleagues as she made her way to the elevator, her footsteps echoing on the polished floor.

As the doors closed, she found herself alone with Dr. Jonathan Evans, her longtime friend and colleague.

"Morning, Jonathan," she said, offering a warm smile. "Ready to push the boundaries of reality today?"

Dr. Evans adjusted his wire-rimmed glasses, his calm demeanor a stark contrast to the frenetic energy around them. "Always, Rachel. Though I must admit, our latest findings have me both excited and concerned."

Rachel's brow furrowed. "Oh? What's on your mind?"

As the elevator ascended, Dr. Evans explained, "The data from our last expedition suggests a potential instability in the fabric between dimensions. It could have far-reaching implications for our work."

Rachel's mind whirled with the implications. Could this be the breakthrough they'd been waiting for? Or a sign of impending disaster?

"We'll need to approach this carefully," she said, her voice steady despite the surge of adrenaline coursing through her. "Gather the team for an emergency briefing in an hour. We need to analyze every piece of data before we proceed."

The elevator dinged, and they stepped out onto the floor housing the Multiverse Exploration Division. Rachel's gaze swept across the bustling laboratory, pride swelling in her chest at the sight of her dedicated team hard at work.

"Jonathan," she said, turning to her colleague, "I have a feeling today's going to be a game-changer. Let's make sure we're ready for whatever the multiverse throws our way."

As Dr. Evans nodded and headed off to prepare for the briefing, Rachel took a deep breath, steeling herself for the challenges ahead. The mysteries of alternate dimensions beckoned, and she was determined to unravel them, no matter the cost.

3 - 4

The morning sun painted the sleek corridors of the Temporal Research Institute in hues of gold as Dr. Rachel Summers strode purposefully towards the main laboratory. Her lab coat billowed behind her like a cape, a visual testament to her role as a pioneer in multiverse exploration. The rhythmic click of her heels against the polished floor echoed through the hallway, accompanied by the excited murmurs of the researchers trailing in her wake.

As she approached the lab's entrance, Dr. Summers' mind raced with possibilities. Today's experiments could unlock secrets of alternate realities they'd only dreamed of before. She allowed herself a small, determined smile before composing her features into their usual mask of calm authority.

The doors slid open with a soft hiss, revealing a hive of activity within. Dr. Summers paused for a moment, taking in the scene before her. Researchers hunched over computer terminals, their faces bathed in the blue glow of screens displaying complex equations and swirling data patterns. Technicians darted between towering machines, adjusting dials and checking readouts with practiced precision.

"Dr. Evans," Rachel called out, spotting her colleague amidst the bustle. "How are the preparations coming along?"

Dr. Jonathan Evans looked up from the holographic display he'd been studying, his wire-rimmed glasses reflecting the shimmering data points. "Ah, Rachel," he said, his calm voice a counterpoint to the lab's frenetic energy. "We're nearly there. The quantum stabilizers are at 97% capacity, and we've triple-checked the temporal coordinates."

Rachel nodded approvingly. "Excellent work, Jonathan. I knew I could count on you." She paused, noticing a slight furrow in his brow. "Is something troubling you?"

Dr. Evans hesitated for a moment before responding. "It's probably nothing, but... there's an anomaly in the latest data set. It could be a simple calibration error, but if it's not..."

"If it's not," Rachel finished, her voice low, "it could indicate a fundamental shift in our understanding of interdimensional travel." She felt a mix of excitement and trepidation course through her. This was why she'd dedicated her life to this work – the thrill of discovery, the potential to rewrite the laws of physics as they knew them.

"Gather the team," she decided, her eyes gleaming with determination. "We need to analyze this anomaly from every angle before we proceed with today's expedition. The multiverse isn't going anywhere – but we need to ensure we're not walking into a trap of our own making."

As Dr. Evans moved to assemble the researchers, Rachel turned her attention to the pulsing heart of the lab – the Nexus Portal, a shimmering gateway that held the promise of infinite realities. She placed her hand on the cool metal of the control panel, feeling the subtle vibrations of power coursing through it.

"What secrets are you hiding today?" she whispered to herself, a mixture of reverence and challenge in her voice. "We're coming for you, ready or not."

5 - 6

Dr. Rachel Summers surveyed the bustling laboratory, her keen eyes taking in every detail of the controlled chaos before her. The air hummed with the energy of scientific discovery, a tangible excitement that made her heart race.

"Good morning, everyone," she announced, her voice carrying a mix of authority and warmth that immediately commanded attention. "I trust you're all ready for another day of exploration and discovery."

A chorus of enthusiastic responses erupted from the gathered researchers, their faces alight with anticipation. Dr. Summers felt a surge of pride in her team's dedication. She caught Dr. Jonathan Evans's eye across the room, noting the reassuring nod he gave her.

Gesturing towards the center of the lab, Rachel directed their attention to the holographic display. A mesmerizing array of swirling patterns and vibrant colors danced before their eyes, representing the complex tapestry of the multiverse they sought to unravel.

"As you can see," Rachel began, her voice tinged with excitement, "our latest calculations have revealed some intriguing anomalies in the fabric of reality." She zoomed in on a particular section of the display, highlighting a series of pulsating nodes. "These fluctuations could indicate a previously undiscovered pathway between dimensions."

As she spoke, Rachel's mind raced with possibilities. Could this be the breakthrough they'd been seeking for years? The potential implications were staggering, and she felt a familiar thrill of scientific curiosity course through her veins.

"Dr. Evans," she called out, "what's your initial assessment of these readings?"

7 - 8

Dr. Evans stepped forward, his eyes narrowing behind his wire-rimmed glasses as he studied the holographic display. "Fascinating," he murmured, stroking his neatly trimmed beard. "The quantum signatures here suggest a level of interdimensional permeability we've never encountered before."

Rachel nodded, her heart racing with excitement. She turned back to address the team, her voice filled with passion and determination. "Today, we embark on a journey unlike any other," she declared, her eyes sparkling with anticipation. "We stand on the threshold of a new frontier, where the boundaries between reality and imagination blur. Together, we will venture into the unknown, charting a course through the multiverse itself."

A hushed silence fell over the room as the weight of her words sank in. Rachel could feel the energy shift, a palpable sense of anticipation and nervous excitement filling the air. She caught glimpses of wide eyes and quickened breaths among her colleagues.

"Dr. Summers," a young researcher called out, her voice quavering slightly, "are you suggesting we attempt a physical crossing?"

Rachel paused, considering her response carefully. The risks were enormous, but so were the potential rewards. "That's precisely what I'm proposing," she confirmed, her tone steady and resolute. "We've prepared for this moment for years. It's time to put our theories to the test."

With a determined nod, Rachel began issuing instructions, her mind already racing ahead to the myriad preparations required. As her team sprang into action around her, she felt a mix of exhilaration and trepidation. We're really doing this, she thought. We're about to step into the unknown.

9 - 10

Dr. Rachel Summers surveyed the sleek, glass-topped table before her, its polished surface reflecting the determined faces of her top researchers. The hum of anticipation was palpable in the air-conditioned conference room.

"Let's begin," Rachel announced, her voice steady despite the flutter of excitement in her chest. "We need a comprehensive strategy for this expedition. Dr. Evans, your thoughts on viral containment protocols?"

Dr. Jonathan Evans leaned forward, his wire-rimmed glasses catching the light. "I've developed a new nanotech barrier," he explained, his calm voice belying the gravity of his words. "It should protect us from any interdimensional pathogens we might encounter."

Rachel nodded, absorbing the information. Brilliant as always, Jonathan, she thought. Our safety net in the face of the unknown.

"Excellent work, Jonathan," she said aloud. "Dr. Chen, what about our quantum entanglement sensors?"

As Dr. Marcus Chen launched into his explanation, Rachel's mind raced, piecing together the complex puzzle of their mission. We're on the brink of something extraordinary, she mused. The multiverse stretches before us, vast and unexplored.

The discussion flowed, each scientist contributing their expertise. Rachel listened intently, her keen intellect connecting disparate ideas into a cohesive plan. The possibilities seemed endless, exhilarating, and terrifying all at once.

11 - 12

Rachel's gaze swept across the room, taking in the eager faces of her team. She drew a deep breath, her mind crystallizing their next steps.

"We'll need to recalibrate the quantum stabilizers," she said, her voice calm and authoritative. Rachel's fingers traced an invisible pattern on the table's surface as she spoke, visualizing the complex calculations in her mind. "And double-check the temporal coordinates for any discrepancies."

The weight of responsibility settled on her shoulders. One miscalculation could strand them in an unknown reality or worse. We're venturing into uncharted territory, she thought. The risks are immense, but so are the potential discoveries.

Around the table, heads nodded in agreement. Dr. Chen's eyes sparkled with determination as he pulled up a holographic display of the temporal matrix. Jonathan, their resident engineer, leaned forward, his calloused hands already itching to make the necessary adjustments to their equipment.

"I'll run a full diagnostic on the stabilizers," Jonathan offered, his gruff voice tinged with excitement. "We can't afford any surprises once we're out there."

Rachel felt a surge of pride in her team. "Excellent, Jonathan. Your expertise will be crucial for this mission."

As the scientists began discussing the finer points of their preparations, Rachel's mind wandered to the ancient codex sitting in her office. What secrets does it hold? she wondered. And how will they shape our understanding of the multiverse?

13 - 14

Rachel's gaze swept across the room, taking in the determined faces of her team. Her heart swelled with a mixture of pride and anticipation. This is it, she thought. The culmination of years of research, sleepless nights, and relentless pursuit of knowledge.

She stood, her lab coat rustling softly. The quiet murmur of conversation died down as all eyes turned to her. Rachel took a deep breath, steadying herself for the weight of the words she was about to speak.

"Before we adjourn," she began, her voice clear and resolute, "I want to remind you all of something crucial."

Dr. Jonathan Evans leaned forward, his wise eyes twinkling behind wire-rimmed glasses. "What's on your mind, Rachel?" he asked, his tone gentle and encouraging.

Rachel smiled at her mentor, drawing strength from his unwavering support. "Remember, we're pioneers in this field," she said, her voice ringing with conviction. She placed her palms on the table, leaning in to emphasize her words. "Our journey may be fraught with challenges, but together, we will overcome them."

She paused, allowing her gaze to meet each team member's eyes. In her mind, she saw flashes of the worlds they might encounter.

"The fate of the multiverse rests in our hands," Rachel continued, her voice barely above a whisper yet carrying to every corner of the room. "We will not falter in our quest for knowledge and understanding."

A shiver ran down her spine as she spoke those words. The enormity of their mission hit her anew, but instead of fear, she felt a surge of exhilaration. We're about to change everything, she thought. The very fabric of reality is within our grasp.

15 - 16

The lab hummed with energy as the scientists dispersed, their footsteps echoing with purpose across the polished floor. Rachel's heart raced with anticipation as she made her way to the secure vault at the far end of the room. Her fingers trembled slightly as she input the access code, the heavy door sliding open with a pneumatic hiss.

Inside, bathed in soft blue light, lay the ancient book. Rachel approached it reverently, her breath catching in her throat as she gazed upon its weathered leather cover. Gently, she lifted it from its protective case, feeling the weight of centuries in her hands.

"Incredible, isn't it?" Dr. Evans's voice startled her from her reverie. He stood beside her, eyes fixed on the tome. "To think this belonged to Sir Mordred himself."

Rachel nodded, carefully opening the book to reveal intricate patterns etched across its yellowed pages. "It's beautiful," she murmured, tracing a finger along a swirling symbol. "But what secrets does it hold, Jeremy? Could this really be the key to unlocking the multiverse?"

Dr. Evans leaned closer, adjusting his glasses. "If the legends are true, it just might be. But Rachel," he paused, his tone growing serious, "we must tread carefully. The power contained within these pages... it could reshape reality itself."

Rachel met his gaze, determination burning in her eyes. "That's precisely why we need to understand it. Imagine the possibilities, Jeremy. We could prevent catastrophes, save entire worlds."

She turned back to the book, her mind racing with possibilities. What if we could harness this power? she thought. We could rewrite the very fabric of existence. But at what cost?

17 - 18

Rachel sighed, running a hand through her hair as she leaned back in her chair. The ancient book lay open before her, its cryptic symbols seeming to dance mockingly across the page. For weeks, she had pored over every inch of the manuscript, her eyes straining in the dim light of her study as she sought to unravel its mysteries.

"There has to be something I'm missing," she muttered, frustration evident in her voice. She reached for her coffee mug, only to find it empty. Again.

As she stood to stretch her cramped muscles, Rachel's gaze drifted to the window. The setting sun cast long shadows across her cluttered desk, reminding her of how much time she'd spent locked away with this enigma.

"Maybe I need a fresh perspective," she thought, considering calling Dr. Evans. His calm demeanor might help clear her mind.

Just as she reached for her phone, a soft knock echoed through the room. Rachel froze, her heart rate quickening. Who could be here at this hour?

Cautiously, she approached the door. "Hello?" she called out, her hand hesitating on the handle.

No response came. With a deep breath, Rachel steeled herself and opened the door. Her eyes widened as she took in the sight before her: a figure shrouded in shadows, their features obscured by the failing light of dusk.

"Can I help you?" Rachel asked, her scientific curiosity warring with a sudden sense of unease.

19 - 20

"Can I help you?" Dr. Summers inquired, her voice tinged with curiosity. She leaned forward slightly, squinting to make out the features of her unexpected visitor in the fading twilight.

The figure stepped forward, emerging from the shadows like a specter materializing from mist. Rachel's breath caught in her throat as she beheld a young boy of striking appearance. His eyes, an impossible shade of iridescent blue, gleamed with an otherworldly intensity that sent a shiver down her spine. An aura of mystery seemed to cling to him like a second skin, palpable even in the dim porch light.

"Who are you?" Rachel asked, her scientific mind racing to rationalize the inexplicable presence before her. "How did you get here?"

The boy remained silent, his piercing gaze fixed on her with an unnerving steadiness. Rachel felt as though those eyes were peering into the very depths of her soul, probing for secrets she didn't even know she possessed.

Instinctively, she glanced back at her study, where the ancient book lay open on her desk. A surge of protectiveness washed over her. 'Could he possibly know about the manuscript?' she wondered, her heart rate quickening. 'But how? And why would a child be interested in such an arcane text?'

"I... I think you may have the wrong address," Rachel said, attempting to regain control of the situation. Yet even as the words left her mouth, she knew with inexplicable certainty that this boy's appearance was no mere coincidence.

21 - 22

The boy's lips curled into a knowing smile, sending another shiver through Rachel. He spoke, his voice low and melodious, far too mature for his apparent age.

"I believe you possess something of great importance," he said, each word carefully measured. "Something that holds the key to unlocking the secrets of time itself."

Rachel's mind reeled. Her fingers tightened on the doorframe, steadying herself against the sudden vertigo of implications. How could he possibly know about the book? She'd told no one, not even her closest colleagues at the Institute.

"I'm afraid I don't know what you're talking about," she lied, her scientific training warring with the inexplicable certainty that this child was far more than he appeared.

The boy's eyes flickered, a hint of amusement dancing in their otherworldly depths. "Dr. Summers," he said, her name a gentle rebuke on his lips, "surely a woman of your intellect understands the futility of such deceptions."

Rachel's breath caught. She hadn't introduced herself. 'Who is he?' she wondered, her analytical mind grasping for explanations. 'A prodigy sent by a rival institute? Some sort of elaborate prank?'

But deep down, she knew. This was something far beyond the realm of her current understanding. Something that whispered of possibilities she'd only dreamed of in her most ambitious theories.

"How do you know about the book?" she asked, her voice barely above a whisper.

23 - 24

Rachel's heart raced as she studied the young man's face, searching for any clue to his true nature. Her scientific instincts warred with a growing sense that she stood at the threshold of something monumental.

"I don't know what you're talking about," she replied, her tone guarded even as her mind raced through possibilities. "But if you have information that could help me decipher this book, I'm willing to listen."

The words felt hollow as soon as they left her lips. She was admitting too much, revealing her hand to this enigmatic stranger. And yet, the potential knowledge he offered was too tantalizing to ignore.

The young man's lips curved into a smile, a knowing glint in his eyes that seemed to pierce right through her. "I can offer you the answers you seek," he said cryptically. "But first, you must trust me."

Rachel's breath caught in her throat. Trust? How could she possibly trust someone – some*thing* – she couldn't begin to understand? And yet, the ancient codex had resisted all her attempts at decryption. If this boy truly held the key...

'This could change everything,' she thought, her mind spinning with the implications. 'The nature of time, the multiverse – all the theories we've been working on at the Institute...'

She met the young man's gaze, steeling herself for whatever came next. "Trust is earned," she said firmly. "But I'm willing to listen. Tell me what you know about the book."

25 - 26

Rachel's heart pounded as she led the mysterious young man into her study. The ancient book lay open on her desk, its weathered pages seeming to pulse with hidden knowledge. She gestured for him to approach, watching intently as his eyes swept over the intricate symbols.

"Remarkable," he murmured, his fingers hovering just above the parchment. "The Multiverse Manuscript, in the flesh."

Rachel's eyebrows shot up. "You know its name? How?"

The young man's lips quirked in a enigmatic smile. "Let's just say I've... encountered it before. Now, look here." He pointed to a complex diagram near the center of the page. "This isn't just decoration. It's a map of interdimensional pathways."

As he began to explain, Rachel's mind raced to keep up. Her years of theoretical work suddenly crystallized into tangible possibility.

"Wait," she interrupted, leaning closer. "Are you saying these symbols represent actual gateways between realities?"

He nodded. "Precisely. And with the right understanding, they can be accessed."

Rachel's breath caught. "Time travel... it's really possible?"

"More than possible," the young man replied. "It's been happening for millennia. Your work at the Temporal Research Institute has only scratched the surface."

A thrill of excitement coursed through her, tempered by a hint of skepticism. "How do you know about the Institute?"

The young man's eyes twinkled. "Dr. Summers, there's far more to reality than you've yet imagined. Are you prepared to see just how deep the rabbit hole goes?"

Rachel hesitated, her scientific mind warring with the incredible possibilities before her. "I... I think I am," she finally said, her voice barely above a whisper.

27 - 27

Rachel's fingers traced the intricate patterns on the ancient page, her mind reeling with the implications. "If what you're saying is true," she murmured, more to herself than her enigmatic visitor, "then everything we thought we knew about physics, about reality itself..."

"Is just the beginning," the young man finished, his voice resonating with an authority beyond his apparent years.

She looked up, studying his face. There was something familiar about him, yet utterly alien. "Who are you, really?" she asked, her scientific curiosity overriding her initial caution.

He smiled, a flicker of sadness crossing his features. "Someone who's seen the tapestry of time unravel and rewoven more times than I care to count. But right now, I'm your guide to what lies beyond."

Rachel's heart raced. This was the moment she'd dreamed of her entire career - the cusp of a breakthrough that would change everything. Yet a nagging doubt persisted.

"Why me?" she asked, her voice barely above a whisper. "Out of all the researchers in the world, why come to me with this?"

The young man's gaze intensified. "Because, Dr. Summers, you possess something unique. A perspective, an intuition that makes you uniquely suited to navigate the complexities of the multiverse."

Rachel's mind whirled with possibilities, potential experiments, the sheer scope of what lay before her. "If we can harness this," she breathed, "the applications are endless. We could prevent disasters, cure diseases before they even emerge, reshape the very course of human history!"

"And therein lies the danger," the young man cautioned, his tone grave. "The multiverse is not a toy to be trifled with. Every action ripples across realities in ways we can scarcely comprehend."

Rachel nodded, sobered by the weight of responsibility. "So what's our next step?"

The young man's eyes gleamed with a mixture of excitement and trepidation. "We prepare you for your first journey across the boundaries of reality itself."

Ghosts in the Spotlight

Red World – 2024

1 - 2

Detective Holly Kierstead leaned forward; her face bathed in the eerie blue glow of the security monitors. The flickering images reflected in her dark eyes as she scanned each screen with laser focus, searching for a ghost.

"Come on, Gabriel. Show yourself," she muttered, her fingers drumming an impatient rhythm on the desk.

Hours of footage had yielded nothing but mundane hospital routines – nurses making rounds, doctors rushing between patients, visitors shuffling through corridors. Holly's analytical mind catalogued each face, each movement, looking for anything out of place.

Then, a flash of movement caught her attention. Her breath caught in her throat as a figure appeared on the leftmost screen.

"There," she whispered, zooming in on the grainy image.

The man's face was a roadmap of scars, his features twisted and distorted. He moved with a pronounced limp, yet there was a predatory grace to his gait as he navigated the hospital corridors.

Holly's heart raced. "It's him. It's really him."

She watched, transfixed, as Gabriel made his way through the hospital with a clear purpose. Her mind whirled with implications. Drake had been telling the truth all along. Gabriel wasn't just a figment of his imagination or a convenient scapegoat. He was real, flesh and blood, caught on camera.

"But what were you doing there?" Holly mused aloud, her brow furrowing. "And how are you connected to the accident?"

A chill ran down her spine as she considered the possibilities. If Gabriel was real, what else in Drake's fantastic story might be true? The multiverse, the virus, the blood of the chosen one – could it all be more than just the ravings of a grieving man?

Holly shook her head, trying to focus on the concrete evidence before her. "One step at a time, Kierstead," she told herself. "Gabriel's real. That's what matters right now. Everything else is just speculation until we have proof."

She leaned back in her chair, her gaze still fixed on Gabriel's image. "I'm going to find you," she promised the frozen figure on the screen. "And when I do, you're going to tell me everything you know about Drake Miller and that accident."

3 - 4

As Holly's eyes remained fixed on Gabriel's image, her phone suddenly buzzed, vibrating against the desk. She snatched it up, her heart skipping a beat as she recognized the number.

"Kierstead," she answered, her voice taut with anticipation.

"Detective Kierstead," came a crisp, professional voice from the other end. "This is Dr. Samantha Wells from the forensic team. We've completed our analysis of the DNA found in the car from the accident."

Holly's grip tightened on the phone. This could be it – the breakthrough she'd been waiting for. She glanced back at the monitor, Gabriel's disfigured face still frozen on the screen, a silent reminder of the case's complexity.

"Go ahead, Dr. Wells," Holly urged, her free hand reaching for a pen. "What did you find?"

As she listened to the doctor's report, Holly's mind raced. Could this new evidence corroborate Drake's seemingly impossible story? Or would it lead her down an entirely different path? Whatever the results, she knew they would be a crucial piece in this multidimensional puzzle.

5 - 6

Holly's heart thundered in her chest, each beat echoing the gravity of the moment. She leaned forward in her chair, pen poised over her notepad, ready to jot down every critical detail. The bank of monitors surrounding her seemed to fade into the background, all her focus narrowing to the voice on the other end of the line.

This was it. The moment that could unravel the enigma surrounding Drake Miller, his family's tragic fate, and the inexplicable presence of Gabriel. Holly's mind flashed to Drake's haunted eyes as he recounted his impossible tale of parallel worlds and doppelgangers. Could science actually support his fantastical claims?

She drew a deep breath, steeling herself. "And?" Holly prompted, unable to mask the urgency in her voice. Her free hand clenched into a fist, knuckles white with tension. Whatever Dr. Wells was about to reveal, Holly knew it would irrevocably alter the course of her investigation – and perhaps her entire understanding of reality itself.

7 - 8

The forensic analyst's voice crackled through the phone, heavy with disbelief. "The DNA belongs to both Harrison and Drake Miller," she said, the words hanging in the air like a dense fog.

Holly's pen clattered to the desk. She blinked rapidly, her mind struggling to process the information. "Both of them? How is that even possible?" she asked, her voice barely above a whisper.

"I... I don't know, Detective," the analyst replied, sounding as perplexed as she felt. "We've run the tests multiple times. It's as if the DNA is... simultaneously theirs and not theirs. It defies everything we know about genetics."

Holly leaned back in her chair, her gaze unfocused as she stared at the bank of monitors before her. The security footage of Gabriel's disfigured form seemed to mock her from one of the screens. If both Drake and Harrison's DNA were found at the scene of the accident, then it meant they had been in the car together, didn't it? But how could they have been in two cars at once?

She rubbed her temples, a headache forming as she grappled with the implications. "This correlates with Drake's story," she muttered to herself. "But then, why didn't his blood test reveal what he claimed it would?"

"Detective?" the analyst's voice pulled her from her thoughts. "What should we do next?"

Holly took a deep breath, trying to center herself. "Run the tests again," she said firmly. "And then run them a dozen more times if you have to. We need to be absolutely certain about these results."

As she hung up the phone, Holly couldn't shake the feeling that she was standing on the precipice of something far larger and more complex than she had ever imagined. The boundaries of reality itself seemed to be blurring, and she was determined to find out why.

9 - 9

Holly's fingers tapped a restless rhythm against her thigh as she stared intently at the security footage, her mind racing. The image of Gabriel's limping figure burned into her retinas, a constant reminder of the bizarre nature of this case.

"Chief," she called out, her voice tight with urgency. "I need to speak with you."

Chief Franklin Bird strode over, his weathered face etched with concern. "What have you got, Kierstead?"

Holly's eyes never left the screen as she spoke. "We've got DNA evidence placing both Drake and Harrison at the scene, sir. And now this footage of Gabriel... It's all starting to fit together, but in a way that defies logic."

Franklin rubbed his chin, his brow furrowed. "You're thinking multiverse theory, aren't you?"

"I know it sounds crazy, but what if Drake's story about parallel realities is true?" Holly's voice dropped to a whisper. "What if we're dealing with something beyond our understanding of physics?"

The chief sighed heavily. "Kierstead, you know how this sounds. We need hard evidence, not sci-fi theories."

Holly's jaw clenched, her determination surging. "With all due respect, sir, we have the evidence. It just doesn't make sense in our current framework of reality."

She stood up abruptly, her body thrumming with energy. "I need to talk to Dr. Summers. If anyone can make sense of this, it's her."

As Holly moved towards the door, she couldn't shake the feeling that she was on the verge of uncovering a truth that would shake the foundations of their world. Whatever the cost, she would see this through to the end.

Shadows of Chaos

Blue World – 2024

1 - 2

Detective Holly Sharp's knuckles whitened as she gripped the steering wheel, her car slicing through the fog-shrouded night. The winding road before her seemed to twist and writhe like a living thing, each curve a new challenge to her increasingly fragile focus.

"Come on, Holly," she muttered to herself, blinking hard as another wave of dizziness washed over her. "You've faced down interdimensional threats. You can handle a little drive." And now, as she raced towards the Miller house, she could feel her body betraying her.

Sharp coughed violently, the sound echoing in the confines of her car. She fumbled for the bottle of water in the cup holder, her usually steady hands trembling.

I can't give up now, she thought, forcing herself to take a sip. The Millers are counting on me. The whole damn multiverse might be counting on me.

As she rounded another bend, Sharp's vision blurred alarmingly. The road ahead seemed to swim, doubling and tripling before her eyes. She blinked rapidly, desperately trying to focus.

"No, no, no," she growled, fighting against the disorientation. "I've come too far to fail now."

But her body had other ideas. The fever that had been simmering for days now raged through her, turning her skin to fire and her thoughts to mush. Each breath felt like sandpaper in her lungs, and the fatigue that had been nipping at her heels now threatened to drag her down into darkness.

I should pull over, a small, rational part of her mind suggested. But the larger part, the part driven by an almost manic determination, refused to yield.

"Just... a little... further," Sharp gasped, her words barely audible over the pounding of her heart.

As the Miller house finally came into view, a hazy silhouette against the night sky, Sharp felt a surge of triumph. But it was short-lived. The world tilted alarmingly, and she felt herself slipping away, helpless against the onslaught of her illness.

The last thing Detective Holly Sharp saw before unconsciousness claimed her was the Miller house looming ever closer, a silent sentinel holding secrets she had fought so hard to uncover.

3 - 4

Sharp's trembling fingers fumbled for her phone, her vision swimming as she tried to focus on the keypad. "Come on, come on," she muttered, her usually steady voice now raspy and weak.

She managed to dial the first few digits of Dr. Lee's number before her hand went limp, the phone clattering to the floor of the car. Darkness crept in from the edges of her vision, inexorable and suffocating.

"No... I can't... not now..." Sharp's thoughts became fragmented, her iron will finally buckling under the weight of her illness. As consciousness slipped away, a fleeting image of Dr. Lee's concerned face flashed through her mind. "Charles... I'm sorry..."

Then, in an instant, everything changed. The oppressive darkness vanished, replaced by a brilliant, all-encompassing white light. It poured over Sharp like liquid warmth, banishing the fever and pain that had wracked her body moments before.

Sharp's eyes flew open, her breath catching in her throat. "What... what is this?" she whispered, her voice echoing strangely in the vast, luminous expanse.

The light seemed to pulse gently, almost as if in response to her words. Sharp felt weightless, suspended in this ethereal realm that defied all logic and reason.

"Is this... am I dead?" she wondered aloud, her detective's mind struggling to make sense of the inexplicable. But even as the question left her lips, she felt a profound sense of peace settle over her, quieting her racing thoughts.

For a moment, just a moment, Holly Keirstead was no longer Detective Sharp, driven by an insatiable need for justice and truth. She was simply Holly, basking in the serene embrace of the light, free from the burdens that had weighed so heavily upon her.

5 - 6

As Holly drifted in the radiant embrace, a presence materialized beside her. It wasn't a physical form, but rather an essence that emanated from the very light itself. Warm and comforting, it enveloped her like a cocoon of pure benevolence.

"Who... what are you?" Holly whispered, her voice trembling with a mixture of awe and trepidation.

The presence didn't respond with words, but Holly felt a gentle whisper caress her mind. It spoke of hope, of courage, of a purpose greater than she could imagine. The weight of her recent struggles – the virus, the multiverse mystery, the constant danger – began to lift.

"I don't understand," Holly murmured, her brow furrowing. "Am I meant to see this? To feel this?"

Again, no audible answer came, but a wave of reassurance washed over her. Holly felt her troubled mind ease, the relentless drive that had pushed her to the brink softening into something more sustainable.

She closed her eyes, letting the comforting presence surround her. "It's been so hard," she admitted, her usual stoic facade crumbling. "I've felt so alone in this fight."

The light pulsed gently, as if acknowledging her pain. Holly felt a profound sense of connection, of being part of something vast and eternal. It filled her with a courage she had never known before, a hope that burned brighter than any doubt.

"I'm not alone, am I?" she realized, her eyes opening wide. "There's more to this than I ever imagined."

7 - 8

The ethereal radiance that had enveloped Holly began to recede, its warmth fading like the last rays of a setting sun. The comforting presence withdrew, leaving behind a lingering echo of its reassurance. As the light dimmed to a faint glimmer on the horizon of her consciousness, Holly felt herself being pulled back to reality.

The stark contrast of her surroundings hit her like a physical blow. Gone was the infinite expanse of light, replaced by the confines of her car's interior. The dashboard's faint glow cast eerie shadows across the cabin, transforming familiar contours into alien shapes.

Holly blinked slowly, her vision struggling to adjust. Her mind reeled, caught between the fading memory of transcendent beauty and the harsh reality of her current situation. She raised a trembling hand to her forehead, feeling the heat of her fever still burning beneath her skin.

"Was it... real?" she whispered to herself, her voice hoarse and uncertain. The rational part of her mind, honed by years of detective work, rebelled against the impossible experience. "Or am I losing it completely?"

She closed her eyes again, trying to recapture even a fraction of the peace she had felt moments ago. But it slipped away like water through her fingers, leaving only a haunting sense of loss.

"No," Holly murmured, shaking her head slightly. "It was more than a fever dream. It had to be."

The memory of that otherworldly presence lingered, defying her attempts at logical explanation. She had been touched by something beyond her understanding, something that existed outside the boundaries of the realities she had encountered in her investigation.

"What does it mean?" she asked the empty car, her voice barely above a whisper. "What am I supposed to do now?"

9 - 9

Holly Sharp gripped the steering wheel, her knuckles white. The lingering warmth of the ethereal light faded, replaced by the chill of determination settling in her bones.

"Focus, Sharp," she muttered to herself, her voice cutting through the silence. "The Millers need you."

She turned the key, the engine roaring to life. As she pulled back onto the winding road, her mind raced, piecing together the fragments of her investigation.

"Drake's grief, Linda's fear, Harrison's... uniqueness," she mused aloud. "It all connects somehow."

The car's headlights cut through the encroaching darkness, illuminating the path ahead. Holly's eyes darted between the road and the rearview mirror, half-expecting to see that otherworldly glow pursuing her.

"What if this is bigger than just one family?" she wondered, her brow furrowing. "What if the multiverse itself is at stake?"

The weight of responsibility pressed down on her, threatening to overwhelm. But Holly pushed back, drawing strength from the lingering touch of that divine presence.

"Whatever's waiting at the Miller house," she declared, her voice steadier now, "I'm ready for it. Alternate realities, interdimensional threats... bring it on."

As the Miller house loomed in the distance, Holly felt a surge of renewed purpose. She was more than just a detective now. She was a guardian of realities, standing on the precipice of something far greater than herself.

Clarity in Chaos

Green World – 2024

1 - 2

Detective Holly Keirstead's eyes darted around Dr. Monroe's cluttered office, taking in the stacks of research papers and glowing computer screens displaying complex molecular structures. The weight of recent events pressed down on her shoulders like a physical force. She leaned forward, her sharp features etched with concern.

"Dr. Monroe, we need to discuss the virus that was contained in the bomb I disarmed at the amusement park," Holly said, her voice steady despite the churning in her stomach.

Dr. Monroe nodded, his weathered hands adjusting his wire-rimmed glasses. The gesture seemed to age him, revealing the strain of sleepless nights spent analyzing the pathogen. "Yes, Detective. The virus is unlike anything we've seen before. It's highly sophisticated and engineered to spread rapidly through the air."

Holly's mind raced, piecing together the implications. A bioweapon of this magnitude could devastate entire populations. She clenched her fist, feeling the weight of responsibility settle over her.

"How bad are we talking, Doctor?" she asked, her tone measured but urgent.

Dr. Monroe's eyes met hers, a mix of fascination and fear evident in his gaze. "It's beyond anything in our current medical understanding. The virus seems to possess an almost intelligent design, adapting to its environment with unprecedented speed."

Holly felt a chill run down her spine. The image of the crimson mist she'd glimpsed at the amusement park flashed through her mind. "And its potential for harm?"

"Catastrophic," Dr. Monroe replied, his usually soothing voice now tinged with gravity. "If released, it could spread across continents within days, perhaps even jumping between...realities."

Holly's brow furrowed. Realities? The concept seemed absurd, yet the seriousness in Dr. Monroe's eyes told her this was no theoretical exercise. She took a deep breath, steeling herself for what lay ahead.

"Then we need to act fast," she said, her determination evident in every word. "What's our next move, Doctor?"

3 - 4

Holly leaned forward, her eyes narrowing as she absorbed the gravity of the situation. The weight of countless lives pressed upon her shoulders, fueling her resolve. She drew a deep breath, steadying herself before speaking.

"Do we know what kind of virus it is? What are its effects?" Her voice was calm, but her clenched jaw betrayed the tension coursing through her.

Dr. Monroe sighed heavily, his fingers trembling slightly as he flipped through his notes. The rustling of papers seemed unnaturally loud in the oppressive silence of his office. Holly noticed the dark circles under his eyes, evidence of sleepless nights spent analyzing this unprecedented threat.

"We're still analyzing it," he began, his voice weary but professional. "But based on preliminary findings, it appears to be a genetically engineered pathogen designed to cause widespread respiratory illness." He paused, meeting Holly's intense gaze. "It could lead to symptoms ranging from fever and cough to severe respiratory distress."

Holly's mind raced, imagining the chaos such a virus could unleash. She thought of crowded streets, bustling airports, the interconnectedness of modern society - all perfect conduits for a devastating pandemic. The memory of her father, battling smoke and flames to save lives, flashed in her mind. Now it was her turn to be the protector.

"How quickly could it spread?" she asked, her fingers unconsciously tracing the outline of her badge.

5 - 6

Holly's stomach churned, a wave of nausea washing over her as the full implications of Dr. Monroe's words sank in. She leaned forward, her voice low and urgent. "We need to act fast to prevent any further spread. Is there anything else you can tell me about the virus?"

Dr. Monroe's eyes darted away for a moment, his hesitation palpable. Holly's heart rate quickened, sensing there was more to come. She watched as the doctor removed his glasses, polishing them with trembling hands before replacing them on his nose.

"We're also concerned about its potential to mutate," he finally said, his voice barely above a whisper. "Given its engineered nature, it could adapt quickly to evade treatments and become even more dangerous."

The words hit Holly like a physical blow. She gripped the arms of her chair, her knuckles turning white. In her mind's eye, she saw the virus spreading across the city, across the country, morphing and changing, always one step ahead of their efforts to contain it.

"Mutation?" she echoed, her throat dry. "How quickly are we talking about?"

As Dr. Monroe began to explain, Holly's thoughts raced. She imagined the virus as a living, breathing entity, evolving and outsmarting them at every turn. The weight of responsibility settled heavy on her shoulders. It wasn't just about solving a case anymore; it was about saving lives, perhaps even the fate of humanity itself.

"We need to coordinate with public health officials," she said, more to herself than to Dr. Monroe. "Set up containment protocols, start working on potential treatments..." Her voice trailed off as she realized the enormity of the task ahead.

7 - 8

Holly Keirstead strode out of Dr. Monroe's office, her footsteps echoing in the sterile hallway. The fluorescent lights overhead seemed to flicker in sync with her racing thoughts. She needed more information, and she knew exactly who could provide it.

As she pushed through the precinct doors, the familiar cacophony of ringing phones and bustling officers washed over her. Her eyes scanned the room, finally landing on a young officer hunched over his desk.

"Bird," she called out, her voice cutting through the noise. "Break room. Now."

Moments later, Holly found herself sitting across from Franklin Bird in the cramped break room. The smell of stale coffee hung in the air, matching the weariness etched on both their faces.

"Bird, I need to know everything you've uncovered about this virus," Holly said, leaning forward intently.

Franklin's eyes widened slightly, a mix of surprise and determination crossing his features. "Detective Keirstead, I've been digging into this since the amusement park incident. It's... it's not good."

Holly's jaw clenched. "Give it to me straight, rookie. What are we dealing with?"

As Franklin began to speak, Holly's mind whirred with possibilities. Could this virus be connected to the strange occurrences she'd been investigating? The disappearances, the unexplained phenomena... Was it all part of something bigger?

"Detective?" Franklin's voice snapped her back to the present. "Are you alright?"

Holly nodded, forcing herself to focus. "Keep going, Bird. We need to get ahead of this before it's too late."

9 - 10

Franklin Bird leaned forward, his expression serious, his voice dropping to a low, urgent tone. "Detective, the virus was designed to be released into the air, likely causing mass infection among civilians. It's a weapon, pure and simple."

Holly felt her blood run cold, her mind racing with the implications. Images of crowded streets, packed subways, and bustling shopping malls flashed before her eyes. The potential for devastation was almost unfathomable.

"A weapon," she repeated, her voice barely above a whisper. She clenched her fists, feeling the familiar surge of determination course through her veins. "How certain are we about this, Bird?"

Franklin's eyes met hers, unwavering. "The evidence is overwhelming, Detective. The virus's structure, its method of transmission - it's all engineered for maximum spread and impact."

Holly's jaw tightened at the revelation, her body tensing as if preparing for a fight. "We can't let something like this fall into the wrong hands," she said, her voice laced with steel. "We need to track down who's behind it and stop them before it's too late."

As she spoke, Holly's mind was already formulating a plan. Who had the resources, the knowledge, and the sheer disregard for human life to create such a monstrosity? And more importantly, how could they be stopped?

"Bird," she said, locking eyes with the young officer, "I need you to compile everything we have on this virus. Every scrap of data, every lead, no matter how small. We're racing against time here, and we can't afford to miss anything."

11 - 12

Holly's fingers drummed restlessly on the precinct's worn conference table, her eyes fixed on the setting sun through the grimy window. The fading light cast long shadows across the room, mirroring the dark thoughts swirling in her mind.

"We need to move fast," she muttered, more to herself than to Bird. "Every second we waste is a potential life lost."

Bird nodded, his face a mask of grim determination. "I've got the lab running analysis around the clock. We should have more details on the virus's composition by morning."

Holly's gaze snapped back to her colleague. "Morning might be too late. We need to follow every lead we have right now." She paused, a sudden thought striking her. "The Millers. Drake and his son might know something we don't."

Rising abruptly, Holly grabbed her jacket. "I'm heading to the Miller residence. Keep digging, Bird. If anything comes up, anything at all, you call me immediately."

As she strode out of the precinct, the weight of responsibility pressed down on her shoulders. Lives hung in the balance, and she couldn't shake the feeling that time was rapidly slipping away.

Fifteen minutes later, Holly stood on the sidewalk outside the Miller home, her eyes scanning the quiet suburban street. The sun hung low on the horizon, stretching shadows across neatly manicured lawns like grasping fingers.

"What secrets are you hiding, Drake?" she whispered, a chill running down her spine despite the warm evening air. Something about the stillness of the house, the drawn curtains, and the absence of any signs of life set her nerves on edge.

Taking a deep breath, Holly steeled herself for whatever lay ahead. The fate of countless lives might hinge on what she discovered here tonight.

13 - 14

Holly approached the front door, her heart pounding against her ribs. She knocked firmly, the sound echoing in the eerie silence. No response. Frowning, she tried the doorknob, surprised to find it yielding easily under her touch.

"Drake? Harrison?" she called out, pushing the door open cautiously. "It's Detective Keirstead. Is anyone home?"

The house was unnaturally quiet, devoid of the usual hum of life. Holly's footsteps echoed softly on the hardwood floors as she moved through the entryway, her hand instinctively hovering near her holstered weapon.

"Detective Miller? Harrison?" she called again, her voice carrying through the still air. Only silence answered.

As she stepped into the living room, Holly's keen eyes scanned for any signs of disturbance. Everything seemed in order, almost too perfectly so. A framed family photo on the mantle caught her attention – Drake, Harrison, and a woman she assumed was Drake's late wife. Their smiles seemed to mock the current tension.

"Where are you?" Holly muttered, more to herself than anyone else. Her mind raced with possibilities. Had they fled, fearing for their safety? Or had someone gotten to them first?

Moving deeper into the house, Holly couldn't shake the feeling that she was walking into something far more complex than she'd initially imagined. The air felt heavy, charged with an energy she couldn't quite explain.

"Drake? Harrison?" she called out once more, her voice tinged with growing concern. "If you can hear me, please respond. I'm here to help."

As she reached the kitchen, a sudden chill ran down her spine. The back door stood slightly ajar, a gentle breeze causing it to creak softly. Holly approached it cautiously, her senses on high alert.

"What happened here?" she whispered, her eyes narrowing as she surveyed the backyard. The unsettling silence pressed in around her, carrying with it the weight of unanswered questions and looming danger.

15 - 16

Holly stepped into the backyard, her hand instinctively moving to her holstered weapon. The grass was damp beneath her feet, and the air carried a faint metallic scent she couldn't quite place.

"This doesn't make sense," she muttered, her eyes darting from the empty swing set to the neatly trimmed hedges. Everything looked normal yet felt utterly wrong.

Turning back to the house, Holly's gaze locked onto a glint of something on the kitchen windowsill. She moved closer, her heart rate quickening as she identified the object.

"Drake's watch," she breathed, carefully picking up the expensive timepiece. "He wouldn't leave this behind willingly."

A sudden rustling from the nearby bushes made Holly whirl around, her hand tightening on her gun.

"Who's there?" she called out, her voice steady despite the adrenaline coursing through her veins. "Show yourself!"

As the bushes parted, Holly's mind raced. Could it be Drake? Harrison? Or someone – or something – far more sinister?

"Whatever's going on here," she thought, steeling herself for what might emerge, "I'm going to get to the bottom of it. The Millers' lives may depend on it."

17 - 18

Holly's breath caught in her throat as a neighborhood cat slinked out from the bushes, its yellow eyes reflecting the fading daylight. She exhaled sharply, lowering her weapon but remaining on high alert.

"Damn it," she muttered, her mind churning with possibilities. Could the Millers have been taken? The absence of signs of struggle puzzled her, yet the abandoned watch suggested an abrupt departure.

Holly's analytical mind kicked into overdrive. "Someone could have targeted them because of their connection to the bomb and the virus," she reasoned aloud, her voice barely above a whisper. "Or did they flee, knowing the danger they were in?"

The weight of the situation settled in her gut like a cold, heavy stone. Holly knew she needed answers, and fast. With practiced movements, she pulled out her phone and dialed the precinct.

"This is Detective Keirstead," she said, her voice taut with urgency. "I need an APB out on Drake and Harrison Miller immediately. They've vanished from their residence under suspicious circumstances."

As she relayed the details to her colleagues, Holly's eyes never stopped scanning the surroundings. The crimson hues of the setting sun cast long shadows across the yard, and she couldn't shake the feeling that somewhere, lurking just beyond her vision, the answers to this mystery – and perhaps The Virus itself – were waiting to be uncovered.

"I need a forensics team at the Miller residence ASAP," she continued, her tone leaving no room for argument.

Ending the call, Holly stood motionless for a moment, her keen detective's instincts on high alert. "Whatever's happening here," she thought, her jaw set with determination, "I won't let it spread. Not on my watch."

19 - 20

Holly's mind raced as she pocketed her phone, her eyes narrowing with determination. "I'll start with the neighbors," she muttered to herself, striding purposefully towards the house next door. "Someone must have seen something."

As she walked, the weight of responsibility pressed down on her shoulders. The Millers' disappearance wasn't just another case; it was potentially tied to a threat that could devastate countless lives across multiple realities. Holly's fists clenched involuntarily at her sides.

"Time's not on our side," she thought, her pace quickening. "If that virus gets out..."

She shook her head, forcing herself to focus on the immediate task. Reaching the neighbor's door, Holly took a deep breath, composing herself before knocking firmly.

An elderly woman answered, peering at Holly with curiosity. "Can I help you?"

"Ma'am, I'm Detective Keirstead," Holly said, flashing her badge. "I'm investigating the disappearance of your neighbors, the Millers. Have you noticed anything unusual today?"

As the woman spoke, describing a blinding white light she'd seen earlier, Holly's mind whirred with possibilities. Was it a lead, or just another dead end in this increasingly complex case?

"Thank you for your time," Holly said, jotting down the details. As she turned to leave, a chill ran down her spine. The streets seemed eerily quiet, the encroaching darkness more menacing than usual.

"I need to get home," she thought, suddenly aware of her vulnerability. "Regroup, analyze what we know." But even as she headed towards her car, Holly couldn't shake the feeling that time was slipping away, bringing them all closer to an unimaginable catastrophe.

21 - 22

Holly's keys jangled in her hand as she approached her front door, the weight of the day's events pressing down on her shoulders. The porch light flickered, casting an eerie glow across the weathered wood. As she reached for the doorknob, her gaze fell at her clothes, still stained with Drake Miller's blood.

"God, what a mess," she muttered, her fingers absently brushing at the dark splotches on her sleeve.

Suddenly, Holly froze. Under her touch, the dried blood began to shift and ripple, as if awakening from a long slumber. Her eyes widened in disbelief as the flakes transformed into glistening droplets before her very eyes.

"What the hell?" she whispered, her heart racing. "This isn't possible."

Holly's mind reeled, searching for a logical explanation. Had the stress of the case finally gotten to her? Was she hallucinating? She blinked hard, but the impossible sight remained.

"Focus, Keirstead," she told herself, trying to steady her breathing. "There has to be a rational explanation for this."

As she stared at the liquefied blood, a chilling thought struck her. Could this be connected to the virus? To Drake's mysterious disappearance? The implications were staggering.

Holly fumbled for her phone, her fingers trembling slightly as she dialed. "Dr. Monroe? It's Detective Keirstead. I need you to meet me at the lab immediately. Something's happened with Miller's blood sample, and I think... I think we might be dealing with something far beyond what we initially suspected."

As she ended the call, Holly cast one last wary glance at the blood on her sleeve. Whatever was happening, she knew one thing for certain: the case had just taken a turn into uncharted territory, and the clock was ticking faster than ever.

Shadows of the Past

Blue World – 2024

1 - 2

Detective Holly Sharp's hands trembled as she gripped the steering wheel, her vision blurring for a moment. She blinked rapidly, forcing herself to focus on the winding road ahead. The Miller house loomed in the distance, a foreboding silhouette against the dusky sky.

"Get it together, Holly," she muttered, her voice tight with tension. "You've come too far to lose it now."

As she pulled up to the curb, a chill ran down her spine. The curtains were drawn, and an eerie silence hung over the property. Holly's mind raced with possibilities, each more unsettling than the last.

She approached the front door, her footsteps unnaturally loud on the concrete path. The events of the past few days swirled in her mind – alternate realities, mysterious viruses, and the weight of countless lives hanging in the balance.

"Linda?" Holly called out, her voice wavering slightly. "It's Detective Sharp. Are you home?"

No response.

Heart pounding, Holly peered through the living room window. Her breath caught in her throat as she spotted Linda Miller's motionless form sprawled on the floor.

"No, no, no," Holly whispered, adrenaline surging through her veins.

Without hesitation, she threw her shoulder against the door, wincing at the pain as it gave way. She rushed inside, her training kicking in even as her mind reeled with questions.

As she knelt beside Linda, Holly's vision swam again, the room seeming to tilt and blur around her. She gritted her teeth, fighting against the disorientation.

"Focus, damn it," she hissed, reaching out to check Linda's pulse. "Whatever's happening, I can't let it stop me now. There's too much at stake."

3 - 4

"Linda, can you hear me?" Sharp called out, her voice laced with concern as she knelt beside the unconscious woman. Linda's skin was pale, her long hair splayed across the hardwood floor like a halo. Sharp's fingers trembled as she pressed them against Linda's neck, searching for a pulse.

There. Faint, but present.

Linda's chest rose and fell in shallow, labored breaths. Sharp's mind raced, recalling their last conversation about interdimensional threats. Had something followed Linda home?

"Come on, Linda," Sharp whispered, fighting back the rising tide of panic. "Don't you dare give up on me now."

With shaking hands, Sharp fumbled for her phone. The screen blurred before her eyes, and she blinked hard, forcing herself to focus. She couldn't afford to lose control, not when Linda's life hung in the balance.

"This is Detective Holly Sharp," she said as the emergency operator answered, her voice steadier than she felt. "I need an ambulance at the Miller residence immediately. We have an unconscious female, breathing but unresponsive."

As Sharp relayed the details of Linda's condition, her gaze darted around the room, searching for any clues. Nothing seemed out of place, yet the air felt charged, as if reality itself was holding its breath.

"Please," Sharp thought, her free hand clasping Linda's limp fingers. "Just hold on. Whatever's happening, we'll figure it out together. We have to."

5 - 6

Sharp's grip tightened on Linda's hand as she ended the call, her heart pounding in her ears. The silence of the room pressed in around her, broken only by Linda's shallow breaths.

"What happened to you?" Sharp murmured, her voice barely above a whisper. She studied Linda's face, searching for any sign of consciousness. "Were you trying to protect us from something?"

The ticking of a nearby clock seemed to mock Sharp, each second stretching into eternity. She closed her eyes, fighting against the swirling thoughts threatening to overwhelm her.

"I should have been here sooner," Sharp thought, guilt gnawing at her insides. "If I'd just followed my instincts..."

A soft groan escaped Linda's lips, and Sharp's eyes snapped open.

"Linda? Can you hear me?" she asked urgently, leaning closer.

But Linda remained still, her face a mask of peaceful unconsciousness that belied the danger she was in. Sharp's mind raced with possibilities, each more terrifying than the last. Had Linda stumbled upon some interdimensional secret? Was this the work of Gabrial?

In the distance, sirens began to wail, growing steadily louder. Sharp's shoulders sagged with momentary relief.

"Help's coming, Linda," she said, squeezing her friend's hand. "Just hang on a little longer."

As the sirens drew nearer, Sharp's apprehension grew. What if conventional medicine couldn't help Linda? What if this was something beyond their world's understanding?

"We'll figure this out," Sharp promised, her voice steady despite her fears. "Whatever it takes, I'll find a way to bring you back."

7 - 8

Detective Holly Sharp's keen eyes swept across the living room, searching for any detail that might unravel the mystery before her. The fading sunlight cast long shadows across Linda's motionless form, creating an eerie tableau that sent a chill down Sharp's spine.

As she leaned closer to Linda, something caught her attention. Faint lines marred the skin of Linda's forearm, barely visible in the dim light.

"What's this?" Sharp murmured, her brow furrowing as she gently turned Linda's arm for a better view.

Her heart began to race as the markings came into focus. Etched into Linda's flesh were two words that made Sharp's blood run cold.

"Buried alive," she whispered, her voice barely audible over the distant wail of approaching sirens.

Sharp's mind reeled, trying to make sense of the chilling message. "Who did this to you, Linda? What were you mixed up in?"

She traced the markings with a trembling finger, noting their depth and precision. This was no accident or self-inflicted wound.

"Someone wanted you to find this," Sharp thought, her detective instincts kicking into high gear. "But why? What am I missing?"

The words seemed to pulse with an otherworldly energy, and for a moment, Sharp felt as if she were being pulled into their dark promise. She shook her head, trying to clear the unsettling sensation.

"Whatever's going on, I'll get to the bottom of it," she vowed, squeezing Linda's hand. "I won't let you down."

As the sirens grew louder, Sharp couldn't shake the feeling that she had stumbled upon something far more sinister than a simple assault. The words "buried alive" echoed in her mind, a harbinger of the darkness that lay ahead.

9 - 10

With shaking hands, Sharp fumbled for her phone, her fingers slick with sweat as she unlocked the screen. She positioned the camera, focusing on the eerie markings etched into Linda's pale skin.

"Evidence," she muttered, snapping several photos in quick succession. "God, Linda, what happened to you?"

The flash illuminated Linda's motionless form, casting harsh shadows across her face. Sharp's breath caught in her throat as she studied the gentle curves of Linda's features, now twisted in unconscious anguish.

"Who would do this to someone so kind?" she wondered, her mind flashing to the countless times Linda had volunteered at the local shelter, her warm smile a beacon of hope for the downtrodden.

The wail of sirens grew louder, but Sharp barely registered the sound. Her mind raced, piecing together fragments of information.

"Buried alive," she whispered again, her voice trembling. "Is this a threat? A cry for help? Or something more sinister?"

Sharp's eyes darted around the room, searching for any sign of disturbance. Everything looked normal, almost too normal. It was as if Linda had simply collapsed while going about her day.

"What am I missing?" Sharp muttered, frustration creeping into her voice. "There has to be more to this. Linda, what were you trying to tell me?"

As she awaited the ambulance's arrival, Sharp's fingers hovered over her phone, tempted to call for backup. But something held her back. A nagging feeling that this case was far from ordinary, that it might require a more... unconventional approach.

11 - 12

The piercing wail of sirens grew louder, slicing through Sharp's churning thoughts. She tucked her phone away, her steely gaze returning to Linda's still form.

"I'll figure this out, Linda," Sharp murmured, her voice low and determined. "Whatever's going on, I promise I'll get to the bottom of it."

She reached out, gently brushing a strand of hair from Linda's forehead. As her fingers made contact, a jolt of electricity seemed to course through her body. Sharp gasped, her vision suddenly blurring.

"What the—" she started, her words cut short as the room began to spin around her. The walls seemed to close in, the air growing thick and oppressive.

Sharp's heart raced, her breath coming in short, sharp bursts. She reached out, desperately grasping for the edge of the coffee table to steady herself.

"Focus, Holly," she commanded herself, trying to fight the wave of dizziness. "You've faced worse than this. You can handle it."

But even as the words left her lips, she felt her grip on reality slipping. The room tilted and swayed, colors blending into a nauseating swirl.

"Linda," Sharp called out weakly, her voice barely above a whisper. "What's happening to me?"

Her fingers clutched the table's edge, knuckles white with the effort to remain upright. Sharp's mind raced, searching for an explanation, a lifeline to cling to in this sea of confusion.

"Is this... connected?" she wondered, her thoughts fragmenting. "The message... the multiverse... are they real?"

As the world spun faster and faster around her, Sharp closed her eyes, bracing herself for whatever came next. Whatever lay ahead, she was determined to face it head-on, to unravel the mystery that had ensnared them all.

13 - 14

A blinding white light erupted around Sharp, engulfing her completely. The world fell away, leaving her suspended in a void of nothingness. Her body felt weightless, untethered from reality.

"Am I... dead?" Sharp's thoughts echoed in the emptiness.

Time seemed to stretch and compress, seconds feeling like eternity and eons passing in the blink of an eye. Sharp tried to move, to speak, but found herself paralyzed, adrift in the endless white.

Just as suddenly as it began, the light vanished. Sharp's feet hit solid ground, her knees buckling slightly at the impact. She stumbled, catching herself against the rough bark of a nearby tree.

"What in the hell?" Sharp muttered, blinking rapidly to clear her vision.

Towering pines surrounded her, their branches stretching towards a canopy that blotted out most of the sky. The air was thick with the scent of earth and resin, a far cry from the sterile living room she'd occupied moments ago.

Sharp's hand instinctively went to her holster, relieved to find her weapon still there. "Okay, Holly," she whispered to herself, "assess the situation. You're in a forest. How? Why? Details first, questions later."

She took a deep breath, trying to calm her racing heart. The distant call of a bird echoed through the trees, followed by the rustle of unseen wildlife.

"This can't be real," Sharp thought, her mind reeling. "Multiverse travel? It was just a theory, wasn't it?"

15 - 16

Sharp's hand trembled as she reached out to touch the rough bark of a nearby pine, its solidity both reassuring and terrifying. The texture beneath her fingertips felt real enough, but how could this be?

"Focus, Holly," she muttered to herself, her voice sounding unnaturally loud in the eerie quiet of the forest. "There has to be a logical explanation for this."

She took a few tentative steps forward, leaves and twigs crunching beneath her feet. The sound echoed in the stillness, making her wince.

"Hello?" Sharp called out, immediately regretting the decision as her voice carried through the trees. "Is anyone there?"

Only the whisper of wind through the branches answered her.

Sharp's mind raced, trying to piece together what had happened. One moment she was in the Miller home, the next... here. Wherever "here" was.

"Okay, think," she said aloud, finding comfort in the sound of her own voice. "What do I know about multiverse theory?"

As she spoke, Sharp scanned the area, looking for any sign of civilization or familiarity. But in every direction, there was nothing but an endless sea of trees.

"Parallel universes, alternate realities," she continued, her analytical mind kicking into gear despite the surreal situation. "But travel between them? That's impossible. Isn't it?"

A chill ran down Sharp's spine as the full weight of her situation began to sink in. She was alone, in an unknown forest, possibly in an entirely different reality.

"Get it together, Holly," she whispered, fighting back the panic rising in her chest. "You're a detective. Solve this like any other case. First step: find your bearings."

But as Sharp looked around once more, the unchanging landscape of trees stretching as far as the eye could see, she couldn't shake the sinking feeling that she was far, far from home.

17 - 17

Sharp took a deep breath, centering herself. The air was thick and heavy, carrying an unfamiliar scent of damp earth and something... alien. She shook her head, focusing on what she could control.

"Okay, no obvious landmarks," she muttered, her eyes darting from tree to tree. "But there has to be a way out of here."

She patted her pockets, relieved to find her phone still there. Sharp pulled it out, but her momentary hope faded as she saw the "No Service" icon glaring back at her.

"Of course," she sighed, pocketing the device. "When has anything ever been that easy?"

Sharp's training kicked in, urging her to pick a direction and stick to it. She chose what she hoped was north, marked a tree with a notch from her pocketknife, and started walking.

As she moved through the forest, Sharp couldn't shake the eerie feeling of being watched. The shadows seemed to shift and dance in the corners of her vision, but whenever she turned to look, there was nothing there.

"Get a grip," she chastised herself. "You're letting your imagination run wild."

But even as she said it, Sharp couldn't help but wonder if there was more to this place than met the eye. The air seemed to pulse with an otherworldly energy, and the silence was so complete it was almost deafening.

"If this is another world," she mused aloud, pushing aside a low-hanging branch, "then how do I get back to mine?"

The question hung in the air, unanswered, as Sharp pressed on into the unknown depths of the forest.

Whispers of the Forest

Unknown world – Timeline Unknown

1 - 2

Detective Holly Sharp tread softly, her boots sinking into the lush carpet of moss beneath them. A symphony of the forest's life played around her: the whisper of leaves rustling overhead, the distant call of an unseen bird, and the subtle creaking of the ancient trees swaying ever so gently. The towering giants stretched skyward, their branches knitting together to form a verdant canopy that splintered the sunlight into a kaleidoscope of dappled patterns, dancing on the forest floor.

She paused, closing her eyes for a moment, taking in the scents that suffused the air. The robust fragrance of pine needles intermingled with the earthy scent of damp soil, a signature of the woodland's rich, breathing terrain. As she opened her eyes, beams of golden light caught her attention; they pierced the dense foliage above, spotlighting patches of greenery where wildflowers bloomed in vibrant clusters. Their sweet aroma hung delicately in the air, an unexpected contrast to the backdrop of decay and growth that formed the essence of the forest's cycle.

Holly's senses were not just passively registering these details; they were active extensions of her detective's intuition, mapping the environment, noting each anomaly, each pattern that could be a clue or a signpost. Her eyes, sharp and discerning, traced the long shadows thrown across the ground, searching for anything out of place that might lead her further toward the heart of the mystery that had brought her here, deep into the embrace of the untamed woods.

3 - 4

Detective Holly Sharp's boots pressed into the soft loam, her measured strides leaving a faint trail in the underbrush. The ancient woodland cradled her in its emerald embrace, the winding paths unfurling before her like serpents of old, leading her deeper into its secrets. With every step, the whispers of tall ferns accompanied her, nodding their verdant heads as if approving her passage. Their fronds performed a ballet in the gentle breeze, a silent symphony that resonated with the natural cadence of the secluded forest.

The further she ventured, the more the forest seemed to come alive around her. Life thrived in this secluded haven, each organism playing its role in the grand design of nature's tapestry. Birds darted above, splashes of color against the green canopy, their songs a complex chorus that rose and fell in harmonious arcs. She paused, allowing the avian melodies to wash over her, the notes distilling into a sense of clarity within her mind. The sound was a reminder of the world's intricate puzzles, much like the cases she tirelessly pieced together back in the realm of concrete and steel.

Her gaze followed a squirrel as it scampered across the forest floor, its bushy tail a flag of alarm as it zigzagged between the trees. The creature's nervous energy mirrored her own inner tension, the ever-present drive to seek, to find, to understand. These squirrels were the woodland's sentinels, alert to every rustle, every shift in the wind—a trait she recognized in herself.

Sharp knew these woods were more than just flora and fauna; they were a vast, living entity, whispering secrets she yearned to decipher. Each chirp and chitter she cataloged subconsciously, adding to her mental repository of observations. She belonged to the city's rhythms, yet here, amidst untamed wilderness, her senses sharpened—not in spite of nature's symphony but because of it. There was a puzzle here, nestled among the roots and branches, and Holly Sharp would uncover it, one whispering leaf at a time.

5 - 6

The air held still as Sharp's eyes locked onto the dainty imprint of a hoof pressed into the soft loam. She crouched, fingers hovering above the indentation, tracing its outline without touch—a detective's habit honed by years of preserving crime scenes. A gentle rustle drew her gaze upward just in time to see the white tail of a deer disappearing into the thicket. It moved with an elegance that belied the wildness of this place, vanishing as though it had never been.

Straightening, she continued on, her path unwavering even as the underbrush grew denser. A sudden flurry of movement caught her attention, and she stilled, watching a rabbit bolt from its hiding spot. Its form was a blur, a fluid streak of brown and white that melded with the shadows before silence reclaimed the space.

The forest, for all its vibrance and life, seemed reluctant to yield its secrets. Holly's instincts, sharpened by years of navigating the deceptive calm of crime scenes, prickled with awareness. The deeper she ventured, the more pronounced the sensation became—an itch at the back of her mind, a weight upon her shoulders. She paused, casting her gaze around the clearing she found herself in, searching for the source of her discomfort.

Holly took a deep breath, the scent of pine and damp earth grounding her. She had always trusted her intuition, the unspoken language between her senses and the environment. Now, it spoke of unseen observers, of gazes that lingered too long from the cloistered dark. With no concrete evidence to follow, she relied on the intangible—the whisper of intuition that had guided her through countless investigations.

"Show yourself," she murmured, her voice barely louder than the whispers of the forest. There was no reply, only the distant echo of a bird's call, laughing high above the canopy. Shaking her head, Holly moved forward, each step deliberate, her eyes scanning the play of light and shadow that danced across the woodland stage.

She wasn't alone; of that much she was certain. The forest held its breath, and somewhere in the sea of green, eyes were fixed upon her, watching, waiting. Holly Sharp would not be deterred. Whatever specters haunted these woods, she'd face them head-on, armed with nothing but her wits and an indomitable spirit that refused to yield to fear.

7 - 8

Holly's boots crunched upon a carpet of fallen leaves, their brittle fragments a stark counterpoint to the softness of the moss that had earlier muffled her steps. The forest seemed to expand around her, an infinite labyrinth of flora that defied her every effort to orient herself within it. With each stride, the sense of isolation crept closer, wrapping around her like a tangible shroud.

But Holly Sharp was not one to succumb to the whims of fear or solitude. She was a detective, a seeker of truths in even the darkest of corners. Her jaw set with a resolve that matched the steel in her spine, and she pushed forward, her gaze fixed on the path ahead. She bore the weight of unanswered questions, each one fueling her determination to pierce through the mystery that enveloped her.

"Answers are here," she whispered to herself, the words a silent vow to the life she'd been plucked from—a life where logic reigned, and puzzles lay down their pieces under the scrutiny of her keen mind.

The trees watched her progress, ancient sentinels whose bark bore the scars of time. They leaned into one another, forming archways that beckoned her deeper into their domain. Here in this otherworldly expanse, reality seemed a fragile concept, easily twisted by the capricious will of imagination. Holly couldn't help but marvel at the gnarled limbs reaching skyward, entwining to craft a canopy that transformed sunlight into a spectral ballet upon the ground.

"Keirstead," she muttered, testing the name that now shared space with her own identity. It felt strange on her tongue, a reminder that the person she had become in this place straddled two worlds—one of badge and gunpowder, the other of enigmas wrapped in verdant hues.

With each step, the shadows played tricks on her vision, shapes flickering at the periphery, always just beyond clear sight. Yet, Holly remained undaunted. Within the dappled light and shifting silhouettes, she searched for the key to unlock the truth of this realm and the pathway home.

9 - 10

Golden beams pierced the verdure above, casting a kaleidoscope of light that danced across Detective Holly Sharp's path. The forest seemed to exhale with her every step, releasing a symphony of scents; pine and rich loam warred with the intoxicating sweetness of wildflowers. Their vivid hues splashed against the green canvas underfoot, igniting the landscape with color as if nature itself had discarded all restraint in its artistry.

Holly navigated through this dreamscape, her senses alight with wonder yet underscored by the relentless drum of her purpose. She could not falter, not when each clue might lead to the unraveling of this world's mysteries—and to the reality she yearned to reclaim. Her fingers trailed over the rough bark of a tree, grounding herself with the tangible while her mind grappled with the fantastical elements that defied her detective's logic.

As she delved further into the forest's embrace, ruins emerged from the underbrush like ghosts from an age long past. Stone structures, their facades eroded by time, bore silent testimony to lives once lived within their boundaries. Holly stepped closer, eyes tracing the contours of archways and crumbled walls. These monoliths whispered secrets lost to history, their voices muted by the weight of centuries. She listened intently, trying to decipher the tales embedded within the cold stone, for even here, amongst remnants of antiquity, the truth lay shrouded, waiting to be exhumed by her unwavering resolve.

"Who were you?" she asked the silence around her, the question hanging unanswered in the air. Yet Holly needed no reply; she was a seeker of truths—a sentinel against the encroaching fog of mystery that threatened to consume her. With each uncovered secret, she felt the pieces of her dual existence, Sharp and Keirstead, coalesce into a clearer image of the person she was becoming in this enigmatic realm.

11 - 12

Holly Sharp's gaze lifted from the ancient ruins to the vibrant tapestry of life that adorned every inch of the forest. Her detective's instincts, honed for the concrete and steel of her own urban world, now struggled to catalog the plethora of unfamiliar botanical marvels that sprang forth before her. Towering fungi, their stems thick as tree trunks, rose majestically from the loam, their caps mottled with bioluminescent patterns that pulsed gently in the dimness. Awe-struck, Holly circled one of the colossal mushrooms, her hand hovering inches from its glowing surface, daring not to disturb the delicate ecosystem it supported.

"Remarkable," she whispered, the word a puff of vapor in the cool air, acknowledging a beauty that was both alien and captivating.

Her attention then shifted skyward as a flurry of movement caught her peripheral vision. Exotic birds, feathers gleaming with a kaleidoscope of colors, darted between the branches. Their calls, harmonious and clear, resonated through the vast expanse of timber and leaf. Holly remained still, allowing the symphony of chirps and whistles to wash over her, feeling the music tether her to this surreal reality. Her analytical mind attempted to classify each bird by its song, a habit ingrained from years of piecing together the cacophony of city sounds into coherent leads.

Amidst the concert of avian voices, a soft fluttering brushed against her cheek. Holly turned, her eyes catching sight of iridescent butterflies weaving an intricate dance. They twirled around each other, wings catching shafts of sunlight that broke through the canopy, turning their delicate forms into fleeting prisms. The detective felt a smile tug at the corners of her mouth—a rare involuntary reaction—as she observed the graceful ballet.

"Life... finds its canvas," she mused, the realization that even in a world so far removed from her own, the fundamental drive to exist—to flourish—remained unaltered. In this moment, Holly's resolve melded with a newfound wonder; she was not just a seeker of truths but also a witness to the profound resilience of life, no matter how odd or outlandish its guise.

13 - 14

Holly Keirstead's boots sank softly into the moss with a muted squish, the sound almost devoured by the thick silence of the forest. The leaves whispered secrets as she moved, their hushed tones hinting at ancient wisdom shared only with those who dared to listen. Yet, it was not these voices that caused a prickling sensation at the nape of her neck. It was the unseen gazes that seemed to linger upon her, an audience cloaked in shadow and mystery.

Keirstead paused, her breaths steady in the quietude that blanketed the woods. She scanned her surroundings, searching for the source of her unease. Sunbeams played tricks between the branches, casting enigmatic shapes that danced just beyond the edge of clarity. Nothing revealed itself, yet she felt the weight of attention, as palpable as the humid air pressing against her skin.

Despite the spectral scrutiny, serenity wrapped around her like a warm shawl. The forest's heartbeat pulsed in sync with her own, each beat a reassuring thrum that resonated deep within her bones. The towering trees stood sentinel, their roots delving deep, holding the earth's raw energy that ebbed and flowed with a rhythm older than time itself.

With a deep breath, Keirstead shook off the lingering trepidation and continued her trek. Her curiosity, a force as natural to her as breathing, drove her to delve deeper into this enigma. Each stride brought a new detail into focus: the way the leaves caught the light, the intricate patterns on the bark, the subtle shifts in the fragrance of the forest air.

She followed the winding paths, her senses alert to every nuance of this verdant labyrinth. A detective by nature and by trade, Holly Keirstead embraced the need to unravel what lay before her. The whispers of the forest beckoned, pulling her further away from the world she knew, towards a truth that promised to be as transformative as it was elusive.

As the distance between her and the heart of the forest diminished with her steadfast pursuit, so too did the space between question and answer. What would she find in the depths of this enigmatic expanse? Answers hovered at the edge of her consciousness, ready to reveal themselves when she breached the final barrier of understanding. With resolve fueling each step, Keirstead journeyed on, her spirit undaunted by the veiled watchfulness of the forest's unseen denizens.

15 - 16

The underbrush parted with a whisper, revealing the silhouette that had snagged Detective Holly Sharp's attention. She halted mid-step, her every instinct on high alert. The figure, hazy at first through the interplay of light and shadow, moved with an eerie grace between the trees. Sharp's hands clenched into fists at her sides, her eyes narrowing as she focused on the approaching form.

With each deliberate footfall, the shape took on more definition, stepping into shafts of sunlight that painted the forest in strokes of gold and green. The resemblance struck Sharp like a physical blow; it was her own reflection given flesh, wandering through the verdant wilds. The figure wore a coat mimicking the cut and color of Sharp's—a dark fabric that seemed to absorb the forest hues around it.

For a moment, Sharp questioned her sanity, wondering if the forest itself conjured up illusions to ensnare her mind. But no, the figure's gait was unmistakably hers—the same confident, measured steps she'd taken countless times on the beat. It was as though the forest had peeled away a layer of her being and set it loose among the ancient trees.

Yet, as the doppelgänger drew nearer, an otherness clung to it, an aura that seemed out of place, out of time. It was as if the very air around the figure shimmered with a subtle distortion, setting Sharp's nerves on edge.

Her breath misted in the cool air, her throat tight with a mix of fear and fascination. She could not look away, could not move, caught in the impossible reality of facing herself—or something that wore her face—with an otherworldly twist.

17 - 18

The forest hushed as the figure approached, twigs and leaves yielding silently underfoot. Holly Sharp studied the specter's approach, her detective's mind furiously piecing together the enigma before her. The closer it came, the more she noticed the nuances that distinguished this being from herself. Its steps were unburdened by gravity's full pull, gliding across the mossy floor with a grace that was hauntingly beautiful yet altogether alien.

Sharp's gaze locked onto the figure's eyes. They held a boundless depth, like twin pools reflecting a universe of knowledge that stretched far beyond the confines of her own worldly experiences. There was an ancientness in that gaze, a wisdom that whispered of secrets veiled behind the veil of time itself.

A tremor of disquiet rumbled through Sharp's core. Her usual resolve, hardened by years on the force, wavered in the face of such surreal duality. Was this apparition merely a trick of the mind, a figment born of isolation and the eerie embrace of the forest? Or perhaps it was something more—an inhabitant of this world, a mirror image rendered in a different artist's hand, suggesting the existence of parallel lives entwined yet separate.

She swallowed hard against the unease, her instincts as a detective grappling with the fantastic reality unfolding before her. The woods around them seemed to watch in silent anticipation, the natural chorus stilled by the gravity of the moment. In this encounter with the uncanny, Detective Holly Sharp stood at the precipice of an unfathomable discovery, one that could redefine her very understanding of self and world.

19 - 20

Compelled by an unseen force, Detective Holly Sharp edged forward, each step deliberate and measured as if she were navigating the delicate terrain of a dreamscape. Her heartbeat thrummed in her ears, keeping time with the suspense that tightened around her like the coiled spring of a trap waiting to be sprung. The forest itself seemed to hold its breath, the usual rustle of leaves and chirp of birds eerily absent in this moment of reckoning.

The figure, her enigmatic twin, stood serene and expectant, as though it had always known their paths would cross in this manner. A strange kinship tugged at Sharp's heartstrings—a yearning to understand the connection between them, to decipher the riddle presented in human form before her.

She raised her hand, palm outward, her fingers quivering slightly in the cool air that wrapped around them like a cloak. As the gap between them dwindled to mere inches, an electric charge prickled across Sharp's skin, raising goosebumps along her arms. It was as if the very air pulsated with an energy that sought to bridge the space separating the two entities.

Her gaze remained locked on the figure's hand—an outstretched offering that seemed to beckon her closer still. With a cautious bravery, one born from years of facing down the unknown in dimly lit alleyways and behind closed doors, Sharp extended her own hand. The proximity brought a sensory overload, a maelstrom of anticipation and dread swirling within her.

The tips of their fingers met, and a jolt of exhilarating energy surged through Sharp's body, so potent it threatened to unmoor her from reality. Her senses reeled, caught in the throes of an experience that defied logic, yet demanded to be felt in every fiber of her being. It was a dance of atoms and essence, a silent conversation whispered between the touch of two mirrored souls.

21 - 22

The electrifying contact sparked a recognition deep within Detective Holly Sharp, a resonance that vibrated through her core. It was as if an ancient lock had been turned, releasing a part of herself she never knew was imprisoned. Memories she hadn't lived and feelings she hadn't felt rushed forward, filling her with a sense of completeness she couldn't comprehend yet felt undeniably true.

Her eyes, wide with the shock of connection, reflected a storm of emotions. She saw understanding in the depths of the figure's gaze, a mirror to her own confusion and wonder. A warmth spread from the point where their fingers still touched—a warmth that suffused her being, whispering of unity and shared purpose.

In that suspended moment, the forest around them seemed to lean in closer, the rustling leaves hushing their whispers. The air itself grew still, charged with the gravity of the encounter unfolding beneath its watchful embrace.

Suddenly, the world erupted in a cascade of light, pure and consuming. Brilliance enveloped them, obliterating all distinctions between detective and doppelgänger. Within that radiant cocoon, boundaries melted away, and two souls, each a half of a greater whole, fused together in an intimate alchemy. Holly Sharp, the woman who sought truth in the shadows, now found it in the blinding light, merging with a version of herself both familiar and foreign.

Time lost meaning as they stood there, not two but one, their combined essence a beacon in the silent forest. And then, just as quickly as it had flared, the light receded, leaving behind the echo of a union that would forever alter the fabric of their realities.

23 - 24

The dappled light danced across Detective Holly Sharp's face as she gathered her bearings, the world around her coming back into focus. Silence enveloped her like a cloak, the only sound the rustling of leaves above and her own staggered breaths. She was alone—truly alone—in more ways than one.

Memories flooded her consciousness, two lifetimes' worth of experiences converging in her mind with dizzying force. Rebekah's laughter, once a symphony to her ears, now echoed with the hollowness of loss. In one world, they had been partners in life; in another, strangers passing by without a second glance. The love she knew so well was now tempered by the sting of separation.

Sharp's hand hovered in the space where the figure—Kierstead, her other self—had stood moments before. There was nothing there now but air and the memory of contact, yet she felt changed. A fusion had occurred, an intertwining of destinies that left her stronger and more complete. Drake's words about merging with his other self resonated within her, a prophecy fulfilled.

With each step forward, Sharp's resolve hardened. The forest seemed to recognize her transformation, its whispering leaves now sounding like encouragement rather than enigma. She navigated through the thick underbrush, her detective's intuition guiding her past gnarled roots and overhanging branches with ease.

Then, as she parted a curtain of ivy, the landscape before her shifted, revealing an expanse that defied all logic and expectation. It was a clearing unlike any she'd encountered—a place where the forest bowed respectfully around an open space filled with wildflowers that glowed with their own inner light. Fireflies twirled among the blooms, their bioluminescent dance painting trails of luminescence in the twilight air.

Sharp caught her breath, the weight of the revelation still pressing on her chest. Here, in this alien tableau, she found herself straddling realities, both the seasoned detective with a sharp eye for detail and the explorer Kierstead, who sought out the unknown with relentless curiosity. Her heart pounded with the thrill of discovery, even as her mind grappled with the enormity of her journey.

This strange, beautiful meadow, nestled secretly within the embrace of the ancient woods, was a testament to her newfound duality. It held the tranquility of solitude and the promise of mysteries yet to be unveiled. Holly Sharp, now more than ever, was ready to uncover them all.

25 - 26

Stepping clear of the last clinging vines, Detective Holly Sharp's gaze lifted to the resplendent sight before her. A fortress of gold gleamed under the caress of sunlight that somehow broke through the dense canopy. The castle's spires soared, ambitious and unyielding, piercing the blue expanse above like gilded promises of a world unbowed by ordinary constraints. For a moment, the weight of her dual identity—the merger of Sharp and Kierstead—seemed to lighten in the presence of such majesty.

With each step toward the imposing structure, the delicate crunch of gravel underfoot provided a grounding rhythm to her approach. She studied the carvings on the castle's surface, a pantheon of intricate images depicting valiant deeds and epic sagas. Each line, each curve spoke of an artisan's steady hand and a visionary's dream sculpted into permanence. Her fingers itched with the detective's urge to trace the scenes, to feel the history etched into the very stone.

The energy in the air bristled against her skin, a silent thrumming that sang of ancient secrets and stories that transcended time. Sharp drew in a deep breath, taking in the scent of old stone mixed with the vibrant life force that seemed to emanate from the castle walls themselves. It was as though the edifice breathed — a living testament to the realms she had yet to understand, beckoning her to step closer, to listen, to learn.

With a resolve fortified by her experiences and the unshakeable curiosity that now belonged to both of her selves, Detective Holly Sharp moved forward, ready to face whatever lay beyond those grand gates that held whispers of eternity in their golden embrace.

27 - 28

Stepping over the threshold, Holly Sharp's boots met with the cool stone of the castle's inner courtyard. The transition was tangible; the air inside was still and reverent, as if each breath she took was an intrusion upon the solemnity of the place. She moved slowly, her eyes drinking in the high walls that enclosed the space, walls that seemed to lean inwards, privy to the centuries of whispers they contained.

The courtyard was a tapestry of shadows and light, where creeping vines clutched at the stones with green fingers, and the occasional petal drifted down from unseen blooms nestled high above. Sharp listened, the soft rustle of leaves speaking in hushed tones of bygone eras and lost souls. Her detective's mind whirred, piecing together the narratives that lingered in the air, stories that felt familiar yet remained just out of cognitive reach.

She ventured further, drawn by the pull of discovery, her hand grazing the cool surface of a wall as she entered the labyrinth of corridors. The passage wound before her like an unraveling scroll, each turn revealing more of the castle's enigmatic heart. Candelabras hung from the walls, their unlit candles coated in a thick layer of dust, standing sentinel in the silence.

A chill traced the length of Sharp's spine as she traversed the halls, a sensation that was part recognition, part foreboding. It was as though she had been here before, not as Detective Sharp or as Kierstead, but as someone else entirely—a phantom self who had walked these floors under different stars. The memories were like smoke, coiling and twisting around her thoughts, obscuring clarity.

Her footsteps echoed in the empty expanse, a rhythmic counterpoint to the castle's ancient pulse. She moved with purpose, driven by the innate knowledge that something awaited her within these walls—something essential, something that resonated with her very soul. And so Detective Holly Sharp pressed on, deeper into the golden heart of the mystery that called her name with the voice of an old friend.

29 - 30

As Detective Holly Sharp turned the corner, a sliver of golden light beckoned her from the end of the darkened hallway. She quickened her pace, the sense of foreboding that had been her constant companion now vying with a growing curiosity. The hallway opened into an expansive chamber that seemed to swallow her whole, the walls aglow as if the very stones were infused with sunlight.

In the heart of this luminous space stood a throne carved from some lustrous material that shimmered with an inner fire. Its towering backrest was adorned with intricate scrollwork depicting scenes of valor and triumph, each detail painstakingly etched to honor a ruler whose legacy had weathered the sands of time. Atop this seat of power, a figure draped in light sat motionless, its presence both commanding and enigmatic.

Her breath caught at the juxtaposition of splendor and shadow. Each footfall felt like a trespass into sacred silence as she approached the dais. Her fingers brushed over the cool, smooth armrests of the throne, tracing the opulence of an era forgotten. The allure of unveiling the truth—of understanding her inexplicable connection to this place—drew her closer to the veiled sovereign.

The air thickened with anticipation as she reached the penumbra cast by the throne. Shadows clung to the figure like a shroud, obscuring its identity, its essence. Holly's heart thrummed in her ears, a cacophony against the hush that filled the chamber. With a resolve born of her detective's instinct and the undeniable pull of destiny, she extended her hands, her fingertips grazing the diaphanous veil of obscurity that separated her from the answers she sought.

In one swift, yet hesitant motion, she drew back the cloak of shadows, the fabric whispering secrets as it fell away. The revealed countenance before her was a canvas of revelation, as if the mysteries of this castle and its spectral halls had converged upon a singular point of understanding. Holly stood face-to-face with the obscured occupant of the throne, the distance between them now bridged by the audacity of her quest for the truth.

31 - 32

Holly's breath hitched as her gaze locked with the figure's—a mirror image of herself, yet suffused with an otherworldly glow that seemed to radiate from within. The doppelgänger's eyes sparkled with a knowing light, as if they held centuries of wisdom and secrets untold. In this surreal tableau, time stretched and bent, and Holly felt the very fibers of her being resonate with an unspoken truth.

The air in the chamber seemed to shimmer with revelation, vibrating with the resonance of her astounded heartbeat. She stood transfixed, peering into eyes that reflected not only her own physical form but something deeper, a shared essence that defied explanation. It was a recognition beyond the visual, a meeting of souls, a convergence of paths that had been destined to intersect.

"Hello, Holly," the figure spoke, its voice a harmonic echo of her own, yet imbued with the timbre of authority and agelessness. "Welcome to the Nexus."

The words resonated through the grand chamber, reverberating against the gilded walls and filling Holly with a sense of purpose that transcended her initial confusion. It was a greeting that unlocked doors within her mind, flinging wide the gates to understanding she had not known were closed. This place, this Nexus, was more than a physical location—it was a crossroads of reality, a linchpin of existence where the lines of her world and others converged.

Holly's detective instincts, always attuned to the unraveling of enigmas, now grappled with the magnitude of the revelation before her. The Nexus, the throne, the figure that bore her likeness—all were pieces of a cosmic puzzle that Holly was now compelled to solve. Her journey through the forest, the merging with her other self, the quest for answers—every step had led her to this moment of awe-inspiring discovery.

"Who are you?" Holly whispered, though in her heart, she already sensed the answer.

Whispers in the Dark

Apocalypse World – 20 A.C

1 - 2

The crunch of gravel under their feet echoed in the eerie silence as Harrison and Jonathan approached the looming edifice. Harrison's heart pounded; each beat a reminder of the dangers they might face.

"Jon," Harrison whispered, his voice barely audible, "you see what I'm seeing?"

Jonathan nodded; his usually jovial face etched with concern. "Hard to miss, isn't it? Looks like something out of a dystopian nightmare."

Harrison's gaze traveled up the weathered walls, taking in the faded paint and crumbling concrete. The once-gleaming facility now stood as a decrepit monument to forgotten ambitions. Above the entrance, three letters commanded attention: TRI.

Those letters. Why did they seem so familiar? Harrison's mind raced, trying to connect fragments of memory. The amusement park, Gabriel's cryptic warnings, and now this abandoned research facility – it all had to be connected.

"TRI," Harrison murmured, tasting the letters on his tongue. "Temporal Research Institute, maybe?"

Jonathan shrugged, his eyes darting nervously. "Your guess is as good as mine, mate. But whatever it stands for, I've got a feeling we're in way over our heads."

As Harrison opened his mouth to respond, something else caught his eye. Beside the imposing letters, a symbol seemed to writhe with otherworldly energy. A stylized dragon, its serpentine form coiled and ready to strike.

"Jon," Harrison breathed, "that dragon. It's the same as–"

"–the one from the Temporal Guardians," Jonathan finished, his voice tight with tension. "Bloody hell, what have we stumbled into?"

Harrison couldn't tear his gaze away from the dragon's eyes. They seemed to glint with intelligence, as if the creature might come to life at any moment. A shiver ran down his spine as he remembered the chaos at the park, the feeling of time unraveling around them.

"We need answers," Harrison said, steeling his resolve. "Whatever's inside, whatever TRI was working on – it's the key to understanding what happened to Gabriel. And maybe... maybe it's the key to getting him back."

Jonathan placed a hand on Harrison's shoulder, his touch grounding in the face of the unknown. "You really think he might still be alive? After all this time?"

Harrison nodded; his jaw set with determination. "I have to believe it. And if there's even a chance, we owe it to him to find out."

With a shared glance of trepidation and resolve, the two friends stood before the entrance, the dragon's eyes seeming to follow their every move. Whatever lay beyond those doors, Harrison knew their lives would never be the same.

3 - 4

Harrison gripped the rusted handle of the gate, its cold metal biting into his palm. With a deep breath, he pulled, the hinges groaning in protest as the gate swung open. A gust of stale air rushed out, carrying with it the musty scent of abandonment and decay.

"Christ," Jonathan muttered, wrinkling his nose. "Smells like a tomb in there."

Harrison stepped forward, his footsteps echoing in the cavernous entryway. Dust motes swirled in the thin shafts of light that managed to penetrate the gloom. "It feels like one too," he whispered, his voice barely audible.

As they ventured deeper, Harrison's mind raced. Each shadowy corner seemed to hold the promise of revelation, yet also the threat of danger. He couldn't shake the feeling that they were being watched, observed by unseen eyes.

"What do you think they were doing here, Jon?" Harrison asked, his voice tight with a mixture of excitement and apprehension.

Jonathan's lighter danced across the walls, illuminating faded warning signs and cryptic symbols. "Nothing good, I'd wager. Look at this place – it's like something out of a mad scientist's fever dream."

Harrison's fingers traced over a partially destroyed schematic on the wall. "But what if... what if they were onto something revolutionary? What if Gabriel found a way to–"

A sudden crash from deeper within the facility cut him off. Both men froze, hearts pounding.

"What was that?" Jonathan hissed.

Harrison swallowed hard; his mouth dry. "I don't know. But I think we're about to find out if TRI left behind more than just dust and memories."

5 - 6

Harrison's pulse quickened as they pressed on, the metallic clang of their footsteps reverberating through the empty corridors. Each step felt like a challenge to the oppressive silence, a defiant declaration of their presence in this forgotten place.

"It's so... empty," Jonathan whispered, his voice barely audible above the echo of their movements.

Harrison nodded, his eyes darting from shadow to shadow. "And yet, I can't shake the feeling that we're on the verge of something monumental." He paused, running a hand through his hair. "I know it sounds crazy, but it's like the very air is charged with potential."

As they rounded another corner, Harrison caught sight of a faint, pulsing glow in the distance. "Look," he breathed, pointing ahead.

Emergency lights flickered to life as they approached, bathing the corridor in an eerie, intermittent radiance. Harrison's heart pounded with anticipation, each flash revealing tantalizing glimpses of what lay ahead.

"It's like following a trail of dying stars," Jonathan murmured, his voice tinged with awe.

They emerged into a vast chamber, its expanse stretching beyond the reach of their lights. Rows upon rows of hulking machinery loomed before them, silent sentinels guarding long-forgotten secrets.

Harrison's breath caught in his throat. "This is it," he whispered, his eyes wide as he took in the scene. "The heart of TRI's research."

He approached a nearby console, its screen dark and lifeless. As he ran his fingers over the dusty surface, Harrison couldn't help but wonder what discoveries lay dormant within these ancient circuits, waiting to be awakened.

7 - 8

Harrison's fingers hovered over the console, a mixture of excitement and apprehension coursing through him. He turned to Jonathan, his voice barely above a whisper. "What do you think these machines were used for?"

Jonathan shook his head, his brow furrowed. "I'm not sure but look at the complexity of these systems. They're like nothing I've ever seen before."

As they surveyed the room, Harrison felt a chill run down his spine. The dormant machinery loomed over them, their silent forms seeming to hold countless secrets. He couldn't shake the feeling that they were being watched, as if the very walls of the facility were scrutinizing their every move.

"There's something... unsettling about this place," Harrison murmured, his eyes darting from one shadowy corner to another. "It's like we've stumbled into a tomb of lost knowledge."

Jonathan nodded; his face etched with concern. "I know what you mean. But we can't turn back now. Whatever TRI was working on, it's clear it was groundbreaking."

Harrison's mind raced with possibilities. What kind of experiments had been conducted here? And more importantly, how did they tie in to Gabriel's and Drake's disappearance?

"The archives," Harrison said suddenly, his eyes lighting up. "There must be records, research notes... something that can give us answers."

With a shared glance, they silently agreed. Harrison took a deep breath, steeling himself for what lay ahead. "Ready to go deeper into the rabbit hole?"

Jonathan gave a grim nod. "Lead the way, Alice."

As they prepared to venture further into the labyrinthine corridors of TRI, Harrison felt a renewed sense of determination course through him. Whatever truths awaited them in the depths of this facility, he was ready to face them head-on.

"No matter what we find," Harrison said, his voice steady, "we see this through to the end."

"Agreed," Jonathan replied, his tone matching Harrison's resolve.

With one last look at the chamber of silent machines, they set off into the unknown, each step bringing them closer to unraveling the enigma that had brought them here.

9 - 10

Harrison's fingers trembled as he lifted the cover of an ancient leather-bound tome, releasing a cloud of dust that danced in the dim light of the archive. The musty scent of aged paper filled his nostrils as he began to scan the faded text.

"Jonathan, look at this," he whispered, his voice tinged with awe. "These texts... they're talking about bending time and space, traveling between universes. It's incredible."

Jonathan leaned over Harrison's shoulder; his brow furrowed. "Are you sure? That sounds like science fiction, not scientific research."

Harrison's eyes darted across the page, drinking in every word. "I'm telling you, it's all here. Listen to this passage: 'The boundaries between realities are more permeable than once believed. With the right frequency and energy, one can pierce the veil separating worlds.'"

As he spoke, Harrison's mind whirled with implications. Could this be related to Gabriel's disappearance? Was TRI attempting to breach the barriers between universes?

"There's more," he continued, flipping through the pages with growing excitement. "They conducted experiments, Jonathan. Secret experiments pushing the limits of our understanding of reality."

Jonathan's voice was skeptical but intrigued. "What kind of experiments?"

Harrison paused, his finger tracing a complex diagram. "It's not entirely clear, but there are references to test subjects, to... to people crossing over. But the results are cryptic, shrouded in scientific jargon and code."

As he delved deeper into the text, a pattern began to emerge. Symbols and phrases repeated, forming a tantalizing thread of connection between seemingly disparate theories and experiments.

"It's all connected," Harrison murmured, more to himself than to Jonathan. "These aren't just random experiments. They're building towards something... something big."

His heart raced as he pieced together fragments of information, each revelation bringing him closer to a truth that both thrilled and terrified him. Whatever TRI had been working on, it had the potential to change everything they thought they knew about the nature of reality itself.

11 - 12

Harrison's hands trembled as he reached for the next volume, a leather-bound tome with faded gilt lettering on its spine. His fingers brushed against the ancient cover, sending a shiver of anticipation through his body.

"Jonathan," he breathed, his voice barely above a whisper, "I think I've found something extraordinary."

Jonathan leaned in closer, his eyes wide with curiosity. "What is it?"

Harrison carefully opened the book, revealing pages filled with intricate diagrams and densely packed text. "Look at this," he said, pointing to an illustration that seemed to pulse with an otherworldly energy. "It's a map of sorts, but not of any place on Earth."

The diagram depicted a series of interconnected spheres, each one labeled with strange symbols and equations. Lines of force crisscrossed between them, forming a complex web of relationships.

"My God," Jonathan murmured, "Is that what I think it is?"

Harrison nodded; his voice filled with awe. "A map of multiple universes. And not just a theoretical model – this looks like it's based on actual data."

As he studied the illustration, Harrison's mind raced with possibilities. Could this be the key to understanding Gabriel's disappearance? Was it possible that his enemy had somehow crossed over into another reality?

"There's more," Harrison said, flipping through the pages with growing excitement. "Look at these equations. They're describing methods of manipulating the fabric of spacetime itself."

Jonathan's brow furrowed in concentration. "But that's impossible. The energy requirements alone would be astronomical."

"Unless" Harrison countered, his eyes gleaming with the thrill of discovery, "they found a way to harness energy from multiple universes simultaneously."

As he spoke, a memory stirred in the back of Harrison's mind – a fleeting image of Gabriel working late into the night, surrounded by similar equations and diagrams. Had he been on the verge of a breakthrough that could change the very nature of reality?

Harrison's fingers traced the lines of text, each word seeming to pulse with hidden meaning. "Jonathan," he said softly, "I think we've just scratched the surface of something far bigger than we ever imagined. And I have a feeling that understanding this is the key to finding my dad– and uncovering the truth about TRI."

13 - 14

Harrison's heart raced as he carefully closed the ancient tome, its pages filled with secrets that could reshape the very fabric of reality. He turned to Jonathan, his eyes blazing with newfound determination.

"This is it," he breathed, his voice barely above a whisper. "The key to unlocking temporal travel. It's all here – the mathematics, the theoretical framework, even potential blueprints for a device."

Jonathan leaned in, his skepticism warring with curiosity. "But Harrison, even if this is real, the implications are staggering. We're talking about bending the laws of physics."

Harrison nodded, running a hand through his disheveled hair. "I know. But think about it – this could explain everything. Gabriel's and dads disappearance, the strange occurrences at the amusement park, even TRI itself."

He paced the length of the dusty archive, his mind whirling with possibilities. "We're standing on the precipice of something monumental, Jonathan. A discovery that could change the course of human history."

"Or destroy it," Jonathan cautioned, his voice tinged with worry. "Power like this – it's dangerous in the wrong hands."

Harrison paused, meeting his friend's gaze. "You're right. But that's exactly why we can't walk away. We must see this through, to understand it fully. It might be our only chance to find Drake and uncover the truth."

He took a deep breath, squaring his shoulders. "I don't know where this road leads, but I know I have to follow it. Are you with me?"

Jonathan hesitated for a moment, then nodded firmly. "To the end, my friend. Whatever comes next, we face it together."

With a shared look of determination, they gathered the most crucial texts and prepared to leave the archive. As they stepped into the dim corridor beyond, Harrison couldn't shake the feeling that they were crossing a threshold – not just out of the room, but into a vast unknown that would test the very limits of their understanding and courage.

15 - 16

The sudden crackle of static shattered the eerie silence, causing Harrison to whirl around, his heart leaping into his throat. Before he could react further, a squad of armed guards materialized from the shadows, their ancient robes adorned with the familiar emblem of the green dragon. Harrison's blood ran cold as recognition dawned – the same uniform Gabriel had worn on that fateful night.

"Jonathan," he whispered urgently, "those emblems..."

"I see them," Jonathan muttered, his voice tight with tension. "This can't be a coincidence."

The guards moved with practiced precision; their weapons trained on the two intruders. Harrison's mind raced, desperately seeking an escape route, but they were surrounded.

"We should have been more careful," he thought, silently berating himself. "All this knowledge, and we walked right into a trap."

One of the guards stepped forward, his face obscured by an ornate mask. "You have trespassed on sacred ground," he intoned, his voice carrying an otherworldly resonance. "By order of TRI, you are to be detained for questioning."

Harrison's eyes darted between the guards, assessing their stance, their weapons. He could feel Jonathan's apprehension radiating beside him. The weight of the stolen documents seemed to burn in his satchel, a damning piece of evidence.

"TRI?" Harrison ventured, trying to keep his voice steady. "What exactly is TRI? And what does it have to do with Drake Miller?"

The guard's mask betrayed no emotion. "All will be revealed in time. For now, you will come with us."

As the circle of guards tightened around them, Harrison exchanged a glance with Jonathan. The gravity of their situation was painfully clear – they had stumbled into something far larger and more dangerous than they could have imagined. The mystery of Gabriel, the enigma of TRI, the secrets of temporal manipulation – it all converged here, in this moment.

"Whatever happens," Harrison whispered to Jonathan, "we stick together. We'll find a way out of this."

Jonathan nodded grimly; his jaw set with determination. "Into the dragon's lair we go," he murmured.

With no choice but to comply, Harrison and Jonathan allowed themselves to be led deeper into the facility, each step taking them further from the world they knew and closer to the heart of an ancient conspiracy that threatened to unravel the very fabric of reality itself.

17 - 18

The guards' weapons pressed into their backs as they marched down a dimly lit corridor. Harrison's eyes darted from side to side, taking in the strange symbols etched into the metallic walls. Glowing runes pulsed with an eerie blue light, casting flickering shadows that danced across their path.

"Jon," Harrison whispered, his voice barely audible, "those markings... they're similar to the ones in Gabriel's notes."

Jonathan nodded almost imperceptibly; his face taut with tension. "I see them. What do you think they mean?"

Before Harrison could respond, they were shoved into a vast chamber. The air hummed with an unseen energy that made the hairs on the back of his neck stand on end. Bizarre contraptions lined the walls, their functions a mystery but their presence undeniably ominous.

"On your knees," growled one of the guards, pushing them down with unnecessary force.

As Harrison's knees hit the cold floor, his gaze was drawn to the center of the room. There, atop a raised dais, sat an imposing figure on what could only be described as a throne. The dim light obscured their features, but Harrison could feel the weight of their scrutiny.

His mind raced, questions flooding his thoughts. Who were these people? What did they want? And how was all of this connected to Gabriel's disappearance?

"I don't suppose you'd believe we took a wrong turn at the gift shop?" Harrison quipped, his attempt at humor masking his growing fear.

Jonathan shot him a warning glance. "Now might not be the best time for jokes, Harry."

Harrison swallowed hard, his eyes never leaving the shadowy figure on the throne. "You're right. But I need answers. We've come too far to back down now."

He took a deep breath, steeling himself for whatever came next. The secrets of TRI, the truth about Gabriel – it all lay within his grasp. All he had to do was reach out and take it, no matter the cost.

19 - 20

The figure on the throne leaned forward, emerging from the shadows. Harrison's breath caught in his throat as he beheld a woman of ageless beauty, her silver hair cascading over robes adorned with intricate, shimmering patterns. Her eyes, however, were what truly captivated him—twin pools of swirling mercury that seemed to pierce through his very soul.

When she spoke, her voice resonated with an otherworldly timbre that sent chills down Harrison's spine. "Intruders," she intoned, her gaze flicking between Harrison and Jonathan. "You stand before the Keeper of Temporal Wisdom."

Harrison's mind reeled. Temporal Wisdom? Could this be connected to Gabriel's research on time manipulation?

"We didn't mean to intrude," Jonathan began, but Harrison cut him off.

"We're here for answers," he declared, meeting the woman's unsettling gaze. "About TRI, about Gabriel, about all of this." He gestured at the strange machinery surrounding them.

The Keeper's lips curved into a ghost of a smile. "You have trespassed upon sacred ground," she said, her voice carrying the weight of eons. "But fear not, for you stand on the threshold of enlightenment. The secrets of the ancients are within your grasp, should you prove yourselves worthy."

Harrison's heart raced. This was it—the key to unraveling the mystery that had consumed his life. "How?" he asked, his voice barely above a whisper. "How do we prove ourselves worthy?"

As the Keeper regarded him, Harrison couldn't shake the feeling that his entire future hung in the balance of her next words.

21 - 22

With a fluid motion, the Keeper raised her hand, and the guards retreated, their weapons still trained on Harrison and Jonathan. The tension in the air was palpable, a living thing that seemed to pulse with each passing second.

Harrison's eyes met Jonathan's, a silent conversation passing between them. Despite the uncertainty that gripped his heart, Harrison found strength in his friend's unwavering gaze. They had come too far to falter now.

"Whatever comes next," Harrison whispered, his voice barely audible, "we face it together."

Jonathan gave a slight nod, his jaw set with determination. "Always."

The Keeper's voice cut through their moment of solidarity. "Your trial begins now. Tell me, seekers of truth, what drives you to unravel the mysteries of time and space?"

Harrison's mind raced, memories of Gabriel's disappearance flashing before his eyes. He took a deep breath, steadying himself. "It's personal," he began, his voice growing stronger with each word. "My father, Drake... he could travel between different realities and now he's vanished. I need to understand what happened to him, to bring him home if I can."

As he spoke, Harrison's thoughts whirled. What secrets lay hidden within these ancient walls? How deep did the conspiracy surrounding TRI truly run? And Gabriel and Drake... what role did they play in all of this?

The Keeper leaned forward, her mercurial eyes seeming to bore into Harrison's very soul. "And you?" she asked, turning her gaze to Jonathan. "What compels you to walk this perilous path?"

Harrison held his breath, realizing that in all their adventures, he had never truly asked Jonathan why he had chosen to stand by his side through it all.

"I just wanted a sense of adventure."

Welcome to The Nexus

Nexus – outside of space and time

1 - 2

Holly's tentative steps echoed through the cavernous expanse as she crossed the threshold of the golden castle. Gilded arches loomed overhead, intricate tapestries depicting narratives of worlds unknown graced the walls, and the air itself seemed alight with a vibrant hum, an electric undercurrent of enchantment that danced upon her skin. Each breath she took was laden with the scent of ancient stone mixed with something indefinable, a fragrance of power and mystery interwoven.

The throne before her commanded attention, its very presence dominating the vast hall. It was carved from a single, enormous gemstone that pulsed with an inner light, casting a halo of soft, warm luminescence around the figure seated upon it. The presence situated upon the throne now took on a man's silhouette which was both mesmerizing and formidable, his posture effortlessly commanding yet devoid of arrogance.

With each cautious step Holly took toward him, the details of his visage crystallized like the facets of the gemstone throne. He held himself with a grace that belied the strength evident in the broad set of his shoulders, and his features were chiseled with a precision that no mortal hand could achieve. His eyes, as she came closer, were like twin stars captured in the twilight, piercing through her defenses and laying her soul bare.

She felt inexplicably drawn to him, a moth to the flame of his otherworldly beauty. His hair cascaded down his back in waves of midnight, each strand seemingly spun from the night sky itself. His skin glowed as if kissed by the dawn, and the intricate filigree of his royal attire complemented the ethereal atmosphere of the castle. Holly's heart drummed a staccato rhythm against her ribs, her senses sharpening as she realized this man, this vision of splendor, was the most beautiful being she had ever beheld.

The intensity of his gaze did not falter, nor did hers as she drew nearer, feeling the magnetic pull of his presence. She knew not what power he wielded or what wisdom lay behind those ageless eyes, but she understood instinctually that he was a being of significance, a pivot upon which the fate of realms might turn. In that moment, the air between them crackled with an unseen energy, a silent acknowledgment of a connection neither fully understood.

3 - 4

"Welcome, Holly," the man spoke, his voice a symphony of warmth and authority that seemed to vibrate along the mosaic floor tiles and up the gilded walls, filling the vastness of the castle with its reverberation. The words, simple yet laden with meaning, hung in the air like a sacred proclamation.

Holly's pulse thrummed in her ears, a frenetic counterpoint to the stillness of the opulent chamber. With each step toward the throne, her apprehension swelled, mingling with a profound curiosity that tugged at the edges of her thoughts. A part of her—a part she didn't fully recognize—had known it would lead to this: a confrontation with a mystery made flesh.

The distance between them shrank with her halting advance, the regal figure before her becoming more imposing, more impossibly real. His eyes, those twin celestial bodies, held her captive; she was an explorer locked in the gravity of an undiscovered planet. What secrets did they guard? What ancient tales could they recount?

She felt the weight of her destiny pressing down upon her shoulders, a mantle she had not yet agreed to don, even as it wove itself around her with threads of fate. Her breath hitched slightly, caught between the awe of the unknown and the primal urge to flee from the enormity of what awaited.

Yet, with every tentative step closer, reverence bloomed within her chest—a burgeoning respect for the enigmatic sovereign whose mere presence commanded the elements and whispered of untold power. This was no mere ruler of a kingdom; this was a being who shaped the very essence of worlds. She was drawn inexorably forward, compelled by forces beyond her understanding, to stand before the throne and face the weaver of her destiny.

5 - 6

Holly's voice emerged like a thread of silver in the vastness of the golden chamber. "You know my name, but I don't know yours," she said, her words slicing through the silence with an edge of determination. "Who are you?"

The man on the throne unfolded from his regal repose, a soft rustle accompanying the movement of his robes. His eyes, deep and fathomless, held hers with an intensity that promised both comfort and enigma. "I am known by many names, to different people all over the universe," he continued, his voice carrying an air of solemnity that seemed to reverberate against the very stones of the castle. A pause lingered between them, filled with the weight of ages and the breath of stars. "But you may call me Justin."

The name hung in the space between them, simple yet laden with unspoken depth. Holly felt it resonate within her, a key turning in a long-sealed lock. Justin—this was the name of the being who had stepped from the tapestry of myth into the stark reality of her journey.

7 - 8

Holly's fingers twitched at her sides, a silent testament to the whirl of thoughts that tangled like briars in her mind. Justin—a name whispered on the cusp of dreams, echoing across the chasms of her subconscious with a haunting familiarity that eluded her grasp. Her gaze traced the contours of his face, searching for clues within the lines that spoke of timeless wisdom and hidden lore. Behind those piercing eyes, she felt the promise of knowledge vast as the star-strewn sky, secrets that beckoned her towards realms undreamed.

In the quiet grandeur of the throne room, time seemed to fold upon itself, wrapping Holly in a cocoon of suspense. The air itself held its breath, charged with the anticipation of choices yet unmade.

Then, like dawn breaking over a slumbering world, Justin moved, his hand cutting through the stillness, palm upturned in an offer as old as tales—trust, alliance, a shared path. The gesture was simple, unadorned by jewels or artifice, yet it shimmered with an invitation that resonated in the marrow of her bones.

Holly's pulse thrummed in her ears, a counterpoint to the silence that enfolded them. Her instincts, honed by a lifetime of caution, clamored for restraint, whispering of the perils that lay in the embrace of the unknown. But beneath the clamor, a deeper voice called to her, a siren song woven into the very fiber of her being. It sang of destiny not just encountered but seized, of fates not endured but shaped by the boldness of one's heart.

With a breath that tasted of both resolve and recklessness, Holly closed the distance between hesitation and destiny. Her hand, pale against the darker hue of his, lifted as if buoyed by unseen currents. In the moment their fingers touched, a subtle warmth spread from their clasped hands, a harbinger of the odyssey that awaited—a journey charted by the stars, navigated by the courage nestled within the human spirit.

And so, hand in hand with the enigmatic Justin, Holly stepped forward, crossing the threshold from the known into the boundless expanse of the Nexus, where wonders untold unfurled like petals before the morning sun.

9 - 10

Holly's nod was a silent covenant, an unspoken agreement to the mystery that beckoned. Her hand, trembling ever so slightly, found its way into Justin's palm—a lifeline cast across the chasm of uncertainty. The contact was electric, a jolt of unseen power that raced through her bloodstream, setting every nerve alight. It was as though the very essence of the universe pulsed between them, a cosmic symphony that resonated with the rhythm of ancient melodies.

She could feel it then, a connection that defied explanation, tethering her to this enigmatic being before her. It was a bond woven not of silk but of stardust, not of promises but of prophecies long foretold. Holly's breath hitched in her chest as she absorbed this new reality; her destiny had been set adrift upon the tides of fate, and at the helm stood Justin, the navigator of her soul's voyage.

Amidst the grandeur of the golden castle, beneath the opulent arches that soared like a paean to the heavens, Holly lifted her eyes—eyes now shimmering with the reflection of the arcane luminescence that surrounded them. Her gaze locked with his, and in the fathomless depths of Justin's gaze, she found herself adrift, caught in the whirlpool of his inscrutable presence.

"Where... where am I?" The words escaped her lips in a breathy whisper, a fragile echo that seemed to tremble in the air between them. They were the merest wisp of sound, yet they carried the weight of worlds uncharted, of paths untaken—a plea for understanding from the core of her bewildered soul.

11 - 12

The golden light that bathed the throne room shifted subtly, as if responding to the very essence of Justin's revelation. Holly swallowed hard, her hand still clasped in his, a lifeline amidst the onslaught of staggering truths. "The Nexus," she echoed, the name rolling off her tongue with an air of sacred wonder.

Justin's smile deepened, not with arrogance but with the patience of one who had seen eons pass like the fluttering of a moth's wings. "Yes, Holly. Here, the veil is thin, and the fabric of existence is pliable, molded by forces unknown to your world."

Holly felt the weight of his words settle within her, a heavy cloak that was both terrifying and exhilarating. The Nexus. She allowed the concept to seep into her consciousness, to fill the crevices of her understanding with its impossible truth. Around her, the walls of the castle seemed to pulse gently, their surfaces alive with the dance of otherworldly energies.

"Universes converging... intersecting..." she murmured, trying to wrap her mind around the enormity of it all. Her fingertips tingled where they touched Justin's skin, as if tiny currents of the Nexus's power coursed through them, feeding her glimpses of realities beyond her own.

"Indeed," Justin affirmed softly, releasing her hand only to gesture at the air before them. As he moved, the space seemed to ripple, distorting like a reflection upon water disturbed by a pebble's touch. Within the undulations, images flickered—a myriad of landscapes, creatures, and skies filled with unfamiliar constellations—each vision bleeding into the next with mesmerizing fluidity.

"Strange and wondrous worlds," Holly breathed out, her eyes wide with a mix of fear and fascination. Was it possible that among these countless realms lay answers she sought? Or perhaps questions she had yet to form?

"Worlds without end," Justin intoned, his voice imbuing the sights before them with a gravity that anchored Holly to the spot. She stood with him at the nexus of creation, her heart thrumming with the potential that unfolded in endless cascades around them. In this moment, she was acutely aware of her own insignificance—and yet, paradoxically, of her undeniable connection to the grand tapestry unfurling before her eyes.

13 - 14

Holly's feet anchored her to the polished floor, yet she felt as though she were adrift in a sea of stars. Her breath came in short, sharp intakes as her mind grappled with the scope of Justin's revelation. "But... how is this possible?" The words tumbled from her lips, betraying the swirling vortex of confusion and wonder within. "How can such a place exist?"

Justin rose from his throne, the soft golden light playing across his features as he moved. It was as if he were part of the very essence of the Nexus, woven into its incandescent tapestry. He stepped down, closing the distance between them with a grace that seemed to acknowledge the gravity of her questions. The air around him seemed to thrum with unseen energy.

"The Nexus," he began, his voice a serene whisper that nonetheless carried the weight of ancient galaxies, "is a manifestation of the fundamental forces that govern the cosmos." He extended his hand before them, palm up, and the air above it shimmered as if reacting to his presence. Holly watched, transfixed, as motes of light gathered like fireflies coalescing into constellations.

"It is the culmination of countless eons of cosmic evolution," he continued, his gaze locked with hers, a deep well of empathy reflecting at her own wide-eyed astonishment. "A testament to the boundless potential of existence itself." The light in his hand intensified, casting luminous patterns on their faces, dancing reflections of the infinite possibilities housed within the Nexus.

Holly blinked against the brilliance, but she did not look away. She couldn't. Justin's explanation resonated with something deep within her—a truth she had always sensed but never had the context to understand. The Nexus, with its convergence of all conceivable universes, offered a promise of understanding the vastness of being, and within that promise, Holly felt the seed of her purpose beginning to sprout.

15 - 16

Holly's lips parted, a thought taking shape but faltering in the face of Justin's enigmatic presence. Her pulse quickened as she grappled with the reality folding around her, a single question teetering on the brink of utterance. "Am I.... I mean is this place..."

With a fluid motion, Justin raised his hand, silencing her mid-sentence. His fingers seemed to slice through the charged air, commanding both silence and attention. "This place is many things to many people, whatever their beliefs may be. You may simply call it the Nexus."

She stood still, absorbing his words, feeling the weight of his interruption settle over her like the dust of stars that surrounded them. Holly's gaze lingered on his hand, the gesture still hanging in the space between them—a bridge, she realized, between ignorance and enlightenment. The Nexus. The word echoed in her mind, and she sensed its significance reverberate within her soul, as if the name itself were an incantation that unlocked hidden chambers of understanding.

17 - 18

Holly's fingers twitched at her side, the question burning within her like a shard of sunlight through a prism. She took a hesitant step forward on the marble floor, each footfall a silent drumbeat in the hushed expanse of the Nexus.

"Are you... you know, are you him?" she asked, her voice barely more than a breath, a murmur that dared to challenge the silence.

Justin regarded her with an amused twinkle in his eye, his presence as commanding as the ethereal light that framed him. He let out a soft chuckle, the sound reverberating richly against the high walls and vaulted ceilings, filling the space with warmth.

"Oh gosh please, you mean my father. No, I'm simply the living embodiment, the son if you will," he replied, the corners of his mouth curving into a smile that seemed both ancient and infinitely young.

The simplicity of his laughter disarmed her, the grandeur of the Nexus juxtaposed against the human quality of mirth. Holly's tension eased, just slightly, the edges of her awe-frayed nerves being soothed by the notion of kinship, however divine the connection might be.

19 - 20

Holly's gaze lingered on the gentle undulations of light that danced across Justin's features, the laughter fading into a serene stillness that wrapped around her like a cosmic shawl. The air itself seemed to shimmer with latent knowledge, as if every molecule were imbued with the wisdom of ages past and futures yet to unfold.

She inhaled deeply, the scent of ancient stone and starlight filling her lungs, grounding her amidst the opulence that threatened to overwhelm. Her hand subconsciously brushed against the cool surface of a nearby pillar, etched with symbols that whispered secrets she yearned to understand. She felt small in this vast hall of possibilities yet emboldened by the gravity of her presence here.

"But why am I here?" Holly's voice broke through the silence, each word falling like a droplet into the fabric of the Nexus. "What role do I play in all of this?"

Her fingers traced the intricate carvings, seeking solace in their complexity as she awaited an answer that might anchor her adrift spirit. Here, within the beating heart of the universe, questions of destiny and purpose swirled like constellations caught in the tailwind of creation, waiting for her to chart their course.

21 - 22

Justin's expression shifted, the regal lines of his face softening as if he were about to share a secret with an old friend. The golden light that bathed him seemed to grow warmer, more inviting. "You are here because you possess a rare gift," he said, each word deliberate and heavy with meaning.

Holly stood rooted to the spot, her heart pounding against her ribs like a caged bird desperate for flight. A gift? Her mind raced back through her life, cataloging every odd occurrence, every unexplainable event—were they all leading her here?

"A gift that allows you to traverse the boundaries between worlds," Justin continued, his voice a guide in the darkness, "to glimpse the myriad possibilities that lie beyond the veil of reality."

The words hung in the air between them, profound and electrifying. Holly's breath hitched, caught on the hook of potential that those words implied. She had always sensed something more beneath the surface of her mundane existence, a whisper of greatness or perhaps madness. Now, given shape and form by Justin's revelation, it bloomed within her—a flower unfurling its petals to drink in the nourishing sunlight of truth.

She had been chosen, plucked like a single thread from the vast tapestry of life, set apart to weave a new pattern in the fabric of the cosmos. Her lips parted, but no sound emerged; her voice was lost in the enormity of her purpose. Her eyes, wide and glistening, reflected the infinite starscape that surrounded the Nexus. She felt so insignificant, yet paradoxically essential, as though she were a key fashioned for a lock unknown.

The realization dawned on her slowly, like the sunrise creeping over the horizon, casting away shadows of doubt. Holly straightened her spine, her shoulders rolling back as if to bear the weight of this destiny with newfound resolve. She had been chosen, singled out from among countless souls, to embark on a journey that would reshape the very fabric of existence.

Purpose coursed through her veins, a river breaking free from its icebound prison, rushing towards an ocean of infinite possibilities. The Nexus, once a word devoid of meaning, now resonated within her as a calling. Her journey was not just happenstance—it was necessity, woven into the very essence of who she was meant to become.

"Chosen..." The word was a whisper, an echo of the awakening that trembled through her core. The connection might have been undefined, but the path ahead was clear. Holly's gaze met Justin's, a silent vow passing between them that she would rise to meet the challenge of her extraordinary destiny.

23 - 23

Holly's first step echoed in the silence, a solitary sound that seemed to ripple through the void. The Nexus stretched out before her, an endless canvas of swirling nebulas and glittering constellations, each star a distant sun to worlds unseen. She could almost hear the hum of the cosmos, a symphony of celestial whispers beckoning her to delve deeper into its mysteries.

With every breath she took, the air thrummed with the energy of creation, filling her lungs with the dust of stars and the essence of possibility. The Nexus was alive, a living, breathing entity, and she was now part of its grand design.

The expanse of space wrapped around her, not cold and distant as she had once imagined, but warm and inviting. It was as if the universe itself had opened its arms, welcoming her into its fold. A sense of belonging surged within her, the realization that she was not merely an observer of this cosmic dance, but a participant.

Her fingers tingled, a sensation cascaded down her spine, awakening every nerve with the promise of discovery. Each step forward was a leap into the unknown, yet Holly moved with a confidence that belied her former uncertainty. The Nexus was her proving ground, a realm where she would test the limits of her gift and emerge transformed.

A trail of light bloomed beneath her feet, illuminating a path that twisted and turned through the darkness, charting a course only she could follow. Holly understood then, with a clarity that pierced the veil of her previous life, that her journey was etched in the very fabric of the universe. Her destiny was not written in stone, but in the stardust that flowed through her veins.

She paused for a moment, taking in the majesty of the Nexus, feeling its pulse sync with her heartbeat. This was the beginning of her odyssey, a quest that would challenge her understanding of reality and redefine her place within it. A surge of exhilaration filled her chest, and she knew without a doubt that whatever lay ahead, she was ready.

As the golden glow of the Nexus enveloped her, Holly stepped boldly into her future, her eyes alight with the fires of exploration and her spirit soaring on the wings of infinite wonder.

Reunion or Illusion

Red World – 2024

1 - 2

The harsh fluorescent lights flickered overhead as Drake Miller's footsteps echoed through the sterile corridors of the Bridgewater Research Institute. Each step felt heavier than the last, the weight of his quest pressing down on his shoulders like an invisible burden.

Drake's mind raced, recalling the cryptic phone call that had led him here. *What secrets could this place hold?* he wondered, his heart pounding with a mixture of anticipation and dread.

As he approached the entrance, the glass doors slid open with a soft hiss. Drake squinted against the sudden burst of sunlight, his eyes adjusting to reveal a silhouette framed in the doorway. A woman stood there, her posture radiating an aura of authority that made Drake instinctively straighten his back.

She took a step forward, her features coming into focus. Sharp, intelligent eyes studied him intently, and Drake felt as if she were peering into his very soul.

"Drake Miller, I presume?" the woman inquired, her voice carrying a note of curiosity that sent a shiver down Drake's spine.

Drake swallowed hard, his mouth suddenly dry. He opened his mouth to respond, but the words caught in his throat. *This is it,* he thought. *The moment of truth.*

3 - 4

Drake nodded, his gaze meeting hers with a mixture of determination and apprehension. He clenched his fists at his sides, steadying himself against the tumult of emotions threatening to overwhelm him.

"That's right," he replied, his voice surprisingly steady despite the inner turmoil. "You must be Dr. Summers."

A flicker of something—recognition, perhaps? — passed across the woman's face. Her lips curved into a warm smile, her eyes sparkling with a hint of intrigue that both intrigued and unnerved Drake.

"Indeed, I am, but you can call me Rachel," she confirmed, extending her hand in greeting. Drake hesitated for a fraction of a second before grasping it, noting the firm, confident handshake. "It's a pleasure to finally meet you, Mr. Miller. I've heard quite a bit about you."

Drake's eyebrows rose involuntarily. *She's heard about me? What could she possibly know?* His mind raced, trying to piece together the puzzle of his presence here and her apparent knowledge of him.

"I'm afraid you have me at a disadvantage, Dr. Sum— Rachel," Drake said, stumbling slightly over the informal use of her name. "I'm not sure what brings me here, exactly, or what you might have heard about me."

Rachel's eyes twinkled with amusement, and Drake couldn't shake the feeling that she was privy to some secret he had yet to uncover. The weight of the unknown pressed down on him, a mix of curiosity and trepidation churning in his gut.

5 - 6

Drake accepted her handshake with a nod of gratitude, his mind racing with questions that begged to be asked. The cool morning air nipped at his skin, a stark contrast to the warmth of Rachel's grip. He cleared his throat, searching for the right words.

"I'm sorry to impose on such short notice," he began, his voice betraying a trace of uncertainty. "But something tells me that the answers I seek may lie with you."

Rachel's eyes narrowed slightly, a flicker of interest dancing across her features. She released his hand, tucking a stray lock of hair behind her ear as she studied him intently. Drake felt exposed under her scrutiny, as if she could see right through to the core of his being.

What does she see? he wondered. *What secrets does she hold?*

"You're not the first person to come seeking answers," she remarked cryptically, her words carrying a weight that Drake couldn't quite comprehend. A breeze rustled through the nearby trees, carrying with it the scent of pine and possibility. "But perhaps you're the one who will finally uncover the truth."

Drake's heart quickened at her words. *The truth about what?* he wanted to ask, but something held him back. Instead, he opted for a more measured response.

"I'm not sure I understand," he said carefully, watching Rachel's face for any hint of explanation. "What truth are we talking about here?"

Rachel's lips curved into a enigmatic smile, one that spoke of hidden depths and untold stories. "That, Mr. Miller, is precisely what we're here to find out."

7 - 8

With a graceful sweep of her arm, Rachel gestured towards the imposing edifice behind them. "Shall we?" she asked, her voice tinged with anticipation.

Drake nodded, falling into step beside her as they entered the facility. The air inside felt heavy with secrets, each breath laden with the weight of untold histories. As they navigated the winding corridors, Rachel's voice filled the space between them.

"This institute has stood for over a century," she began, her words painting vivid pictures in Drake's mind. "It was founded by a group of scholars who believed that the key to humanity's future lay hidden in its past."

Drake's eyes darted from door to door, each one a potential gateway to knowledge. "And what did they discover?" he asked, his curiosity piqued.

Rachel's laugh echoed off the stark white walls. "Oh, more than they bargained for, I assure you. Did you know that in 1937, an expedition from this very institute unearthed an artifact that defied all known laws of physics?"

Drake's eyebrows shot up. "What kind of artifact?"

"The kind that makes you question everything you thought you knew about the universe," Rachel replied, her eyes twinkling with mischief.

As they delved deeper into the labyrinth of hallways, Drake found himself captivated by Rachel's tales. Each story seemed to peel back another layer of mystery surrounding the institute, revealing glimpses of a world beyond his wildest imagination.

Could it be true? Drake wondered, his mind reeling. *Or is this all an elaborate ruse?*

Finally, they came to a stop before an unassuming wooden door. Rachel paused, her hand on the handle, and turned to face Drake.

"Are you ready?" she asked, her voice barely above a whisper.

Drake swallowed hard, his heart pounding in his chest. "As I'll ever be," he replied, steeling himself for whatever lay beyond.

With a soft click, the door swung open, revealing a dimly lit chamber that took Drake's breath away. Row upon row of towering bookshelves stretched into the shadows, each one laden with ancient tomes and mysterious manuscripts. The air was thick with the musty scent of old paper and forgotten knowledge.

Drake's fingers twitched at his sides, itching to reach out and touch the weathered spines of the books. His eyes darted from shelf to shelf, drinking in the sight of countless secrets waiting to be uncovered.

"My God," he breathed, taking a tentative step into the room. "It's incredible."

9 - 10

Dr. Summers' voice cut through the reverent silence, her words laced with both awe and caution. "Welcome to the archives, Mr. Miller. Here, amidst the annals of time, you will find the answers you seek. But be warned — knowledge comes at a price, and not all truths are meant to be uncovered."

Drake's gaze swept across the room, his mind racing with possibilities. He turned to Rachel; his eyes alight with curiosity. "How long has this place existed?" he asked, his voice barely above a whisper.

"Longer than you might imagine," she replied cryptically. "Some say these archives predate the institute itself."

Drake nodded, absorbing her words as he took a tentative step forward. The floorboards creaked beneath his feet, and he couldn't shake the feeling that the very air around him was charged with untold secrets.

This is it, he thought, his heart pounding. *The key to everything I've been searching for could be right here, hidden among these ancient texts.*

Undeterred by Dr. Summers' cautionary words, Drake moved deeper into the room. His fingers trailed along the spines of leather-bound volumes, each touch sending a shiver of anticipation through him.

"Where do I even begin?" he asked, turning back to Rachel.

She smiled enigmatically. "Trust your instincts, Dr. Miller. The answers you seek have a way of finding those who are truly ready to receive them."

Drake nodded, feeling a newfound sense of purpose coursing through him. With each passing moment, he felt himself drawing closer to the elusive truth that had eluded him for so long—a truth that lay at the heart of this enigmatic research institute, waiting to be discovered amidst the sands of time.

I'm close, he thought, his eyes scanning the shelves with renewed determination. *I can feel it. Whatever brought me here, whatever connection I have to this place—the answers are within my reach.*

11 - 12

Dr. Summers' eyes never left Drake's face as she reached into an ornate wooden box, her movements deliberate and reverent. As she withdrew an ancient tome, Drake's breath caught in his throat.

"My God," he whispered, his voice barely audible over the thundering of his own heart.

The book was a masterpiece of antiquity, its leather cover cracked and faded, yet still emanating an otherworldly aura. But it was the emblem emblazoned on its face that sent a jolt of recognition through Drake's entire being—a dragon, its sinuous form achingly familiar.

There it is again, he thought, a chill racing down his spine. *That symbol... it's everywhere. But why? What does it mean?*

"This," Dr. Summers said, her voice hushed with reverence, "is Sir Mordred's Codex." She carefully opened the tome, its pages whispering secrets as they turned. "We discovered it in the ruins of Cadbury Castle."

Drake leaned in, drawn by an inexplicable pull. "Cadbury Castle? Isn't that supposed to be—"

"The site of Camelot, yes," Rachel finished, a glimmer in her eye. "This book, Dr. Miller, is said to contain the secrets of time and space itself."

Drake's mind reeled, struggling to process the implications. *A relic from Arthurian legend? Here? And that dragon symbol...*

"How is this possible?" he asked, his fingers hovering just above the fragile pages, yearning to touch but afraid of damaging such a priceless artifact.

Dr. Summers smiled enigmatically. "That, my dear Drake, is precisely what we're hoping to uncover. And I have a feeling you may be the key to unlocking its mysteries."

13 - 14

Drake's eyes widened in astonishment as he beheld the intricate runes and faded illustrations that adorned the pages of the book. His heart raced, each beat echoing the gravity of the moment. Amidst the faded ink and crumbling parchment, his gaze locked onto a series of symbols that seemed to pulse with an otherworldly energy.

"This can't be," he whispered, his voice barely audible. His fingers traced the air above a particular set of runes, afraid to touch the fragile page. "These characters... they're my name."

Dr. Summers leaned in, her eyes sparkling with curiosity. "Your name? Are you certain?"

Drake nodded, his mind whirling. *How is this possible? An ancient text bearing my name?* He swallowed hard, trying to piece together the fragments of understanding that danced just out of reach.

"It's right here," he said, pointing to the symbols. "Drake Miller, clear as day. But how? Why?"

He turned to Dr. Summers, his eyes searching her face for answers. "What does this have to do with me?" The question escaped his lips in a hoarse whisper, laden with equal parts fear and fascination.

As he awaited her response, Drake's thoughts raced. *First the dragon symbol, now this. It can't be coincidence. But what am I missing?* He felt as though he stood on the precipice of a vast, unknown world, one that both terrified and exhilarated him.

15 - 16

Dr. Summers met his gaze with a knowing smile, her eyes twinkling with a hint of mischief. "That, Mr. Miller, is the question, isn't it?" she replied enigmatically. Her fingers brushed the edge of the ancient tome, sending a small cloud of dust into the air. "But I believe the answer lies within the pages of this book. For you see, when translated, the book has one defining key message."

Drake's heart raced, his palms growing damp with anticipation. He leaned forward, drawn inexorably towards the weathered pages. *A key message? About me?* His mind reeled with possibilities, each more fantastic than the last.

"Which is?" he asked, his voice barely above a whisper. The weight of the moment pressed down on him, making the air feel thick and heavy. Drake's eyes darted between Dr. Summers' face and the mysterious text, searching for any clue that might prepare him for what was to come.

As he waited for her response, Drake's fingers twitched, longing to reach out and touch the ancient codex. He held back, afraid that even the slightest contact might cause the fragile pages to crumble, taking their secrets with them. *Whatever this message is,* he thought, *it's going to change everything.*

17 - 18

Dr. Summers' eyes locked with Drake's, her expression grave. "Stop the virus, find Drake Miller in 2024."

The words hit Drake like a physical blow, sending his mind reeling. *A virus? And my name... in a book this old?* His throat constricted, making it difficult to breathe. "That's... that's impossible," he managed to choke out, his voice barely audible.

Dr. Summers remained silent, watching him intently as he grappled with the revelation. Drake's gaze fell to the ancient tome, its leather cover seeming to pulse with an otherworldly energy. Unable to resist any longer, he reached out with trembling hands.

His fingertips brushed the weathered surface, tracing the outline of the dragon emblem. A jolt of electricity seemed to course through him at the contact. *This can't be real,* he thought, yet the tangible presence of the book beneath his touch argued otherwise.

"How?" Drake whispered, his eyes never leaving the codex. "How can this book know about me? About a virus?" His mind raced, trying to reconcile the impossible with what lay before him.

Dr. Summers leaned in, her voice low and urgent. "That's what we need to find out, Mr. Miller. This text... it's the key to unlocking secrets we've only begun to understand."

Drake nodded slowly, a mix of awe and trepidation washing over him. *My past... my future... it's all here, waiting to be uncovered.* He took a deep breath, steeling himself for whatever revelations lay ahead.

19 - 20

Drake's fingers trembled as he carefully turned the fragile pages of Sir Mordred's Codex. Each crackle of parchment sent a shiver down his spine, as if the very book itself was whispering ancient secrets. His eyes darted across the intricate symbols and faded illustrations, drinking in every detail.

"I've never felt anything like this," Drake murmured, more to himself than to Dr. Summers. "It's as if... as if the book is alive somehow."

Dr. Summers leaned in; her eyes gleaming with curiosity. "What do you see, Mr. Miller?"

Drake's brow furrowed in concentration. "I'm not sure. These symbols are unlike anything I've ever encountered. And yet..." He trailed off, lost in thought.

*Why does this feel so familiar? * He wondered, his heart racing. *It's like a half-remembered dream, just out of reach. *

As he turned to another page, a gasp escaped his lips. There, sprawled across the yellowed parchment, was a series of intricate diagrams and equations that seemed to defy logic itself.

"This is incredible," Drake breathed, his voice filled with awe. "These formulas... they're describing something I thought was purely theoretical. Time dilation, quantum entanglement... but with a level of detail that shouldn't be possible."

Dr. Summers nodded, her expression grave. "That's what we believed too, Mr. Miller. But there's more."

She reached out, gently turning to a specific page. Drake's eyes widened as he beheld the strange, flowing script that covered the parchment.

"This is written in what we believed to be a bygone ancient language," Dr. Summers said, her voice barely above a whisper.

Drake stared at the text, a strange sensation of déjà vu washing over him. *Why does this seem so familiar?* he thought, his mind reeling. *It's almost as if...*

He shook his head, unable to complete the thought. The implications were too staggering to contemplate.

21 - 22

Drake's fingers traced the intricate symbols, his brow furrowing as recognition dawned. His heart hammered against his ribcage as he looked up at Dr. Summers, his eyes wide with disbelief.

"No, not ancient," he said, his voice barely above a whisper. "It's written in a language created by my son Harrison. So was this symbol." He tapped the dragon emblem on the cover. "But how could this be if you said it belonged to Sir Mordred?"

His mind raced, grappling with the impossible. Mordred, another Arthurian figure connected to the green dragon, a symbol of the Knights of the Round Table. But this... this was unmistakably Harrison's creation; a fantasy language Drake had dismissed as childish imagination.

Dr. Summers leaned in; her eyes gleaming with curiosity. "Your son created this language? Fascinating. But how can you be certain?"

Drake ran a hand through his hair, his thoughts a maelstrom of confusion and nascent hope. "I'd recognize it anywhere. We spent countless nights inventing it together. But it doesn't make sense. How could it be here, in this ancient text?"

He paused, a new thought striking him. "Wait," he said, his voice sharp with sudden realization. "How could you decipher this without the key? It was lost with my son."

The words hung in the air, heavy with implication. Drake's heart clenched, a mixture of hope and fear coursing through him. *Could it be possible?* he wondered, scarcely daring to believe. *After all this time?*

23 - 24

Dr. Summers' lips curved into a enigmatic smile. "It's best I let my friend explain that to you." She turned towards the back hallway, gesturing towards the staircase shrouded in shadow.

Drake's eyes followed her movement, his pulse quickening. Who could possibly know about Harrison's code? He took an involuntary step forward, hands clenched at his sides.

The soft sound of footsteps echoed from the stairwell, growing louder with each passing second. Drake held his breath, a storm of emotions churning within him – hope, fear, disbelief, and a desperate longing he'd suppressed for years.

A figure began to emerge from the darkness, silhouetted against the dim light. Drake's breath caught in his throat, his vision tunneling to focus solely on the approaching form. Time seemed to slow, each heartbeat stretching into eternity.

It can't be, he thought, even as a part of him dared to hope. *After all this time, all the searching...*

The figure took another step forward, features becoming clearer. Drake's legs trembled, threatening to give way beneath him. His mind reeled, unable to process what his eyes were telling him.

"Is this real?" he whispered, more to himself than anyone else. "Or have I finally lost my mind?"

25 - 26

"Harrison..." Drake murmured, his voice choked with emotion as he took in the sight of his son standing before him, alive and whole. The young man's familiar eyes, so like his own, stared back at him from a face that had matured but was still unmistakably Harrison's. Drake's hands trembled at his sides, fingers flexing with the urge to reach out and touch, to confirm this wasn't some cruel illusion.

Harrison's eyes met his father's, and for a moment, the air between them crackled with unspoken words—words that hung heavy with the weight of all they had lost and all they had yet to gain. The silence stretched, filled with years of absence, of questions unanswered and explanations unspoken.

Drake swallowed hard, his mind racing. *How is this possible? Where has he been all this time?* His throat constricted, making speech nearly impossible. "I thought... we all thought..." he managed, unable to finish the sentence.

Harrison shifted his weight, a flicker of uncertainty crossing his features. "I know, Dad," he said softly, his voice deeper than Drake remembered. "I'm sorry. There's so much to explain."

Drake nodded, a thousand questions bubbling up inside him. But for now, he simply drank in the sight of his son, alive and standing before him. The miracle he'd stopped believing in had finally come true.

27 - 28

Harrison's voice quavered slightly as he spoke, his eyes glistening with unshed tears. "It's good to see you, Dad," he said softly, his tone a mixture of relief and uncertainty. "I... I didn't know if I'd ever get the chance to see you again."

The words hung in the air, laden with years of separation and unspoken truths. Drake felt his heart constrict, a maelstrom of emotions threatening to overwhelm him. *My boy, my brilliant boy,* he thought, *alive and here before me.*

Without thinking, Drake stepped forward, his arms outstretched. He enveloped Harrison in a fierce embrace, pulling him close as if afraid he might vanish again. The familiar scent of his son - a mix of old books and something uniquely Harrison - filled his senses, confirming this wasn't just another cruel dream.

"Harrison," Drake choked out, his voice muffled against his son's shoulder. "I never stopped looking for you. Never stopped hoping."

As he held his son, Drake's mind raced. *How did he survive? What connection does he have to Sir Mordred's Codex?* But for now, those questions could wait. In this moment, all that mattered was that his son had returned - a living testament to the resilience of the human spirit and the enduring power of hope.

29 - 30

Drake slowly released Harrison from his embrace, his hands lingering on his son's shoulders as he took a step back to drink in the sight of him. Harrison's face had matured, lines of worry etched around his eyes, but his gaze still held that familiar spark of curiosity and intelligence.

"Dad," Harrison began, his voice thick with emotion, "there's so much I need to tell you, about the Codex, about where I've been—"

Drake nodded, a wave of calm washing over him. "We have time now," he said softly, a small smile playing at the corners of his mouth. "Time to unravel all these mysteries together."

He glanced down at the ancient tome on the nearby table, its dragon emblem seeming to shimmer in the dim light of the archives. *To think,* Drake mused, *that my son's creation led us here, to this moment of infinite possibility.*

Dr. Summers cleared her throat gently, reminding them of her presence. "Gentlemen," she said, her eyes twinkling with a mix of excitement and trepidation, "shall we begin our journey through time and space?"

Drake met Harrison's gaze, seeing his own determination reflected there. "Together," Drake affirmed, reaching for the Codex. "Whatever trials lie ahead, we face them as a family."

As his fingers brushed the weathered cover, Drake felt a surge of courage. *We're no longer lost,* he thought. *We've found our path forward, right here in these dusty archives.*

Castle of Wonders

Nexus – outside of space and time

1 - 2

Holly's fingers trailed along the cool, golden walls as she followed Justin through the winding corridors. Her eyes darted from one marvel to the next, drinking in every detail of the castle's opulence. Intricate carvings of mythical beasts and ancient heroes adorned every archway, their features so lifelike she half-expected them to spring into motion.

Shimmering tapestries depicting epic battles and long-forgotten legends hung between towering windows, their threads glinting in the soft light. Holly's heart raced with a mixture of awe and disbelief. How could such a place exist? And why had she, of all people, been brought here?

As they rounded another corner, an ornate golden throne came into view, its high back etched with swirling patterns that seemed to move of their own accord. Holly gasped, her steps faltering.

"This place is incredible," she breathed, her eyes wide with wonder as she took in the opulence surrounding her. She turned to Justin, searching his face for some explanation. "How is this possible? It's like something out of a fairytale."

Holly's mind whirled with questions. Was this all real, or had she somehow stumbled into an elaborate dream? The weight of the situation pressed upon her, a mix of excitement and trepidation churning in her stomach. Whatever lay ahead, she knew her life would never be the same after this moment.

3 - 4

Justin's eyes sparkled with warmth as he met Holly's gaze, a smile playing at the corners of his mouth. For a moment, he seemed to drink in her wonder, as if seeing the castle anew through her eyes.

"It's been my home for as long as I can remember," he said, his voice tinged with a hint of nostalgia. "I know every nook and cranny like the back of my hand."

Holly's brow furrowed slightly. "How long exactly have you lived here?" she asked, curiosity getting the better of her.

Justin chuckled, a sound that echoed off the gilded walls. "Longer than you might believe," he replied cryptically, before gently guiding her down another corridor. "But come, let me show you more."

As they walked, Justin's voice took on a rhythmic cadence, weaving tales of the castle's past. "These very halls have seen the rise and fall of great dynasties," he began, gesturing to a particularly ornate tapestry. "See there? That's King Aldric the Brave, who single-handedly defended the castle against an army of shadow creatures."

Holly's imagination ignited, picturing the scenes Justin described. She could almost hear the clash of swords and the roar of mythical beasts. "And what about that one?" she asked, pointing to a mural of a knight kneeling before a radiant figure.

"Ah, that's the tale of Sir Galahad and the Celestial Queen," Justin explained, his eyes twinkling. "A story of valor, sacrifice, and a love that transcended realms."

With each step, Holly felt herself being drawn deeper into the rich tapestry of history surrounding her. The weight of countless stories seemed to press in on her, both exhilarating and overwhelming.

"It's all so much," she murmured, half to herself. "I feel like I've stepped into another world entirely."

Justin's hand found her shoulder, steadying her. "In a way, you have," he said softly. "But fear not, Holly. You're exactly where you're meant to be."

5 - 6

Holly's breath caught in her throat as they stepped into a cavernous space that seemed to stretch endlessly upward. Shafts of sunlight pierced through towering stained-glass windows, painting the stone floor in a kaleidoscope of vibrant hues. The sheer scale of the room made her feel impossibly small.

"Oh, Justin," she whispered, her eyes wide with awe. "This is... it's beyond anything I could have imagined."

Justin's smile was warm as he watched her reaction. "This is the Great Hall," he said, his voice reverent. He swept his arm in a grand gesture, encompassing the vast space. "It's the very heart of the castle. Here, we gather for our grandest feasts and most important celebrations."

Holly turned slowly, trying to take in every detail. "I can almost hear the echoes of all those gatherings," she mused. "The laughter, the music..."

"Indeed," Justin nodded. "If these walls could speak, they'd tell tales to rival any bard. It's where our greatest stories are shared, where legends are born and kept alive through the ages."

A thought struck Holly, and she turned to Justin with curiosity burning in her eyes. "Have you been part of many of those celebrations?" she asked. "What's it like when this place is full of people?"

7 - 8

Holly's imagination sparked to life as she pictured the hall filled with revelers. "I can almost see it," she said, her voice hushed with wonder. "The long tables laden with food, torches flickering on the walls, nobles in their finest attire..."

Justin chuckled, a warmth in his eyes as he gazed at her. "You're not far off," he said. "Though I'd add the minstrels in the corner, their music competing with the boisterous laughter of knights sharing tales of their latest quests."

Holly closed her eyes for a moment, letting the imagined sounds wash over her. "And the clink of goblets," she added, "raised in toast after toast."

"Precisely," Justin agreed. "You have quite the vivid imagination, Holly."

She opened her eyes, meeting his gaze. "This place inspires it," she said softly. "It's like... like stepping into a storybook."

As they moved further into the hall, Holly's curiosity began to bubble over. "Justin," she began, her brow furrowed slightly, "you mentioned the Nexus earlier. What exactly is it? How does it relate to this castle, to... well, everything?"

Justin's expression grew thoughtful. "The Nexus," he said slowly, "is both simpler and more complex than you might imagine. It's a convergence point, a place where realities intersect."

Holly's mind reeled at the implications. "Realities? As in... multiple worlds?"

"Precisely," Justin nodded. "The castle serves as a sort of... waypoint, if you will. A nexus of nexuses, you might say."

As they walked, Holly found herself hanging on Justin's every word, her heart racing with the thrill of discovery. "So there are other worlds out there?" she asked, her voice barely above a whisper. "And this place connects them?"

9 - 10

Holly's mind whirled with possibilities. She stopped walking, turning to face Justin fully. Her eyes searched his face, seeking answers to questions she was only beginning to formulate.

"Justin," she said, her voice quiet but intense, "I need to know. So why was I brought here?"

Justin's expression softened, a mix of compassion and determination in his eyes. He placed a gentle hand on Holly's shoulder, his touch both reassuring and weighty with significance.

"You're here to save humanity," he said simply, his voice resonating with conviction.

Holly's breath caught in her throat. She blinked rapidly, trying to process his words. Save humanity? Her? But how could she possibly...

"I don't understand," she whispered, her mind racing. "I'm just... me. How could I possibly save humanity?"

Justin's grip on her shoulder tightened slightly. "Because, Holly, you have a strength within you that you've yet to fully realize. A potential that transcends the boundaries of a single world."

Holly's heart pounded in her chest. She looked around the grand hall, its golden splendor suddenly feeling overwhelming. "But what does that mean?" she asked, her voice trembling slightly. "What am I supposed to do?"

Justin's eyes never left hers as he spoke. "It means that the fate of not just one world, but many, rests in your hands. The details will become clear in time, but for now, you must trust in yourself and in the path that has brought you here."

Holly took a deep breath, trying to steady herself. Save humanity. The words echoed in her mind, both terrifying and exhilarating. She looked back at Justin, seeing the unwavering belief in his eyes.

"I... I'll try," she said softly, her voice growing stronger with each word. "I don't know if I can do it, but I'll try."

11 - 12

Holly's brow furrowed in confusion as Justin's words sank in. "Save humanity?" she echoed, disbelief coloring her tone. "But how?"

Her mind raced, trying to grasp the enormity of what he was suggesting. She, Holly, an ordinary girl thrust into an extraordinary world, was somehow meant to be the savior of humanity? It seemed impossible, laughable even.

Justin's eyes softened, seeming to sense her inner turmoil. He took a step closer, his presence both comforting and intimidating in the vastness of the golden hall.

"You must find and deliver a gift to Drake Miller," he said, his voice low and urgent.

Holly's heart skipped a beat at the mention of Drake's name. She remembered him from her world - enigmatic, brilliant, and now apparently crucial to humanity's survival.

"A gift?" she asked, her voice barely above a whisper. "What kind of gift could possibly-"

She cut herself off, realizing the futility of questioning the logic of this strange new reality. Instead, she focused on the task at hand, her mind already whirring with possibilities and potential obstacles.

"How am I supposed to find him?" she asked, her tone more determined now. "And what exactly am I delivering?"

As she waited for Justin's response, Holly couldn't shake the feeling that she was standing on the precipice of something monumental. Whatever this gift was, whatever role she was meant to play, she knew that nothing would ever be the same again.

13 - 14

Holly ran her fingers through her hair, a nervous habit she'd never quite shaken. "And what gift could I possibly give to Drake Miller that would make a difference?" she asked, her voice tinged with both curiosity and skepticism.

Justin's warm demeanor shifted, his expression growing solemn as he met her gaze. The sudden change sent a shiver down Holly's spine. She found herself holding her breath, waiting for his response.

"There is a virus," Justin began, his voice low and grave, "that threatens to spread across the multiverse. It's unlike anything humanity has ever seen before." He paused, letting the weight of his words sink in.

Holly's mind reeled. A virus? Across the multiverse? The concept seemed too vast, too terrifying to fully comprehend. She opened her mouth to speak, but no words came out.

Justin continued, his eyes never leaving hers. "It's a threat to all existence, and only Drake has the power to stop it."

The enormity of the situation crashed over Holly like a tidal wave. She stumbled back a step, her hand instinctively reaching out to steady herself against a nearby golden pillar. The cool metal beneath her fingers grounded her, reminding her that this was real, not some fantastical dream.

"But... how?" she finally managed to whisper; her voice barely audible in the cavernous hall. "How can Drake stop something like that? And what does it have to do with me?"

15 - 16

Holly's heart began to race, pounding so hard she could feel it in her throat. A mixture of fear and determination coursed through her veins, setting her nerves on fire. She took a deep breath, trying to calm the storm of emotions raging within her.

"This is... it's overwhelming," she admitted, her voice shaky. "But I can't just turn my back on this, can I? Not when so much is at stake."

Justin nodded solemnly, his eyes reflecting a glimmer of pride. "You're stronger than you know, Holly."

She squared her shoulders, steeling herself for what was to come. The weight of responsibility settled upon her, heavy yet somehow invigorating. The fate of countless worlds hung in the balance, and somehow, she was at the center of it all.

"What do I need to do?" Holly asked, her voice steadier now despite the turmoil swirling within her. She clenched her fists at her sides, nails digging into her palms. "Tell me how I can help."

As she waited for Justin's response, Holly's mind raced with possibilities. What could she, an ordinary woman, possibly do to save the multiverse? The enormity of the task ahead threatened to overwhelm her, but she pushed the fear down, focusing instead on the determination burning in her chest.

17 - 18

Justin's hands moved to the folds of his robes, his movements slow and deliberate. Holly's breath caught in her throat as he produced a small, intricately carved box. The golden surface gleamed in the light, its intricate patterns seeming to shift and dance before her eyes.

"Inside this box," Justin said, his voice low and reverent, "lies a relic of great power." He held it out to her, the weight of history and destiny evident in his gestures. "It's a key that will pave the way for a brighter future."

Holly's eyes widened; her gaze fixed on the ornate container. She could almost feel the energy radiating from it, pulsing with untold potential.

Justin's next words sent a shiver down her spine. "You must deliver it to Drake Miller and trust that he will know what to do."

Holly hesitated for a moment, her mind reeling. Drake Miller - the name echoed in her thoughts, carrying with it a sense of both mystery and importance. How could he possibly wield whatever power lay within this small box?

With trembling fingers, Holly reached out and took the box from Justin's outstretched hand. It was heavier than she expected, as if the fate of worlds truly did rest within its golden confines. The responsibility of it all threatened to crush her, but she steeled herself against the doubt.

"I won't let you down," she vowed, her voice finding a firmness she didn't know she possessed. Holly clutched the box to her chest, feeling its warmth seep into her skin. "I'll do whatever it takes to save the world."

As the words left her lips, Holly realized the truth of them. She may not have asked for this role, may not have ever imagined herself as anything more than ordinary, but now, with the weight of the multiverse in her hands, she knew she would stop at nothing to see this through.

19 - 20

Justin's eyes softened as he gazed at Holly, a mixture of pride and concern etched across his features. With a nod of affirmation, he offered her a reassuring smile. "I believe in you, Holly," he said softly. "Now go and may the fate of the multiverse rest in your hands."

The gravity of the situation crashed over Holly like a tidal wave. Her heart raced, and she clutched the ornate box tighter, as if it might slip away at any moment. A thousand questions swirled in her mind, each more urgent than the last.

"But how do I get back?" she blurted out; her voice tinged with panic. "And how do I find Drake Miller? He's gone in both worlds." Holly's breath caught in her throat as she voiced her final, most terrifying concern. "I'm also infected with the virus and will most likely die soon."

As she spoke, Holly felt a wave of dizziness wash over her. The golden walls of the castle seemed to waver and blur. Was it the virus already taking hold, or simply the overwhelming weight of her newfound responsibility? She steadied herself against a nearby pillar, her eyes never leaving Justin's face, desperately seeking answers in his enigmatic gaze.

21 - 22

Justin's eyes softened with understanding. He stepped closer to Holly, his presence radiating a calming energy that seemed to still the chaos in her mind. Gently, he placed his hand on her shoulder, his touch warm and reassuring.

"I have a way," Justin said, his voice low and filled with quiet conviction. "Do you trust me?"

Holly's gaze locked with Justin's, searching the depths of his eyes. There was something there, something ancient and powerful, yet infinitely kind. It stirred a feeling deep within her, a sense of recognition that she couldn't quite explain.

Her mind raced, weighing the enormity of what she was being asked to do against the inexplicable connection she felt to this man. Could she really trust him with her life, with the fate of entire worlds?

As if in answer to her unspoken question, a wave of warmth washed over her. It was as if the very air around them was infused with love and compassion, emanating from Justin in palpable waves. In that moment, Holly knew with absolute certainty that this man was more than he appeared – he was a protector, a guide, perhaps even something divine.

"I do," Holly whispered, her voice barely audible but filled with unwavering conviction. "I trust you."

23 - 24

Justin's eyes softened with gratitude at Holly's trust. With a fluid motion, he reached into the folds of his robe and produced a small crystal vial filled with a luminous red liquid. The sight of it made Holly's heart skip a beat.

"This is my blood," Justin said, his voice resonating with power as he held out the vial. "Drink of me and you will be saved. It is the gift of life I bestow upon you."

Holly's eyes widened, her mind reeling at the implications. She reached out with trembling fingers, feeling the weight of the vial in her palm. The liquid within seemed to pulse with an otherworldly energy, casting a faint red glow on her skin.

A thousand questions raced through her mind, but only one made it past her lips. "And what will it do to me?" she asked, her voice barely above a whisper.

As she awaited Justin's response, Holly couldn't shake the feeling that she stood on the precipice of something monumental. Whatever his answer, she knew her life would never be the same after this moment.

25 - 26

Justin's eyes shimmered with an otherworldly light as he spoke, his voice carrying the weight of ages. "Whoever feeds of my flesh and drinks my blood has eternal life. Drink up, child, and you will be saved. With this, you will be able to find your heart's desire."

Holly's hand trembled as she raised the vial to her lips. Is this really happening? Am I about to drink his blood? The questions swirled in her mind, but a deeper instinct urged her forward. With a deep breath, she tipped the vial back and let the liquid flow into her mouth.

The taste was unlike anything she had ever experienced—sweet and rich, with an undercurrent of power that seemed to course through her very being. As the last drop passed her lips, a wave of warmth spread from her core to the tips of her fingers and toes.

Suddenly, Holly felt enveloped by an overwhelming sense of love, so pure and intense that it brought tears to her eyes. "Oh," she gasped, her voice choked with emotion. "I've never felt anything like this before."

The tears flowed freely now, but they were tears of joy, of profound peace. Holly looked up at Justin, her vision blurring. "Thank you," she whispered, her heart overflowing with gratitude.

Before Justin could respond, a brilliant white light began to surround Holly. She felt herself being lifted, transported. As the golden halls of the castle faded from view, a singular thought crystallized in her mind: Find Drake Miller.

The light intensified, and Holly closed her eyes, surrendering to its power. When she opened them again, she knew she would be back in her world, forever changed and with a critical mission ahead.

Suffocating Darkness

Green World – 2024

1 - 2

The darkness pressed against Linda's skin like a suffocating blanket, each breath a labored wheeze in the confined space. Her fingers, once frantically clawing at the wooden walls of her prison, now lay limp at her sides. A curious calm settled over her, washing away the panic that had consumed her for what felt like an eternity.

"Is this... how it ends?" Linda whispered to herself; her voice barely audible in the stale air. She tried to swallow, her throat parched and raw from screaming. "After everything... just silence?"

Her mind, once racing with desperate plans for escape, now drifted lazily. The fear that had gripped her heart loosened its hold, replaced by an odd sense of acceptance. Linda's eyelids fluttered, heavy with exhaustion.

I should be terrified, she thought. But I'm not. Why aren't I scared anymore?

She inhaled deeply, wincing at the burn in her lungs. The air was growing thinner, each breath less satisfying than the last. Linda's heart, once pounding furiously against her ribcage, now beat a slow, steady rhythm.

"I fought," she murmured, a hint of pride in her weak voice. "I fought so hard."

Her fingers twitched, remembering the frantic scratching, the desperate pounding. But now, as consciousness began to slip away, Linda felt a strange peace settling over her. The darkness no longer seemed threatening, but almost... comforting.

I did everything I could, Linda thought, her mind growing hazy. No one can say I didn't try.

With a soft sigh, she closed her eyes against the oppressive blackness. The fight was over. Whatever came next, Linda knew she had given her all. As the last wisps of awareness faded, a small smile played on her lips.

"It's okay," she breathed, barely audible even to herself. "It's okay to let go now."

And with that final whisper, Linda surrendered to the inevitable, slipping into a darkness deeper than any she had known before.

3 - 4

In the stillness, memories flickered like an old film reel behind Linda's closed eyelids. Sunlight dappled through leaves as she and Drake danced at their wedding, his warm brown eyes crinkling with laughter. Harrison's first steps, tiny hands reaching for her as she coaxed him forward.

"My boys," Linda whispered, her voice barely a rasp in the confines of the coffin. "I'm so sorry."

She imagined Drake's strong arms around her, heard the echo of his deep voice. "You have nothing to be sorry for, sweetheart. We love you. Always."

A tear slipped down Linda's cheek. "I love you too. Both of you. So much."

In her mind's eye, she saw Harrison's gap-toothed grin, felt the warmth of his small body as he snuggled close for bedtime stories.

"Mom," his voice seemed to say, "remember when we built that epic sandcastle? The one that lasted through high tide?"

Linda's lips curved in a faint smile. "How could I forget, sweetie? You were so determined."

The memories swirled, bittersweet. Family game nights. Holiday dinners. Quiet moments of shared understanding. Each one a treasure she'd carry with her, no matter what came next.

Suddenly, Linda's eyes snapped open. In the oppressive silence, she could have sworn she heard... something. A faint scraping sound, like...

"Hello?" she called out, her voice hoarse. "Is someone there?"

The sound came again, louder this time. Unmistakable. The scrape of a shovel against wood.

Linda's heart, which had slowed to a sluggish beat, began to race. "I'm here!" she cried, mustering all her remaining strength. "Please, I'm down here!"

She pressed her palms against the coffin lid, straining to hear more. Was it real, or just a dying hallucination? Linda held her breath, desperate for any sign of hope in the darkness.

5 - 6

Linda's pulse thrummed in her ears as she strained to listen. The scraping sound continued, growing louder and more distinct with each passing moment.

"Drake?" she called out, her voice raspy and weak. "Harrison? Is that you?"

No response came, but the sounds persisted. Linda's mind raced, hope warring with doubt. Could it really be her family, or had her oxygen-starved brain conjured this cruel illusion?

"Please," she whispered, pressing her palms against the coffin lid. "Please be real."

As if in answer, a muffled voice filtered through the wood and earth above her. The words were indistinct, but the tone was urgent, determined.

Linda's breath caught in her throat. "I'm here!" she cried out, summoning the last of her strength. "I'm still alive!"

The digging intensified, accompanied by more voices. Linda's heart soared even as her vision began to dim around the edges. She was so close to rescue, but her body was failing her.

"Stay with me," she murmured to herself, echoing Drake's favorite phrase of encouragement. "Just... stay... with me."

As consciousness slipped away, Linda allowed herself to believe. To hope. Her lips moved in a silent prayer of gratitude, to whatever force had brought her would-be rescuers.

"Thank you," she breathed, her eyes fluttering closed. "Thank you for not letting me die alone."

And as darkness claimed her, Linda felt a profound sense of peace. Whatever happened next, she knew she'd faced her fears with courage. She'd held onto love until the very end.

Echoes of a Distorted Reality

Green World – 2024

1 - 2

Holly's lungs burned as she sprinted through the eerily quiet streets, her footsteps echoing off the too-green houses. The world around her felt wrong, distorted, like a funhouse mirror version of reality.

"This can't be happening," she gasped between ragged breaths. "Linda can't be..."

But she had seen the empty Miller house with her own eyes. The family photos still adorning the walls, a half-finished cup of coffee on the kitchen counter - signs of life abruptly halted. Holly's mind raced, trying to make sense of it all.

She rounded a corner, nearly losing her footing on the slick grass that seemed to cover every surface. The cemetery loomed ahead, a sinister silhouette against the unnaturally vibrant sky.

"Please, let this all be some horrible mistake," Holly pleaded to no one in particular as she pushed herself to run faster.

Her legs trembled with exertion as she stumbled through the wrought iron gates. Row after row of gravestones stretched before her, but one plot stood out - freshly turned earth piled high, the headstone gleaming as if brand new.

Holly's breath caught in her throat as she approached, her steps slowing to a hesitant shuffle. Each footfall seemed to echo in the oppressive silence.

"No... it can't be," she whispered, her voice trembling.

But there it was, etched in cold, unforgiving stone: "Linda Miller, Beloved Wife and Mother."

Holly's knees became weak as the full weight of the situation crashed over her. She reached out a shaking hand, her fingertips hovering just above the carved letters.

"I don't understand," she choked out, tears welling in her eyes. "How can you be here when I just saw you? What's happening to this world?"

The silence of the cemetery offered no answers, only the faint whisper of an unnatural breeze rustling through unnaturally green leaves.

3 - 4

Holly's fingers trembled as they traced the harsh edges of Linda's name on the headstone. Her mind raced, desperately trying to make sense of the impossible situation.

"This can't be real," she murmured, her voice barely a whisper. "Linda was alive, I saw her... but this grave..."

She closed her eyes, forcing herself to think. The pieces began to fall into place, memories of conversations with Drake flooding back. And then the message she seen carved on Lindas arm only moments ago, 'Buried alive.'

"The green world," she gasped, her eyes flying open. "Oh god, Linda!"

Holly's heart pounded as realization dawned. "She's not dead - she's trapped here, in this twisted version of reality. Drake warned me about this, but I never thought..."

She stood abruptly, scanning the cemetery with newfound urgency. "I have to find a way to get her out. If I don't act fast, she could be stuck here forever."

Holly's mind raced with possibilities, her determination growing with each passing second. "Hold on, Linda," she whispered fiercely. "I'm not leaving you here. I'll find a way to bring you home."

5 - 6

Without hesitation, Holly dropped to her knees, her fingers clawing desperately at the freshly turned earth. The soil was soft, still damp from recent rain, and it clung to her hands as she dug frantically.

"I'm coming, Linda," she panted, her voice raw with determination. "Just hold on."

Her nails caught on roots and small stones, tearing as she burrowed deeper. The pain was irrelevant; all that mattered was reaching Linda before it was too late.

"This can't be how it ends," Holly muttered, pausing briefly to wipe sweat from her brow. "Not after everything we've been through."

Memories of their friendship flashed through her mind, fueling her resolve. She redoubled her efforts, ignoring the burning in her muscles and the dirt caking her skin.

"Come on, come on," she urged, desperation creeping into her voice as she dug deeper.

Suddenly, her fingers brushed against something solid. Holly's heart leapt.

"Please, let this be it," she whispered, clearing away more soil with renewed vigor.

As she uncovered more of the object, its shape became clear - a wooden coffin, buried just beneath the surface. Holly's breath caught in her throat, a mix of relief and fear washing over her.

"I found you, Linda," she said softly, her hands trembling as they rested on the coffin's surface. "Now, let's get you out of here."

7 - 8

With trembling hands, Holly gripped the edges of the coffin lid, her heart racing as she summoned the strength to pry it open. The wood creaked in protest, but slowly yielded to her desperate efforts. As the lid lifted, a musty odor wafted out, making Holly's stomach churn.

"Oh God," she gasped, her eyes widening in horror as she beheld Linda's pale, motionless form inside.

Linda lay there, her skin ashen and her chest barely moving. But she was alive – miraculously, impossibly alive. Holly's vision blurred as tears welled up in her eyes, a cocktail of relief and fear coursing through her veins.

"Linda," Holly whispered, her voice breaking. She reached out, her dirt-caked hand hovering over her friend's face. "What have they done to you?"

Holly's mind raced, recalling Drake's warnings about the green and blue world and their cruel tricks. This place had buried Linda alive, trapping her between realities. The injustice of it all made Holly's blood boil.

"I'm not letting you go," she declared, her voice gaining strength. "Do you hear me, Linda? I'm getting you out of here."

Holly placed her hands on Linda's shoulders, giving her a gentle shake. When there was no response, panic began to set in.

"Linda, wake up!" she pleaded, her heart pounding so hard she could hear it in her ears. "Please, you have to wake up. We don't have much time!"

9 - 10

Linda's eyelids fluttered, her brow furrowing as consciousness slowly returned. Her eyes, once vibrant, now appeared dull and unfocused as they blinked open. "Holly?" she murmured, her voice barely above a whisper and raspy from disuse. "What's happening?" Linda's gaze darted around; confusion etched across her face as she tried to make sense of her surroundings.

Holly's heart leapt with relief, but the urgency of their situation kept her from celebrating. She grasped Linda's cold hands, helping her sit up in the coffin. "We don't have time to explain," Holly replied, her voice low and intense. "We need to find a way to escape this world before it's too late."

As Holly spoke, she scanned the cemetery, her mind racing. How long did they have before this reality realized its mistake and tried to correct it? The thought sent a chill down her spine.

"This... world?" Linda echoed, her brow furrowing as she struggled to comprehend. She gripped the edges of the coffin, her knuckles white with the effort of staying upright.

"I know it doesn't make sense right now," Holly said, gently pulling Linda to her feet. She wrapped an arm around her friend's waist, supporting her weight. "But we're in danger here. We need to move."

Linda stumbled; her legs weak from disuse. "I don't understand," she mumbled, leaning heavily on Holly. "How did I get here? Where's my family?"

Holly bit her lip, torn between the need for haste and the desire to comfort her friend. "I promise I'll explain everything once we're safe," she said, guiding them towards the cemetery gate. "Right now, I need you to trust me. Can you do that?"

11 - 11

Linda nodded weakly, her eyes darting around the cemetery with growing alarm. "I trust you, Holly," she whispered, her voice trembling. "But where are we going?"

Holly's gaze swept across the rows of tombstones, searching for anything that might offer a clue. "I'm not entirely sure," she admitted, her heart pounding. "But there has to be a way out of this place, a portal or something that can take us back."

They stumbled forward, their footsteps crunching on the gravel path. Holly's mind raced, recalling everything Drake had ever told her about the green world. There had to be something she was missing, some detail that could save them.

"Holly," Linda gasped, her legs buckling slightly. "I feel... strange. Like I'm fading."

Panic surged through Holly. "Hold on," she urged, tightening her grip on Linda. "Focus on me, on my voice. We're going to make it out of here together."

As they neared the cemetery gate, Holly noticed something odd. The air seemed to shimmer faintly, like heat rising from pavement on a scorching day. Could this be it? The way back?

"Linda, look," Holly said, pointing towards the distortion. "Do you see that? I think it might be our ticket home."

Linda squinted, her face pale with exhaustion. "I... I think I see it," she murmured. "But what if it's not safe?"

Holly swallowed hard, steeling herself. "We don't have a choice," she said, her voice firm despite her own doubts. "Whatever's on the other side has to be better than staying here."

With renewed determination, they pressed forward, each step bringing them closer to the shimmering air and, hopefully, their way back to the world they once knew.

Shadows of Tension

Apocalypse World – 20 A.C.

1 - 2

The air in the dimly lit room hung thick with tension, each breath a struggle against the oppressive atmosphere. Harrison's heart thundered in his chest as he squinted into the shadows, desperately trying to make out the figure emerging before them. Beside him, Jonathan stood rigid, his presence a small comfort in the face of the unknown.

A sliver of light from a crack in the wall caught the edge of a familiar silhouette, and Harrison's world tilted on its axis. Time seemed to slow as the figure stepped fully into view, revealing a face he'd only seen in faded photographs and distant memories.

"Mom?" The word escaped Harrison's lips in a strangled whisper, disbelief etched into every syllable. His mind reeled, struggling to reconcile the impossible reality before him with everything he thought he knew.

Linda Miller stood just feet away, her presence as surreal as it was undeniable. Harrison's eyes darted over her features, drinking in details he'd feared lost forever – the curve of her cheek, the set of her jaw, the depth of her gaze. She looked older, wearier than in his memories, but unmistakably alive.

This can't be real, Harrison thought, his palms slick with sweat. *I watched her die. I mourned her. How is she here, in this desolate place?*

"Harrison," Linda breathed, her voice carrying a weight of emotion that threatened to overwhelm him. "My boy..."

He took an unsteady step forward, torn between the urge to run to her and the fear that she might vanish if he moved too quickly. "Is it really you?" he asked, hating how small and uncertain his voice sounded. "How... how is this possible?"

Linda's eyes shimmered with unshed tears as she regarded him. "It's a long story, one I'm not sure I fully understand myself. But yes, it's me. I'm here."

Harrison's mind raced, grasping for explanations. The multiverse, the strange energies that seemed to permeate this world – could they have somehow brought his mother back? Or had she never truly died at all?

"I don't understand," he said, his voice cracking. "We thought... I saw..." He trailed off, unable to voice the painful memories.

Linda took a tentative step closer, her hand half-raised as if to touch him before falling back to her side. "I know, sweetheart. I'm so sorry for everything you've been through. But we don't have much time. There's so much I need to tell you, so much you need to know."

Harrison glanced at Jonathan, seeing his own confusion mirrored in his friend's face. He turned back to Linda, a thousand questions burning on his tongue. But before he could voice any of them, a distant rumble shook the building, sending a shower of dust cascading from the ceiling.

Linda's expression hardened, a fierce determination replacing the sorrow in her eyes. "We need to move," she said urgently. "It isn't safe here. Come with me, both of you. I'll explain everything I can, but first, we need to get somewhere secure."

Harrison hesitated for just a moment, years of caution warring with the desperate hope blooming in his chest. Then, with a quick nod to Jonathan, he stepped forward to follow his mother into the unknown.

3 - 4

Linda's haunted gaze swept over Harrison and Jonathan, her weathered features a map of untold hardships. The dim light filtering through the cracks in their prison walls cast deep shadows across her face, accentuating the weariness etched into every line. Yet beneath that exhaustion, a fierce spark of determination blazed in her eyes, defying the oppressive darkness surrounding them.

"Harrison," Linda whispered, her voice barely audible as it echoed softly against the cold, unforgiving walls. "I never thought I would see you again."

Harrison's mind reeled, a maelstrom of emotions threatening to overwhelm him. How could she be here? After all this time, all the grief and loss... His throat constricted, making it difficult to speak.

"Mom," he finally managed, his voice trembling. "How... how is this possible?"

Linda's lips curved into a sad smile, her eyes glistening with unshed tears. "It's a long story, sweetheart. One I'm not sure I fully understand myself."

Harrison took a halting step forward, his hand reaching out instinctively before falling back to his side. "We thought you were dead. I saw... I saw you die."

A flash of pain crossed Linda's face. "I know. And I'm so sorry for the pain you've endured. But there are forces at work here beyond our comprehension. The multiverse is vast and full of mysteries."

Harrison's mind raced, trying to reconcile the impossible reality before him with everything he thought he knew. "But why now? Why here, in this... this prison?"

Linda's expression hardened, that spark of determination flaring brighter. "Because the fate of all realities hangs in the balance, Harrison. And you... you may be the key to saving them all."

5 - 6

The weight of Linda's words hung heavy in the air, laden with unspoken emotion. For a moment, silence reigned supreme as mother and son regarded each other across the expanse of the room, each grappling with the enormity of the reunion.

Harrison's mind whirled, a tempest of questions and conflicting emotions. He opened his mouth to speak, but found himself at a loss for words. Instead, he studied his mother's face, drinking in every detail he thought he'd never see again.

"I don't understand," he finally managed, his voice barely above a whisper. "How can I be the key to saving... everything?"

Linda's eyes softened, a mixture of pride and concern evident in her gaze. "You've always been special, Harrison. Even as a child, you saw connections others missed. Your father and I... we knew you were destined for something greater."

Harrison felt a familiar pang at the mention of his father. He swallowed hard, pushing the thought aside. "But I'm just... me. I'm not some chosen one or superhero."

From the corner of his eye, Harrison noticed Jonathan shift uneasily. His friend had remained uncharacteristically quiet, watching the exchange with a mixture of astonishment and curiosity. Harrison could almost see the gears turning in Jonathan's analytical mind, piecing together fragments of information.

"You okay, Jon?" Harrison asked, suddenly aware of how surreal this must be for his friend.

Jonathan nodded, his gaze flickering between Harrison and Linda. "It's just... I've heard you speak of your mother, of her fate in the other world. But to see her now, alive and in the flesh... it's a revelation I never anticipated."

Linda's attention shifted to Jonathan, her expression softening. "You must be Jonathan. Harrison's told me about you... in a manner of speaking."

Harrison's brow furrowed. "What do you mean, 'in a manner of speaking'?"

His mother's eyes met his, a flicker of something – hesitation? fear? – passing through them. "There's so much to explain, Harrison. So much you need to know. But we don't have much time. The forces aligned against us are growing stronger by the moment."

7 - 8

Harrison's heart pounded against his ribcage, a tempest of emotions threatening to overwhelm him. He stared at his mother, drinking in every detail of her face – the same face he'd seen lifeless and cold in another world. His voice trembled as he finally found the words.

"Mom," he choked out, his eyes glistening with unshed tears. "How... how is this possible? I thought you were..."

The words died in his throat, the unthinkable reality too painful to vocalize. Harrison's mind reeled, grappling with the paradox before him. He had watched her die, had mourned her loss, had carried the weight of her absence for so long. And yet, here she stood, alive and breathing, defying everything he thought he knew about the world – about reality itself.

Linda's eyes softened, a mix of sorrow and understanding etched across her features. She took a step towards him, her hand outstretched as if to touch him, but hesitated.

Harrison's thoughts raced, each more bewildering than the last. How could she be here? Was this some cruel trick of the multiverse? A doppelganger from another timeline? Or had everything he'd experienced been a lie?

"I know this must be overwhelming for you," Linda said softly, her voice anchoring him amidst the storm of his thoughts. "I can only imagine what you've been through, what you've seen."

Harrison swallowed hard, fighting to keep his voice steady. "I saw you die," he whispered, the words hanging heavy in the air between them. "In another world, another time. How can you be here now?"

He searched her face for answers, for some sign that might unravel the mystery of her impossible presence. The very fabric of reality seemed to stretch and warp around them, challenging everything he thought he understood about the multiverse and his place within it.

9 - 10

Linda offered her son a sad smile, her expression tinged with sorrow. "There are many things you do not yet understand, Harrison," she said softly. "But know this – I am here now, and I will do whatever it takes to keep you safe."

The weight of her words pressed against Harrison's chest, a mix of comfort and unease. He wanted desperately to believe her, to throw himself into her arms and forget the nightmare of losing her. But caution held him back, the lessons of multiple realities etched deep into his psyche.

"How can I trust that you're really my mother?" Harrison asked, his voice barely above a whisper. "I've seen so many versions, so many possibilities..."

Linda's eyes glistened with unshed tears. "I know, sweetheart. The multiverse is vast and cruel sometimes. But feel this," she said, gently taking his hand and placing it over her heart. "This is real. I'm real."

Harrison felt the steady rhythm beneath his palm, a tangible connection to the woman before him. His own heart raced in response, a cocktail of hope and fear surging through his veins.

Jonathan shifted uncomfortably beside them, a silent reminder of the dangers that still lurked. Harrison glanced at his companion, noting the mix of awe and wariness on his face.

"We can't stay here," Harrison said, reluctantly pulling his hand away. "It's not safe. There are people... things... hunting us."

Linda nodded, her posture straightening with resolve. "Then we'll face them together. Whatever comes, whatever trials lie ahead, we'll overcome them as a family."

Her words hung in the air, a solemn vow that echoed through the darkness. And as Harrison and Jonathan stood before her, enveloped in the weight of her presence, they knew that whatever trials lay ahead, they would face them together, bound by a bond that transcended time and space.

Harrison's mind raced with possibilities, with questions still unanswered. But for now, in this moment, he allowed himself to feel a flicker of hope. Whatever the multiverse had in store for them, they would navigate it together.

11 - 12

Linda's eyes narrowed as she studied Harrison, her gaze tracing the contours of his face with an intensity that made him want to squirm. The dim light cast long shadows across her features, accentuating the worry lines etched around her eyes and mouth.

"Mom?" Harrison ventured, his voice barely above a whisper. The word felt strange on his tongue, filled with a mixture of hope and uncertainty.

Linda reached out, her hand hovering inches from Harrison's cheek. He could feel the warmth radiating from her palm, a stark contrast to the cool, stale air of their surroundings.

"Harrison," she began, her voice soft yet tinged with uncertainty. "You... you're not the same..."

Harrison's heart clenched. How could he explain? His mind raced, searching for the right words. "I'm still me, Mom," he said, fighting to keep his voice steady. "Just... a different version."

Linda's brow furrowed, her eyes searching his face. "How is this possible?" she murmured, more to herself than to him.

Harrison swallowed hard, acutely aware of Jonathan's presence beside him. "It's complicated," he admitted. "I'm not even sure I understand it all myself."

As Linda's hand finally made contact with his cheek, Harrison leaned into her touch, closing his eyes briefly. The familiar scent of her perfume – a mix of lavender and vanilla – washed over him, stirring memories he thought long buried.

"Whatever's happened," Linda said, her voice gaining strength, "we'll figure it out together. You're my son, no matter what version of you stands before me."

Harrison nodded, fighting back the tears that threatened to spill. In this moment, surrounded by the unknown dangers of this world, he allowed himself to feel a glimmer of hope. Whatever lay ahead, he wasn't alone anymore.

13 - 14

Linda's hand trembled as it fell away from Harrison's face, her eyes never leaving his. The silence between them was thick with unspoken questions, the air heavy with the weight of impossibility.

Harrison watched as his mother's gaze flickered over his features, drinking in every detail. He could almost see the gears turning in her mind, trying to reconcile the boy before her with the man she thought she knew.

"How..." Linda's voice cracked, and she cleared her throat before continuing. "How can this be? The Harrison I know, he's..." She trailed off, unable to finish the thought.

Harrison took a deep breath, steeling himself for the conversation ahead. His heart raced, pounding against his ribcage like a caged bird seeking freedom. How could he explain something he barely understood himself?

"I know I look different," he said quietly, his voice barely above a whisper. The words felt inadequate, but he pressed on. "But I assure you, I'm still your son – just from a different time."

As the words left his lips, Harrison studied his mother's face, searching for a sign of understanding, of acceptance. The familiar crease between her brows deepened, a telltale sign of her inner turmoil.

Linda's eyes widened, a mix of confusion and wonder swirling in their depths. "A different time?" she echoed, her voice tinged with disbelief.

Harrison nodded, feeling the weight of the multiverse on his shoulders. He glanced briefly at Jonathan, drawing strength from his friend's silent support, before turning back to his mother.

"It's hard to explain," he began, choosing his words carefully. "But I'm from a reality where things... happened differently. Where I'm still the boy you remember, not the man you've known here."

15 - 16

Linda's brow furrowed deeper, her mind racing to make sense of the revelation. "A different time?" she echoed, her voice tinged with incredulity. "What do you mean?"

Harrison swallowed hard, his throat suddenly dry. He could feel the weight of his mother's gaze upon him, a mixture of confusion and concern etched across her familiar features. The air in the dimly lit room felt thick, charged with the tension of unspoken questions and impossible truths.

"Mom," he began, his voice wavering slightly. "I know this sounds crazy, but..." He paused, gathering his courage. "I'm from the year 2024."

Linda's eyes widened, her lips parting in silent shock. Harrison pressed on, his words measured yet filled with conviction. "I was... I was surrounded by a white light, and when I woke up, I found myself here."

As he spoke, Harrison's mind raced with memories of that fateful moment - the blinding flash, the sensation of falling through endless space, the disorientation upon awakening in this strange, familiar world. He watched his mother carefully, searching for any sign of understanding or acceptance.

Linda remained silent, her eyes never leaving Harrison's face. He could almost see the gears turning in her mind, trying to reconcile the impossible truth before her with everything she thought she knew about the world - about her son.

"I know it's hard to believe," Harrison added softly, reaching out to touch his mother's hand. "But I'm still me, Mom. Just... a different version of me."

17 - 18

Linda's fingers twitched beneath Harrison's touch, her warm hand a stark contrast to the chill that seemed to permeate the room. She drew in a shaky breath, her eyes searching his face with an intensity that made Harrison's heart ache.

"Time travel," she whispered, the words hanging in the air between them like a fragile bubble. "My God, Harrison."

The weight of his revelation hung heavy in the air, the implications sinking in with a profound sense of understanding. Linda's mind raced as she processed the information, piecing together the fragments of the puzzle before her. Harrison could almost see the thoughts whirling behind her eyes, a maelstrom of confusion, wonder, and maternal concern.

"So you've traveled through time," she mused, a note of wonder creeping into her voice. "But why? How is that even possible?"

Harrison swallowed hard, his throat suddenly dry. "I wish I knew, Mom. One moment I was in my own time, and the next..." He gestured helplessly at their surroundings. "I ended up here, in this world that's both familiar and completely alien."

Linda's brow furrowed, her expression a mixture of fascination and worry. "This is... it's beyond anything I could have imagined," she said softly. "My son, a time traveler."

As she spoke, Harrison couldn't help but marvel at his mother's resilience. Even faced with such an earth-shattering revelation, she maintained her composure, her innate warmth and strength shining through. It was so quintessentially Linda that it made his chest tighten with emotion.

"I'm still trying to figure it all out myself," Harrison admitted, running a hand through his hair. "But I think... I think there's a reason I'm here. Something I'm meant to do."

19 - 20

Harrison shook his head, his expression grave. The weight of uncertainty pressed down on him, but he felt compelled to voice his thoughts. "I don't have all the answers," he admitted, his voice barely above a whisper. "But I believe there's a greater purpose to all of this – a reason why I've been brought here, to this place and time."

As he spoke, Harrison's mind raced with possibilities. Was he meant to prevent some catastrophic event? To save someone? The responsibility felt overwhelming, and he clenched his fists at his sides, trying to ground himself in the moment.

Linda's eyes softened as she regarded her son. Despite the years and dimensions that separated them, she could still read the turmoil in his features. She reached out, placing a gentle hand on his arm. "Oh, Harrison," she said, her voice a soothing balm to his frayed nerves. "You've always had such a strong sense of purpose, even as a child."

Harrison looked up, meeting his mother's gaze. In her eyes, he saw a mixture of concern and determination that mirrored his own feelings. "Mom, I... I'm scared," he confessed, the words tumbling out before he could stop them. "What if I'm not up to the task? What if I fail?"

Linda's grip on his arm tightened slightly, her touch anchoring him. "We'll face this together," she said firmly, her voice filled with unwavering resolve. "Whatever lies ahead, whatever challenges we must overcome, we'll do it as a family."

As she spoke, Harrison felt a surge of warmth in his chest. Despite the impossible situation they found themselves in, despite the uncertainty that loomed before them, he knew that with his mother by his side, they could face anything. Their bond, it seemed, truly did transcend the boundaries of time and space.

21 - 22

"We'll figure it out," she said firmly, her voice infused with resolve. "Whatever it takes, we'll find a way to set things right – for you, for me, and for everyone caught up in this tangled web of fate."

Harrison nodded, drawing strength from his mother's words. He glanced around the dimly lit chamber, its shadows seeming to pulse with untold secrets. The air felt thick with possibility and danger in equal measure.

"But where do we even start?" he asked, his mind racing with questions. "We're in a world that's not our own, facing threats we don't fully understand."

Linda's eyes gleamed with determination. "We start by trusting each other," she said, squeezing his hand. "And by using every resource at our disposal."

As they stood there, Harrison felt a profound sense of connection to his mother, despite the years and realities that separated them. He realized that their reunion, as inexplicable as it was, held the key to unraveling the mysteries that surrounded them.

"You're right," he said, straightening his shoulders. "Together, we can do this. We have to."

They shared a look of understanding, both aware that their journey was only beginning. With each step forward, they would uncover truths hidden within the very fabric of time itself. The weight of their task was immense, but Harrison felt ready to face it – with his mother by his side, he could conquer anything. Meanwhile Jonathan had sauntered off in search of the key to everything.

23 - 24

Jonathan's fingers trembled as they traced the intricate patterns etched into the tome's weathered leather cover. The dim emergency lights of the abandoned research facility cast an eerie glow across the ancient text, its secrets seemingly pulsing beneath his fingertips.

"I can't believe I actually found it," he whispered, his voice barely audible over the pounding of his heart. The corridors around him stretched into darkness, filled with unseen dangers.

With each step, Jonathan's mind raced. What if he was caught? What if the book's power was too much for him to control? The weight of his stolen prize seemed to grow heavier with each passing moment.

"Focus," he muttered to himself, forcing his breathing to slow. "You've come too far to falter now."

As he rounded a corner, a flicker of movement caught his eye. Jonathan pressed himself against the wall, the rough concrete cool against his back. He held his breath, straining to hear any sign of pursuit.

After a moment of tense silence, he allowed himself to relax slightly. "Just shadows," he reassured himself, though the tremor in his voice betrayed his lingering fear.

Jonathan's gaze fell once more to the book in his hands. Its presence filled him with a mix of awe and trepidation. This was no ordinary text – it was a key to unlocking the very fabric of reality itself.

"With this," he murmured, running a hand over the cover, "we might actually have a chance to set things right." The enormity of the situation threatened to overwhelm him, but Jonathan steeled himself against the tide of doubt.

He took a deep breath, steadying his nerves. "One step at a time," he reminded himself. "First, get out of here. Then... then we figure out how to use this thing."

With renewed determination, Jonathan pushed off from the wall and continued his stealthy journey through the shadowy corridors, the stolen tome clutched tightly to his chest – a beacon of hope in a world teetering on the brink of chaos.

25 - 26

Jonathan reached the threshold of the facility, his hand hovering over the door handle. The weight of the ancient tome pressed against his chest, a constant reminder of the monumental task that lay ahead. He paused, casting a wary glance over his shoulder into the darkness behind him.

"This is it," he whispered to himself, his voice barely audible. "No turning back now."

The night air that seeped through the cracks in the doorframe hung heavy with an oppressive stillness, as if the very atmosphere was holding its breath in anticipation. Jonathan's fingers tightened around the handle, his knuckles turning white with the pressure.

A fleeting image of the dangers that awaited him beyond these walls flashed through his mind. The desolate landscape, the unknown threats, the weight of responsibility that came with possessing such powerful knowledge – it all threatened to overwhelm him.

But deep within, a fire burned. A singular purpose that had driven him this far and would carry him forward. Jonathan closed his eyes, drawing strength from that inner flame.

"Whatever it takes," he murmured, a quiet mantra to steel his resolve. "Whatever it takes to make things right."

With a silent prayer on his lips, Jonathan pushed open the door and stepped out into the cool embrace of the night. The crisp air filled his lungs, carrying with it the faint scent of decay and abandonment that seemed to permeate this world.

His footsteps echoed against the cracked pavement, each sound a stark reminder of his solitude in this desolate place. Above him, the sky stretched out in an endless expanse of inky blackness, punctuated only by the flickering light of distant stars.

As Jonathan began his journey into the unknown, guided only by instinct and the faint hope of salvation, he couldn't help but wonder aloud, "Where do I go from here? How do I even begin to unravel the secrets of the multiverse?"

The silence that answered him was both comforting and unnerving. In this moment, suspended between worlds and realities, Jonathan felt the full weight of his mission settle upon his shoulders. Yet with each step forward, his resolve only grew stronger.

27 - 28

Jonathan's fingers tightened around the ancient tome as he trudged through the desolate landscape. The weight of the book seemed to grow heavier with each step, a physical reminder of the burden he now carried.

As he navigated around a cluster of abandoned vehicles, their rusted frames glinting dully in the starlight, He paused, scanning the horizon with keen eyes. The silhouette of a dilapidated building loomed in the distance, its broken windows like vacant eyes staring back at him. Jonathan steeled himself, squaring his shoulders.

"I'm finally here," he said firmly, his voice gaining strength. "This knowledge... it's too important. I can't let it fall into the wrong hands, no matter the cost."

With renewed determination, Jonathan pressed forward, each step purposeful and resolute. The tome pulsed with an otherworldly energy against his chest, as if responding to his unwavering commitment.

"Whatever dangers lie ahead," he vowed, his eyes fixed on the path before him, "I'll face them. For the sake of all realities, I have to succeed."

29 - 30

Jonathan's breath caught in his throat as the first rays of dawn pierced the horizon, casting long shadows across the desolate landscape. The stolen book seemed to grow heavier with each passing moment, its ancient knowledge a tangible weight against his chest.

"Almost there," he muttered, his voice raspy from exhaustion. "Just a little further."

As he crested a small hill, the full expanse of his destination came into view - a sprawling, abandoned research facility, its weathered walls a testament to the passage of time. Jonathan's eyes narrowed, scanning for any signs of movement or danger.

"This has to be it," he whispered, his heart pounding. "This is where I get my family back."

With cautious steps, Jonathan approached the facility's perimeter fence. His fingers brushed against the rusted metal, sending a shiver down his spine.

"What secrets are you hiding?" he mused, addressing the silent building before him. "And at what cost will I uncover them?"

As if in response, the tome pulsed with an otherworldly energy, causing Jonathan to gasp. He clutched it tighter, his resolve strengthening.

"No turning back now," he declared, his voice firm despite the weariness etched on his face. "Whatever lies beyond those walls, I'm ready to face it."

With a deep breath, Jonathan began to search for an entry point, his eyes alert for any sign of danger. The weight of his duty pressed upon him, but his spirit remained unbroken, driven by a purpose that transcended his own existence.

31 - 32

Jonathan slipped through a gap in the fence, his heart racing as he entered the facility's grounds. The eerie silence was broken only by the crunch of gravel beneath his feet and the whisper of wind through abandoned structures.

As he approached the main building, a flicker of movement caught his eye. He froze, pressing himself against a wall, his breath caught in his throat.

"Who's there?" a familiar voice called out, tinged with both hope and fear.

Jonathan's eyes widened in recognition. "Megan?" he whispered, scarcely believing it.

Stepping out from his hiding place, he saw Megan Johnson standing in a doorway, her face a mixture of relief and confusion. But it was the figure beside her that made Jonathan's heart skip a beat.

"Lucian?" he breathed, taking in the sight of the figure cloaked in black who stood protectively close to his master.

Megan's gaze locked onto Jonathan, her eyes narrowing as she assessed the situation. "Jonathan? Did you finally bring it?" she asked, her voice a blend of steel determination and wariness.

Jonathan held up the ancient tome, his voice thick with emotion. "I found it, your highness. The key to understanding all of this. But we need to move quickly. They'll be coming for it."

As Megan gazed upon Jonathan, a flicker of recognition danced in her eyes, mingling with a profound sense of sorrow and longing. Here stood a man, the one she tasked with finding the codex. He was older, more innocent, touched by the trials and tribulations of the years that had passed since the multiversal collision.

Jonathan watched the silent exchange between Megan and Lucian, his mind racing. How could he explain the complexities of their situation? The weight of his newfound purpose pressed upon him, urging him to action.

"Your royal Highness," he said softly, "I know this is confusing, but we don't have much time. We need to get somewhere safe where I can explain everything."

33 - 34

Linda's eyes glistened with unshed tears as she cupped Harrison's face in her hands. The dim light of their surroundings cast long shadows across her features, accentuating the lines of worry etched into her brow.

"Harrison," she began, her voice a gentle whisper that seemed to hang in the air between them. "You're still so young, so full of promise. There's still time for you to choose the right path, to remain true to yourself and the values that define who you are."

Harrison swallowed hard, his mind reeling. He wanted to speak, to ask the thousand questions that burned within him, but found himself frozen under his mother's intense gaze.

Linda's hand trembled slightly as she brushed a stray lock of hair from Harrison's forehead. The tender gesture sparked a memory within him - of simpler times, of a childhood unmarred by the complexities of multiple realities.

"You have the chance to stay pure, to not make the same mistakes again." Linda continued, her voice soft but resolute. "To hold onto the goodness that resides within you. The world may be a dark and dangerous place, but you have the power to shine brightly amidst the shadows, to be a beacon of hope in a sea of uncertainty."

Harrison's throat tightened with emotion. How could he tell her about the challenges he'd already faced? The weight of responsibility that pressed down upon his young shoulders.

"Mom," he managed to choke out, "I don't know if I can be what you're asking. Everything's so complicated now."

Linda's eyes softened with understanding. "I know, sweetheart. But that's precisely why you must hold onto your core values. They'll be your compass when the path ahead seems unclear."

35 - 36

Linda's words hung in the air, a silent plea that resonated through the dim room. Harrison felt their weight settle on him, a mixture of hope and trepidation swirling in his chest. He took a deep breath, the musty air of their surroundings filling his lungs.

"I'll try, Mom," he said softly, his voice barely above a whisper. "But how can I be sure I'm making the right choices when everything around me keeps changing?"

Linda's eyes, filled with a mother's love and worry, searched his face. "Trust your instincts, Harrison. They've guided you this far."

As she spoke, Harrison's gaze drifted to the cracked walls surrounding them, shadows dancing in the corners. The ever-present threat of the unknown pressed in, a constant reminder of the perilous journey ahead.

"But what if my instincts aren't enough?" he asked, his voice catching. "What if I'm not strong enough to face what's coming?"

Linda reached out; her hand warm against his cheek. "You are stronger than you know, my dear boy. I see it in your eyes – the same determination, the same fierce spirit you've always had."

Harrison leaned into her touch, allowing himself a moment of vulnerability. In his mind, memories flickered – of laughter echoing through their old home, of quiet evenings spent reading together. How far away those moments seemed now, separated by the vast expanse of time and reality.

"I'm scared, Mom," he admitted, the words tumbling out before he could stop them. "Everything's changing so fast, and I don't know if I can keep up."

Linda's expression softened, a mix of pride and sorrow etched across her features. "Fear is natural, Harrison. It's what you do in the face of that fear that defines you. And I know, in my heart, that you have the strength to overcome whatever lies ahead."

As she spoke, Harrison felt a spark of resolve ignite within him. He straightened his shoulders, meeting his mother's gaze with newfound determination. "I won't let you down," he promised, his voice steady despite the uncertainty that still lingered.

37 - 38

With a gentle smile, Linda placed a hand on Harrison's shoulder, her touch a silent reassurance of her unwavering faith in him. "Remember, my son," she said, her voice tinged with warmth and affection, "no matter what challenges you may face, you are never alone. You carry within you the light of hope and the power of love – and with those by your side, you can conquer anything that stands in your way."

Harrison felt a lump form in his throat, overwhelmed by the depth of his mother's love and belief in him. He swallowed hard, trying to find the right words to express the tumult of emotions swirling within him.

"But how can you be so sure?" he asked, his voice barely above a whisper. "The multiverse is vast, and there's so much we don't understand. What if I make the wrong choice?"

Linda's eyes shimmered with unshed tears, but her smile never wavered. "Because I know you, Harrison. I've seen your kindness, your resilience, your unwavering desire to do what's right. Those qualities transcend any reality or timeline."

As she spoke, Harrison's mind raced through the myriads of possibilities that lay before him. The weight of responsibility pressed down on his shoulders, but alongside it, he felt a growing sense of purpose.

"I'll try," he said, his voice growing stronger with each word. "For you, for Dad, for everyone caught up in this mess. I'll find a way to make things right."

Linda nodded, pride radiating from her entire being. "That's my boy," she whispered, pulling him into a tight embrace.

And as Harrison met his mother's gaze once more, he felt a flicker of hope ignite within his soul, a spark of determination that burned brighter than ever before. For in that moment, he knew that no matter what the future held, he would face it with courage and conviction, guided by the wisdom and love of the woman who had given him life.

39 - 39

Linda's eyes hardened with resolve as she released Harrison from her embrace. "Now let's go find your father."

The words hung in the air, charged with purpose and a hint of trepidation. Harrison's heart raced, a mix of anticipation and fear coursing through his veins. He swallowed hard, picturing his father's weary face, those piercing eyes that always seemed to carry the weight of unsolved mysteries.

"Do you know where he is?" Harrison asked, his voice barely above a whisper.

Linda's gaze flickered to the shadowy corners of the room. "I have a feeling, but it's dangerous. Drake's been working with some powerful people, and they won't take kindly to our interference."

Harrison's fingers twitched nervously at his sides. "What if... what if he doesn't recognize me? This version of me, I mean."

His mother's expression softened. "Your father's love transcends time and space, just like mine. He'll know you, Harrison. Deep in his soul, he'll know."

As they moved towards the exit, Harrison's mind raced with possibilities. Would they find his father in this world, or would their search take them across the boundaries of reality itself? The thought both thrilled and terrified him.

"Mom," he said, pausing at the threshold, "whatever happens... I'm glad I found you."

Linda's smile was tinged with sadness and hope. "So am I, sweetheart. Now, let's bring our family back together."

Whispers in the Abandoned Hospital

Apocalypse World – 20 A.C.

1 - 2

The abandoned hospital loomed before them, a decaying monolith against the muted green sky. Harrison's breath caught in his throat as he took in the crumbling façade, windows like hollow eyes staring back at him. Beside him, Linda's hand tightened on his arm.

"Mom," he whispered, his voice barely audible above the eerie silence, "are you sure about this?"

Linda nodded, swallowing hard. "We have to, Harrison. The answers we need... they're in there somewhere."

They approached cautiously, each step crunching on debris-strewn ground. Harrison's mind raced with possibilities. What would they find inside? Would it lead them closer to his father, or just raise more questions?

As they neared the entrance, a flicker of movement caught Harrison's eye. A shadowy figure emerged from the darkness, heading towards what looked like a hidden chamber.

"Mom, did you see that?" Harrison hissed, his heart pounding.

Linda nodded; her eyes wide. "Who could that be?"

Harrison's curiosity battled with his apprehension. "I don't know, but we should follow them. They might know something."

"Be careful, sweetheart," Linda cautioned, her motherly instincts kicking in. "We don't know what kind of dangers lurk here."

Harrison took a deep breath, steeling himself. "I know, Mom. But we've come too far to turn back now."

As they crept closer, Harrison's mind whirled with possibilities. Could this mysterious figure be connected to his father's wearabouts? Or were they just another lost soul in this desolate world?

"Stay close," he murmured to Linda, his eyes never leaving the spot where the figure had vanished. "Whatever happens, we face it together."

Linda squeezed his hand in response, her touch a reminder of the unbreakable bond between them. With hearts racing and senses on high alert, mother and son ventured deeper into the unknown, the hospital's ominous silence engulfing them with each step.

3 - 4

The air crackled with tension as Harrison and Linda crouched behind a crumbling pillar, their eyes fixed on the chamber entrance. A surge of people materialized from the shadows, their voices rising in a cacophonous blend of shouts and jeers.

"What in the world?" Harrison whispered; his brow furrowed. The crowd's frenzy was palpable, a stark contrast to the eerie silence that had enveloped them moments ago.

Linda's grip on Harrison's arm tightened. "I've never seen anything like this," she murmured, her voice tinged with awe and fear.

As the mysterious figure stepped into view, the crowd's fervor intensified. Harrison leaned forward, straining to make out details through the sea of bodies.

"They seem... different," he observed, his curiosity piqued. "Look at how they move, Mom. It's like they're not even fazed by all this chaos."

Indeed, the figure moved with an otherworldly grace, each step purposeful and unhurried. The crowd parted before them, their frenzied cries seeming to slide off an invisible barrier.

"It's almost as if..." Harrison's voice trailed off, his mind racing. Could this person be connected to the multiverse somehow? To his father?

Linda's soft voice broke through his thoughts. "What are you thinking, sweetheart?"

Harrison shook his head, uncertainty clouding his features. "I'm not sure, but something tells me they're important. We need to find a way to talk to them."

As the figure disappeared into the chamber, Harrison's resolve solidified. "Come on, Mom. We didn't come this far to just watch from the sidelines. We need answers."

With a deep breath, he stood, helping Linda to her feet. Together, they stepped out from their hiding place, ready to plunge into the unknown depths of the abandoned hospital and the mysteries it held.

5 - 6

Harrison's heart raced as he squinted through the crowd, desperate to catch a glimpse of the enigmatic figure's face. The throng of people surged and swayed, obscuring his view at every turn.

"I can't see them clearly," he muttered, frustration edging his voice. "Who are they? What could possibly bring someone like that to a place like this?"

Linda's grip on Harrison's arm tightened, her fingers trembling slightly. "Be careful, sweetheart," she whispered, her eyes never leaving the scene before them. "There's something... different about this person. Can't you feel it?"

Harrison nodded, a shiver running down his spine. The air around them seemed charged, crackling with an energy he couldn't quite explain. It reminded him of the moments before a thunderstorm, when the world held its breath in anticipation.

"Yeah, I feel it too," he replied, his voice low. "It's like the whole universe is watching, waiting to see what happens next."

Linda's eyes widened, her maternal instincts on high alert. "Harrison, maybe we should-"

"No, Mom," he interrupted gently, placing his hand over hers. "We need to know. This could be connected to Dad, to everything we've been through. We can't turn back now."

As they watched, the figure raised a hand, and the crowd fell silent. The sudden hush was almost more deafening than the previous clamor.

"Whatever's about to happen," Harrison murmured, his curiosity warring with caution, "I think it's going to change everything."

7 – 8

Stood before the figure was a chamber, a machine that Harrison couldn't quiet comprehend. What did it do? What were the onlookers expecting to witness. Suddenly armed guards come out form behind the masked figure, dragging a someone with them. The bound figure's face was covered in a black hood. They wore the same white robe as everyone in the crowd.

The guards placed the figure inside the chamber and sealed the door. The figure did not object to this punishment. Suddenly as soon as they masked figure was sealed in their tomb the figure who Harrison and his mother had been following, approached the chamber. They spoke to the person that was sealed away. Then as silence fell over the crowd, the figure pulled a lever on a control panel and as blinding as a flash of lightning a white light emitted before Harrisons eyes. As soon as the light appeared it quickly faded, and the masked figure was gone. Leaving behind a empty chamber.

Harrison's eyes swept across the sea of faces, his heart pounding with a mixture of anticipation and dread. The crowd's murmurs faded to white noise as his gaze locked onto a figure at the forefront, and suddenly, the world narrowed to a single point. The figure lowered his hood to speak, to address his onlookers but Harrison quickly interrupted.

"Dad?" The word escaped his lips in a hoarse whisper, barely audible even to himself. But as recognition dawned, Harrison's voice found its strength. "Dad!" he called out, louder this time, his cry cutting through the din of the crowd.

There, standing beside a woman Harrison didn't recognize, was Drake Miller. His father's familiar silhouette, the set of his shoulders – it was unmistakable. A maelstrom of emotions surged through Harrison: disbelief, hope, fear, and an overwhelming sense of longing.

"It can't be," Harrison muttered, his mind reeling. "How is this possible?" He took an involuntary step forward, his eyes never leaving his father's form.

Drake turned at the sound of Harrison's voice, his eyes widening as they met his son's. For a moment, father and son stood frozen, separated by a gulf of impossibility and the press of bodies between them.

"My son..." Drake's voice carried across the space, filled with a mixture of wonder and disbelief. "I found you." His words trailed off, as if he couldn't quite believe what he was seeing.

Harrison watched as emotions played across his father's face – shock, joy, and a deep, aching vulnerability that he had never seen before. Drake's arms opened, reaching out towards him, and Harrison felt an irresistible pull.

"Dad, I..." Harrison's voice caught in his throat. He wanted to run to his father, to close the distance between them, but fear held him back. What if this wasn't real? What if it was another trick of this strange, fractured reality?

As if sensing his hesitation, Drake took a step forward. "It's really me, Harrison," he said, his voice thick with emotion.

Drake's expression shifted, a mix of determination and weariness etching lines into his face. "It's a long story, son. One I'm not sure I fully understand myself. But I promise, I'll explain everything. We will meet again, and I assure you I will tell you everything then, not in this time though."

As Harrison stood there, caught between the urge to embrace his father and the caution born of their extraordinary circumstances, he felt a gentle touch on his arm. Linda had moved to stand beside him, her presence a comforting anchor in the storm of emotions.

"Drake?" Linda's voice was barely more than a whisper, filled with a tentative hope that mirrored Harrison's own feelings.

The reunion hung in the balance; a moment suspended in time. Harrison knew that whatever happened next would change everything. The mysteries of the multiverse, the dangers they had faced, the long-awaited answers to their questions – it all paled in comparison to this moment of connection, of a family reunited against impossible odds.

9 - 10

Harrison couldn't contain himself any longer. With a choked sob, he rushed forward, his heart thundering in his chest. Tears blurred his vision as he closed the distance between them, years of longing and uncertainty melting away with each step.

"Dad," he gasped, colliding with Drake's outstretched arms. The familiar scent of his father – a mix of sandalwood and something distinctly otherworldly – enveloped him. Harrison clung to Drake, his fingers digging into the worn fabric of his father's robe. Then Harrison recognized the robe, with its embroidered Green Dragon symbol. This was Gabriels robe.

Drake's embrace was fierce, protective. "My boy," he murmured, his voice breaking. "I've missed you so much."

As they held each other, Harrison's mind whirled. How many realities had his father traversed to find them? What dangers had he faced? The questions bubbled up, but he pushed them aside, focusing on the warmth of his father's arms, the solid reality of his presence.

"I thought... I thought I'd never see you again," Harrison admitted, his words muffled against Drake's shoulder. He pulled back slightly, searching his father's face. "There's so much I need to tell you, so much that's happened."

Drake nodded, his eyes shining with unshed tears. "I know, son. And I promise, we'll have time for everything. But right now..." He glanced around at the crowd surrounding them, his expression growing serious. "Right now, we need to focus on getting somewhere safe."

Harrison followed his father's gaze, suddenly remembering where they were – the abandoned hospital, the mysterious chamber, the watching crowd. The weight of their situation came crashing back, but now, with his father by his side, Harrison felt a renewed sense of purpose and strength.

"You're right," he agreed, straightening his shoulders. "Lead the way, Dad. I trust you."

11 - 12

Drake's hand rested firmly on Harrison's shoulder as he guided them through the throng of onlookers. The air crackled with an energy that seemed to transcend the physical realm, a reminder of the multiverse's ever-present influence.

"I can't believe you're really here," Harrison whispered, his voice tinged with awe. "How did you find us?"

Drake's eyes darted around, vigilant even in this moment of reunion. "It's a long story, son. One that spans more realities than I care to count. But I never stopped looking, never gave up hope."

As they moved, Harrison noticed the subtle changes in his father - the new lines etched around his eyes, the slight gray at his temples. Yet beneath it all, he saw the same determined set of Drake's jaw, the same piercing gaze that had always made him feel safe.

"Dad," Harrison began, his throat tightening with emotion, "I need you to know, I've tried to be strong, to protect Mom and-"

Drake cut him off, pulling him close once more. "You've done more than I could have ever asked, Harrison. You've become a man I'm incredibly proud of."

The world around them seemed to fade, the cacophony of the crowd dulling to a distant hum. In this moment, suspended between realities, father and son found an anchor in each other.

"Whatever comes next," Drake said, his voice low and intense, "we face it together. The multiverse has thrown its worst at us, but it underestimated the strength of our bond."

Harrison nodded, feeling a surge of determination. "Together," he echoed, gripping his father's arm. "No matter what."

Curiosity and Apprehension

Green World – 2024

1 - 2

Holly's fingers traced the worn edge of Linda's kitchen table, her eyes fixed on the swirling patterns in the wood grain. The soft tick of the wall clock punctuated the heavy silence between them. She lifted her gaze to meet Linda's, noting the mixture of curiosity and apprehension in her friend's warm eyes.

Taking a deep breath, Holly steeled herself for what was to come. The memory of the Nexus still pulsed within her, a kaleidoscope of impossible colors and whispered echoes. How could she possibly convey the magnitude of what she'd experienced?

"Linda," Holly began, her voice low but steady, "I know this is going to sound unbelievable, but I need you to hear me out." She paused, searching Linda's face for any sign of doubt or dismissal. Instead, she found only patience and an open heart—qualities that had always defined Linda.

Holly's hand clenched involuntarily as she continued, "While I was at your house earlier, something extraordinary happened to me." The words felt inadequate, unable to capture the true weight of her experience. "I found myself transported to another world—a place beyond space and time called the Nexus."

As she spoke, Holly watched Linda's expression closely. The other woman's brow furrowed slightly; her hands clasped tightly in her lap. But there was no outright disbelief, no immediate rejection of Holly's fantastic claim. Instead, Linda leaned forward slightly, her posture radiating concern and attentiveness.

Holly's mind raced, grappling with how to describe the indescribable. How could she paint a picture of that realm of infinite possibility, where reality itself seemed to shimmer and dance? The memory of it tugged at her, both exhilarating and terrifying in its implications.

"I know it sounds crazy," Holly added, her voice softening. "If I hadn't experienced it myself, I wouldn't believe it either. But Linda, I swear to you, it was real."

3 - 4

Linda's brow furrowed deeper, her kind eyes flickering with a mixture of confusion and concern. "Another world?" she echoed; her voice soft yet tinged with skepticism. "What do you mean, Holly?"

The detective took a deep breath, steeling herself. She could see the struggle in Linda's face—the desire to believe warring with the sheer implausibility of it all. Holly's fingers drummed nervously on her knee as she searched for the right words.

"I know it sounds impossible," Holly began, her voice steady despite the tumult of emotions churning within her. "But I was there, Linda. I saw it with my own eyes." She leaned forward, her gaze intense. "It was a place where realities converge, where the very fabric of existence seems to shift and bend."

Linda remained silent, her expression a mask of careful neutrality. Holly could almost see the gears turning in her friend's mind, trying to reconcile this fantastical tale with the grounded, rational world she knew.

Holly nodded, her expression grave as she continued. "Yes, another world. And in this world, I met a man named Justin." The memory of his peaceful eyes flashed through her mind. "He told me about a terrible virus spreading across the multiverse—a virus that threatens to destroy everything in its path."

As the words left her mouth, Holly felt the weight of them settle in the air between them. She watched Linda's face, searching for any sign of disbelief or rejection. Instead, she saw only a deepening concern, a flicker of fear igniting in those kind eyes.

5 - 6

Holly took a deep breath, her heart pounding as she watched the shift in Linda's expression. The skepticism that had initially clouded her friend's eyes was slowly giving way to a mixture of concern and dawning comprehension.

"Justin gave me a gift to deliver to Drake," Holly continued, her voice low and urgent. She leaned forward, her hands clasped tightly together. "He said that Drake is the key to stopping the virus, but I need to find him in another timeline."

The words hung heavy in the air; each syllable laden with the weight of countless lives across countless realities. Holly's mind raced, trying to anticipate Linda's reaction. Would she believe her? Or would this be the moment when her incredible tale finally stretched the bounds of credibility too far?

Linda's eyes widened, her lips parting in surprise. "Another timeline?" she breathed, her voice barely above a whisper. "But how? And why Drake?"

Holly could see the struggle playing out on Linda's face – the desire to trust her friend warring with the sheer impossibility of what she was hearing. She yearned to reach out, to offer some tangible proof of her journey, but all she had were her words and the conviction burning in her chest.

"I don't fully understand it myself," Holly admitted, running a hand through her short dark hair. "But I know what I experienced, Linda. And I know that somehow, Drake is at the center of all this."

7 - 8

Holly took a deep breath, her piercing gaze locked onto Linda's face. The weight of Justin's words pressed down on her, urging her to convey the gravity of the situation.

"I don't know all the answers, Linda," Holly said, her voice low and urgent. She leaned forward, her shoulders tense. "But Justin was clear about one thing: Drake holds the key to stopping the virus. Delivering this gift to him..." She paused, her hand instinctively moving to her pocket where the mysterious object lay. "It's crucial to our survival. To everyone's survival."

As she spoke, Holly's mind raced through the implications. How could Drake, a man she barely knew, be pivotal in stopping a multiversal plague? The enormity of it all threatened to overwhelm her, but she pushed the feeling aside, focusing on the task at hand.

Linda sat motionless for a moment; her eyes distant as she processed Holly's words. Holly could almost see the gears turning in her friend's mind, piecing together this new reality where her husband held the fate of countless worlds in his hands.

Suddenly, Linda's expression shifted. The confusion and fear melted away, replaced by a steely determination that Holly had never seen before. Linda's jaw set firmly as she met Holly's gaze.

"Then we'll find a way to get to Drake," Linda declared, her voice unwavering. "No matter what it takes."

Holly felt a surge of relief and admiration. She had known Linda as a gentle, caring woman, but now she saw a fierce protector emerging, ready to face the impossible for the sake of her husband and the greater good.

"It won't be easy," Holly cautioned, even as she felt bolstered by Linda's resolve. "We're talking about crossing timelines, facing dangers we can't even imagine."

"I don't care," Linda responded, her eyes flashing with determination. "If Drake is the key to stopping this virus, then nothing else matters. We have to try."

9 - 9

Holly nodded, a mixture of relief and determination washing over her. The dim light of the room cast long shadows across Linda's face, accentuating the newfound resolve etched into her features.

"I never thought I'd say this," Holly began, her voice barely above a whisper, "but we're about to embark on a journey across realities. It's... it's terrifying, Linda."

Linda reached across the space between them, grasping Holly's hand. Her touch was warm, grounding. "Nothing terrifies me anymore Holly. Just moments ago I was at home cleaning and then suddenly I wake up in another world buried alive. If you say this will be terrifying then I say so be it. We are in this together."

Holly squeezed Linda's hand in return, drawing strength from the connection. Her mind raced, trying to piece together a plan. "We need to figure out how to access these other timelines. Justin didn't exactly leave me with an instruction manual."

A wry smile tugged at Linda's lips. "No interdimensional GPS, huh?"

Despite the gravity of the situation, Holly couldn't help but chuckle. "I'm afraid not. But maybe..." She paused, her detective's instincts kicking in. "Maybe there are clues in the gift Justin gave me for Drake. We should examine it more closely."

As Holly spoke, her gaze drifted to the window, where the familiar skyline of their world stood in stark contrast to the unimaginable vastness of the multiverse that now lay before them. The weight of their mission pressed down on her, a mixture of exhilaration and dread coursing through her veins.

"Whatever we find," Holly said, turning back to Linda, "we have to be prepared for anything. The fate of existence itself might rest on our shoulders."

The Weight of Grief

Apocalypse World – 20. A.C

1 - 2

The air in the dimly lit room felt heavy, thick with the weight of Harrison's words. Drake's weathered face, etched with lines of grief and determination, shifted as he absorbed the gravity of his son's tale. His piercing eyes, once filled with disbelief, now burned with a grim resolve.

"My God, Harrison," Drake breathed, his voice barely above a whisper. "You've been through hell and back."

Harrison nodded; his throat tight. The memories of the apocalyptic wasteland still haunted him, the acrid smell of ash and decay lingering in his nostrils. He watched his father's expression, searching for any sign of doubt or rejection.

Drake leaned forward, his muscular frame tense with barely contained energy. "I believe you, son. Every word. And I swear to you, we'll figure this out together."

A flood of relief washed over Harrison. He opened his mouth to respond, but before he could speak, a sharp knock echoed through the room.

"Drake, it's Dr. Summers," a female voice called out, cutting through the heavy silence.

The door swung open, revealing a woman whose presence immediately commanded attention. Dr. Summers strode into the room, her keen eyes taking in the scene before her. Her tailored robe and neatly styled hair contrasted sharply with the disheveled state of the Millers. This was the woman on stage with Drake only moments ago.

Harrison's mind raced. Who was this woman? How did she fit into the complex tapestry of realities he'd stumbled into?

Drake stood, his posture straightening as he addressed the newcomer. "Rachel, I'm glad you're here. We've got a situation that's right up your alley."

Dr. Summers raised an eyebrow, her gaze settling on Harrison. "I can see that. You must be Harrison. We've met before. I've heard... quite a lot about you."

Harrison tensed, unsure how to respond. The weight of multiple realities pressed down on him, and he found himself longing for the simplicity of his own world, however ravaged it might be.

3 - 4

Dr. Summers extended her hand towards Harrison, a warm smile gracing her lips as she spoke. "It's a pleasure to meet you again, Harrison. I've heard a great deal about you. My god you haven't aged a day since we first met."

Harrison hesitated for a moment, studying the woman's face. Her eyes held a depth of knowledge that both intrigued and unnerved him. He reached out, clasping her hand firmly.

"Can't say I can say the same thing, Dr. Summers," Harrison replied, his voice tinged with curiosity and a hint of wariness. "What brings you here?"

As he spoke, Harrison's mind raced. How much did this woman know? Was she friend or foe in this labyrinth of realities? He glanced at his father, searching for any clue in Drake's expression.

Dr. Summers released his hand, her smile unwavering. "I'm here because of you, Harrison. Your arrival has set quite a few things in motion."

Harrison's muscles tensed involuntarily. He'd learned the hard way that being the center of attention in any reality rarely boded well. "Set things in motion?" he echoed; his tone cautious. "What kind of things?"

He noticed Dr. Summers exchange a quick look with Drake, a silent communication passing between them. It only heightened Harrison's sense of unease.

"Perhaps we should sit down," Dr. Summers suggested, gesturing towards the chairs. "This may take some explaining."

5 - 6

Dr. Summers turned her gaze towards Drake, her expression shifting to one of grave intensity. The air in the room seemed to thicken with the weight of her words.

"I've been studying the phenomenon of parallel universes for quite some time now," she began, her voice steady and measured. "And I believe that Harrison's sudden appearance in this world may hold the key to unlocking the mysteries of interdimensional travel."

Harrison's breath caught in his throat. Interdimensional travel? His mind reeled, trying to process the implications. He glanced at his father, searching for a reaction.

Drake's brow furrowed deeply, his eyes narrowing as he struggled to grasp the enormity of Dr. Summers' statement. "Interdimensional travel?" he repeated, his voice a mix of disbelief and cautious hope. "You mean to tell me that there's a way for Harrison to return to his own timeline?"

Harrison's heart began to race. Return to his own timeline? The possibility both thrilled and terrified him. He'd seen so much, lost so much. Could he really go back? And if he did, what would he be returning to?

"It's... complicated," Dr. Summers replied, her gaze moving between father and son. "But yes, theoretically, it may be possible."

Harrison leaned forward; his voice tight with urgency. "How? What would it take?"

As Dr. Summers began to explain, Harrison's mind whirled with possibilities and dangers. The thought of navigating between realities was dizzying. What if he ended up in the wrong place? Or worse, lost between worlds? He clenched his fists, steeling himself for whatever lay ahead. No matter the risks, he knew he had to try. The fate of multiple realities might depend on it.

7 - 8

Dr. Summers nodded; her eyes alight with determination. The corners of her mouth tightened as she spoke, her voice carrying the weight of scientific expertise. "Yes, but it won't be easy. The fabric of reality is delicate, and traversing between worlds is fraught with peril."

Harrison's pulse quickened, his mind racing with images of shimmering portals and swirling vortexes. He leaned forward, hanging on to every word.

"However," Dr. Summers continued, her gaze meeting Harrison's, "I believe that with the right knowledge and resources, we can find a way to send you back to where you belong."

A surge of hope coursed through Harrison's veins, electric and intoxicating. His fingers twitched, longing to reach out and grasp this chance at returning home. But beneath the excitement, a nagging doubt gnawed at him.

He turned to his father, studying the lines of worry etched on Drake's face. The man before him was both familiar and a stranger – a version of his father he'd never known. Harrison's voice wavered as he asked, "What about you, Dad? What will happen to you?"

As the words left his mouth, Harrison felt torn between two worlds, two realities. The possibility of going home filled him with longing, but the thought of leaving this version of his father behind twisted his gut with guilt and uncertainty.

9 - 10

Drake's gaze softened as he looked upon his son, a mixture of pride and sadness shimmering in his dark eyes. The harsh fluorescent lights of the lab seemed too dim, casting shadows across his weathered features.

"Don't worry about me, Harrison," Drake said, his voice low and reassuring. He reached out, placing a hand on Harrison's shoulder. "My place is here, but yours is out there—in your own world."

Harrison's throat tightened, a lump forming as he processed his father's words. He wanted to argue, to insist that they could find a way to stay together, but the determined set of Drake's jaw told him it was futile.

"But Dad, I just found you," Harrison whispered, his voice catching. "How can I leave you behind?"

Drake's grip on his shoulder tightened. "You're not leaving me behind, son. You're honoring the memory of the father you lost and the life you built. That's where you belong."

Harrison's gaze darted between his father and Dr. Summers, who stood quietly observing their exchange. The weight of the decision pressed down on him, threatening to crush his resolve.

"It's going to be dangerous, isn't it?" Harrison asked, turning to Dr. Summers.

She nodded solemnly. "Crossing dimensional boundaries is never without risk. But we'll do everything in our power to ensure your safe return."

Harrison closed his eyes, drawing in a deep breath. When he opened them again, a flicker of determination had ignited within him—a small flame pushing back against the darkness of uncertainty.

"Okay," he said, straightening his shoulders. "I'm ready to do whatever it takes."

Drake's eyes shone with a mixture of pride and sorrow. "That's my boy," he murmured, pulling Harrison into a tight embrace.

As they separated, Harrison felt a renewed sense of purpose. The journey ahead would be difficult, fraught with unknown dangers, but he wasn't facing it alone. With Dr. Summers' guidance and his father's unwavering support, that small flame of hope grew stronger, becoming a beacon to light his way through the mysteries of the multiverse.

11 - 12

As Dr. Summers spoke those words, a chill swept through the room. Harrison felt a shiver run down his spine, his skin prickling with goosebumps. The air seemed to grow heavy, pressing down on him with an unseen weight.

"Temporal madness," Dr. Summers said, her voice barely above a whisper.

Harrison's mind reeled. He'd encountered that term before, but only in the darkest corners of online forums and in hushed movie dialogue. Now, hearing it spoken aloud in this sterile room, it took on a new, terrifying reality.

His eyes darted between Dr. Summers and his father, searching their faces for any sign that this was some kind of cruel joke. But their grim expressions offered no such comfort.

"What do you mean, temporal madness?" Harrison asked, his voice cracking slightly. He swallowed hard, trying to keep the rising panic at bay. "I've heard of it, but... it's real?"

As he waited for Dr. Summers to respond, Harrison's thoughts raced. Images from sci-fi films flashed through his mind - people driven insane by time travel, their minds fractured and broken. Was that his fate? Had his journey through the multiverse already set him on an irreversible path to madness?

He clenched his fists, willing himself to stay calm. There had to be more to it. There had to be a way to prevent it, or cure it, or... something. Anything.

"Dr. Summers," he said, forcing his voice to remain steady. "Please, I need to know what we're dealing with here."

13 - 14

Dr. Summers' eyes met Harrison's, her gaze filled with a mix of compassion and scientific detachment. She took a deep breath, her shoulders tensing visibly as she prepared to deliver the harsh truth.

"Temporal madness is far more than science fiction, Harrison," she began, her voice low and measured. "It's a very real phenomenon that occurs when an individual spends an extended period in a world that isn't their own." She paused, her fingers tracing invisible patterns on the table's surface. "It begins subtly – distortions in how you perceive reality, lapses in memory that you can't quite explain."

Harrison's stomach churned. He thought back to the moments of disorientation he'd experienced since arriving in this timeline. Had it already begun?

Dr. Summers continued, her tone growing grimmer. "Over time, these symptoms escalate. The boundaries between what's real and what isn't... they blur. Eventually, it can lead to full-blown psychosis. The afflicted individual becomes unable to distinguish truth from illusion."

The room seemed to spin around Harrison. He gripped the edge of the table, steadying himself. "How long?" he managed to choke out, his voice barely above a whisper. "How long do I have before it takes hold? Is there anything – anything at all – we can do to stop it?"

As he spoke, Harrison's mind raced with possibilities. Could they find a cure? Was there a way to reverse the effects? Or was he doomed to lose himself, piece by piece, in this unfamiliar world?

15 - 16

Dr. Summers' eyes met Harrison's, a flicker of compassion softening her usually composed features. She shook her head slowly, her brow furrowing. "It's difficult to say with any certainty," she admitted, her voice tinged with frustration. "Temporal madness manifests differently in each individual. The onset can vary wildly depending on a multitude of factors we don't yet fully understand."

Harrison felt his breath catch in his throat. He clenched his fists, fighting against the rising tide of panic threatening to overwhelm him. How much time did he have left before his grip on reality began to slip?

Dr. Summers leaned forward; her gaze intense. "However, I can tell you this with absolute certainty: the longer you remain in this world, the greater the risk becomes. Every moment here increases the chances of irreversible damage to your psyche."

The weight of her words settled over the room like a suffocating blanket. Harrison's mind reeled, imagining himself lost in a maze of fractured realities, unable to discern truth from delusion. He opened his mouth to speak but found himself at a loss for words.

Suddenly, Drake's voice cut through the oppressive silence. "Then we won't waste any time," he declared, his tone resolute. Harrison turned to face his father, seeing a fierce determination burning in the older man's eyes. "We'll find a way to send Harrison back to his own timeline, before it's too late."

Harrison felt a surge of conflicting emotions – hope, fear, and a deep gratitude for his father's unwavering support. He swallowed hard, forcing himself to focus on the path ahead rather than the terrifying possibilities that loomed over him.

17 - 18

Harrison's gaze locked with his father's, a silent understanding passing between them. He took a deep breath, steeling himself for what was to come.

"Dad, I... thank you," Harrison managed, his voice thick with emotion. "I don't know if I could face this alone."

Drake's expression softened, a hint of vulnerability breaking through his typically stoic demeanor. "You'll never have to, son. We're in this together."

Dr. Summers cleared her throat, drawing their attention back to the matter at hand. "While your bond is admirable, we must act quickly. Drake, you mentioned a plan?"

Harrison watched as his father's face hardened once more, the attorney in him taking over. Drake paced the room, his words measured and precise.

"There's someone who you must meet – Meghan Johnson. She's... well, let's just say she has unique insights into the multiverse. But reaching her won't be easy."

A chill ran down Harrison's spine as his father continued. "She's in the badlands – a lawless wasteland where danger lurks at every turn. It's a place where the fabric of reality itself seems to fray at the edges."

Harrison's mind raced, trying to reconcile this apocalyptic vision with the world he knew. He pictured vast, desolate landscapes and crumbling ruins, a far cry from the bustling metropolis outside their window. Meghan Johnson he thought, why was that name so familiar. Then realization dawned on Harrison, Meghan was the young girl that Gabriel kidnapped and held at the abandoned amusement park along with Harrison himself. So she did have a greater connection to all this he thought.

"And you want me to go there?" Harrison asked, his voice barely above a whisper.

Drake nodded grimly. "I'm afraid it has to be you, son. Your... unique situation makes you our best chance at navigating the badlands safely."

Harrison felt the weight of responsibility settle heavily on his shoulders. He thought of the temporal madness threatening to consume him, of the mysterious Meghan who held the key to their next steps. The enormity of the task before him was overwhelming.

Yet, as he looked at his father's unwavering resolve and felt Dr. Summers' quiet confidence, a spark of determination ignited within him. He might be lost in a world not his own, but he wasn't alone.

"Alright," Harrison said, squaring his shoulders. "Tell me everything I need to know about the badlands and Meghan Johnson. If she's our best shot at getting me home, I'll find her."

19 - 20

Harrison's heart pounded as he met his father's intense gaze. The weight of the mission ahead pressed down on him, but a surge of determination steeled his resolve.

"Meghan is a dangerous individual. No matter what she tells you, you can't trust her in this timeline or the next. She has a friend of ours held captive, what she means to do with him we do not know. Only that it can't be good. We need you to free him as he holds the key to bringing you back to your present day."

"I'll do it," Harrison declared, his voice strong despite the tremor of fear in his chest. "I'll find Meghan and bring your friend back safely."

Drake's eyes softened, a mixture of pride and worry etched across his face. He placed a hand on Harrison's shoulder, squeezing gently. "Be careful, son," he said, his tone grave. "The badlands are a treacherous place, and Meghan is resourceful. But I trust that you'll do whatever it takes to bring him home."

Harrison nodded, his mind racing with questions. What exactly would he face out there? And how bad was this Meghan, really? He took a deep breath, steadying himself.

"What should I expect in the badlands?" Harrison asked, trying to keep his voice level. "And how will I even find Meghan?"

Drake's brow furrowed as he considered the question. "It's a desolate wasteland out there," he explained. "Harsh terrain, unpredictable weather, and desperate survivors. Trust no one but yourself."

Harrison felt a chill run down his spine. This was so far removed from anything he'd ever experienced. Yet, a part of him - the part that had always craved adventure - felt a thrill of excitement.

"As for Meghan," Drake continued, "she has a safehouse near the old power plant. A research facility much like this place. Start there but be cautious. She's... changed since you last saw her. She's not the wife you'll fall in love with. Remember keep your heart barred from her, don't let her damage you again."

Harrison's eyebrows shot up. "Last saw her? But I've never-" He stopped, remembering the complexities of his situation. "Right, alternate timeline. Got it."

As he prepared himself mentally for the journey ahead, Harrison couldn't shake the feeling that this mission would change everything. For better or worse, he was about to step into a world beyond anything he could have imagined.

Drake and Dr. Summers took in the sight of Harrison as he began to venture out on his own. "Be cautious of your surroundings. And may Justin be with you on your journey through time. See you soon."

21 - 22

The merciless sun beat down on Harrison as he trudged through the barren wasteland, each step kicking up a small cloud of dust. Jagged rock formations loomed in the distance, their silhouettes wavering in the heat haze. His eyes scanned the horizon, alert for any sign of movement or danger.

"What have I gotten myself into?" Harrison muttered, wiping sweat from his brow. The weight of his mission pressed heavily on his shoulders, a constant reminder of what was at stake.

As he navigated a particularly treacherous stretch of rocky terrain, his thoughts drifted to Meghan. The woman who would become his wife in another life, another timeline. A stranger, yet somehow intimately connected to his fate.

"I wonder what she's like here," he mused aloud, his voice barely audible over the crunch of gravel beneath his feet. "Is she still the same person I... will meet?"

The memory of their brief encounter in his own timeline flashed through his mind - both of them bound and separated by Gabriel's machinations. He shuddered, pushing the unsettling image away.

"Focus, Harrison," he chided himself. "Find Meghan, get the information, and figure out how to get back home before temporal madness sets in."

As he crested a small hill, the ruins of what must have been the old power plant came into view. Harrison's heart raced with a mixture of anticipation and apprehension.

"Alright, Meghan," he whispered, steeling himself for whatever lay ahead. "Let's see what secrets you're hiding in this godforsaken place."

23 - 24

A flicker of movement caught Harrison's eye, jolting him from his thoughts. He instinctively dropped into a crouch, his hand flying to the weapon at his side. Squinting against the harsh glare of the sun, he peered at a shadowy figure emerging from behind a crumbling concrete wall.

"Don't move!" Harrison called out, his voice steady despite the adrenaline coursing through his veins. "Identify yourself!"

As the figure drew closer, Harrison's grip on his weapon loosened. "Meghan?" he whispered, more to himself than to her.

The woman before him was undoubtedly Meghan Johnson, but not as he remembered her. Her once vibrant features were now drawn and weary, etched with the harsh realities of this desolate world. Yet her eyes - those he recognized instantly. They burned with a fierce determination, tinged with an anger that caught him off guard.

Harrison stood, his mind reeling. This was Meghan, but older, hardened by experiences he could only imagine. The stark contrast between the girl he'd glimpsed in his own timeline and this battle-worn woman before him was jarring.

"What happened to you?" he murmured, taking a tentative step forward. "What has this world done to make you look at me like that?"

25 - 26

"Meghan," Harrison called out, relief flooding through him as he rushed forward to meet her. His heart pounded, a mix of excitement and apprehension coursing through his veins. The badlands stretched out around them, a desolate canvas of rust-colored earth and jagged rocks.

Meghan's expression softened at the sight of him, a fleeting smile gracing her lips as she clasped his hand in hers. The touch was electric, familiar yet foreign. "I knew you would come," she replied, her voice tinged with gratitude. "But you're so different... so much younger...."

Harrison's brow furrowed, his mind racing to process her words. He studied her face, noting the fine lines etched around her eyes, the weariness that seemed to settle on her shoulders like a heavy cloak. This Meghan was older, hardened by experiences he couldn't begin to fathom.

"How long has it been for you?" he asked, his voice barely above a whisper. The implications of time's fluidity across realities hit him anew, leaving him dizzy with the possibilities.

Meghan's eyes clouded, a shadow of pain flickering across her features. "Too long," she murmured, her grip on his hand tightening. "But that doesn't matter now. You're here, and we have work to do."

Harrison nodded, pushing aside his swirling thoughts. "My father sent me to find you," he explained, scanning their surroundings for any signs of danger. The badlands were treacherous, and he couldn't shake the feeling that they were exposed. "He said you had something that could send me back to my own world."

Meghan's gaze sharpened, a spark of the fierce determination he'd glimpsed earlier reigniting. "I do," she confirmed, her voice low and urgent. "But it's not safe to talk here. We need to move."

As they set off across the barren landscape, Harrison's mind raced with questions. What secrets did this older Meghan hold? And how would they impact his journey through the tangled web of realities that threatened to unravel around him?

27 - 27

The harsh crack of gunfire shattered the air, sending Harrison's heart into overdrive. He instinctively dropped to a crouch, pulling Meghan down with him as bullets whistled overhead.

"Scavengers," Meghan hissed, her eyes darting across the desolate landscape. "They must have followed you."

Harrison's mind raced, assessing their options. "We need cover," he muttered, spotting a cluster of rusted-out vehicles about fifty yards away. "Can you make it to those cars?"

Meghan nodded grimly. "On your mark."

As they sprinted toward safety, Harrison's thoughts tumbled over each other. Who were these attackers? How did they fit into the complex tapestry of this world? He pushed the questions aside, focusing on the immediate threat.

They reached the vehicles, sliding behind a battered pickup truck just as another volley of shots peppered the ground around them. Harrison's breath came in quick gasps, adrenaline surging through his veins.

"Any weapons?" he asked Meghan, his eyes scanning their meager shelter.

She produced a small pistol from her waistband. "Limited ammo," she warned, her face set in determined lines. "We can't stay here long."

Harrison nodded, his mind already formulating a plan. The curiosity that had always driven him now sharpened into tactical analysis. "How many of them?" he asked, straining to hear movement beyond their hideout.

"At least five," Meghan replied, her voice tight with tension. "Maybe more."

As Harrison weighed their options, a chilling realization struck him. This wasn't just about survival – it was a test. Every challenge, every threat in this world was pushing him further along his path. The weight of his family's legacy, the complexities of the multiverse – it all converged in this moment.

"We're getting out of here," he declared, meeting Meghan's gaze with newfound resolve. "Together. And then you're going to tell me everything you know about fixing this mess of a timeline."

Shadows of the Enchanted Castle

Apocalypse World – 20 A.C.

1 - 2

The once-cheerful murals of knights and dragons twisted into grotesque shapes as Harrison followed Meghan through the castle's winding corridors. This place used to be a research facility, now turned into a shrine of past triumphs. Each step echoed hollowly; the sound swallowed by an oppressive silence that hung in the air like a shroud.

Harrison's fingers twitched, longing to reach out and touch the walls, to confirm their solidity in this increasingly surreal environment. But he kept his hands at his sides, acutely aware of Meghan's rigid posture as she led the way.

"Where exactly are we going?" he asked, his voice barely above a whisper.

Meghan didn't answer, her stride never faltering. Harrison frowned, studying the back of her head. Something was off, but he couldn't quite put his finger on what. The familiar feeling of curiosity warred with a growing sense of unease in his gut.

As they rounded another corner, Harrison's eyes widened. The heart of this so-called castle loomed before them – a cavernous chamber that seemed to pulse with an otherworldly energy. Shadows danced along the walls; their movements eerily independent of any visible light source.

Meghan came to an abrupt halt, turning to face him. The sadness etched into her features made Harrison's breath catch in his throat.

"Harrison," she began, her voice soft yet underlined with steely resolve, "I have to tell you something."

Harrison's mind raced, a thousand possibilities flashing through his thoughts. Was this about his parents? The virus? The strange occurrences that had been plaguing multiple realities? He forced himself to remain outwardly calm, even as his heart hammered against his ribcage.

"What is it, Meghan?" he asked, striving to keep his tone even.

A flicker of something – regret? pain? – passed across Meghan's face. Harrison wanted to reach out, to offer comfort, but something held him back. The air between them seemed to crackle with an unseen tension.

3 - 4

Harrison braced himself, his fingers curling into fists at his sides. The knot in his stomach tightened as he waited for Meghan to speak, sensing the weight of her impending words. His mind, ever curious, raced through possibilities, each more unsettling than the last.

"I miss you," Meghan finally confessed, her eyes brimming with a potent mixture of longing and sorrow that pierced Harrison to his core. "But you're not mine to keep. You're not the same version that left me moments ago. And I can't bear to lose you again."

The words hit Harrison like a physical blow. He stumbled back a step, his mind reeling as he processed their implications. "What do you mean, not the same version?" he asked, his voice barely above a whisper. The concept of multiple realities wasn't new to him, but to be confronted with it so personally, so viscerally, left him feeling adrift.

Meghan reached out, her hand hovering in the space between them before falling back to her side. "You're from another timeline, Harrison. I can see it in your eyes. The way you move, the way you speak – it's all just slightly off."

Harrison's gaze darted around the chamber, taking in details he'd overlooked before. The shadows seemed to writhe with newfound menace, and even the familiar contours of the castle walls felt alien. "How is this possible?"

he murmured, more to himself than to Meghan. "I remember everything – our first meeting, our adventures, all of it."

"Those memories aren't real," Meghan said softly. "And they're not yours. Not exactly." She took a deep breath, her shoulders sagging under an invisible weight. "I've seen this before, Harrison. The multiverse is fracturing, and you're caught in the middle of it. You're experiencing the onset of temporal madness."

5 - 6

Harrison's heart sank, the weight of Meghan's words pressing down upon him like a leaden weight. He understood the gravity of the situation—that he was a stranger in this world, a mere echo of the Harrison she once knew. The realization sent a chill through him, his fingers curling into fists at his sides.

"I understand," he replied quietly, his voice tinged with resignation. He swallowed hard, forcing himself to meet Meghan's gaze. "But what do you plan to do?"

As he waited for her response, Harrison's mind raced. He thought of the countless worlds he'd glimpsed, the infinite possibilities stretching out before him. Yet here he stood, trapped in a reality that wasn't his own, facing a version of Meghan who saw him as both familiar and foreign.

Meghan hesitated, her eyes flickering with emotion Harrison couldn't quite place. "I don't know," she admitted, her voice barely above a whisper. "Part of me wants to keep you here, safe. But I know that's not right, not fair to you or... or to him."

Harrison nodded slowly, a lump forming in his throat. "We need to find a way to set things right," he said, his natural curiosity and sense of duty pushing through the fog of confusion. "There must be a reason I ended up here, in this specific reality."

7 - 8

Meghan's gaze flickered with uncertainty, her fingers twisting nervously at her side. The silence stretched between them, heavy with unspoken words and impossible choices. Finally, she spoke, her voice barely above a whisper.

"I'm sorry, Harrison," she murmured, the words seeming to cost her greatly. "But I can't let you go back."

Harrison's heart plummeted, a cold dread seeping into his bones. "Meghan, please," he began, reaching out to her. "We can figure this out together. There has to be another way. Dad told me you could help me go back. Like you said I need to set things right."

But before he could say more, Meghan turned away, her shoulders set in a rigid line. The soft tap of her footsteps against the cold stone floor echoed hollowly as she began to walk, leading him deeper into the castle's depths.

With each step, Harrison's mind raced. He thought of the multiverse, of the infinite possibilities that had led him to this moment. He wondered about the Harrison of this world; the man Meghan couldn't bear to lose again. What had happened to him? He had visions of his future self, of the conquest of this land that he promised to Meghan. But were they real? These visions of love between the two of them, of the betrayal he did to others for her. His thoughts were graphic at times, was this actually who he would become if he didn't set things right.

"Where are we going?" he asked, his voice steady despite the fear gnawing at his insides.

Meghan didn't answer, her silence more chilling than any words could have been. As they descended a winding staircase, the air grew colder, damper. Harrison's heart sank as realization dawned.

The dungeon. She was taking him to the dungeon.

With a heavy heart, Harrison followed, each step feeling like a betrayal of his own free will. He knew his fate was sealed—he was destined to remain imprisoned in this world, a captive of circumstances beyond his control.

"I hope you'll forgive me someday," Meghan whispered, her words almost lost in the oppressive silence of the stone corridors.

9 - 10

The heavy iron door clanged shut behind him, plunging Harrison into darkness. A bone-deep chill seeped through his clothes, making him shiver involuntarily. He pressed his palm against the damp stone wall, its rough surface grounding him in this new, terrifying reality.

"Meghan?" he called out, his voice echoing in the empty chamber. No response came.

Harrison's mind whirled with questions. Why had she done this? What did she hope to achieve by keeping him here? He slumped down against the wall, drawing his knees to his chest.

"Think, Harrison," he muttered to himself. "There has to be a way out of this."

As his eyes slowly adjusted to the gloom, Harrison began to make out vague shapes in the darkness. Shadows upon shadows, each one seeming to hold a potential threat or salvation.

Suddenly, a whisper cut through the silence. "Psst... over here."

Harrison's head snapped up, his heart racing. "Who's there?" he called out, straining to locate the source of the voice.

Silence fell again, heavy and oppressive. Harrison held his breath, wondering if he had imagined the voice. The weight of his situation pressed down on him, threatening to crush his spirit.

"I can't give up," he thought, clenching his fists. "My journey isn't over. There's too much at stake."

As he steeled himself to face whatever challenges lay ahead, Harrison couldn't shake the feeling that something significant was about to happen. In this world of uncertainty and shadows, he knew one thing for certain: his adventure was far from over.

11 - 12

A flicker of movement caught Harrison's eye. From the deepest shadows of the dungeon, a figure emerged – a silhouette that seemed to absorb what little light filtered through the narrow slits in the walls. As the figure drew nearer, Harrison's breath caught in his throat. The man's features were obscured, but there was an undeniable aura of quiet strength radiating from him.

Harrison's mind raced. Was this a friend or foe? A fellow prisoner or something more sinister? He pushed himself to his feet, muscles tense, ready to act if necessary.

"Who are you?" Harrison asked, his voice a mixture of curiosity and wariness. Despite his caution, he couldn't shake an inexplicable feeling of familiarity. Something about this stranger stirred a deep-seated sense of trust within him.

The figure paused, just out of clear sight. Harrison squinted, trying to make out any distinguishing features, but the dim light refused to yield its secrets.

"I could ask you the same question," the man replied, his voice low and measured. "But I suspect we both have more pressing concerns than formal introductions."

Harrison's brow furrowed. "What do you mean? Do you know why I'm here?"

As he waited for a response, Harrison's mind whirled with possibilities. Could this mysterious figure hold the key to unraveling the complexities of the multiverse? Or was he simply another pawn in this intricate game of realities?

13 - 14

The man paused; his gaze fixed upon Harrison with an intensity that seemed to pierce through the darkness itself. "I am a friend," he replied, his voice resonating with a warmth and sincerity that washed over Harrison like a gentle embrace.

Harrison's shoulders relaxed slightly, his guard lowering despite the bizarre circumstances. There was something in the stranger's tone that felt achingly familiar, like a half-remembered dream.

"A friend?" Harrison echoed, his voice barely above a whisper. He took a tentative step forward, squinting to make out more of the man's features. "How can I be sure?"

The stranger remained still; his silhouette unwavering in the dim light. "Trust your instincts, Harrison. They've guided you this far."

A chill ran down Harrison's spine at the use of his name. How did this man know who he was? And yet, despite the questions swirling in his mind, Harrison felt an inexplicable sense of calm settling over him.

"I don't understand," Harrison admitted, his brow furrowing. "But I... I feel like I can trust you. Why is that?"

As he spoke, Harrison's mind raced through possibilities. Was this some latent ability tied to his unique bloodline? A trick of this strange world? Or something deeper, a connection that transcended the boundaries of reality itself?

The man's reply came softly, "Because in every world, in every version of reality, there are constants. Some bonds are too strong to be broken by mere shifts in the fabric of the universe."

15 - 16

Harrison's heart raced, his curiosity battling with caution. He inhaled deeply, the musty air of the dungeon filling his lungs as he gathered his courage.

"What do you want from me?" Harrison asked, his voice trembling slightly as he awaited the man's response. The weight of his family's legacy pressed upon him, reminding him of the responsibility he carried across realities.

The dim light caught the stranger's face as he shifted, revealing a reassuring smile that seemed to brighten the gloomy dungeon. Harrison found himself instinctively leaning forward, drawn to the warmth emanating from this mysterious figure.

"I want to help you," the man replied, his voice soft yet filled with conviction. "But first, you must trust me."

Harrison's mind whirled with possibilities. Help him how? To escape? To find his way home? To unravel the mysteries that had plagued his family for generations? He clenched his fists, feeling the familiar surge of determination that had carried him through countless challenges.

"Trust is a rare commodity in a world like this," Harrison said, his tone a mixture of hope and wariness. "But I'm willing to listen. What exactly do you mean by 'help'?"

17 - 18

Harrison hesitated, his mind racing with a thousand questions and doubts. The damp chill of the dungeon seeped into his bones, but it was nothing compared to the cold uncertainty gripping his heart. He studied the stranger's face, searching for any sign of deception or malice.

"How can I be sure?" Harrison whispered, more to himself than to the man before him. "In a multiverse full of shadows and illusions, how can I trust anyone? I can't even trust my own mind anymore."

The stranger's eyes seemed to soften, reflecting a depth of understanding that transcended the confines of their gloomy surroundings. "You've been thrust into a world of chaos and uncertainty, Harrison," he said gently. "But sometimes, a leap of faith is all we have."

Harrison's gaze locked onto the man's, and in that moment, he felt a profound connection. It was as if those eyes held the wisdom of countless ages, of realities beyond imagination. A flicker of hope ignited within him, pushing back the encroaching darkness.

"I've seen so much deception," Harrison murmured, his voice thick with emotion. "Across timelines, across worlds. But there's something about you..." He trailed off, unable to articulate the inexplicable sense of trust building within him.

The stranger nodded, a gesture of infinite patience. "Trust your instincts, Harrison. They've guided you this far."

With a deep breath, Harrison squared his shoulders. The weight of his family's legacy, the fate of multiple realities – it all seemed to converge in this moment. He took a step forward, his heart filled with a newfound sense of courage.

"I trust you," he whispered, his voice barely audible above the echoing silence of the dungeon. The words felt right, as if he were finally aligning with some greater purpose.

19 - 20

The stranger's hand extended, offering a small crystal vial. Its contents shimmered faintly in the dim dungeon light, like liquid starlight captured in glass. Harrison reached out, his fingers trembling slightly as they closed around the cool surface.

He stared at the vial, mesmerized by its ethereal glow. The weight of countless possibilities pressed upon him, each potential future branching out from this singular moment. Harrison's mind raced, recalling the myriad worlds he'd traversed, the faces of those he'd left behind, and the ever-present shadow of his family's enigmatic past.

"What is it?" he asked, his voice barely above a whisper. The words seemed to hang in the stale dungeon air, heavy with significance.

The stranger's eyes gleamed with an otherworldly knowledge. "A key," he replied simply, "to unlock the paths between realities."

Harrison's brow furrowed, his natural curiosity battling with the weight of uncertainty. He rolled the vial between his fingers, feeling its smooth surface, watching the liquid within swirl and dance. A thousand questions bubbled up within him, but one rose above the rest, demanding to be asked.

"How will this really help me find my way home?" Harrison looked up at the man, his voice a mixture of hope and doubt. The enormity of his quest – to navigate the treacherous waters of the multiverse, to find his true place – seemed to press down upon him, threatening to overwhelm.

21 - 22

The man nodded solemnly, his eyes reflecting a depth of understanding that seemed to transcend the confines of the dungeon. "It will," he replied, his voice filled with an unwavering confidence. "But you must trust in yourself, Harrison. Trust that you have the strength to overcome whatever challenges may lie ahead."

Harrison's mind raced, grappling with the weight of the stranger's words. He thought of all the worlds he'd seen, the versions of himself he'd yet to encounter – some broken, some triumphant. Could he truly be the one to make a difference?

"And if I'm not strong enough?" Harrison asked, his voice barely audible, giving voice to the doubt that had plagued him since this journey began.

The stranger's expression softened. "You are the son of heroes, Harrison. But more than that, you are your own person. Your choices, your determination – that's what will guide you home."

Harrison's fingers tightened around the vial, feeling its coolness against his skin. He took a deep breath, steeling himself for what was to come. With trembling hands, he uncorked the vial and brought it to his lips. The liquid within glimmered like liquid starlight, seeming to pulse with an otherworldly energy.

He hesitated for a moment, his heart pounding in his chest. The faces of those he loved flashed before his eyes – his parents, lost to the mysteries of the multiverse; Dr. Summers, her wisdom a guiding light; even Meghan, despite her betrayal.

"For them," Harrison whispered, resolve hardening in his voice. "For all of us."

With that, he tipped back his head and swallowed the contents in a single gulp.

23 - 24

The effect was instantaneous. A rush of warmth flooded through Harrison's body, spreading from his core to the tips of his fingers and toes. His senses sharpened, the dim dungeon suddenly coming into vivid focus. Every shadow, every crevice in the stone walls seemed to pulse with newfound significance.

Harrison gasped, his eyes widening as a kaleidoscope of images flashed through his mind. Fragments of memories – some his own, some unfamiliar – danced at the edges of his consciousness. He saw glimpses of bustling cities bathed in red light, desolate landscapes shrouded in eerie green mist, and a shimmering nexus pulsing with cosmic energy.

"It's... incredible," he breathed, his voice filled with awe. The weight of uncertainty that had been pressing down on him for so long seemed to evaporate, replaced by a surge of purpose and clarity. He turned to the mysterious stranger, a spark of determination igniting in his eyes.

"Thank you," Harrison said earnestly, handing the empty vial back to the man. His fingers lingered for a moment, as if reluctant to break this tenuous connection. "I won't forget this. Whatever happens next, whatever I have to face – I'll remember this moment."

As he spoke, Harrison could feel the elixir continuing to work its way through him, each heartbeat seeming to resonate with newfound strength. He squared his shoulders, feeling as though he could take on the entire multiverse if need be.

*I can do this, * he thought, a wave of resolve washing over him. *I have to. *

25 - 26

The man's weathered face creased into a smile, his eyes twinkling with a mixture of pride and concern. "You carry the hopes of many upon your shoulders, Harrison," he said, his voice resonating with a solemn gravity that made Harrison's breath catch in his throat. "But remember, you are never truly alone. Trust in yourself, and you will find your way home."

Harrison nodded, swallowing hard against the lump forming in his throat. The weight of responsibility settled over him like a heavy cloak, but there was comfort in the stranger's words. He wasn't just fighting for himself anymore; he was fighting for countless others across the multiverse.

"I'll try," Harrison whispered, his voice barely audible in the oppressive silence of the dungeon. "But how can I be sure I'm making the right choices?"

The man's expression softened, and he placed a reassuring hand on Harrison's shoulder. "You must concentrate on your objective and where you want to go," he explained, his voice taking on an urgent tone. "First, you must find Dr. Summers – your Dr. Summers. She holds a key, a book that will help you save the world."

Harrison's mind raced, piecing together the fragments of information. "Dr. Summers," he repeated, thinking of the brilliant scientist he knew from this world. "But how will I know which version of her to find?"

As the man began to fade back into the shadows, his final words echoed in the chamber: "Trust your instincts, Harrison. They will guide you true."

Left alone in the dimly lit dungeon, Harrison closed his eyes, focusing on the image of Dr. Rachel Summers and the mysterious book she possessed. *I'm coming, * he thought with grim determination. *Whatever it takes, I'll find you and that book. The fate of everything depends on it. *

27 - 28

Harrison opened his eyes, a newfound resolve burning within him. The dank dungeon walls seemed to press in less oppressively now, as if responding to his surge of courage. He clenched his fists, feeling the weight of responsibility settle on his shoulders.

"Alright," he muttered to himself, his voice echoing softly in the chamber. "Dr. Summers, the book, save the world. I can do this."

He scanned the dungeon, searching for any sign of an exit. His gaze fell upon a rusty grate in the far corner, barely visible in the dim light. Harrison approached it cautiously, his footsteps echoing on the stone floor.

*This has to be the way out, * he thought, running his fingers along the cold metal. *But how do I open it? *

As if in response to his unspoken question, he felt a slight give in one of the bars. Harrison's heart raced as he applied more pressure, feeling the grate slowly swing open with a protesting creak.

"I guess sometimes the simplest solution is the right one," he chuckled nervously, peering into the dark tunnel beyond.

Taking a deep breath, Harrison steeled himself for whatever lay ahead. The mysterious man's words echoed in his mind: *Trust in yourself. *

"Here goes nothing," he whispered, ducking into the tunnel. As he crawled forward, leaving the dungeon behind, Harrison couldn't shake the feeling that this was only the beginning of a much greater journey.

29 - 29

As Harrison emerged from the tunnel, a blinding light enveloped him. He squinted, raising a hand to shield his eyes. The dungeon's oppressive darkness melted away, replaced by an ethereal glow that seemed to pulse with energy.

"What's happening?" he gasped, his voice lost in the swirling vortex of light.

Harrison felt his feet leave the ground; his body weightless as he was drawn into the heart of the luminescence. His mind raced, trying to make sense of the surreal experience.

*Is this what the mysterious man meant? Am I on my way to find Dr. Summers? *

As the light intensified, Harrison heard a familiar voice cut through the whirlwind of energy. The mysterious man's words, clear and resolute, reached his ears:

"I forgive you."

Harrison's brow furrowed in confusion. "Forgive me? For what?" he called out, but his words were swallowed by the radiant cocoon surrounding him.

*What could I have done that needs forgiveness? * Harrison wondered, a knot of unease forming in his stomach. *And why does his voice sound so... familiar? *

Suddenly a memory reoccurred to him, he must find the friend of his fathers that Meghan held captive and release him. Was the mysterious man the friend his father told him about. He must have been.

Before he could turn back and help his savior, the light began to fade. Harrison felt a tugging sensation, as if reality itself was shifting around him. His last coherent thought before the world dissolved into a blinding flash was tinged with both determination and trepidation:

Return to the Lab

Red World – 2024

1 - 2

The blinding light faded, and Harrison found himself standing in a familiar corridor, its polished floors reflecting the sterile white walls like a mirror. His heart raced as he recognized the unmistakable surroundings of Dr. Summers' research facility.

"I'm back," he whispered, his voice echoing in the empty hallway. The sudden shift from the ethereal glow of the Nexus to this stark, clinical environment left him reeling.

Harrison ran a hand through his tousled hair, his fingers trembling slightly. The weight of his recent journey through the multiverse pressed heavily on his shoulders. He straightened his jacket, a futile attempt to compose himself.

*How long have I been gone? * he wondered, glancing at his watch. The digital display flickered erratically, unable to reconcile the time disparities between realities.

With a deep breath, Harrison approached Dr. Summers' office door. The nameplate gleamed under the fluorescent lights, a beacon of familiarity in a sea of uncertainty. He raised his hand to knock, hesitating for a moment.

Pushing aside his doubts, Harrison rapped his knuckles against the door. The sound seemed to reverberate through his very being, marking a pivotal moment in his journey.

"Hello?" Dr. Summers' voice called from within, steady and authoritative as ever.

Harrison's hand hovered over the doorknob. "Here goes nothing," he muttered, steeling himself for whatever lay beyond.

Suddenly the door opened and there stood Dr. Summers, a much younger version then when he first met her. "Can I help you?"

3-4

Dr. Summers circled her desk, her eyes never leaving his face. "How long has it been for you?"

Harrison laughed softly; the sound tinged with weariness. "I'm not entirely sure. Time moves differently across the multiverse. It could have been months, maybe years."

"The multiverse?" Dr. Summers breathed, her scientific curiosity igniting. "You've actually traversed different realities?"

"I have," Harrison confirmed, sinking into a nearby chair. "And I've seen things you wouldn't believe. But I've also uncovered dangers that threaten not just our world, but all of them."

Dr. Summers leaned against her desk, her brow furrowing. "Tell me everything, Harrison. We have a lot of work ahead of us."

As Harrison began recounting his experiences, he felt a mix of relief and trepidation. He was home, but the journey was far from over. The fate of the multiverse hung in the balance, and he knew that his next steps with Dr. Summers would be crucial in unraveling the mysteries that lay ahead.

5-6

Dr. Summers listened intently, her eyes widening as Harrison recounted his incredible journey through the multiverse. Her fingers tapped rhythmically on her desk, a habit that surfaced whenever her brilliant mind was processing complex information.

"The Ancient Codex," she murmured, more to herself than to Harrison. "It's connected to all of this, isn't it?"

Harrison nodded, leaning forward. "It's the key, Dr. Summers. The language within it... it's mine. Somehow, the code I created as a child is woven into the fabric of reality itself."

Dr. Summers' gaze sharpened. "Your language? That's... extraordinary. But how—"

7 - 8

Harrison's eyes widened as he leaned over the ancient codex, his breath catching in his throat. The faded ink on the weathered pages formed intricate runes and symbols, but it wasn't their antiquity that stunned him. It was their familiarity.

"This can't be," he muttered, tracing a finger along the delicate curves of a particularly elaborate glyph. His mind reeled; memories of childhood afternoons spent inventing his own secret language flooding back.

Dr. Summers looked up from her notes, her brow furrowed. "What is it, Harrison?"

He swallowed hard, his voice barely above a whisper. "Dr. Summers, look," Harrison exclaimed, his excitement palpable as he pointed to a particularly intricate passage. "This... this is the language I invented when I was a child. I never thought I'd see it written in a book like this."

His hands trembled slightly as he turned the page, revealing more of the mysterious script. How was this possible? The codex predated him by centuries, yet here was his childhood creation, etched into its very fabric.

"Are you certain?" Dr. Summers asked, leaning in closer, her sharp eyes scrutinizing the text.

Harrison nodded emphatically. "Absolutely. Every curve, every dot – it's exactly as I designed it. But how? Why?" His mind raced with possibilities, each more outlandish than the last. Was this some cosmic joke? Or was there a deeper connection between him and the multiverse than he'd ever imagined?

9 - 10

Dr. Summers leaned in closer, her eyes alight with curiosity as she studied the ancient text. "You created this language?" she marveled; her voice tinged with awe. "That's remarkable, Harrison. It must hold great significance if it's found its way into such an important artifact."

Harrison felt a shiver run down his spine. The weight of Dr. Summers' words settled heavily on his shoulders. He traced the elegant curves of the script with his fingertip, lost in thought. The familiar symbols seemed to pulse with an otherworldly energy beneath his touch.

"I always thought it was just a game, something I did to pass the time," he admitted, his voice barely above a whisper. Harrison's mind reeled, trying to reconcile his childhood memories with the profound implications of their discovery. "But now... now it feels like it's connected to something much larger, something beyond my wildest imagination."

He looked up at Dr. Summers, searching her face for answers. "How is this even possible? I created this language when I was ten years old, in my bedroom back in... in my original timeline." The words caught in his throat, a reminder of all he had lost.

Dr. Summers' brow furrowed in concentration. "The multiverse works in mysterious ways, Harrison. Perhaps your creation of this language wasn't as random as you thought. It could be a key to understanding the very fabric of reality itself."

Harrison nodded slowly, his fingers still tracing the ancient text. "It's like... it's like I've always been a part of this, somehow. Even before I knew about multiple realities or time travel." He paused, a realization striking him. "Do you think this is why I was able to travel between worlds in the first place?"

The possibilities swirled in his mind, both exhilarating and terrifying. What did it all mean for his past, his future, and the fate of the multiverse itself?

11 - 12

Harrison's eyes darted across the intricate symbols, his heart racing with a mixture of excitement and trepidation. The weight of responsibility settled on his shoulders like a heavy cloak. He took a deep breath, steadying himself.

"Dr. Summers," he said, his voice barely above a whisper, "I think I can decipher this. But... what if what we find is beyond our comprehension?"

Dr. Summers placed a reassuring hand on his shoulder. "That's the nature of discovery, Harrison. We push the boundaries of knowledge, no matter how daunting it may seem."

Harrison nodded, his resolve strengthening. He leaned in closer, squinting at a particularly complex passage. "This part here," he murmured, "it's talking about... intersecting realities? Like threads in a tapestry."

As he spoke, the words seemed to dance before his eyes, revealing their secrets. "It's describing a way to navigate between worlds, Dr. Summers. Not just randomly jumping, but with precision and purpose."

Dr. Summers' eyes widened. "That's incredible, Harrison. If we can understand this mechanism, it could revolutionize our understanding of the multiverse."

Harrison's mind raced with the implications. Could this be his ticket home? A way to prevent the catastrophes he'd witnessed in other realities? He pushed the thoughts aside, focusing on the task at hand.

"There's more," he said, his finger tracing a complex diagram. "It mentions something about 'anchors' between worlds. Points of stability in the chaos of the multiverse."

As they delved deeper into the codex, Harrison felt a growing sense of purpose. This wasn't just about finding his way home anymore. It was about understanding the very fabric of reality itself.

13 - 14

Harrison's breath caught in his throat as he turned the page, revealing an intricate diagram etched in shimmering ink. "Dr. Summers, look at this," he whispered, his voice thick with awe.

The page depicted a complex machine, its components labeled in the same cryptic language he had created as a child. Gears and crystals intertwined with symbols of power, all converging on a central chamber.

"It's... it's a time machine," Harrison breathed, his fingers tracing the delicate lines. "But not just for traveling through time. This device... it's designed to traverse the boundaries between worlds."

Dr. Summers leaned in; her eyes alight with fascination. "Extraordinary," she murmured. "The level of detail is remarkable. But what's this notation here?" She pointed to a small inscription near the central chamber.

Harrison squinted, deciphering the text. His eyes widened. "It says... 'Activated by the lifeblood of the chosen.' Dr. Summers, this machine requires a specific person's blood to function."

As the implications sank in, Harrison felt a chill run down his spine. Who was this chosen one? And what price would they have to pay to unlock the secrets of the multiverse?

Dr. Summers straightened, a look of triumph on her face. "Fascinating," she said, her voice brimming with excitement. "The very key to interdimensional travel lies right here in these pages. I have finally done it."

Harrison nodded but couldn't shake the feeling that they were standing on the precipice of something far greater and more dangerous than they could possibly imagine.

15 - 16

Harrison ran a hand through his hair, his brow furrowing as he considered the implications. "But first you need the chosen one's blood for it to work," he pointed out, his voice tinged with a mix of awe and trepidation. The weight of this discovery pressed down on him, and he found himself grappling with a whirlwind of emotions.

Dr. Summers tilted her head, her eyes gleaming with curiosity. "And who might that be, I wonder?" she mused, tapping her chin thoughtfully.

Harrison's mind raced, considering the possibilities. Could it be someone they knew? Or perhaps a historical figure lost to time? The uncertainty gnawed at him, and he couldn't shake the feeling that they were teetering on the edge of something monumental.

"I'm not sure," he admitted, his gaze drifting back to the intricate diagrams. "But whoever they are, they hold the key to unlocking the multiverse. It's... it's a bit overwhelming, isn't it?" He let out a nervous chuckle, trying to mask the anxiety bubbling up inside him.

Dr. Summers nodded; her expression serious. "Indeed, it is, Harrison. We're dealing with forces beyond our comprehension. The responsibility that comes with this knowledge is immense."

As they stood there, surrounded by the ancient wisdom of Sir Mordred's codex, Harrison couldn't help but wonder what other secrets lay hidden within its pages – and what consequences they might face in uncovering them.

17 - 18

Harrison's eyes narrowed as he leaned closer to the ancient text, his heart pounding in his chest. The faded ink seemed to shimmer under his intense gaze, revealing a familiar name that sent a jolt through his entire body.

"It's my father," he breathed, his voice barely above a whisper. The realization hit him like a thunderbolt, sending his mind reeling with implications.

Dr. Summers leaned in; her brow furrowed. "Your father? Are you certain?"

Harrison nodded, his finger tracing the delicate script. "Look here," he said, his voice trembling slightly. "I can't believe I didn't see it before."

As Dr. Summers peered at the page, Harrison's mind raced. His father, the chosen one? The key to unlocking the mysteries of the multiverse? It seemed impossible, yet there it was, written in ink centuries old.

"Find Drake Miller in 2024," he read aloud, the words feeling strange on his tongue. A mix of emotions washed over him – confusion, excitement, and a twinge of fear. "But how? Why?"

Dr. Summers placed a comforting hand on his shoulder. "It seems, Harrison, that your connection to this mystery runs deeper than we ever imagined."

Harrison nodded; his throat tight. "I always knew Dad was special, but this... this is beyond anything I could have dreamed." He paused, taking a deep breath to steady himself. "We have to find him. Whatever's happening, he's at the center of it all."

Shadows of Worry

1 - 2

The golden afternoon light filtering through Dr. Summers' office windows cast long shadows across Drake Miller's face, deepening the lines of worry etched there. Harrison leaned forward in his chair; his hands clasped tightly in his lap as he met his father's piercing gaze.

"Dad, I know it sounds impossible," Harrison began, his voice barely above a whisper. He could feel the weight of his father's scrutiny, the familiar mixture of love and skepticism that had defined their relationship since that fateful day. "But I swear, everything I'm telling you is true."

Drake's brow furrowed; his lips pressed into a thin line as he processed his son's words. Harrison could almost see the gears turning in his father's brilliant legal mind, searching for some rational explanation for the extraordinary tale he'd just heard.

"So let me get this straight," Drake said, his voice tinged with incredulity. "You're telling me that you found yourself in some post-apocalyptic wasteland, and this mysterious stranger helped you find your way back here?"

Harrison nodded, fighting the urge to look away. He knew how it sounded – like the ravings of a madman, or perhaps the desperate fantasy of a grieving son. But he also knew what he had experienced, the bone-deep certainty that what he had seen was real.

As his father's words hung in the air, Harrison's mind raced back to that desolate world. The acrid taste of ash on his tongue, the eerie silence broken only by the crunch of debris beneath his feet. And then, that figure emerging from the shadows of the dungeon, a beacon of hope in a world devoid of it.

"I know it's hard to believe," Harrison said softly, his voice thick with emotion. "But Dad, you have to trust me. What I saw, what I experienced – it was real. And I think it's connected to everything that's happened to us, to Mom…"

He trailed off, the pain of their shared loss hanging heavy between them. Drake's expression softened for a moment; a flicker of the man he had been before tragedy struck their family.

"Harrison," Drake began, his tone gentler now. "I want to believe you. But you have to understand how this sounds. What if you're experiencing temporal madness like the Dr. Summers you met had mentioned. What if you never experienced any or all of what you claim?"

Harrison leaned back in his chair; his heart heavy. How could he make his father understand? How could he convey the truth of what he had seen, what he had felt? The fate of not just their world, but countless others, hung in the balance.

"Then explain how I'm sitting here with you now when in this world mom and I are dead?"

3 - 4

Harrison leaned forward, his eyes locking with his father's. "That's right, Dad. It sounds crazy, I know, but it happened." His voice trembled slightly, but his conviction remained unwavering. "This person – I couldn't see their face, but their voice… It was like nothing I've ever heard before. They sounded so angelic; it was a voice you knew you could trust."

As he spoke, Harrison's mind flashed back to that moment in the apocalyptic wasteland. The air had been thick with ash, the silence deafening, but that voice had cut through it all like a beacon of hope. He suppressed a shudder, focusing on conveying the gravity of his experience to his father.

Drake ran a hand through his hair, his brow furrowed in deep thought. The attorney in him wanted to dissect every detail, to find the logical explanation that surely must exist. But the father in him saw the earnestness in his son's eyes, the conviction in his voice.

"And you're sure they were trying to help you?" Drake asked, his tone a mixture of concern and skepticism. "They weren't leading you into some kind of trap?"

Harrison could see the internal struggle playing out on his father's face. He knew that Drake, ever the analytical lawyer, was grappling with the impossible nature of his story. But he also sensed a glimmer of hope, a desire to believe that there might be more to their reality than they had ever imagined.

"I'm sure, Dad. His gift, this liquid sent me here. I thought about finding Dr. Summers and just like that I was teleported here in her office. That gift led me straight to you. You told me to find your friend and help them, sadly I failed as I didn't see it at the time. But they did help me." Harrison replied, his voice steady despite the tumult of emotions within him. "I know it's hard to accept, but we have to trust that there are forces out there working to help us. To guide us through this... this predicament we've found ourselves in."

5 - 6

Harrison hesitated, his fingers tracing the outline of the small container in his pocket. The weight of it seemed to grow heavier with each passing second, a tangible reminder of the incredible journey he'd undertaken. He took a deep breath, steeling himself for his father's reaction.

"I don't know, Dad. I guess it's hard to say for certain," he began, his voice tinged with a mixture of doubt and hope. "But they gave me something – this vial."

"They said it would help me find my way home," he added softly, his gaze still fixed on the memory of the vial.

"And you believe them?" Drake asked, his tone a mixture of curiosity and caution. "You trust them enough to take whatever's inside?"

As he spoke, Drake's hand instinctively moved towards the vial, his fingers hovering just inches away from its smooth surface. Harrison could see the internal struggle playing out on his father's face – the desire to protect his son warring with the need to uncover the truth.

7 - 8

"I did, Dad," he said, his voice steady. "I know it's a risk, but I had to believe that this is our best chance of getting back to where we belong."

As he spoke, Drake's mind flashed to the haunting landscapes of the other worlds they'd traversed – the eerie green twilight, the oppressive red dystopia, the desolate blue wasteland. Each memory strengthened his determination to find a way home.

Drake ran a hand through his hair, a gesture that betrayed his inner turmoil. His eyes, usually sharp and focused, now held a mixture of concern and uncertainty.

"I want to believe you, Harrison. I do," Drake said, his voice heavy with the weight of their shared experiences. He paused; his gaze distant as if seeing beyond the confines of Dr. Summers' office. "But after everything we've been through – with Gabriel, with the accident – I can't help but be skeptical."

Harrison felt a pang of frustration. He understood his father's hesitation, but the urgency of their situation gnawed at him. How could he make Drake understand the gravity of their predicament?

"Dad, I know it sounds crazy," Harrison began, leaning forward in his chair. "But we've seen things that defy explanation. We've crossed between worlds. Is this really so hard to believe?"

Drake's expression softened slightly, a flicker of recognition passing across his features. For a moment, Harrison saw a glimpse of the man his father had been before the accident – open, curious, willing to embrace the unknown.

9 - 10

Harrison reached out, placing a hand on his father's shoulder. The warmth of the contact seemed to bridge the gap between them, father and son united in their extraordinary circumstances.

"I understand, Dad," Harrison said softly, his voice tinged with empathy. "But we can't afford to let doubt hold us back. We have to take this chance – for Mom, for everyone."

As he spoke, Harrison's mind flashed to the faces of those they'd left behind in other realities – his mother's gentle smile, the friends they'd made, the lives that hung in the balance. The weight of their responsibility pressed down on him, but it also fueled his resolve.

Drake's eyes met Harrison's, and in that moment, a silent understanding passed between them. The attorney's posture straightened; his jaw set with determination.

"You're right," Drake admitted, his voice low but steady. "We've come too far to turn back now."

Harrison felt a surge of relief wash over him. He hadn't realized how much he'd needed his father's support until this moment.

Drake took a deep breath, squaring his shoulders. "Alright, Harrison," he said, a mixture of pride and apprehension gleaming in his eyes. "Let's do it. Let's see where this takes us."

As his father spoke those words, Harrison felt a curious blend of excitement and trepidation. They were about to embark on a journey that could change everything – or cost them everything. But they would face it together.

11 - 12

The air in Dr. Summers' office seemed to crackle with an electric charge, making the hairs on Harrison's arms stand on end. He glanced at his father, noting the tightness in Drake's jaw as they both leaned forward, hanging on to Dr. Summers' every word.

Dr. Summers' eyes gleamed with an almost feverish intensity as she spoke, her voice dropping to a near-whisper. "Gentlemen, what I'm about to share with you will change everything we thought we knew about the fabric of reality itself."

Harrison felt his heart rate quicken. What could possibly be more earth-shattering than what they'd already experienced? He swallowed hard; his throat suddenly dry.

"According to the ancient texts," Dr. Summers continued, her fingers tracing the worn leather of Sir Mordred's codex, "this machine is capable of harnessing the power of the multiverse. It's a device of unimaginable potential."

Drake's brow furrowed. "Harnessing the power of the multiverse? What exactly does that mean, Doctor?"

Harrison's mind raced. Could this be the key to saving his mother? To fix the chaos that had torn their lives apart?

Dr. Summers leaned in closer, her voice barely above a whisper. "It means, Mr. Miller, that with this machine, we could potentially navigate between realities at will. We could reshape the very fabric of existence. Just think a world where Hitler was never born, a world wear JFK was never assassinated. The possibilities are endless, we could create the perfect dystopian future."

Harrison's breath caught in his throat. The implications were staggering. He turned to his father, seeing his own mix of hope and fear reflected in Drake's eyes.

"But," Dr. Summers added, her tone grave, "it requires a very specific catalyst to activate its full capabilities."

Harrison couldn't contain himself any longer. "What kind of catalyst?" he asked, his voice trembling with a mixture of excitement and dread.

As Dr. Summers opened her mouth to respond, Harrison felt as if he were standing on the edge of a precipice, about to plunge into the unknown. Whatever she said next, he knew their lives would never be the same.

13 - 14

Harrison exchanged a glance with his father, their shared apprehension palpable in the air between them. Drake's jaw tightened; his piercing eyes fixed on Dr. Summers as he voiced the question, they both dreaded to ask.

"And what is this catalyst?" Drake's whisper was barely audible, his usual authoritative tone replaced by a tremor of uncertainty.

Dr. Summers paused, her composed demeanor faltering for a moment. She took a deep breath, her fingers unconsciously tracing the edges of Sir Mordred's codex as if drawing strength from its ancient wisdom.

"The blood of the chosen one," she finally replied, her words hanging heavy in the air.

Harrison felt a chill run down his spine, his mind reeling with the implications. He watched his father's face, noting the subtle tightening around Drake's eyes that betrayed his inner turmoil.

Dr. Summers continued, her voice taking on a reverent quality. "The texts speak of an individual who possesses a unique genetic makeup, a lineage that traces back through the ages. It's believed that only someone with this bloodline can unlock the full potential of the machine."

Harrison's thoughts raced. Could this be connected to the strange experiences he'd had? The visions of other worlds, the inexplicable knowledge that sometimes flooded his mind? He glanced at his father again, wondering if Drake was harboring similar suspicions.

"A chosen one?" Drake echoed; his skepticism evident. "That sounds more like fantasy than science, Doctor."

Dr. Summers smiled wryly. "In my experience, Mr. Miller, the line between fantasy and reality becomes increasingly blurred when dealing with the mysteries of the multiverse."

Harrison found himself nodding in agreement, memories of impossible worlds flashing through his mind. "But how do we find this person?" he asked, leaning forward. "And what exactly does their blood do to activate the machine?"

As Dr. Summers prepared to answer, Harrison felt a strange tingling sensation in his veins, as if his very blood was responding to the weight of her words.

15 - 16

A chill raced down Harrison's spine, his skin prickling with goosebumps as Dr. Summers' words hung in the air. He watched his father intently, noting the subtle shift in Drake's posture - a slight straightening of his back, a tightening of his jaw.

Drake's voice was barely above a whisper, tinged with disbelief. "And you believe that person is me?"

Harrison's heart hammered in his chest. Could it be true? His father, the chosen one? Images of Drake's unwavering determination, his ability to navigate impossible situations, flashed through Harrison's mind. It made a strange sort of sense, and yet...

Dr. Summers shook her head, her piercing gaze fixed on Drake. "No, Mr. Miller. The texts make it clear that the chosen one is someone else – someone with a connection to the ancient lineage. Someone like you."

The air in the room seemed to thicken, charged with electric tension. Harrison's thoughts whirled, pieces of a cosmic puzzle clicking into place. He remembered the mysterious figure in the apocalyptic world, the angelic voice that had guided him home. Could they be connected to this ancient lineage?

"Someone like me?" Drake repeated, his brow furrowed. "What exactly does that mean, Doctor?"

Harrison leaned forward, his curiosity overriding his apprehension. "Is it possible there are others out there with this... this special blood?" he asked, his voice hushed with awe.

17 - 18

Drake's eyes widened in astonishment, the weight of the revelation settling upon him like a mantle. The fluorescent lights of Dr. Summers' office seemed to flicker, casting dancing shadows across his face. "But why me?" he asked, his voice laced with uncertainty.

Harrison watched his father closely, noting the slight tremble in Drake's usually steady hands. It was rare to see his father so shaken, and it sent a chill down Harrison's spine.

Dr. Summers leaned forward, her lab coat rustling softly as she moved. She offered Drake a reassuring smile, her eyes softening with empathy. "That's what we hope to discover, Mr. Miller," she said, her voice calm and measured. "But for now, we must focus on finding a way to activate the machine. And to do that, we need someone with similar blood to you. Or the very least we need to find a way to reactivate you special blood genetics."

Drake's jaw tightened, his gaze darting between Dr. Summers and Harrison. "My blood?" he echoed, his voice barely above a whisper. "How exactly do we get my abilities back. I had my blood tested; I lost my connection to the multiverse."

Harrison's mind raced, recalling the vial he'd been given in the apocalyptic world. Could there be a connection? He wanted to speak up, to share his suspicions, but something held him back. The weight of the unknown pressed down on him, stifling his words. "But my blood didn't," he said. "Listen I drank from the vial, I believe the mysterious figure was the chosen one and he gave me the ability to transverse worlds like my dad used to be able to do. If we don't find the chosen one, if dads blood is no longer effective. Then that means... we use mine."

Dr. Summers' fingers drummed lightly on her desk as she chimed in. "Your blood, with its unique properties, could be the key to unlocking its full potential."

Drake ran a hand through his hair, a gesture Harrison recognized as a sign of his father's inner turmoil. "And if I refuse? What if I say we don't use Harrisons blood then what?" Drake asked, his voice tight with tension.

Harrison felt a surge of protectiveness. He wanted to reach out, to reassure his father, but he held back, sensing that Drake needed to make this decision on his own.

Dr. Summers' expression remained neutral, but her eyes flickered with a hint of urgency. "The choice is yours, Mr. Miller. But remember, the fate of not just our world, but countless others, may hang in the balance."

The silence that followed was deafening. Harrison could almost hear the gears turning in his father's mind, weighing the risks against the potential consequences of inaction. He held his breath, waiting for Drake's response, knowing that whatever decision his father made would irrevocably alter the course of their lives – and perhaps the fate of the multiverse itself.

19 - 20

Harrison's gaze flicked between his father and Dr. Summers, the tension in the room palpable. He could see the conflict etched in Drake's furrowed brow, the way his jaw clenched as he processed the weight of the decision before him. Harrison's own heart raced, a mix of anticipation and fear coursing through his veins.

Drake's eyes met Harrison's, and in that moment, a silent understanding passed between them. Harrison saw the flicker of determination ignite in his father's gaze, a resolve that he had come to associate with Drake's unwavering pursuit of justice in the courtroom.

"Dad," Harrison began, his voice soft but steady, "whatever you decide, I'm with you."

Drake nodded, a ghost of a smile touching his lips. He turned back to Dr. Summers, his shoulders squaring as he made his decision.

"We'll do whatever it takes," Drake said, his voice steady and resolute. "If your blood can help us save the world, then I won't hesitate."

Harrison felt a swell of pride in his chest, mixed with a twinge of fear for what lay ahead. He watched as his father rolled up his sleeve, offering his arm to Dr. Summers.

"How much do you need?" Drake asked, his tone businesslike, reminiscent of his courtroom demeanor.

As Dr. Summers prepared the equipment, Harrison's mind raced with questions. What would this mean for them? For the multiverse? And what dangers might they face along the way? But beneath his doubts, a spark of hope flickered to life. Together, they would face whatever challenges lay ahead, their bond stronger than any force that might try to tear them apart.

21 - 22

Harrison's heart swelled with admiration as he watched his father, the man who had always been his anchor, prepare to face the unknown. The sterile office faded into the background as Harrison's focus narrowed to Drake's determined expression.

"You know, son," Drake said softly, his eyes meeting Harrison's, "I never imagined we'd be here, on the brink of something so... vast." He paused, a wry smile tugging at the corner of his mouth. "But I suppose life rarely follows the path we expect."

Harrison nodded; his throat tight with emotion. "We've come a long way from legal briefs and court appearances, huh? I mean that as both you being a lawyer and a Detective. You've had quiet the career."

Drake chuckled, the sound warm and familiar in the tense atmosphere. "That I have. But in a way, this isn't so different. I'm still fighting for what's right, just on a much larger scale."

As Dr. Summers approached with the needle, Drake's expression grew somber. "Harrison, there's something I need to tell you about what I learned in the other timelines."

Harrison leaned forward; curiosity piqued. "What is it, Dad?"

Drake took a deep breath, his words heavy with disbelief and resignation. "In the other timelines, I discovered something remarkable about my blood. It contained not one, but three distinct DNA profiles."

Harrison's mind reeled, trying to process this new information. "Three profiles? How is that even possible?"

23 - 24

Harrison leaned forward, his brow furrowing with intrigue. "Three profiles?" he echoed, his mind racing with possibilities. The sterile office seemed to fade away as he focused intently on his father's face, searching for answers in the lines etched by experience and hardship.

Drake nodded solemnly; his piercing eyes distant as if looking through the veil of time itself. "Yes. One of those profiles, it seemed, was imbued with a unique ability – the ability to absorb high levels of radiation." He paused, his gaze refocusing on Harrison as he continued, "It was this radiation that allowed people to traverse between dimensions, to move freely between the worlds. I guess you could say it was a cosmic radiation."

Harrison's heart raced, a mix of awe and trepidation coursing through him. Could this be the key to understanding their family's connection to the multiverse? He found himself unconsciously leaning closer, as if proximity might help him grasp the magnitude of this revelation.

"But how?" Harrison asked, his voice barely above a whisper. "How did you discover this? And what does it mean for us now?"

Drake ran a hand through his hair, a gesture Harrison recognized as a sign of his father's inner turmoil. "In the Blue World," Drake explained, "I underwent extensive testing. The Doctors wanted to help me with my blackouts." His voice trailed off, the weight of memories evident in his tone.

Harrison's mind whirled with implications. If his father's blood held such power, what did that mean for him? For their mission? He opened his mouth to ask another question, but Drake held up a hand, silencing him with a look that spoke volumes.

"There's more, Harrison," Drake said, his lawyer's composure cracking slightly. "This ability... it's not just a gift. It's a responsibility. One that I'm not sure you're ready for."

25 - 26

Harrison's eyes widened with realization as he processed his father's words. "So, your blood was the original key," he murmured, the pieces of the puzzle slowly falling into place. His mind raced with possibilities, imagining the power to traverse dimensions at will. A shiver ran down his spine, both thrilling and terrifying.

Drake nodded, a bitter smile playing at the corners of his lips. "It seems so," he replied. His gaze drifted to the window, where the perpetual crimson haze of the Red World cast an eerie glow across the cityscape. "But since waking up in this world – the red world, as I call it – something has changed." His expression grew pensive, a shadow passing over his features. "My blood is no longer the same. It's... normal."

Harrison felt his stomach drop, the weight of his father's words sinking in. He watched Drake's face, noting the mixture of relief and regret etched in the lines around his eyes. The constant wail of sirens in the distance seemed to grow louder, as if underscoring the gravity of the moment.

"How can, you be sure?" Harrison asked, his voice barely audible over the city's omnipresent hum. He clenched his fists, fighting against the tide of disappointment threatening to overwhelm him.

Drake turned back to his son, his piercing gaze softening. "I said I've had it tested, Harrison. Multiple times. Whatever properties my blood possessed in the other worlds... they're gone now." He paused, swallowing hard. "It's as if this world... this reality... has stripped away that part of me."

Harrison's mind raced, grappling with the implications. Had they lost their only chance to navigate the multiverse? To find a way home? He took a deep breath, the faint metallic scent of the Red World filling his lungs, grounding him in this harsh reality.

27 - 28

Harrison's heart sank at the realization, a sense of loss washing over him like a tide. The bustling sounds of the Red World's metropolis seemed to fade away, leaving only the heavy silence between him and his father. "You mean..." he began, his voice barely above a whisper, unable to finish the thought that terrified him most.

Drake met his son's gaze, his eyes reflecting a mixture of sorrow and acceptance. The flickering neon lights from the window cast shifting shadows across his face, emphasizing the weariness etched in his features. "I'm afraid so, son," he replied, his voice heavy with regret. Drake ran a hand through his dark hair, a gesture Harrison recognized as a sign of his father's inner turmoil. "Without the unique properties of my blood, I fear we may have lost our only chance of returning to the other worlds. You would be our only hope, if it works at all."

Harrison felt his chest tighten, the weight of their predicament pressing down on him. He clenched his fists, fighting against the wave of despair threatening to engulf him. "There has to be another way," he muttered, more to himself than to Drake. "You can't just be stuck here, can you? When Gabriel kidnapped me, he gave me his blood and suddenly I was transported to the apocalypse world for the first time. When I met the strange figure in the cell I believe it was blood he gave me to be able to traverse worlds and come here and find you. Maybe I can give you my blood and you'll have your powers back."

Drake's expression softened, his legal training giving way to fatherly concern. "I wish I had better answers for you, Harrison. I wish it was that easy. But right now, we need to focus on what we can control." He placed a comforting hand on his son's shoulder, the gesture bridging the gap between them. "We may be in the Red World, but we're together. And that's not nothing."

29 - 30

Harrison nodded, swallowing hard against the lump in his throat. The room seemed to close in around him, the bustling city beyond the window a stark reminder of their isolation in this unfamiliar reality. He gazed at the glowing neon signs, their harsh light a poor substitute for the warmth of home.

"I know, Dad," he said, his voice barely above a whisper. "It's just... I can't help but think of Mom, of everyone we left behind. What if we never see her again?"

Drake's eyes clouded with emotion, but he squeezed Harrison's shoulder reassuringly. "We can't think like that. Your mother is strong, and so are we. We've faced impossible odds before."

Harrison closed his eyes, drawing a deep breath. The metallic scent of the city filled his nostrils, grounding him in this harsh reality. When he opened his eyes again, there was a newfound determination in their depths.

"You're right," he said, straightening his posture. "We've come too far to give up now. There has to be another way, and we're going to find it."

Drake nodded, a hint of pride gleaming in his eyes. "That's the spirit. We may have lost one path, but that doesn't mean there aren't others. We just need to look harder, think outside the box."

Harrison's mind raced, his natural curiosity kicking into overdrive. "What if we start by retracing our steps? There might be clues we missed, connections we didn't see before. Just hear me out, what if we find Gabriel and use his blood? He gave me limited powers the first time."

As he spoke, Harrison felt a familiar surge of energy coursing through him. It was the same feeling he'd experienced in the face of every challenge across the multiverse – a mix of fear and excitement, fueled by an unwavering resolve to protect those he loved.

31 - 32

The shrill ring of Drake's phone shattered the moment, its harsh tone slicing through the air like a siren's wail. Harrison watched as his father's brow furrowed, a mix of trepidation and hope flashing across his features. Drake's hand trembled slightly as he reached for the device, his fingers hovering for a split second before answering.

"Detective Bird," Drake said, his voice a carefully controlled blend of anticipation and apprehension.

Harrison leaned in, straining to catch any fragments of the conversation. His heart raced; each beat a thunderous reminder of how much hinged on this call. Could this be the breakthrough they desperately needed?

Drake's eyes darted back and forth as he listened, his free hand clenching and unclenching at his side. Harrison recognized the gesture – a telltale sign of his father's inner turmoil, a battle between the coolly logical attorney and the desperate father fighting for his family's future.

"What could this Detective Bird have found?" Harrison wondered, his mind spinning with possibilities. "A new lead? Evidence that could exonerate us? Or something worse?"

The seconds stretched into an eternity as Harrison watched his father's face, searching for any clue to the nature of the call. He longed to reach out, to grab the phone and demand answers, but he held himself in check. Years of watching his father work had taught him the value of patience, even when every fiber of his being screamed for action.

33 - 34

Drake's expression suddenly shifted, a flicker of recognition crossing his features. His eyes widened, and he leaned forward in his chair, his entire body tensing.

"You found something?" he inquired; his voice tight with barely contained excitement. Harrison could hear the surge of adrenaline in his father's words, feel the electric anticipation crackling in the air.

Harrison's heart began to pound even harder, his palms growing slick with sweat. He watched intently as his father listened, hanging on every subtle change in Drake's expression. The furrow in his brow deepened, then relaxed, only to deepen again.

"This could be it," Harrison thought, his mind racing. "The key to unraveling everything – the accident, the other worlds, Gabriel's involvement. Maybe even a way back..."

He found himself holding his breath, afraid that even the slightest sound might break the spell of this moment. The fate of not just their world, but countless others, could hinge on whatever information Detective Kierstead was sharing.

"Dad," Harrison whispered, unable to contain himself any longer. "What is it? What did she find?"

Drake held up a hand, silencing his son as he continued to listen intently. But his eyes met Harrison's, and in that moment, a spark of hope passed between them – a fragile, precious thing that neither dared to fully embrace just yet.

35 - 36

Drake's face suddenly broke into a rare smile, relief washing over him like a wave. His shoulders relaxed, the tension draining from his body as he listened to Detective Bird's words.

"You were right, Drake," he repeated, his voice filled with a mixture of awe and validation. "The blood sample on the robe – it matches yours and Harrison's. We also have video evidence of Gabriel matching the description you provided on the hospital surveillance."

Harrison's breath caught in his throat, his mind reeling with the implications. He leaned forward, trying to catch every word of the conversation.

Drake's eyes widened with astonishment, the pieces of the puzzle finally falling into place. "Gabriel..." he murmured; his gaze distant as his mind raced with newfound clarity. "He's been one step ahead of us this whole time."

Turning to Harrison, Drake's expression was a mix of triumph and trepidation. "They found him, son. We have proof."

Harrison's heart pounded. "What does this mean, Dad? For us, for... everything?"

Drake ran a hand through his hair, a habit Harrison recognized as a sign of his father's intense focus. "It means we're not crazy. It means all of this – the other worlds, the accidents, it's all connected to Gabriel somehow."

"But how?" Harrison pressed, leaning forward. "How could he be in multiple places, multiple realities?"

Drake's eyes narrowed, his lawyer's mind dissecting the problem. "I don't know yet. But this is the break we've been waiting for. We can finally start putting the pieces together."

As he spoke, Harrison couldn't help but notice the determined set of his father's jaw, the fire rekindled in his eyes. For the first time in what felt like ages, Drake Miller looked like his old self – the unstoppable force Harrison had always admired.

"We're going to find him," Drake declared, his voice low and intense. "And we're going to get answers, no matter what it takes."

37 - 38

Detective Bird's voice crackled through the phone, his tone sharp with urgency. "But not anymore," he declared, his words ringing with determination. "So, what do we do now? What happened next in the other worlds?"

Drake's grip tightened on the phone, his knuckles whitening as the weight of their situation bore down on him. He glanced at Harrison, seeing the mix of anticipation and fear in his son's eyes. The memory of countless alternate timelines flashed through Drake's mind, each one a kaleidoscope of possibilities and dangers.

"The Johnsons," Drake said, his voice barely above a whisper. He turned to Harrison; his gaze steely with purpose. "We need to find the Johnsons," he stated, his tone brooking no argument. "And we need to protect Meghan Johnson at all costs. Those were Gabriel's next victims."

Harrison's eyes widened, his mind racing. "The Johnsons? His Meghan Johnson? How do she fit into all this?"

Drake's jaw clenched, the memories of other worlds flooding back. "In every timeline where Gabriel succeeded, the Johnsons were his key targets. Meghan especially. I don't know why, but she's crucial to his plans."

As he spoke, Drake's free hand unconsciously moved to his chest, where the weight of his unique blood – now seemingly ordinary – felt like a phantom limb. He couldn't shake the feeling that they were missing something vital, something that could unravel this entire mystery.

"Dad," Harrison said, his voice steady despite the tremor in his hands, "if we do this, if we go after the Johnsons... we're changing the timeline. Are we ready for what that might mean?"

Drake met his son's gaze, seeing the reflection of his own determination and fear. "We have to be," he replied, the weight of words resting on his shoulders. "It's our only chance to stop Gabriel and find our way back home."

39 - 40

Harrison nodded, his heart pounding as he rose from his chair. The magnitude of their mission settled over him like a heavy cloak, but he refused to let it paralyze him. "Alright, Dad. Where do we start?"

Drake pocketed his phone, his attorney's mind already piecing together a plan. "We need to locate the Johnsons first. I'll reach out to some contacts, see if we can get an address. It's possible they don't live in the same address in this world as they did in others."

As they moved towards the door, Harrison's mind raced with possibilities. "What if Gabriel's already found them? What if we're too late?"

Drake paused, his hand on the doorknob. "We can't think like that, son. We have to believe we can make a difference."

The corridors of the building seemed to stretch endlessly before them as they hurried towards the exit. Harrison couldn't shake the eerie feeling that they were being watched, shadows dancing at the corners of his vision.

"Dad," he whispered, "do you ever feel like we're just pawns in some cosmic game? Like no matter what we do, fate's already decided?"

Drake's stride faltered for a moment, his expression softening as he looked at his son. "I used to, Harrison. But then I realized something." He placed a hand on Harrison's shoulder, his touch grounding them both in the present. "We may not control the game, but we choose how we play it. And right now, we're choosing to fight."

As they stepped out into the crisp night air of the Red World, Harrison felt a surge of determination course through him. The neon-lit streets pulsed with life, oblivious to the multiversal drama unfolding in their midst.

"So," Harrison said, a hint of a smile playing at his lips, "ready to save the world? Or worlds, I guess?"

Drake chuckled, the sound a welcome respite from the tension. "One step at a time, son. First, we find the Johnsons. Then... we change destiny."

Crimson Reflections

1 - 2

Detective Kierstead's reflection flickered across the rain-streaked window as she paced her office, the neon signs from the street below casting an eerie red glow across her face. Her fingers trembled slightly as she clutched a crumpled printout, her mind whirling with the implications of what she'd just discovered.

"This changes everything," she muttered, her eyes darting to the clock on the wall. Time was slipping away, and with it, their chance to prevent another tragedy.

She strode to her desk, snatching up her phone and punching in Detective Bird's number with practiced efficiency. As the line began to ring, Kierstead's free hand drummed an anxious rhythm on the worn surface of her desk.

Come on, Franklin. Pick up.

Her gaze drifted to the case board on the far wall, a sprawling web of photos, notes, and red string that seemed to pulse with newfound significance in light of her discovery. The pieces were falling into place, revealing a picture far more complex and sinister than she'd initially imagined.

The ringing continued, each unanswered tone ratcheting up Kierstead's anxiety. She knew Bird was thorough, methodical – qualities that made him an invaluable partner. But right now, she needed his quick thinking and decisive action.

"Where are you, Chief?" she whispered, her voice barely audible over the steady patter of rain against the window. The urgency of the situation pressed down on her like a physical weight, each passing second feeling like an eternity.

Finally, mercifully, there was a click as the call connected. Kierstead's heart leapt into her throat, her words tumbling out before Bird could even speak.

3 - 4

"Detective Bird," she greeted briskly, her voice laced with urgency. "I need you to listen carefully. I've just reviewed the hospital security footage, and there's something you need to see."

Franklin's deep, gravelly voice rumbled through the line. "Kierstead? What's going on?"

She took a steady breath, her mind racing to organize the flood of information. "The footage shows our suspect entering the hospital at 2:37 AM, but here's the kicker - they're wearing a nurse's uniform that doesn't match the current staff attire. And Franklin, their face... it's distorted somehow. Like it's shifted. Like it's been burned and disfigured and put back together."

As she spoke, Kierstead's free hand traced the path of red string on her case board, connecting the hospital to a photo of their prime suspect. She could almost feel the pieces clicking into place.

"Shifting?" Franklin's tone sharpened, his usual stoic demeanor giving way to a hint of disbelief. "What do you mean, shifting?"

Kierstead closed her eyes, recalling the eerie footage. "It's like... their features are constantly in flux. One moment they look like a middle-aged woman, the next a young man. I've never seen anything like it."

She heard Franklin's sharp intake of breath, could picture his brow furrowing with concern. The implications of her findings hung heavy in the air between them.

"This changes everything," Franklin muttered, more to himself than to her. "If they can alter their appearance at will..."

"Exactly," Kierstead interjected, her mind already racing ahead. "We're not just dealing with a skilled impostor. This is something... else. Something beyond our usual scope."

The silence that followed was thick with tension. Kierstead's heart pounded in her chest as she awaited Franklin's response, knowing that their next move could make or break the entire investigation.

5 - 6

"Got it," Detective Bird replied, his voice dropping to a gravelly whisper. His fingers tightened around the phone, knuckles whitening. "I'll head over to the Johnsons' residence right away and conduct a wellness check. If there's any sign of trouble, I'll handle it."

Franklin's mind raced, cataloging potential scenarios and strategies. A shape-shifting suspect meant conventional tactics might be useless. He'd need to rely on his instincts, honed by years on the force.

"Be careful, Franklin," Kierstead urged, her concern evident even through the phone line. "This isn't like anything we've faced before."

"I know," he responded, already reaching for his coat. "But someone's got to do it. And if not us, then who?"

Kierstead nodded, a surge of gratitude welling up within her. Detective Bird was one of the best – resourceful, diligent, and unwavering in his commitment to justice. She trusted him implicitly to handle this task with the utmost professionalism.

"You're right," she admitted, her voice softening. "Just... keep your eyes open. And Franklin?"

"Yeah?"

"Thank you. I couldn't ask for a better partner in all this madness."

Franklin allowed himself a small smile, the first one in days. "We'll crack this case, Holly. Together. No matter what reality-bending nonsense we're up against."

Franklin took a deep breath, steeling himself for whatever lay ahead at the Johnsons' residence. The weight of responsibility settled on his shoulders, but it was a familiar burden – one he'd carry gladly in the pursuit of truth and justice.

7 - 8

"Keep me updated," Kierstead instructed, her voice firm with resolve. She gripped the phone tighter, her knuckles whitening. "And be careful out there. We don't know what we're dealing with yet."

A chill ran down her spine as she considered the implications of their discovery. The hospital footage had revealed more than just a suspicious figure; it had shown a glimpse into a world she'd only theorized about until now.

"I will," Detective Bird's voice crackled through the line. "You know me, always cautious."

Kierstead allowed herself a wry smile. "That's what worries me, Franklin. Your idea of caution and mine are worlds apart."

As she ended the call, Kierstead's mind raced ahead to the next steps. The Johnsons' residence could be a nexus point, a place where realities collided. But what if it was more than that? What if it was a gateway?

"Whatever's waiting for us," she murmured to herself, "we have to face it. For the Johnsons, for this city... for every possible version of reality."

9 - 10

Detective Bird's calloused fingers brushed the cool metal of his car key, a familiar sensation that usually brought comfort. Not today. The hairs on the back of his neck stood on end, an instinct honed by years on the force screaming danger.

"Something's not right," he muttered, eyes darting to scan the parking lot.

That's when he felt it—a sharp, sudden prick at the base of his skull. Alarm surged through him, his heart rate skyrocketing.

"What the—" Bird's hand flew to his neck, fingers probing the spot. They came away wet, a smear of crimson stark against his skin. "Blood?"

The world began to tilt, reality warping around him like a funhouse mirror. Bird gripped the steering wheel, knuckles white, fighting to stay upright.

"Kierstead," he gasped, fumbling for his phone. "Got to warn... got to..."

His vision swam, the parking lot blurring into a kaleidoscope of muted colors. Was this how it ended? Not with a bang, but with a whimper in a department-issued sedan?

"No," Bird growled, his trademark determination kicking in. "Not like this. Not when we're so close."

But even as he fought, a creeping numbness spread through his limbs. Whatever had pierced his skin was potent, designed to work fast.

"Whoever you are," he slurred, addressing his unseen attacker, "you've made a big mistake. We don't go down easy in this department."

The words were brave, but Bird's thoughts raced with fear. What if this was more than a simple attack? What if Drake's theories about parallel worlds were true? What if he was about to be pulled into another reality entirely?

As consciousness began to slip away, Bird's last coherent thought was of his partner. "Stay safe, Kierstead. And for God's sake, be careful."

11 - 12

Bird's eyelids fluttered, each blink a herculean effort against the encroaching darkness. The world around him seemed to pulse, reality bending at the edges like a photograph curling in flames.

"Got to... fight it," he mumbled, his normally authoritative voice reduced to a whisper. His fingers, numb and uncooperative, fumbled for the door handle. "Get... help."

But his body betrayed him, muscles turning to lead. The steering wheel, his last anchor to consciousness, began to slip from his grasp.

In that moment, as oblivion beckoned, Bird's mind raced with a lifetime of regrets and unfinished business. Cases left unsolved, lives he couldn't save, the perpetual dance between justice and chaos that defined his career.

"I'm sorry," he whispered to no one and everyone. "I tried... I really..."

With a final, futile effort, Bird attempted to lift his head, to peer into the rearview mirror, to catch a glimpse of his assailant. But the darkness was absolute now, swallowing him whole.

As consciousness fled, his body slumped forward, forehead coming to rest against the steering wheel with a soft thud. In the eerie silence that followed, only the faint tick of the cooling engine marked the passage of time, a stark counterpoint to the momentous event that had just transpired.

13 - 13

The world outside faded into a kaleidoscope of blurred shapes and muted colors, as if reality itself was dissolving around Detective Bird. His eyelids fluttered, each blink a desperate attempt to cling to consciousness.

"Who... why..." he mumbled, his words slurring as he fought against the encroaching darkness.

In his mind's eye, fragmented images flashed by, the hospital security footage, Detective Kierstead's urgent call, the Johnsons' residence waiting for his arrival. Each memory felt like a puzzle piece, tantalizingly close yet impossible to grasp.

Bird's fingers twitched against the steering wheel, a feeble attempt to regain control. "Got to... warn... Kierstead," he gasped, but his voice was barely audible over the soft hum of the idling engine.

As his consciousness ebbed away, a fleeting thought crossed his mind: Could this be connected to the multiverse? The cases they'd been investigating, the strange occurrences that defied explanation – it all seemed to converge in this moment of vulnerability.

"The virus..." he whispered, his final coherent thought before the darkness claimed him completely.

In that last instant of awareness, Detective Bird's racing mind grasped at straws, desperately seeking answers. Who had targeted him? Was it Gabriel, the scarred enigma with unknown motives? Or something even more sinister, reaching across realities to silence him?

The questions lingered, unanswered, as Bird's consciousness slipped away into the void, leaving behind only the soft tick of the engine and the weight of unresolved mysteries.

Syringe of Suspense

Red World – 2024

1 - 2

The syringe felt like a live wire in my hand, pulsing with malevolent potential. I lay still in the backseat of Detective Bird's cruiser, every nerve ending on high alert. The faint crimson glow of the virus within the syringe cast an eerie light across my fingers.

I remained silent, my eyes fixed on the back of his head. His salt-and-pepper hair was neatly trimmed, belying the chaos that was about to unfold.

My fingers tightened around the syringe. If only he knew the true scale of what was coming. The multiverse itself would tremble.

Bird sighed heavily as he settled into the driver's seat, broad shoulders filling out his jacket. I watched him adjust the rearview mirror, his sharp eyes briefly meeting mine. In that moment, I saw a flicker of the man he used to be - the small-town cop with an unwavering moral compass. How far we'd both come.

As Bird turned the key in the ignition, I slowly extended my arm, the syringe glinting ominously in the dim interior light. My heart raced, knowing the devastating power I held in my grasp. One quick motion and everything would change.

3 - 4

With a swift, practiced motion, I plunged the needle into the side of Detective Bird's neck. He let out a startled gasp, his body tensing as the virus surged into his bloodstream.

"What the—" Bird's voice was cut short as he instinctively reached for the injection site.

I withdrew the now-empty syringe, my heart pounding. "I'm sorry, Franklin," I whispered, though I knew my words rang hollow. "But this is bigger than both of us."

As I watched him struggle, I could feel the air in the car grow heavy, thick with an unseen malevolence. The virus was taking hold, its power radiating outward in invisible waves.

Bird's breathing grew labored as he fought against the virus's effects. "Why?" he managed to choke out, his eyes meeting mine in the rearview mirror one last time.

I closed my eyes, feeling the weight of my actions. "Because sometimes, to save a world, you have to be willing to destroy it first."

5 - 6

As Bird's head lolled forward, his body slumping against the steering wheel, a wave of grim satisfaction washed over me. The once-formidable detective was now just another victim..

"You were a good man, Franklin," I muttered, watching his shoulders heave with labored breaths. "But good men can't save us from what's coming."

Bird's fingers twitched spasmodically, grasping at nothing. His voice, now barely a whisper, rasped out, "You... you've doomed us all."

I leaned forward, studying the changes overtaking him. A faint crimson mist began to emanate from his pores, the telltale sign of the virus's progression.

"No, Chief," I replied, my voice steady despite the turmoil in my gut. "I've given us a chance at a new beginning."

Bird's only response was a pained groan as he slid further down in his seat. I settled back, a sinister grin playing at the corners of my mouth. The die was cast; there was no turning back now.

"You know," I mused, more to myself than to the rapidly deteriorating detective, "they say the multiverse is infinite. Endless possibilities, endless worlds. But what happens when you introduce chaos into that system?"

I chuckled softly, the sound hollow in the confines of the car. "I guess we're about to find out."

7 - 8

The neon sign of Meghan Johnson's bedroom flickers, casting an eerie blue glow across the rain-slicked street. I stand in the shadows, my eyes fixed on the figure visible through the living room window. Meghan sits behind the counter, her face bathed in the soft light of her phone, oblivious to the world beyond her four walls.

"Oh, Meghan," I whisper, my breath fogging in the cool night air. "If only you knew what's coming."

A car passes, its headlights momentarily illuminating my face. I duck deeper into the alley, heart pounding. When I peek out again, Meghan hasn't moved.

I clench my fists, battling the urge to rush in and warn her. "No," I mutter to myself. "Not yet. She's not ready."

My mind races with possibilities. In her, I see a strength that could reshape worlds, a determination that could stand against the coming storm. But as I watch her laugh at something on her screen, her innocence strikes me like a physical blow.

"I should leave," I think, even as my feet refuse to move. "Let her have these last moments of peace."

But I can't. The protective instinct that's been growing since I first learned of her whereabouts roots me to the spot. I've set something terrible in motion, and Meghan may be the only one who can thrive from this.

"God help me," I whisper, taking a step towards the store. "I hope I'm doing the right thing."

9 - 10

The weight of destiny settles upon my shoulders as I stare at Meghan through the window. My voice is barely audible as I murmur, "For in you lies the key to a new world, my queen."

I pause, my hand hovering over the door handle. The metal feels cool against my skin, grounding me in this moment of hesitation. My thoughts race, a tumultuous mix of ambition and concern.

"We could reshape reality itself," I whisper, my breath fogging the glass. "But at what cost?"

A distant siren wails, snapping me from my reverie. My eyes dart to the shadows stretching across the pavement, imagining threats lurking in every corner. The urgency of the situation crashes over me like a wave.

"No," I growl, resolve hardening my voice. "I won't let them touch her."

With silent determination, I move closer to the entrance, my footsteps soundless against the concrete. The distance between us shrinks, each step bringing me closer to our shared destiny. As I reach for the door, a sense of purpose propels me forward.

My hand trembles slightly as I grasp the handle. "Forgive me, Meghan," I whisper, steeling myself for what's to come. "But your safety comes first. Always."

11 - 12

With a steady hand, I turn the doorknob, the door swinging open soundlessly before me. The warm glow of the living room washes over me as I step inside, my eyes immediately locking with Meghan's. Her expression shifts from surprise to a complex mix of fear and recognition.

"Who are you?" she gasps, her voice barely above a whisper. "How did you—"

I hold up a hand, cutting her off. "There's no time to explain," I say, my voice low and urgent. My eyes scan the room, searching for any signs of danger. "We need to leave. Now."

Meghan rises from her seat, her brow furrowed in confusion. "What's going on? Why are you here?"

As I move closer, I can see the flicker of emotions across her face—uncertainty, curiosity, and something else I can't quite place. My heart races, torn between the need to protect her and the weight of the truths I must reveal.

"You're in danger," I explain, reaching out to grasp her arm gently. "There are forces at work beyond your imagination, Meghan. Forces that want to use you for their own ends."

She doesn't pull away, instead searches my face intently. "And you? What do you want?"

The question hangs in the air between us, loaded with unspoken implications. I swallow hard, my resolve wavering for a moment under the intensity of her gaze.

"I want to keep you safe," I say finally, my voice thick with emotion. "Whatever it takes."

For a heartbeat, time seems to stand still. The soft hum of the television fades into the background, and all I can see is Meghan—her eyes wide, her breath quickening. In that moment, I feel the weight of our shared destiny, the invisible threads of fate that bind us together across realities.

My mind races with the magnitude of what lies ahead—the chaos, the danger, the potential for a new world order. But as I look at Meghan, I know with unwavering certainty that I will do whatever it takes to protect her, to shield her from the storm that's coming.

"Do you trust me?" I ask, extending my hand to her.

Chaos in the Office

Green World – 2024

1 - 2

The acrid scent of ozone assaulted Holly's senses as she burst into Dr. Monroe's office, her eyes widening at the chaos before her. Papers fluttered in the air like wounded birds, settling among the wreckage of overturned furniture and shattered glass.

"Dr. Monroe!" Holly's voice cracked with urgency as she spotted the crumpled form of her mentor amid the debris. Her heart hammered against her ribs as she rushed to his side, her detective's instincts cataloging every detail even as fear threatened to overwhelm her.

Kneeling beside the unconscious scientist, Holly's fingers trembled as she reached for his neck. "Come on, come on," she muttered, her breath catching in her throat. The faint flutter beneath her fingertips sent a wave of relief through her body.

He's alive. Thank God.

"Dr. Monroe, can you hear me?" Holly gently patted his cheek, her eyes fixed on the angry gash marring his forehead. Blood matted his silver hair, a stark contrast to the unnatural pallor of his skin.

What the hell happened here? Holly's mind raced, piecing together the scene. Signs of a struggle, but no obvious weapon. Whoever did this knew what they were after.

"Hold on, Dr. Monroe. I'm going to get you help," Holly assured him, her voice steady despite the turmoil in her chest. She fumbled for her phone, her fingers leaving smears of the doctor's blood on the screen.

As she dialed for emergency services, Holly's gaze swept the room once more. The familiar office, once a bastion of scientific progress, now stood as a testament to violation and violence. Her jaw clenched, determination pushing back against the tide of fear.

I'll find who did this, Dr. Monroe. I promise you that.

3 - 4

Holly's eyes darted across the ransacked office, her detective instincts kicking into overdrive. Papers scattered like fallen leaves, overturned furniture, shattered glass—each detail screamed of a frantic search. But for what?

Her gaze locked onto the empty space on Dr. Monroe's desk, and her heart plummeted. "No," she whispered, the word barely audible. "It can't be."

The reinforced containment unit that had housed the virus sample was gone.

"Damn it!" Holly slammed her fist against the desk, the sharp pain a welcome distraction from the horror unfolding in her mind. She turned to the unconscious scientist; her voice tight with urgency. "Dr. Monroe, who was here? Who took the virus?"

Silence answered her, broken only by the doctor's labored breathing.

Holly's mind raced; each possibility more terrifying than the last. "Someone who knows what they're dealing with," she muttered, pacing the room. "Someone willing to cross lines to get it."

She paused, her gaze falling on a crumpled note near the doctor's outstretched hand. With trembling fingers, she unfolded it, revealing a hastily scrawled message: "The key to all worlds."

"Oh God," Holly breathed, the implications hitting her like a physical blow. "They're going to try to weaponize it across realities."

The enormity of the threat loomed before her, a tidal wave of potential devastation. Holly's fists clenched, her resolve hardening even as fear threatened to overwhelm her.

5 - 6

Holly's fingers trembled as she punched in Franklin Bird's number, her breath catching in her throat with each ring. "Come on, Chief," she muttered, scanning the chaos around her. "Pick up, pick up..."

"Bird here," came the gruff response, tinged with a hint of concern.

"Bird, it's Holly," she blurted, her words tumbling out in a rush. "We've got a situation at Dr. Monroe's lab. He's been attacked, and the virus sample... it's gone."

A sharp intake of breath came through the line. "How bad?"

"Critical," Holly replied, her free hand clenching into a fist. "Whoever did this knew exactly what they were after. We're not dealing with some random thief, Rookie. This is big."

"I'm on my way," Franklin said, his voice tight with determination. "Secure the scene, Holly. Don't let anyone—"

His words were cut off as a blinding flash of light erupted in the center of the room. Holly stumbled back, shielding her eyes. "What the—"

The world around her began to warp and twist, reality itself seeming to bend and fracture. Colors bled into one another, forming a swirling vortex that threatened to engulf her.

"Holly? Holly!" Franklin's voice crackled through the phone, distorted and distant.

"Chief, something's happening!" Holly shouted, her heart pounding in her chest. "I don't know what—"

The vortex surged forward, enveloping her in a maelstrom of light and shadow. Holly felt herself being pulled apart, molecule by molecule, as she hurtled through what felt like the very fabric of existence.

"Hold on!" she screamed, though whether to herself or to the world she was leaving behind, she couldn't say. The force of her journey intensified, and Holly clung desperately to her sense of self as reality dissolved around her.

7 - 8

The kaleidoscopic tunnel of light and shadow whirled around Holly, threatening to tear her consciousness apart. She gritted her teeth, forcing herself to focus on a single image: Drake Miller. His face materialized in her mind's eye, strong and determined, a beacon in the chaos.

"Drake," Holly whispered, her voice lost in the maelstrom. "I won't let you down."

She pictured his piercing eyes, the slight quirk of his smile when he was onto something. The timbre of his voice echoed in her memory, steady and reassuring.

"We're in this together, Holly," Drake's voice seemed to say. "You can do this."

Holly's fingers splayed out, reaching for something solid in the swirling void. "I'm coming, Drake. Just hold on."

The vortex pulsed, as if responding to her determination. Colors shifted, coalescing into recognizable shapes. A building here, a street there. The world was reforming around her.

With a final, dizzying lurch, Holly felt solid ground beneath her feet. She stumbled, catching herself against a nearby wall. The cacophony of city life assaulted her senses – car horns blaring, people chattering, the sizzle of food from a nearby vendor.

Holly blinked, her vision clearing. She stood on a bustling sidewalk, surrounded by towering skyscrapers and hurrying pedestrians. A woman bumped into her, muttering an apology without breaking stride.

"Where am I?" Holly breathed, her eyes darting around, searching for anything familiar. "Drake, are you here?"

9 - 10

Holly's heart raced as she tried to process her surroundings. The city was bustling, alive with energy, but completely alien to her. She took a deep breath, inhaling the mix of exhaust fumes and street food aromas.

"This can't be real," she muttered, her voice barely audible above the urban din. "Did I actually...?"

A businessman in a crisp suit brushed past her, nearly knocking her off balance. Holly instinctively reached out to steady herself, her hand brushing against the small box in her pocket. The touch of it sent a jolt through her, grounding her in the reality of her situation.

She pulled the box out, examining it with a mix of wonder and trepidation. Its smooth surface gleamed in the sunlight, a stark contrast to the gritty cityscape around her.

"Justin said this would help me find Drake," Holly thought, her mind racing. "But how? And where do I even start looking?"

She glanced up at the towering buildings, feeling suddenly small and overwhelmed. A digital billboard caught her eye, displaying the date and time. Her breath caught in her throat as she realized it matched her own timeline perfectly.

"I'm in the right when," she mused, "but is this the right where?"

With a determined set to her jaw, Holly gripped the box tightly and stepped into the flow of pedestrian traffic.

"Only one way to find out," she said to herself, her voice barely above a whisper. "Drake, I hope you're ready. Because ready or not, here I come."

Masterpiece of Destruction

Green World – 2024

1 - 2

The makeshift bomb looms before me, a twisted masterpiece at the heart of Bridgewater, Maine. Its crude assembly belies the devastating power contained within, a testament to my ingenuity and determination. I run my scarred fingers along its cool metal surface, savoring the moment.

"At last," I whispered, my voice raspy with anticipation. "Years of careful planning, all for this."

My disfigured face reflects in the bomb's polished casing, a constant reminder of the price I've paid to reach this point. The scars that mar my features are badges of honor, each one representing a step closer to my ultimate goal.

With practiced precision, I begin adjusting the dials and switches on the control panel. The device responds to my touch, humming softly as if eager to fulfill its purpose. I can't help but smile, a rare expression that feels foreign on my twisted lips.

"Soon, the world will understand," I murmur to myself, lost in the intricate dance of my fingers across the panel. "They'll see the truth that spans across realities."

As I work, memories of countless worlds flash through my mind – the perpetual twilight of the Green World, the neon-drenched streets of the Red World, the desolate silence of the Apocalypse World. Each one a piece in the cosmic puzzle I've spent my life unraveling.

The timer blinks to life, ready to begin its countdown. I pause, my hand hovering over the final switch. For a fleeting moment, doubt creeps into my mind.

"Is this truly the path?" I ask aloud, my voice echoing in the empty space. "Am I prepared for the consequences?"

But as quickly as it appears, the doubt dissipates. I straighten my posture, ignoring the twinge of pain from my ever-present limp. My resolve hardens, forged by years of struggle and sacrifice.

"No," I declare firmly. "This is my destiny. The multiverse itself has led me to this moment."

With a decisive motion, I flip the switch. The bomb comes to life, its quiet hum growing more insistent. I step back, watching as the countdown begins, each second bringing me closer to the realization of my vision.

"Bridgewater," I say, my voice filled with a mixture of anticipation and something akin to reverence. "You will be the catalyst for change across all realities."

As the numbers tick down, I stand tall, ready to embrace the chaos that will soon engulf this unsuspecting city – and with it, the very fabric of the multiverse itself.

3 - 4

I take a step back, my eyes drawn to the unassuming canisters affixed to the bomb's exterior. Their innocuous appearance belies the devastating power within—the fruit of years of clandestine research and experimentation.

"The Multiverse Pathogen," I murmur, running a finger along the cool metal surface. "My magnum opus."

Inside these vessels lies a potent viral gas, engineered to transcend the barriers between realities. As I gaze upon my creation, I can't help but marvel at its elegance.

"You'll spread like wildfire," I whisper, a note of pride in my voice. "Infecting not just this world, but every possible version of it."

My mind races with visions of the impending chaos. The streets of Bridgewater, usually so quaint and predictable, will soon descend into madness. I can almost hear the screams, smell the acrid tang of fear in the air.

A twisted smile curls upon my lips. "And in the midst of it all, I'll rise." My voice grows stronger, more assured. "A god among mortals, with power absolute and unquestioned."

I pace the room, my limp barely noticeable in my excitement. "They'll beg for salvation," I continue, gesturing grandly. "And I alone will hold the key to their survival."

As the countdown ticks away, I savor these final moments of anticipation. Soon, the multiverse itself will tremble at my feet.

5 - 6

As I stand there, basking in the glow of my impending triumph, a sudden chill runs down my spine. The voice in my head, once a faint whisper, now grows louder, more insistent.

"Is this truly what you want?" it asks, cutting through my euphoria like a knife.

I shake my head, trying to dispel the unwelcome thoughts. "Of course it is," I mutter, but the words sound hollow even to my own ears.

My eyes drift to the bomb's control panel, its digits steadily counting down. Each passing second brings me closer to my goal, yet paradoxically, further from certainty.

"Countless innocents," the voice persists. "Children, families, entire worlds..."

I clenched my fists, nails digging into my palms. "They're necessary sacrifices," I argue, but my voice wavers.

For a moment, I see not the glorious future I've envisioned, but the faces of those I'm condemning. Their terror, their suffering—all because of me.

"I can't..." I whisper, my hand hovering over the abort switch.

But then, like a ray of light piercing through storm clouds, my ambition reasserts itself. I straighten, squaring my shoulders.

"No," I declare, my voice steady and resolute. "This is my destiny. My chance to reshape reality itself."

I turn away from the bomb, gazing out at the city below. "I will transcend mortality," I proclaim. "And in doing so, I'll create a new order—one of my own design."

The doubt recedes, banished by the fire of my conviction. I am ready to embrace my role as the architect of a new multiverse.

7 - 7

With a deep breath, I turn back to the bomb. My hand no longer trembles as I reach for the final activation button. The smooth surface is cool beneath my fingertip, a stark contrast to the inferno of determination burning within me.

"Forgive me," I whisper, though I'm not sure to whom I'm speaking. Perhaps to the universe itself, or to the countless versions of myself across the multiverse who lack the courage to take this step.

I press down, feeling the satisfying click of the button. Immediately, the control panel springs to life, a cascade of lights flickering across its surface like a sinister constellation.

"It's done," I breathe, a mixture of exhilaration and dread coursing through my veins.

The countdown begins, each second ticking away with ominous precision. I step back, my eyes fixed on the device that will soon tear reality asunder.

"And so it begins," I murmur, a grim smile playing at the corners of my mouth. "The end of one world, the birth of another."

I turn to face the sprawling cityscape of Bridgewater, bathed in the golden light of a sun that will soon be extinguished. The weight of what I've set in motion settles over me like a heavy cloak, but I refuse to buckle beneath it.

"I am become Death," I intone, the ancient words resonating with newfound meaning. "The destroyer of worlds... and their creator."

As the countdown continues its relentless march towards zero, I stand tall, arms outstretched. Ready to embrace the chaos, the destruction, and the terrible, glorious future that awaits.

Awakening in the Abyss

Red World – 2024

1 - 2

Holly's eyes snapped open, her vision assaulted by a kaleidoscope of swirling crimson and amber. The world around her pulsed with an eerie, otherworldly glow that set her nerves on edge. This wasn't the muted greens of the isolation world or the washed-out blues of the virus-ravaged reality she'd come to know. No, this was something entirely different—and utterly terrifying.

Her heart hammered in her chest as she took in her surroundings. Towering skyscrapers loomed overhead, their glass facades reflecting the blood-red sky. The air thrummed with a metallic scent, mingling with the acrid smell of smoke and decay. In the distance, sirens wailed, their mournful cries echoing through the concrete canyons.

"Where the hell am I?" Holly muttered, her voice barely above a whisper. She stumbled forward, her athletic frame tensed for action. The memory of her conversation with Detective Bird surged to the forefront of her mind. The Johnsons. She had to find them, had to uncover the truth behind this madness.

With trembling fingers, Holly reached for her phone. It felt like a lifeline in this strange, hostile world. She pulled up Drake's number, hesitating for a moment before hitting the call button. As the line began to ring, Holly's thoughts raced.

What if Drake doesn't answer? What if I'm truly alone here?

The phone rang once, twice. Holly's breath caught in her throat. On the third ring, a familiar voice crackled through the receiver, distorted but unmistakably Drake's.

"Holly?" His voice was tense, laced with an undercurrent of worry that made Holly's stomach clench.

She opened her mouth to respond, but the words caught in her throat. How could she even begin to explain this bizarre situation? The unfamiliar landscape, the otherworldly hues, the palpable sense of danger that hung in the air like a toxic mist?

3 - 4

"Drake, it's me, Holly," she said, her words rushed and urgent. "I need to know where you are, right now." Her free hand clenched into a fist, knuckles whitening as she fought to keep her voice steady.

The silence on the other end of the line stretched for what felt like an eternity. Holly's heart pounded in her chest, each beat echoing in her ears like a thunderclap. She could almost picture Drake's face, his brow furrowed in concentration as he processed her words.

Is he in danger too? Holly wondered, her detective's mind already racing through possible scenarios. Or is he safe in our world, oblivious to the nightmare I've stumbled into?

Finally, Drake's voice came through, laced with concern. "Holly, what's going on? Where are you?" His tone carried the sharp edge of a lawyer preparing for cross-examination, but there was an unmistakable tremor beneath the surface.

Holly opened her mouth to respond, but the words died on her lips. How could she possibly explain the inexplicable? Her gaze darted around the alien landscape, searching for anything familiar, anything that might ground her in this surreal reality.

5 - 6

Holly swallowed hard; her throat dry. "I... I'm not sure," she admitted, her voice wavering. Her free hand brushed against the cold, metallic object in her pocket—the item she'd found just before the world shifted. "I ended up in a place that's unlike anything I've ever seen before. It's like... like another dimension."

The landscape before her shimmered with an otherworldly hue, the air thick with an electric charge that made her skin tingle. Shadowy structures loomed in the distance, their architecture defying the laws of physics she knew.

"I need to speak to you," Holly continued, urgency creeping into her tone. "I have something you may need." Her fingers tightened around the object in her pocket, its weight a constant reminder of the bizarre turn her investigation had taken.

Drake's response was immediate, his lawyer's pragmatism kicking in. "Stay where you are, Holly. I'll come to you. Just give me your coordinates."

Holly's heart raced. How could Drake possibly reach her here, in this impossible place? And yet, his confident tone sparked a flicker of hope within her. If anyone could navigate the complexities of multiple realities, it was Drake Miller.

"Drake," she whispered, "how will you—"

7 - 8

"Listen, Holly. Bird called earlier, hes on his way to retrieve Meghan Johnson before Gabriel gets to her first. I'll come to you and you can explain everything to me. Theres so much I have to tell you."

As Holly relayed her coordinates and ended the call the gravity of her situation barrelled down on her. She remembers the Nexus and Justin, she remembers her mission to find Drake. She remembers saving Linda from her earthly grave and then leaving her behind. She knows shes not Rookie cop Detective Kierstead or seasoned officer Detective Sharp, no shes someone new yet entirely familiar. She remembers everything from all three lives, this was a new world entirely as Justins blood gift has finally merged her conscious into this realm. She has found Drake and he is coming for her.

Awakening Shadows

Red World – 2024

1 - 2

Detective Franklin Bird's eyes fluttered open, the world around him a hazy blur of muted colors. His head pounded with a fierce intensity, each throb sending shockwaves of pain through his body. A dry, raspy cough tore from his chest, leaving him gasping for air in the confines of his car.

"What... what happened?" he muttered, his usually authoritative voice now weak and strained.

As he struggled to push himself upright, memories began to flood back. The prick of a needle, sharp and sudden. The encroaching darkness that followed. His stomach churned with a sickening realization.

Fighting against the fever that burned through his veins, Franklin forced his eyes to focus. His gaze fell to the backseat, where a glint of metal caught his attention. A syringe lay innocently on the floor, its presence anything but benign.

"No," he whispered, panic rising in his chest. "This can't be happening."

His mind raced, trying to piece together the fragments of his memory. Who had done this? Why? The questions swirled in his fevered brain, each one more urgent than the last.

Franklin clenched his jaw, determined to maintain his composure despite the fear threatening to overwhelm him. "Stay calm, Bird," he told himself. "Assess the situation. Like you've done a thousand times before."

But this was different. This wasn't a crime scene he could objectively analyze. He was the victim, and whatever was coursing through his system was rapidly breaking down his defenses.

With trembling hands, he reached for the syringe, careful not to touch the needle. "Evidence," he muttered. "Need to... preserve it."

As he grasped the syringe, a wave of nausea washed over him. The world tilted precariously, and Franklin found himself slumping against the car door, his breath coming in short, ragged gasps.

"Got to... get help," he managed, his thoughts becoming increasingly disjointed. "Before it's... too late."

The gravity of the situation bore down on him. Someone had deliberately targeted him, injected him with an unknown substance. As a detective, he'd made his fair share of enemies, but this... this felt different. More sinister. More calculated.

Franklin's eyes darted around the car, searching for his phone. He needed to call for backup, to alert his team. But as another coughing fit seized him, he realized with growing dread that he might not have much time left.

"Come on, Bird," he growled, mustering every ounce of strength he had left. "You've faced worse. You can beat this."

But even as the words left his lips, Franklin knew he was facing a battle unlike any he'd encountered before. Whatever was flowing through his veins was potent, dangerous, and completely unknown. And for the first time in his long career as a detective, Franklin Bird found himself truly, utterly afraid.

3 - 4

With trembling hands, Detective Bird reached for his phone, fingers fumbling as he dialed the number for the hospital. Every movement sent waves of nausea crashing over him, but he pushed through, his determination overriding the debilitating sickness that threatened to consume him.

"Stay... focused," he muttered, his usually commanding voice now a feeble whisper. The phone felt impossibly heavy in his hand, each number taking an eternity to press. Franklin's mind raced, analyzing the situation even as his body rebelled against him. Who had done this? Why? And what exactly had he been injected with?

As the line connected, Franklin steeled himself. He was Detective Franklin Bird, dammit. He'd stared down criminals, solved impossible cases. He wouldn't let this beat him.

"Emergency," he rasped into the phone, his voice hoarse and strained. "I need... I need help. Something's wrong... I've been... I've been exposed to something."

The words tasted like ash in his mouth, each syllable a monumental effort. Franklin's vision swam, the interior of his car blurring into a nauseating kaleidoscope of colors. He gripped the steering wheel with his free hand, anchoring himself to reality.

"Detective Bird," he managed, forcing authority into his tone. "Possible... poisoning. Unknown substance. I'm at—"

Another coughing fit seized him, cutting off his words. As he fought for breath, Franklin's mind raced. This wasn't just an attack on him. It was an attack on justice itself. Someone wanted him out of the picture, and he'd be damned if he'd let them succeed.

5 - 6

A soothing voice filtered through the phone, cutting through the haze of Franklin's pain. "Stay calm, Detective Bird. We're dispatching an ambulance to your location now. Can you describe your symptoms?"

Franklin's jaw clenched, his teeth grinding as he fought against the waves of nausea. "Fever... dizziness... can barely... stand," he grunted, each word a battle. His eyes darted to the rearview mirror, half-expecting to see his attacker lurking in the shadows. "Weakness... throughout my body."

As the dispatcher continued asking questions, Franklin's mind raced. Every second felt like an eternity, and the realization hit him like a punch to the gut. He couldn't wait.

"I can't... stay here," he interrupted, his voice gravelly but determined. "Too dangerous. I'm driving... to the hospital."

"Detective, I strongly advise against—"

Franklin cut the call, his trembling fingers fumbling with the phone. He'd made tougher calls in worse situations. This was no different. Just another case to solve, another challenge to overcome.

With a herculean effort, he forced his body to move. Every muscle screamed in protest as he dragged himself toward the driver's seat. The world tilted and swayed around him, dark spots dancing at the edges of his vision.

"Come on, Bird," he muttered to himself, gritting his teeth. "You've faced worse than this. Push through."

As he collapsed back into the driver's seat, Franklin's mind flashed to the countless times he'd driven these streets. The familiarity of the wheel under his hands provided a small comfort. He had to focus, had to stay alert. Lives depended on him solving this case, on surviving this attack.

With shaking hands, he turned the key in the ignition. The engine roared to life, the vibrations sending fresh waves of pain through his body. Franklin squinted at the road ahead, willing the world to stop spinning.

"One turn at a time," he whispered, easing the car into drive. "Just get to the hospital. Then... then we solve this case."

As the car lurched forward, Franklin's determination burned brighter than the fever ravaging his body. He was Detective Franklin Bird, and he wouldn't go down without a fight.

The Ancient Codex Secrets

Red World – 2024

1 - 2

The Ancient Codex pulsed with an eerie, otherworldly glow as Harrison and Dr. Summers hunched over its weathered pages. The faint shimmer cast dancing shadows across their faces, etching lines of worry into their features.

Harrison's fingers traced the intricate symbols, his brow furrowing deeper with each passing moment. The weight of their discovery pressed down on him, threatening to crush his spirit. How could something so small threaten the entire fabric of reality?

"Dr. Summers," he murmured, his voice barely above a whisper, "these warnings... they can't be real, can they?" He glanced up, searching her face for any sign of reassurance.

Dr. Summers adjusted her wire-rimmed glasses, her sharp gaze fixed on the cryptic text. "I'm afraid they are, Harrison. The evidence is undeniable."

Harrison's heart raced as he absorbed the gravity of her words. A virus capable of destroying not just one world, but countless realities across the multiverse. The implications were staggering.

He ran a hand through his tousled hair, a nervous habit he'd never quite shaken. "But how?" he asked, his voice tinged with a mixture of awe and dread. "How could a virus spread across worlds and timelines?"

As he awaited Dr. Summers' response, Harrison's mind whirled with possibilities. Was this the reason for his father's disappearance? Had Drake stumbled upon this terrifying truth during his own explorations of the multiverse?

The silence stretched between them, broken only by the soft rustle of ancient parchment as Dr. Summers carefully turned another page of the Codex. Harrison felt the weight of countless lives resting on their shoulders, the fate of entire universes hanging in the balance.

3 - 4

Dr. Summers, her expression grave, exchanged a somber glance with Dr. Patal before turning back to Harrison. "It's a phenomenon known as interdimensional contagion," she explained, her voice soft but resolute. "The fabric of reality is fragile, and the boundaries between worlds are porous. When a virus gains a foothold in one timeline, it can potentially spread across the multiverse, infecting countless worlds and civilizations."

Harrison's fingers trembled as they traced the intricate symbols on the ancient page. His mind reeled, trying to comprehend the enormity of what Dr. Summers was saying. "Like a cosmic plague," he whispered, more to himself than anyone else.

Dr. Summers nodded, her eyes reflecting a mix of scientific fascination and deep concern. "Precisely. Imagine a tapestry of interconnected realities, each thread representing a different world. This virus... it's like a corrosive agent, eating away at those threads, unraveling the very fabric of existence."

Harrison's heart sank, a cold dread settling in his stomach. He thought of the Blue World, already ravaged by disease, and imagined that devastation multiplied across infinite realities. The implications were staggering—a single virus could spell the end of everything they knew, plunging countless worlds into chaos and destruction.

"My God," he breathed, running a shaky hand through his hair. "How... how do we even begin to fight something like that?" The weight of responsibility pressed down on him, threatening to crush his spirit. But beneath the fear, a spark of determination flickered to life. This was why he'd inherited his father's gift, why he could traverse realities. He had to believe there was a purpose to it all.

Dr. Summers placed a reassuring hand on his shoulder, her touch grounding him in the moment. "One step at a time, Harrison. We have the Codex, we have your abilities, and we have a team of brilliant minds working on this. We'll find a way."

Harrison nodded, drawing strength from her confidence. He turned his attention back to the ancient text, his eyes scanning the cryptic symbols with renewed focus. Somewhere in these pages lay the key to saving not just one world, but all of them. And he was determined to find it, no matter the cost.

5 - 6

Dr. Patal cleared her throat softly, drawing Harrison's attention. Her eyes, normally bright with curiosity, were now shadowed with concern. "There's more we need to consider," she said, her voice barely above a whisper.

Harrison felt a chill run down his spine. What could be worse than what they already knew? He braced himself, nodding for Dr. Patal to continue.

"In a vast and diverse multiverse," she began, her words measured and careful, "each universe teems with its own life forms, civilizations, and unique physical laws. However, a catastrophic event unfolds when a deadly virus emerges in one universe, unlike any pathogen ever encountered."

As Dr. Patal spoke, Harrison's mind raced. He imagined countless worlds, each vibrant and unique, suddenly plunged into chaos. The weight of responsibility pressed down on him, almost suffocating in its intensity.

"This virus," Dr. Patal continued, "possesses the ability to traverse the barriers between parallel universes, exploiting quantum phenomena or extradimensional pathways that connect different realms."

Harrison's fists clenched involuntarily. "But how?" he interrupted, his voice tight with frustration and fear. "How does something like that even come into existence?"

Dr. Patal's gaze met his, her expression grave. "The origin of the virus is uncertain. It may have originated from a highly advanced civilization experimenting with quantum manipulation or extradimensional travel. Alternatively, it could have arisen from a natural source, such as a cosmic anomaly or a rift in the fabric of space-time."

Harrison's mind reeled. The implications were staggering. He thought of his own ability to traverse realities – a gift he had only begun to understand. Could something like that be twisted into a weapon of such devastating power?

"But how do we stop it?" he asked, his voice tinged with desperation. "How do we prevent such devastation?"

The silence that followed his question was deafening. Harrison looked from Dr. Patal to Dr. Summers, searching their faces for any sign of hope. The fate of not just one world, but countless realities, hung in the balance. And he, Harrison, with his unique abilities, might be the key to it all.

The weight of that responsibility threatened to crush him, but he stood straighter, squaring his shoulders. They had to find a way. The alternative was unthinkable.

7 - 8

Dr. Summers' eyes locked with Dr. Patal's, a silent conversation passing between them. Harrison's heart raced, anticipation and dread warring within him as he awaited their response.

Finally, Dr. Summers turned to him, her voice cutting through the tension. "We need to find the source of the virus, the origin point where it first emerged," she said, her tone firm and resolute. "Only then can we hope to contain it and prevent further spread."

Harrison's fingers tightened on the edge of the table, his knuckles turning white. He could feel the weight of countless lives pressing down on him, threatening to suffocate him. But beneath the fear, a spark of determination ignited.

"How do we even begin to track something like that?" he asked, his voice steadier than he felt. "We're talking about an infinite number of realities."

Dr. Summers' lips quirked in a grim smile. "That's where you come in, Harrison. Your ability to traverse dimensions might be our best shot at tracing the virus back to its source."

Harrison nodded, his mind racing with the enormity of the task before them. Images flashed through his mind - worlds ravaged by the crimson mist, civilizations crumbling, the very fabric of reality unraveling. He clenched his fists, pushing back against the tide of despair threatening to overwhelm him.

"I'll do whatever it takes," he said, meeting Dr. Summers' gaze with determination. "The fate of the multiverse rests in our hands, and failure is not an option."

9 - 10

Harrison ran his fingers through his hair, a nervous habit that betrayed his inner turmoil. His vibrant eyes, a striking blend of his parents' features, darted between Dr. Summers and the ancient codex before them.

"But Dr. Summers," he said, his voice tinged with a mix of frustration and desperation, "how do we find the source if it hasn't reached our world yet? How do we stop something we particularly know nothing about?"

Dr. Summers adjusted her wire-rimmed glasses, her sharp gaze focused on the weathered pages of the codex. The faint glow emanating from certain sections cast an otherworldly light across her face.

"That's the challenge we face, Harrison," she replied, her tone measured and calm despite the gravity of the situation. "We're in uncharted territory, but this codex might hold the key."

Harrison leaned in, studying the intricate symbols that seemed to shift before his eyes. His mind raced with possibilities, each more daunting than the last. How could they possibly hope to prevent a catastrophe of this magnitude?

With a deep breath, he steeled himself. "Alright, let's break this down. What do we know so far?"

As Dr. Summers began to outline their findings, Harrison felt a renewed sense of purpose surge through him. He might be young, but he was a Miller. His family had faced impossible odds before, and he wouldn't let them down now.

Together, they poured over the ancient text, their determination growing with each passing moment. Time was their enemy, but Harrison was ready to fight. No matter the cost, they would find a way to save the multiverse.

Reflections of Stress

Green World – 2024

1 - 2

Linda stared at her reflection in the bathroom mirror, her pale face a stark contrast against the muted green tiles. The world around her seemed to pulse and waver, like a mirage in the desert.

"It's just stress," she whispered, her voice trembling slightly. "You've been through worse, Linda. Pull yourself together."

But even as the words left her lips, a wave of nausea crashed over her, sending her stumbling backward. She gripped the edge of the sink, knuckles white, as she fought to steady herself.

I shouldn't feel this way. It's been days since... since...

The memory of being trapped, buried alive, flashed through her mind. Linda squeezed her eyes shut, willing the image away. When she opened them again, the room seemed to spin.

"Drake?" she called out, forgetting for a moment that her husband wasn't there. That he couldn't be there. The silence that answered her was deafening.

Linda pushed herself away from the sink, determined to make it to the kitchen. Maybe some water would help. She took one step, then another, each movement feeling like she was wading through molasses.

"Come on," she urged herself. "One foot in front of the other."

As she reached the doorway, a sharp pain lanced through her temples. Linda gasped, pressing her palm against her forehead. The pressure behind her eyes built, threatening to split her skull apart.

What's happening to me?

She stumbled into the hallway, the familiar contours of her home suddenly alien and threatening. The air felt thick, oppressive, as if it were actively trying to smother her.

"This isn't right," Linda murmured, her words slurring slightly. "Something's wrong."

She tried to take another step, but her legs gave way beneath her. As she collapsed to the floor, her last coherent thought was of her family, lost to her in a world that now seemed impossibly far away.

3 - 4

Linda gritted her teeth, pushing herself up from the cold floor. Her arms trembled with the effort, but she refused to give in to the weakness that threatened to consume her.

"Just... a passing thing," she whispered, her voice hoarse. "It'll be over soon."

But even as the words left her lips, doubt gnawed at her resolve. The room swam before her eyes, the familiar contours of her living room warping and twisting like a funhouse mirror.

Linda stumbled to the couch, collapsing onto its soft cushions. She closed her eyes, trying to steady her breathing.

"Harrison?" she called out weakly, knowing her son wouldn't answer but unable to stop herself. "Drake?"

The silence that greeted her was oppressive, weighing down on her like a physical presence. Linda opened her eyes, surveying the dimly lit room. Shadows seemed to creep along the walls, reaching out with grasping fingers.

"Stop it," she chided herself. "You're just... imagining things."

But the fear that had taken root in her heart refused to be silenced. It whispered of isolation, of abandonment, of a world where she was utterly alone.

Linda hugged herself tightly, trying to ward off the chill that seemed to emanate from within. "I can get through this," she murmured. "I've faced worse. I've survived worse."

Yet even as she spoke the words, a part of her wondered if this time, she might not be so lucky.

5 - 6

Linda's gaze fell upon a framed photograph on the side table, capturing a moment of happiness that now felt like it belonged to another lifetime. Drake's warm smile, Harrison's mischievous grin—frozen in time, tantalizingly close yet impossibly far away.

"I miss you both so much," she whispered, her voice cracking. "I don't know if I can do this alone."

The room tilted suddenly, and Linda gripped the edge of the couch to steady herself. Her stomach churned, threatening to expel what little she'd managed to eat that day.

"I need... I need help," she realized, the admission tearing at her usually self-reliant nature.

With shaking hands, Linda reached for her phone on the coffee table. The sleek device felt alien in her grip, her fingers clumsy as they attempted to navigate the familiar interface.

"Come on," she muttered, squinting at the screen as she tried to focus on the emergency contact numbers. "Just... need to call someone."

But even as she managed to punch in the first few digits, a wave of dizziness crashed over her. The phone slipped from her grasp, clattering to the floor with a sound that seemed to echo in the empty house.

"No," Linda gasped, reaching out feebly. "Please, I can't—"

The darkness that had been hovering at the edges of her vision rushed in, consuming everything in its path. As consciousness slipped away, Linda's last coherent thought was a desperate plea:

"Someone... anyone... help me."

7 - 7

As the world faded to black, Linda's mind conjured vivid images of her family. Drake's warm smile, the gentle strength of his embrace. Harrison's infectious laughter, his eyes shining with youthful exuberance. The memories swirled around her, a bittersweet reminder of all she had lost.

"Drake... Harrison..." she murmured, her voice barely a whisper in the emptiness of the room. "I need you..."

In her mind's eye, Linda saw them reaching out to her, their faces etched with concern and love. She tried to grasp their hands, but they remained just out of reach, like wisps of smoke slipping through her fingers.

"Please," she pleaded silently, her heart aching with longing. "Just one more moment together. One more chance to tell you how much I love you."

As consciousness continued to slip away, Linda's thoughts turned to the future they had once planned together. Family vacations, watching Harrison grow up, growing old side by side with Drake. All of it now seemed like a cruel mirage, shimmering on the horizon of a reality she could no longer reach.

With her last ounce of strength, Linda formed a silent prayer, her lips barely moving as she thought, "If anyone can hear me, please... don't let it end like this. I'm not ready to leave them behind."

The darkness enveloped her completely, and Linda's body went limp on the floor. Her final conscious thought was a fervent hope that somehow, across the vast expanse of the multiverse, her family could feel her love – and that someone, anyone, would find her before it was too late.

Descent into Chaos

Blue World – 2024

1 - 2

Chief Franklin Bird's calloused hands gripped the rusty railing, his knuckles white as he surveyed the desolate cityscape. The acrid stench of smoke assaulted his nostrils, a constant reminder of the world's descent into chaos.

"God almighty," he muttered, his gravelly voice barely audible over the distant wail of sirens. His eyes narrowed as he spotted movement in the streets below—a figure darting between abandoned cars, hunched and furtive.

Franklin's jaw clenched. Another scavenger, or something worse? He'd seen too many good people reduced to animals by the Virus, their humanity stripped away layer by layer until nothing remained but primal hunger.

A sudden screech pierced the air, causing Franklin to flinch. His hand instinctively moved to the holster at his hip, fingers brushing cool metal. The cry came again, closer this time, accompanied by the sound of shuffling feet.

"Dispatch, this is Chief Bird," he spoke into his radio, eyes scanning the perimeter. "Possible infected individual approaching the precinct from the east. Send a containment team."

Static crackled in response. Franklin cursed under his breath. Of course, the comms were down again. Nothing worked reliably anymore.

As he turned to head back inside, a flash of crimson caught his eye. His breath caught in his throat as he recognized the telltale mist—harbinger of the Multiverse Pathogen.

"Not here," he whispered, a prayer and a command. "Not now."

But even as the words left his lips, Franklin knew it was too late. The Virus had found them, just as it had found countless other realities. He thought of the faces he'd seen transformed—friends, colleagues, civilians he'd sworn to protect. Their vacant eyes and twisted expressions haunted his dreams.

With a heavy heart, Franklin reached for the alarm. Its shrill cry would alert the few remaining officers, signaling the beginning of emergency protocols they'd drilled countless times but hoped never to use.

As the siren blared, Franklin allowed himself one moment of doubt. How long could they hold out against an enemy that defied the laws of nature itself? But he pushed the thought aside, squaring his shoulders.

"Time to get to work," he growled, heading for the stairs. Whatever came next, he'd face it head-on. It was all he knew how to do.

3 - 4

Franklin descended the stairs two at a time, his footsteps echoing through the empty stairwell. As he burst into the precinct's main floor, he was met with a scene of controlled chaos. Officers scrambled to their stations; the air thick with tension.

"Chief!" Detective Athena Martinez called out, her voice strained. "We've got reports of fires breaking out all over the eastern sector. The containment teams are overwhelmed."

Franklin's jaw clenched. "Damn it," he muttered. Louder, he ordered, "Get every available unit out there. Priority is evacuation, not firefighting. We can't risk losing more people to this thing."

As officers rushed to comply, Franklin's gaze swept over the room. The precinct, once a bastion of order, now felt like a crumbling fortress. Papers littered the floor, and the acrid smell of smoke seeped through the windows.

"Sir," a young officer approached, his face pale. "What about... what about the infected? They're starting to gather near the evacuation routes."

Franklin's heart sank. He'd hoped for more time before facing this impossible choice. "We hold the line," he said, his voice steady despite the turmoil in his gut. "Use non-lethal force, if possible, but... protect the civilians at all costs."

As the officer nodded and turned away, Franklin allowed himself a moment of doubt. "What would you do, Meridith?" he whispered, thinking of his wife, lost to the virus. "How do we fight something that's rewriting the very fabric of our world?"

The crackle of the radio interrupted his thoughts. "Chief! We've got a situation at Memorial Hospital. The fire's spread to the west wing, and we've got patients trapped inside!"

Franklin snapped back to the present. "I'm on my way," he barked into his radio. As he headed for the door, he caught his reflection in a cracked window. The man staring back at him looked haunted but determined.

"One crisis at a time," he muttered to himself. "That's how we'll make it through this. One damn crisis at a time."

5 - 6

Franklin clenched his fist, the cool metal of his wedding band a stark reminder of all he had to fight for. He strode across the rooftop, his eyes scanning the ruined cityscape below. Despite the devastation, a fierce determination welled up within him.

"We're not done yet," he growled, his voice carrying the weight of his resolve. "This city's seen dark days before, and we've always come back stronger."

Officer Martinez approached; concern etched on her face. "Chief, the remaining civilians are panicking. What should we tell them?"

Franklin turned to her, his gaze steady. "The truth, Martinez. That we're still here, still fighting. That hope isn't lost as long as we stand together."

He paused, considering his next words carefully. "Get on the emergency broadcast system. Tell everyone who can hear that we're establishing a safe zone at City Hall. We'll make our stand there."

As Martinez hurried off, Franklin's mind raced. How many could they save? How long could they hold out? The uncertainty gnawed at him, but he pushed it aside.

"Rachel would've had a plan," he thought, a pang of longing for his wife hitting him. "She always saw the angles I missed."

Shaking off the memory, Franklin squared his shoulders and headed for the roof access door. Each step felt heavier than the last, but he refused to falter.

"One foot in front of the other, Bird," he muttered to himself. "That's how we'll rebuild this world. One step, one life, one day at a time."

As he reached for the door handle, a flicker of movement caught his eye. In the distance, a faint light pulsed, different from the fires ravaging the city. For a moment, it looked almost... blue?

Franklin blinked, and it was gone. But as he descended into the chaos below, that fleeting glimpse of something unexplained kindled a spark of hope in his chest. Maybe, just maybe, there was more to this fight than met the eye.

Unveiling Secrets

Red World – 2024

1 - 2

Drake's eyes widened as Holly's words washed over him, each revelation more staggering than the last. The weight of her tale seemed to press down on his shoulders, threatening to crush him under its immensity.

"I know it sounds impossible," Holly said, her voice steady despite the tremor in her hands. "But I swear to you, Drake, every word is true."

Drake ran a hand through his dark hair, his mind reeling. The lawyer in him wanted to dissect every detail, to find the logical flaw in her story. But the part of him that had already witnessed the impossible knew better.

"Tell me again about this Nexus," he urged, leaning forward in his chair. "What did it look like? How did it feel?"

Holly's eyes grew distant, as if seeing beyond the confines of his office. "It was... indescribable. Colors that shouldn't exist, sounds that felt more like vibrations in my soul. And the energy, Drake. It was like standing at the center of creation itself."

Drake's heart raced, a mixture of fear and exhilaration coursing through his veins. He thought of his wife and son, their loss still a raw wound in his chest. Could this be the key to understanding their fate?

"And you're certain it was my blood that brought you there?" he asked, his voice barely above a whisper.

Holly nodded, her gaze locking with his. "Without a doubt. The moment it touched me, it was like... like being unmade and remade in an instant."

Drake stood abruptly, pacing the length of his office. His mind whirled with possibilities, each more terrifying than the last. If his blood held such power, what did that mean for him? For the world?

"So you're saying that my blood somehow transported you to this nexus, merging you with your counterpart from another world?" Drake's voice was laced with disbelief, but beneath it simmered a growing sense of urgency. He turned to face Holly, his eyes burning with intensity. "And now there's a virus threatening not just our world, but countless others?"

Holly rose to meet his gaze, her posture mirroring his determination. "Yes, Drake. And I believe you're the key to stopping it."

Drake's hands clenched at his sides, his mind racing with the implications. He thought of the courtroom battles he'd faced, the cases he'd won against impossible odds. But this... this was beyond anything he'd ever encountered.

"I don't know if I'm ready for this, Holly," he admitted, vulnerability creeping into his voice. "But I know I can't turn my back on it either."

Holly placed a comforting hand on his arm. "You're not alone in this, Drake. We'll face it together."

Drake nodded, drawing strength from her words. Whatever lay ahead, he knew one thing with certainty: the battle for the multiverse had only just begun.

3 - 4

Holly nodded solemnly, her dark eyes reflecting a mix of awe and trepidation. "Yes, that's exactly what happened. And in the nexus, I met Justin, who tasked me with delivering a gift to you." She reached into her pocket, her movements deliberate and careful.

Drake's breath caught in his throat as Holly produced a small, intricately carved box. Its surface gleamed with an otherworldly sheen, adorned with mysterious symbols that seemed to shift and dance beneath his gaze. The attorney in him wanted to demand more information, to cross-examine Holly about every detail of her extraordinary journey. But another part of him, the part that had been irrevocably changed by the loss of his family, recognized the weight of this moment.

His fingers twitched at his sides, itching to reach out and take the box, to unravel its secrets. Instead, he forced himself to remain still, his analytical mind kicking into overdrive. What could this object mean? How was it connected to the inexplicable events surrounding his blood?

"And what did Justin say about this gift?" Drake pressed, his curiosity piqued. He leaned forward slightly, his piercing eyes fixed on the enigmatic box. The familiar thrill of pursuing a challenging case coursed through him, momentarily overshadowing the grief that had become his constant companion.

5 - 6

Holly's grip tightened on the box, her knuckles whitening. "He said that it was meant to help you," she replied, her voice barely above a whisper. "That it holds the key to combating the virus and saving countless lives across the multiverse."

Drake's eyes widened, the implications of her words hitting him like a physical blow. He stumbled back a step, his hand reflexively reaching out to steady himself against the nearby desk. The smooth wood beneath his fingers grounded him as his mind reeled.

"The multiverse?" he echoed, his tone a mix of disbelief and dawning comprehension. "You mean the other worlds out there, all threatened by this... this virus?"

Holly nodded gravely, her detective's instincts clearly on high alert as she watched Drake's reaction. "I've seen it, Drake. The crimson mist, the devastation. It's unlike anything we've ever faced."

Drake's thoughts churned like a maelstrom, memories of courtroom victories and legal strategies giving way to visions of apocalyptic destruction spanning countless realities. The weight of responsibility settled on his shoulders, heavier than any case he'd ever taken on.

"My God," he muttered, running a hand through his dark hair. "The fate of not just one world, but countless worlds... it's all hanging in the balance." His gaze snapped back to Holly, a newfound determination blazing in his eyes. "We can't afford to hesitate. Whatever's in that box, whatever it takes, we need to act now."

7 - 8

Drake's piercing gaze locked onto the intricate box in Holly's hands, its mysterious symbols seeming to pulse with hidden meaning. He drew in a deep breath, squaring his shoulders as he made his decision.

"Thank you, Holly," Drake said, his tone resolute. He reached out, carefully taking the box from her. Its weight felt significant in his hands, as if burdened with the fate of countless realities. "You've done more than you know by bringing this to my attention. Now, we need to find a way to stop this virus before it's too late."

Holly nodded, her expression a mix of relief and determination. "What's our next move?" she asked, her detective's instincts clearly kicking in.

Drake's fingers traced the intricate carvings on the box as he considered their options. "I need to unlock the secrets this box holds," he mused, more to himself than to Holly. "There has to be a connection between this and the virus, something we can use."

He glanced up, meeting Holly's intense gaze. "I'll need to work on this alone for now. Can you discreetly gather any information you can about unusual outbreaks or unexplained phenomena? Anything that might be linked to this interdimensional threat?"

"Consider it done," Holly replied, already moving towards the door with purpose.

As she left, Drake's mind raced with possibilities. He set the box on his desk, staring at it intently. The fate of the multiverse might hinge on what lay within, and he was determined to unravel its mysteries. With a deep breath, he reached for the lid, steeling himself for whatever revelations awaited.

9 - 10

The front door crashed open, the sound reverberating through the house like a thunderclap. Holly burst in, her chest heaving as if she'd sprinted the entire way home. Her eyes, wild with a mix of emotions, darted around until they locked onto Rebekah in the kitchen.

Rebekah's head snapped up, wooden spoon frozen mid-stir over a gently simmering pot. "Holly?" she asked, her voice laced with concern.

Holly's mind raced, the weight of everything she'd learned pressing down on her. How could she possibly explain the enormity of what she'd just experienced? The multiverse, the virus, Drake's blood – it all seemed too fantastical, even to her analytical mind.

"I..." Holly started, then faltered. She took a deep breath, steadying herself. "Rebekah, something's happened. Something big."

Rebekah set the spoon down, her brow furrowing as she stepped towards Holly. "What is it? Are you okay?"

Holly's hand instinctively went to her pocket, feeling the small velvet box nestled there. Her heart hammered against her ribs, a cocktail of adrenaline and love coursing through her veins.

"I'm fine," Holly assured her, managing a small smile. "But everything's changed. I've seen... things. Things that change everything we thought we knew about reality."

Rebekah's eyes widened, concern deepening in her gaze. "Holly, you're scaring me. What's going on?"

Holly crossed the room in three quick strides, taking Rebekah's hands in her own. She looked into the eyes of the woman she loved, seeing confusion, worry, and unwavering support reflected back at her.

"I promise I'll explain everything," Holly said, her voice steady despite the turmoil inside. "But first, there's something I need to ask you. Something that can't wait, not even for a second longer."

11 - 12

Holly's arms encircled Rebekah in a fierce embrace, her fingers gripping the soft fabric of Rebekah's sweater. The familiar scent of lavender and vanilla enveloped her, grounding her in this moment amidst the swirling chaos of multiverse revelations.

"I need to tell you something," Holly whispered, her voice quavering with the weight of her emotions. "Something incredible and terrifying and... life-changing."

She felt Rebekah stiffen momentarily in her arms, then relax, returning the embrace with equal intensity. Holly's mind raced, grappling with how to convey the enormity of what she'd experienced. The Green World's isolation, the Nexus's ethereal glow, the looming threat of the virus – it all seemed too vast, too unbelievable.

Rebekah's hands moved in soothing circles on Holly's back, a silent gesture of support and love. Holly's throat constricted, overwhelmed by the unconditional acceptance radiating from the woman in her arms.

I can't lose her, Holly thought fiercely. Not to a virus, not to alternate realities, not to anything.

As she pulled back slightly to meet Rebekah's gaze, Holly saw apprehension mingled with curiosity in those familiar eyes. Rebekah remained silent, patient, her very presence urging Holly to continue.

Holly opened her mouth, prepared to unleash the torrent of impossible truths, but found herself hesitating. How could she possibly begin to explain?

13 - 14

Holly's heart pounded as she gazed into Rebekah's eyes, finding strength in their unwavering trust. She took a deep breath, steadying herself for what she needed to say.

"Rebekah," Holly began, her voice low but firm, "No matter what happens in the coming days, no matter what we face or what challenges lie ahead, I want you to know that I love you." Her words gained momentum, fueled by the intensity of her emotions. "I don't ever want to lose you again."

Confusion flickered across Rebekah's features, her brow furrowing slightly. "Again? Holly, what do you mean?"

But before Rebekah could voice any further questions, Holly felt an overwhelming urgency. Her analytical mind, usually so adept at piecing together clues, now raced with a different kind of clarity. In that moment, surrounded by the warmth of their kitchen and faced with the uncertainty of multiple realities, Holly knew exactly what she needed to do.

With trembling fingers, she reached into her pocket, her hand closing around the small velvet box she'd been carrying. The weight of it seemed to ground her, reminding her of all they'd been through and all that was yet to come.

I've faced alternate worlds and cosmic threats, Holly thought. This shouldn't terrify me so much. And yet her heart raced as she slowly lowered herself to one knee.

Rebekah's eyes widened, a mix of surprise and dawning realization spreading across her face. Holly's fingers shook as she opened the box, revealing the shimmering diamond ring nestled within.

15 - 16

"Rebekah Sharp, will you marry me?" Holly's voice quivered with raw emotion, her heart pounding so hard she was sure Rebekah could hear it. The kitchen suddenly felt both vast and intimate, the familiar scents of home mingling with the charged atmosphere of this life-altering moment.

Holly's mind raced, recalling the harrowing journey through alternate realities that had led her to this point. She'd faced unimaginable dangers, but nothing compared to the vulnerability she felt now, kneeling before the woman she loved.

Rebekah stood frozen, her eyes wide with shock and disbelief. The wooden spoon she'd been holding clattered to the floor, forgotten. For a moment that seemed to stretch into eternity, the only sound was their shared, rapid breathing.

Please say something, Holly thought desperately, her detective's instincts kicking in as she searched Rebekah's face for any clue to her thoughts. Have I misjudged? Is this too soon after everything we've been through?

But then, as if emerging from a trance, Rebekah's expression transformed. A radiant smile spread across her face, tears glistening in her eyes, catching the light like tiny crystals. Holly felt her own eyes well up in response, a mixture of relief and overwhelming love washing over her.

17 - 18

"Yes, Holly," Rebekah whispered, her voice barely above a breath. "Yes, of course, I'll marry you."

The words hung in the air for a moment, crystalline and perfect. Holly's heart soared, a euphoria unlike anything she'd ever experienced flooding through her. With tears of joy streaming down her cheeks, she surged to her feet, wrapping Rebekah in a fierce embrace.

"I love you," Holly murmured against Rebekah's hair, inhaling the familiar scent of lavender shampoo. "God, I love you so much."

Rebekah's arms tightened around her. "I love you too," she said, her voice thick with emotion.

As they pulled apart slightly, Holly's detective instincts couldn't help but notice the way Rebekah's eyes darted to the ring, still nestled in its velvet box. With trembling fingers, Holly plucked it out and slid it onto Rebekah's finger.

"It's beautiful," Rebekah breathed, admiring the way the diamond caught the light.

Holly cupped Rebekah's face in her hands, overcome with a sense of rightness. This is what I've been fighting for, she realized. This moment, this love, this future.

Their lips met in a tender kiss, and Holly felt as if the very fabric of reality shifted around them. In that moment, she knew with absolute certainty that no matter what trials lay ahead—interdimensional threats, world-ending viruses, or the everyday challenges of life—they would face them together, united in love and unwavering in their commitment to each other.

As they broke apart, both breathless and grinning, Holly's mind raced with the enormity of what lay ahead. But for now, in this perfect moment, she allowed herself to simply be present, to bask in the love and joy that surrounded them like a protective cocoon against the chaos of the multiverse.

19 - 20

The harsh fluorescent lights flickered overhead as Drake's footsteps echoed through the sterile corridors. His hand tightened around the small wooden box, its weight a constant reminder of the burden he carried. The familiar scent of antiseptic and ozone filled his nostrils, a stark contrast to the earthy aroma emanating from the box.

As he reached the makeshift laboratory, Drake paused, taking a deep breath to steady his nerves. What if this isn't enough? The thought flashed through his mind, unbidden. He pushed it aside, squaring his shoulders before stepping through the doorway.

Harrison's head snapped up at his entrance, eyes wide with anticipation. Dr. Summers turned more slowly, her composed demeanor belying the intensity in her gaze. Drake offered them a reassuring smile, though his heart hammered against his ribs.

"Well?" Harrison blurted out, unable to contain himself. "Did you find it?"

Drake nodded, his throat suddenly dry. "I think so," he managed, his voice rough with emotion. "But I'm not entirely sure what 'it' is."

Dr. Summers stepped forward, her eyes fixed on the box in Drake's hand. "May I?" she asked, extending her palm.

As Drake placed the box in her hand, he couldn't help but notice the slight tremor in her fingers. It was oddly comforting to see that even the brilliant Dr. Summers wasn't immune to the gravity of their situation.

"What do you think it contains?" Drake asked, watching as she turned the box over in her hands, examining its intricate carvings.

Dr. Summers' brow furrowed in concentration. "I'm not certain, but these symbols... they're unlike anything I've ever seen before. They seem to pulse with an energy of their own."

Harrison moved closer, peering over Dr. Summers' shoulder. "Can we open it?" he asked, practically vibrating with curiosity.

Drake felt a surge of protectiveness. "I'm not sure that's wise," he cautioned, even as his own fingers itched to unlock the box's secrets. "We don't know what kind of safeguards might be in place."

Dr. Summers nodded approvingly. "Drake's right. We need to approach this carefully. Whatever's inside could be the key to saving countless lives across the multiverse."

As they huddled around the mysterious box, Drake's mind raced with possibilities. What if this is the breakthrough we've been searching for? he thought, hope and fear warring within him. And if it is, are we truly ready for what comes next?

21 - 22

Drake took a deep breath, steadying his nerves. "I believe I may have what we've been searching for," he announced, his voice tinged with cautious optimism.

Harrison's eyes lit up instantly, a spark of excitement igniting in their depths. Dr. Summers, ever the composed scientist, leaned forward, her gaze sharp and intent as it locked onto the box in Drake's hand.

With trembling fingers, Drake lifted the lid. The soft click of the opening mechanism seemed to echo in the tense silence of the lab. As the contents were revealed, he heard Harrison's sharp intake of breath.

Nestled within the velvet-lined interior was a single vial, its glass surface gleaming under the harsh fluorescent lights. The liquid inside shimmered with an otherworldly iridescence, seeming to pulse with a life of its own.

"Is that..." Harrison's voice trailed off, awe evident in his tone.

Drake's heart raced. Could this really be it? The key to unraveling the mysteries of the multiverse? He fought to keep his voice steady as he replied, "I think so. But I'm not entirely sure what we're dealing with here."

Dr. Summers extended her hand, hesitating just short of touching the vial. "May I?" she asked, her professional demeanor barely concealing her excitement.

As Drake nodded his assent, he couldn't help but wonder: What have I unleashed by bringing this here? And are we truly prepared for the consequences?

23 - 24

Harrison leaned in closer, his vibrant eyes wide with curiosity. "What is it?" he asked, his voice barely above a whisper. The young man's lean frame was taut with anticipation, his fingers drumming an erratic rhythm on the lab bench.

Drake watched intently as Dr. Summers reached out, her slender fingers brushing against the cool glass of the vial. With utmost care, she lifted it from its velvet nest, cradling it as if it were the most precious artifact in existence.

"Careful," Drake cautioned, his heart racing. What if this is our only chance? What if we damage it?

Dr. Summers' sharp gaze focused on the label, her brow furrowing in concentration. As she read, her eyes widened, and she drew in a sharp breath. The sudden change in her demeanor sent a jolt of both excitement and fear through Drake's body.

"Rachel?" Drake's calm voice cut through the tension. "What do you see?"

Drake's mind whirled with possibilities. Could this truly be the key to saving not just their world, but countless others? The weight of responsibility settled heavily on his shoulders as he waited for Dr. Summers' response.

25 - 26

Dr. Summers' eyes remained fixed on the vial, her voice barely above a whisper as she spoke. "It's blood," she murmured, her tone filled with awe and wonder. "But not just any blood. This... this is the key."

Drake's heart skipped a beat, his breath catching in his throat. Could it really be? He watched as realization dawned on Dr. Summers' face, her expression shifting from shock to excitement.

"The key?" Drake echoed, his voice hoarse with emotion. "You mean...?"

Dr. Summers nodded, her eyes gleaming with newfound purpose. "This blood sample contains properties I've only theorized about. It could be the missing link we've been searching for."

Relief washed over Drake, unlike anything he had ever known. His knees felt weak, and he gripped the edge of the lab bench to steady himself. We might actually have a chance now, he thought, hope blossoming in his chest for the first time in what felt like ages.

"I can't believe it," Drake breathed, shaking his head in disbelief. "All this time, and it was right there in that box."

Dr. Summers carefully placed the vial in a secure holder, her movements precise and reverent. "We'll need to run extensive tests, of course," she said, her scientific mind already racing ahead. "But if my suspicions are correct, this could change everything."

Drake nodded, his mind reeling with the implications. "Where do we start?" he asked, ready to throw himself into action.

27 - 28

Harrison's brow furrowed, his lean frame taut with tension as he leaned forward. His gaze darted between Drake and Dr. Summers, eyes alight with a mixture of hope and apprehension.

"The key to what?" Harrison pressed, his voice carrying a hint of urgency. He paused, carefully choosing his next words. "What exactly are we unlocking here?"

Drake felt a surge of sympathy for Harrison. The young man's curiosity was palpable, tempered by the weight of responsibility he carried. Before Drake could respond, Dr. Summers turned to face them both, her wire-rimmed glasses catching the harsh laboratory light.

"The key to unlocking the machine," Dr. Summers explained, her tone steady despite the gravity of her words. She took a deep breath, her composure a stark contrast to the monumental revelation she was about to share. "The key to opening the rifts between worlds."

Drake's heart raced as he processed her words. The rifts between worlds. The concept he'd only dared to dream about was now within reach. He glanced at Harrison, noting the younger man's widened eyes and slightly parted lips.

Swallowing hard, Drake allowed himself a moment to contemplate the enormity of what lay ahead. We're really doing this, he thought. We're about to breach the barriers between realities. The possibilities - and dangers - seemed endless.

"Dr. Summers," Drake began, his voice barely above a whisper, "are you absolutely certain? The implications of this..."

He trailed off, unable to fully articulate the mix of excitement and trepidation swirling within him. The lab suddenly felt too small, too confined for the cosmic significance of their discovery.

29 - 29

Drake's fingers tightened around the small wooden box, feeling its weight anew. He looked at Harrison and Dr. Summers, their faces a mix of anticipation and resolve. A surge of determination coursed through him, pushing aside his doubts.

"We have a responsibility," Drake said, his voice gaining strength. "Not just to our world, but to every world threatened by this virus."

Harrison nodded, his eyes shining with a mix of fear and excitement. "Dad, what's our next move?"

Drake turned to Dr. Summers, who was already moving towards her workstation with purposeful strides. "Rachel, how soon can we prepare the machine?"

Dr. Summers' fingers flew over her keyboard, bringing up schematics on the large monitor. "With this key, we can begin the calibration process immediately. But Drake," she paused, meeting his gaze, "we're venturing into uncharted territory. The risks are immeasurable."

Drake felt a familiar ache in his chest, thoughts of his lost wife and new found son flashing through his mind. He pushed the pain aside, focusing on the task at hand.

"We've come too far to turn back now," he said, his jaw set with determination. "Whatever challenges we face, we face them together."

As he spoke the words, Drake felt a profound sense of purpose wash over him. This was bigger than his personal loss, bigger than any one of them. They stood on the precipice of something monumental, with the fate of countless worlds hanging in the balance.

Race Against Time

Red World – 2024

1 - 2

The harsh fluorescent lights of the hospital corridor assault Holly's eyes as she sprints through the automatic doors, her heart pounding in sync with her footsteps. The acrid smell of disinfectant fills her nostrils, a stark reminder of the gravity of the situation.

Holly's mind races, replaying the frantic phone call that brought her here. Each labored breath echoes in her ears as she rounds the corner, her detective's instincts on high alert despite the personal nature of this visit.

She bursts into the room, her eyes immediately locking onto the frail figure in the hospital bed. Detective Franklin Bird, her mentor and friend, lies there, his usually commanding presence diminished by illness. His face is ashen, a sheen of sweat glistening on his brow as another violent cough wracks his body.

Holly's throat tightens, a lump forming as she takes in the scene. She's seen Bird in tough situations before, but never like this. Never so... vulnerable.

"Holly," Detective Bird rasps weakly as she approaches, "I'm glad you're here."

She moves to his bedside, her hand hovering uncertainly over his. Part of her wants to grab it, to offer some tangible comfort, but another part hesitates, afraid of causing him more pain.

"Chief," she manages, her voice thick with emotion. "What happened? How did you end up here?"

As Bird opens his mouth to respond, another coughing fit overtakes him. Holly winces, feeling utterly helpless as she watches him struggle for breath.

This is bad, she thinks, her analytical mind already cataloging symptoms and potential causes. *Whatever's affecting him, it's aggressive and fast-acting. We need answers, and we need them now.*

When the coughing subsides, Bird's eyes meet hers, filled with a mix of pain and determination. "Holly," he wheezes, "there's something you need to know. Something... important."

Holly leans in, her senses on high alert. Despite his weakened state, she can see the urgency in Bird's eyes. Whatever he's about to tell her, she knows it will be crucial to unraveling the mystery that's brought them to this point.

"I'm listening, Chief," she says softly, her voice steady despite the turmoil in her heart. "Whatever it is, we'll face it together. Just like we always have."

3 - 4

Holly's eyes fill with concern as she takes his hand, her grip firm yet gentle. "What happened, Franklin? What did they inject you with?"

Detective Bird struggles to speak, his words barely audible between coughs. "It was Gabriel... he... injected me with... something."

Holly's heart races, her mind reeling at the implications. Gabriel. The name sends a chill down her spine, conjuring images of the disfigured man with his cold, calculating demeanor.

Of course it was Gabriel, she thinks, anger and fear warring within her. *But what could he possibly gain from this?*

"Easy, Chief," she soothes, her thumb tracing circles on the back of his hand. "Take your time. Can you remember anything else? Any details about what he used?"

Bird's face contorts in concentration, fighting against the fog of illness. "A vial," he manages. "Glowing... faintly. Never seen anything... like it before."

Holly nods, committing every word to memory. Her detective's mind is already piecing together the puzzle, connecting this new information with what they know about Gabriel's plans for the multiverse.

"You're doing great, Franklin," she encourages, masking her growing dread with a calm exterior. "We're going to figure this out, I promise. Just hold on."

As Bird's eyes flutter closed, exhaustion overtaking him, Holly's resolve hardens. She may not understand the full scope of what they're facing, but one thing is clear: time is running out, and the fate of not just their world, but countless others, hangs in the balance.

5 - 6

Holly leans in closer, her voice low and urgent. "Franklin, this is crucial. Do you have the vial? Did you manage to keep it?"

Detective Bird's eyes snap open, a flicker of determination cutting through the haze of his illness. He nods weakly, his gaze darting to the pillow beneath his head.

With trembling hands, Bird reaches underneath, his movements slow and labored. Holly's heart pounds in her chest, each second feeling like an eternity. Finally, his fingers emerge, clutching a small glass container.

"This..." he croaks, his voice barely above a whisper. "This is what he injected me with."

Holly's eyes widen as she takes in the sight of the vial. Its contents shimmer with an otherworldly glow, casting faint, ethereal patterns across Bird's pallid skin. The liquid inside seems to dance and swirl of its own accord, defying the laws of physics.

My God, Holly thinks, a mixture of awe and terror coursing through her. *What kind of substance is this? And what does Gabriel plan to do with it on a larger scale?*

She reaches out, her hand hovering hesitantly over the vial. "May I?" she asks, her voice tight with apprehension.

Bird nods, relinquishing his grip on the container. As Holly takes it, she's surprised by its weight and the subtle warmth emanating from within. It feels alive, somehow, pulsing with an energy she can't quite comprehend.

"Thank you, Franklin," she says, carefully pocketing the vial. "You've done more than you know. Now rest, please. I'll make sure this gets to the right people."

As Bird's eyes drift closed once more, Holly's mind races with possibilities and fears. She knows that in her hands, she holds not just a potential key to saving her friend, but perhaps the fate of the entire multiverse.

7 - 8

Holly's fingers curl protectively around the vial in her pocket as she strides purposefully through the hospital corridors. The rhythmic beeping of machines and hushed voices fade into background noise as she focuses on her mission.

"Hold on, Franklin," she mutters under her breath. "We're going to figure this out."

Her footsteps quicken as she approaches the hospital's laboratory wing. Holly's heart pounds, each beat a reminder of the urgency of her task. As she reaches for the door handle, a wave of dizziness washes over her, the weight of responsibility momentarily overwhelming.

Pull yourself together, Keirstead, she chides herself. *The entire multiverse is at stake.*

Taking a deep breath, Holly pushes through the doors. The sterile environment of the lab greets her, a stark contrast to the chaos swirling in her mind.

"Dr. Ramirez?" she calls out, scanning the room for the lead researcher she knows from previous cases. "I need your help. It's urgent."

A bespectacled woman emerges from behind a row of centrifuges, her eyebrows raised in surprise. "Detective Keirstead? What brings you here at this hour?"

Holly withdraws the vial, holding it up to the fluorescent lights. "This," she says, her voice taut with tension. "I need you to analyze it immediately. I fear it might be the key to stopping a catastrophe beyond our imagination."

9 - 10

The lab bustles with frantic energy as Dr. Summers' team races against time, their fingers flying over keyboards and adjusting complex machinery. In the center of this controlled chaos, Drake Miller stands rigid, his piercing gaze fixed on Dr. Summers as she carefully examines the vial of blood.

The crimson liquid seems to shimmer unnaturally under the harsh laboratory lights. He suppresses a shudder, his mind racing with the implications of what they might discover.

"Holly says she went to this realm called the Nexus after coming into contact with remnants of my blood," Drake explains, his voice tight with tension. "Says in this world she was connected with her other self and there she met Justin. The man told her to trust him and she drank of his blood and was cured of the virus herself. There he gave her this vial and said that I would know what to do with it."

Dr. Summers looks up from her microscope, her brow furrowed in concentration. "Fascinating," she murmurs, her eyes meeting Drake's. "The composition is unlike anything I've ever seen before."

Drake's heart skips a beat. Could this be the breakthrough they've been desperately searching for? He thinks of his lost family, of the countless lives at stake across the multiverse. *If this blood really holds the key to stopping the virus...*

"What exactly are we looking at, Dr. Summers?" he asks, struggling to keep his voice steady. "Could this be the cure we need?"

As Dr. Summers opens her mouth to respond, Drake notices a flicker of uncertainty cross her face. It's brief, almost imperceptible, but it sends a chill down his spine. Whatever they've discovered, he realizes, it's going to change everything.

11 - 12

Dr. Summers takes a deep breath, her eyes gleaming with a mixture of excitement and apprehension. "This blood," she begins, her voice measured, "like yours, it consists of one DNA profile. But the components..." She trails off, shaking her head in disbelief.

Drake leans in, his pulse quickening. "What about the components?"

"They suggest that it contains high levels of cosmic radiation," Dr. Summers finishes, her gaze fixed on the vial.

Drake's mind races, memories of his experiences in other worlds flooding back. The strange sensations, the inexplicable abilities he'd gained. "So like mine in the other worlds did," he murmurs, more to himself than to Dr. Summers.

Could this be the missing piece? Drake wonders, a spark of hope igniting in his chest. *If this blood is similar to what I carried in those other realities, maybe it holds the key to stopping Gabriel and saving the multiverse.*

"Exactly," Dr. Summers nods, her excitement palpable. "But there's something more to this sample. Something I can't quite put my finger on yet."

Drake's hands clench involuntarily, the weight of their discovery settling on his shoulders. "What's our next step?" he asks, ready to take action, to do whatever it takes to unravel this mystery and protect the worlds he's come to care for.

13 - 14

Dr. Summers furrows her brow, her eyes narrowing as she peers intently at the sample through her microscope. The lab falls silent, the hum of equipment fading into the background as everyone holds their breath, waiting for her next words.

"Exactly, only this is different," she says, her voice barely above a whisper. Drake leans in closer, hanging on her every word. "While a normal human being consists of 46 chromosomes, this blood only consists of 24. 23 from the mother and one from the father."

Drake's mind reels, trying to grasp the implications. "What does that mean?" he asks, his voice tight with tension.

Dr. Summers looks up from the microscope, her eyes wide with a mixture of awe and disbelief. "It's truly extraordinary," she breathes. "I believe we are looking at the blood of the chosen one indeed."

The revelation sends a shiver down Drake's spine, and he can see the same reaction rippling through the others in the room. Dr. Summers' words hang heavy in the air, each syllable echoing with profound implications.

The chosen one, Drake thinks, his heart pounding. *If Justin's blood is indeed the key we've been searching for, it means that the fate of not just one world, but the entire multiverse rests in our hands.*

He glances around the room, taking in the stunned expressions of his colleagues. Dr. Monroe, usually so composed, looks visibly shaken. The gravity of the situation is palpable, pressing down on all of them like a physical weight.

"So what now?" Drake asks, breaking the charged silence. "How do we use this information to stop Gabriel and save the multiverse?"

15 - 16

Harrison's eyes widened, his breath catching in his throat as he absorbed the magnitude of Dr. Summers' discovery. The room seemed to spin around him, reality bending under the weight of this revelation. His gaze darted from the vial of glowing liquid to Dr. Summers' intense expression, then back again.

Justin... the chosen one? Harrison's mind raced, images of the mysterious figure from Holly's account flashing before his eyes. *How could one person hold such power?*

He gripped the edge of the lab table, steadying himself as he tried to process the implications. The fate of countless worlds, infinite versions of reality, all potentially hinging on this single vial of blood. It was almost too much to comprehend.

"What does this mean?" Harrison finally managed to ask, his voice barely above a whisper. He cleared his throat, struggling to articulate the storm of questions swirling in his mind. "For us, for the multiverse... for everything?"

As he spoke, Harrison's gaze locked onto Dr. Summers, searching her face for answers, for reassurance, for anything that might make sense of this earth-shattering revelation. His fingers tightened on the table, knuckles white with tension, as he waited for her response.

Could this really be the key? he wondered silently. *The solution to the virus, to Gabriel's plan, to saving all of existence?* The weight of possibility - of responsibility - settled heavily on his shoulders, and Harrison found himself holding his breath, poised on the edge of a moment that could change everything.

17 - 18

Dr. Summers turned to Harrison, her expression grave yet determined. The lines around her eyes deepened as she met his gaze, her voice steady despite the weight of their situation.

"It means that we have a chance," she said, each word carefully measured. "It means that Justin may hold the key to unlocking the machine and restoring balance to the multiverse."

Harrison's heart leapt in his chest, hope surging through him like an electric current. He released his grip on the table, flexing his fingers as he processed her words.

"A chance," he repeated, tasting the possibility on his tongue. "But how? What makes Justin's blood so special?"

Dr. Summers gestured to the vial, its contents shimmering faintly under the harsh lab lights. "The unique genetic structure, the cosmic radiation... it's unlike anything we've ever seen. If our theories are correct, it could be the catalyst we need to stabilize the rifts between realities."

As she spoke, Harrison's mind raced ahead, imagining the implications. *If we can harness this power, we might be able to stop Gabriel, to save not just our world, but all worlds.*

"So what's our next move?" he asked, a newfound determination hardening his voice. "How do we use this to our advantage?"

Dr. Summers' eyes gleamed with a mix of scientific curiosity and cautious optimism. "We need to run more tests, to understand exactly how Justin's blood interacts with the machine. And we need to find him – the man himself might be crucial to unlocking its full potential."

The gravity of her words sank in, and Harrison felt a surge of hope amidst the uncertainty. If Justin's blood truly was the missing piece of the puzzle, then perhaps there was still a chance to set things right, to undo the damage that Gabriel had wrought.

We're not beaten yet, Harrison thought, a spark of determination igniting within him. *We can still fight back.*

19 - 20

Harrison's brow furrowed, his eyes distant as a memory suddenly surfaced. He inhaled sharply, his hand instinctively reaching for the spot on his arm where he'd once felt the pinch of a needle.

"Wait," he said, his voice tinged with a mix of excitement and trepidation. "In the wasteland, I found a man in a dungeon. He gave me a vial too, told me to drink it and I'd find my way back home." Harrison's gaze locked onto Dr. Summers, his words tumbling out faster now. "That's how I came here, how I found you and eventually Dad. Could it... could it have been the same man that Holly met?"

Dr. Summers leaned forward, her eyes widening with interest. "A man in a dungeon? In the wasteland?" she echoed, her scientific mind already whirring with possibilities.

As Harrison nodded, Drake's posture suddenly stiffened. His eyes glazed over, unfocused, as if seeing something far beyond the sterile walls of the lab.

The acrid smell of decay. Ash swirling in air thick with despair. Skeletal buildings looming against a slate-gray sky.

Drake's voice was barely above a whisper when he spoke, "The Black World."

"Dad?" Harrison's concerned voice cut through the vivid memory.

Drake blinked, his eyes refocusing on the present. "I remember it," he said, his tone grave. "That apocalyptic landscape. I dubbed it the Black World during my brief visit there." He shuddered involuntarily, the weight of that desolate reality still palpable. "If this mysterious man is connected to that place... we might be dealing with something far more complex than we initially thought."

21 - 22

Drake took a deep breath, his brow furrowing as he processed the implications. He looked at Harrison, then back to Dr. Summers, his eyes filled with a mix of determination and trepidation.

"All I know is we have to trust him," Drake said, his voice steady despite the uncertainty swirling in his mind. "He saved Holly and brought you home to me, Harrison. That has to count for something."

Holly, who had just arrive and been listening intently, stepped forward. Her detective's instincts were on high alert, but she couldn't deny the truth in Drake's words. "You're right," she agreed, her tone resolute. "But we can't just blindly follow. We need to understand what we're dealing with."

Dr. Summers nodded, her analytical mind already racing ahead. "Agreed. Which brings us to the next crucial step," she said, gesturing towards the vial of Justin's blood. "So how do we test to see if the blood actually works?"

The question hung in the air, heavy with possibility and danger. Drake felt a familiar tension coiling in his gut, the same feeling he'd had before every major breakthrough in this multiversal mystery.

How much are we willing to risk? he thought, his eyes darting between the faces of his companions. *And what happens if we're wrong?*

"We need a controlled environment," Holly suggested, her detective's mind already formulating a plan. "Something that allows us to observe the effects without putting anyone at unnecessary risk."

Drake nodded, appreciating Holly's cautious approach. But a part of him knew that at some point, they'd have to take a leap of faith.

23 - 24

Dr. Summers' brow furrowed in concentration, her fingers tapping rhythmically against the lab bench. "We need to find a sample of the virus," she declared, her voice a mixture of excitement and trepidation. "If my theory is correct, then Holly should be infected with the virus still, although not contagious as the blood should have killed it." Her gaze shifted to Kierstead. "Do you think you can lend us a sample of your blood?"

Drake's heart raced at the suggestion. The thought of Holly being a carrier, even if dormant, sent a chill down his spine. He opened his mouth to respond, but before he could, Holly's voice cut through the tense atmosphere.

"How about a sample of the virus itself?"

Holly's presence commanding instant attention. Drake's breath caught in his throat as he saw the determined set of her jaw, the fire in her eyes. She marched across the room, her steps purposeful and urgent.

"The virus has made its way to this world," Holly announced, her voice tight with barely contained anger and fear. "Gabriel infected Franklin with it, and it's only a matter of time before the virus spreads further."

Drake's mind reeled at the implications. *Gabriel's here? And he's already started?* The weight of their mission suddenly felt crushingly heavy on his shoulders. He looked at Holly, seeing the strain etched in the lines around her eyes, the tension in her shoulders.

"Holly," he said softly, reaching out to her. "Are you alright? How's Franklin?"

She met his gaze, and for a moment, her tough exterior cracked, revealing the worry underneath. "He's... fighting," she replied, her voice catching slightly. "But we don't have much time."

Dr. Summers stepped forward, her eyes wide with a mixture of scientific curiosity and grave concern. "You have a sample? Holly, this could be crucial. But we need to be extremely careful in handling it."

Drake nodded in agreement, his mind racing through potential scenarios. *If the virus is already here, we're in more danger than we realized. But this could also be the breakthrough we need.*

"What's our next move?" he asked, looking between Holly and Dr. Summers, ready to face whatever challenges lay ahead in their fight to save not just their world, but all of reality.

25 - 26

Holly's hand trembled slightly as she extended the vial towards Dr. Summers. The faintly glowing liquid inside seemed to pulse with an otherworldly energy, a stark reminder of the threat they faced.

"Here," Holly said, her voice tight with urgency. "Be careful. This is all we have."

Dr. Summers gingerly accepted the vial, her eyes widening as she examined its contents. "Extraordinary," she breathed, her scientific curiosity momentarily overriding her concern. "This could be the key to understanding how the virus operates across different realities."

As the gravity of the situation settled over the room, Harrison stepped forward, his brow furrowed with worry. "So what happens if we don't stop this virus in time? What does it look like for our world, for all worlds?"

The question hung in the air, heavy with implications. Harrison mind raced, recalling the desolation he'd witnessed in other realities. *The empty streets, the silence, the overwhelming sense of loss...*

"It's... it's unimaginable," Holly finally said, her voice barely above a whisper. "I've been shown worlds torn apart by this virus. Entire civilizations wiped out. If we fail here, it's not just our reality at stake. It's everything."

Drake nodded grimly, his jaw set with determination. "Then we won't fail," he stated, his voice carrying a resolve that belied the fear Holly could see in his eyes. "We've come too far to give up now."

As Dr. Summers carefully secured the vial, Holly felt a surge of hope amidst the dread. *We have a chance,* she thought. *As long as we're still fighting, there's hope.*

27 - 28

Dr. Chen swept into the room, his normally composed demeanor tinged with an uncharacteristic urgency. The air seemed to thicken as he began to speak, his words painting a vivid and terrifying picture of cosmic annihilation.

"The collapse of the multiverse is a cataclysmic event unlike anything humanity has ever witnessed," he began, his voice low and intense.

As Dr. Chen continued his chilling description, Drake felt a cold dread seeping into his bones. He envisioned reality fracturing like shattered glass, worlds colliding in a chaotic dance of destruction. The image of swirling vortexes consuming everything in their path made his stomach churn.

This can't be happening, Drake thought, his mind reeling. *How can we possibly hope to stop something so vast, so incomprehensible?*

The room fell into an eerie silence as Dr. Chen finished speaking. The weight of his words pressed down on everyone present, the gravity of their situation more apparent than ever.

Drake's analytical mind, honed by years of legal practice, desperately sought a foothold in this sea of cosmic chaos. He latched onto a detail that had been nagging at him, something concrete he could grasp amidst the abstract horror.

"If I had three strands of DNA in my blood in the other worlds," Drake finally spoke up, his voice cutting through the oppressive silence, "how could that have been possible?"

As he voiced the question, Drake's eyes darted between Dr. Chen and Dr. Summers, searching their faces for any hint of an explanation. *There has to be some logic to this,* he thought. *Some pattern we can understand and use to our advantage.*

29 - 30

Dr. Chen turned to Drake, his eyes gleaming with a mixture of fascination and concern. "That's easy to explain," he said, his voice calm despite the gravity of the situation. "You see, you carried a DNA strand for each universe you existed in."

Drake leaned forward, his brow furrowing as he tried to process this information. *Each universe I existed in? How many could there be?*

Dr. Chen continued, his words painting a vivid picture of diverging realities. "There's a universe where you didn't die in the car accident that claimed the lives of your wife and son. There's the main reality, the one where the accident occurred, and then there's the two possible scenarios where your wife or son survived."

The mention of his family sent a sharp pang through Drake's chest. He could almost see them - his wife's warm smile, his son's infectious laughter. Parallel worlds where they still lived, where their family wasn't torn apart. The thought was both comforting and agonizing.

"Only three universes," Drake said, his voice barely above a whisper. A chill ran down his spine as the implication of his words sank in. "You mean I died in the rest?"

As he voiced the question, Drake felt a strange disconnect, as if he were discussing someone else's fate rather than his own. *How many versions of me are there? How many have already been lost?* The enormity of the multiverse suddenly felt oppressive, each possibility a weight on his shoulders.

31 - 32

Dr. Chen's eyes softened with understanding as he regarded Drake. "It's quite possible you survived in those ones too, but later died from unrelated circumstances." He gestured towards Harrison, who had been listening intently, his young face a mix of fascination and concern. "Like Harrison here, he traveled to a world where he's dead. It's quite possible if you hadn't lost your abilities, you would have been able to do the same."

Drake's gaze shifted to Harrison, seeing his son in a new light. The boy had already experienced so much, traversing realities Drake could only imagine. A surge of pride mingled with his worry.

Suddenly, a memory flashed through Drake's mind - searing pain, the acrid smell of gunpowder. His hand unconsciously moved to his side where the phantom wound still ached. "When I was shot," he began, his voice tight with tension, "my bullet wound traveled over from one universe to the next."

The implications of this realization hit him like a physical blow. Drake's mind raced, piecing together the fragments of his experiences across realities. "If I had died in one universe, I could have died in the other." He paused, swallowing hard against the lump forming in his throat. "So if I'm dead in all other realities, why am I not dead here?"

As he voiced the question, Drake felt a chill run down his spine. He was walking, talking, breathing - but was he living on borrowed time? The room seemed to spin slightly as he grappled with the enormity of his situation.

Am I just an anomaly? Drake wondered, his heart pounding. *A glitch in the multiverse that hasn't been erased yet?* He looked at Harrison, seeing the concern etched on his son's face, and felt a fierce determination well up inside him. Whatever the answer, he had to stay alive - for Harrison, for all the versions of his family he couldn't save.

33 - 34

Dr. Chen's voice cut through Drake's spiraling thoughts. "It's quite possible again that when you became connected across the multiverse, that was when you carried over the bullet," he explained, his tone clinical yet tinged with fascination. "Much like how Detective Kierstead could bring a box with her across multiple dimensions. So could you bring a bullet wound."

Drake's brow furrowed, his mind struggling to grasp the implications. He paced the room, his footsteps echoing in the tense silence. The weight of the multiverse seemed to press down on his shoulders, each step heavy with the burden of understanding.

A box is one thing, he thought, *but a wound? My own death?* The concept was dizzying, like trying to hold smoke in his hands.

He turned back to Dr. Chen, his piercing gaze filled with a mix of confusion and desperate need for answers. "This still doesn't fit quite right with me," Drake said, his voice low and gravelly with frustration. "How did I not wake up shot here?"

As he spoke, Drake's hand unconsciously moved to his side again, probing for a wound that wasn't there. The phantom pain flared, a stark reminder of the reality—or realities—he had experienced.

Am I whole in this world? he wondered, a surge of doubt coursing through him. *Or am I just a patchwork of different versions of myself, stitched together by some cosmic accident?*

The room fell silent, the weight of Drake's question hanging in the air. He looked from face to face, searching for an answer that could make sense of the impossible situation he found himself in.

35 - 36

Dr. Summers stepped forward, her eyes filled with a mix of scientific curiosity and compassion. "You lost your connection to the other worlds," she explained, her voice steady and measured, "and you were transported back in time to the moment you woke up from the accident. The bullet wound hadn't occurred in this reality yet."

Drake's mind reeled at the implications. He ran a hand through his disheveled hair, trying to process the information. The scar on his forehead seemed to throb, a reminder of the accident that now existed both in memory and reality.

Back in time? Before the bullet, before... everything? His thoughts raced, hope and fear intertwining in a dizzying dance.

"So, I have a chance to change things?" Drake asked, his voice barely above a whisper. The possibility of saving his family, of rewriting their tragic fate, bloomed in his chest like a desperate flower.

But as quickly as the hope had risen, a chilling realization washed over him. His eyes widened, and he turned to Dr. Summers, his expression a mask of dawning horror.

"But what you're saying is," Drake began, his voice trembling slightly, "there's a possibility that I will soon be shot again or that I'll explode?"

The room seemed to hold its breath, waiting for Dr. Summers' response. Drake's hands clenched at his sides, bracing for an answer that could shatter his newfound hope or plunge him into an even more terrifying uncertainty.

37 - 38

Dr. Summers' eyes met Drake's, her expression a mixture of sympathy and scientific detachment. "Only if you become connected to the multiverse again," she replied softly.

Drake's shoulders sagged with momentary relief, but his mind was already racing ahead. The possibility of reconnection hung over him like a sword of Damocles. He paced the room, his footsteps echoing in the tense silence.

Connected to the multiverse again, he thought. *But how? And why?* The questions swirled in his mind, each one leading to another, more daunting query.

Suddenly, a memory flashed through his mind - Gabriel, that enigmatic figure with the disfigured face and piercing eyes. Drake spun to face Dr. Summers, his heart pounding.

"And why did Gabriel have Harrison's and my DNA?" he demanded, his voice tight with urgency.

The question hung in the air, heavy with implications. Drake's fists clenched at his sides as he awaited an answer, his mind conjuring increasingly disturbing scenarios. Whatever the reason, he knew it couldn't be good. Gabriel's manipulations had already cost them so much. What more did he have planned?

39 - 40

Dr. Summers took a deep breath, her eyes flickering with a mix of concern and scientific fascination. "It would seem that when one is injected or comes into contact with the blood of a person who can travel, then they too can obtain the ability to travel," she explained, her voice measured and calm despite the weight of her words.

Drake's mind reeled, images of Gabriel's white-robed figure flashing before his eyes. He could almost feel the phantom pain of a needle piercing his skin. When had Gabriel obtained his blood? The implications made his stomach churn.

"I presume that at some point you gave Gabriel your blood," Dr. Summers continued, her gaze steady on Drake. "He in turn obtained two markers from your blood which allowed him to travel the same worlds as you could. He obtained copies of your DNA, Mr. Miller."

Drake's throat tightened, a bitter taste rising in his mouth. He hadn't willingly given Gabriel anything, let alone his blood. The violation felt deeply personal, an intrusion into the very essence of his being.

"But I never..." Drake started, his voice trailing off as a horrible realization dawned on him. The accident. The hospital. There had been so many tests, so many samples taken. Had Gabriel somehow accessed those?

His thoughts were interrupted by Harrison's voice, tense with concern. "And what about me? How did he obtain my DNA?"

Drake's head snapped up, his protective instincts flaring. He hadn't even considered that Harrison might be involved in this twisted genetic manipulation. The thought of Gabriel having access to his son's DNA made his blood run cold.

What have I dragged you into, Harrison? Drake thought, his heart heavy with guilt. He looked at his son, seeing not just the determined young man before him, but the innocent child he had once been. The weight of their shared trauma, of all they had endured, pressed down on him like a physical force.

41 - 42

Dr. Chen's eyes darted between Drake and Harrison, a flicker of unease crossing his face. He hesitated, his fingers drumming nervously on the edge of his clipboard.

"That I cannot surmise, Mr. Miller," he said finally, his voice low and careful. "But I think the answer is something you wouldn't like if I were to speculate."

Drake's jaw clenched, a surge of protective anger rising within him. The implications of Dr. Chen's words hung heavy in the air, each possibility more unsettling than the last. He opened his mouth to demand more information, but Harrison's voice cut through the tension.

"When Gabriel had me tied up," Harrison said, his words coming out in a rush, "he could vanish into thin air, much like I could when I came into contact with the mysterious man's blood."

Drake's head whipped around to stare at his son, his heart pounding. The memory of Harrison's abduction was still raw, a wound that hadn't fully healed. But this new information... it changed everything.

Gabriel had powers like Harrison's? How? When? Drake's mind raced, trying to piece together the fragments of this cosmic puzzle. He couldn't shake the feeling that they were missing something crucial, some key piece of information that would make everything fall into place.

"Harrison," Drake said, his voice tight with barely contained emotion, "why didn't you tell me this before?"

43 - 44

Holly's voice cut through the tense silence, her words measured but tinged with a hint of urgency. "And much like I could when I drank of Justin's blood," she added, her eyes flickering between Drake and Harrison.

The revelation hung in the air, heavy with implication. Drake felt a chill run down his spine as he processed Holly's words, his mind racing to connect the dots. The mysterious Justin, the blood with extraordinary properties, the ability to traverse realities - it was all interconnected in ways they were only beginning to understand.

Harrison's brow furrowed, his lean frame taut with tension as he leaned forward, eyes alight with a mixture of curiosity and concern. "Is it possible that Gabriel also came into contact with Justin's blood at some point in time?" he asked, his voice low and urgent. "Is it not possible to surmise that Gabriel can also travel to more than just the three worlds we've been to?"

Drake's heart hammered in his chest as he considered the implications of Harrison's questions. The thought of Gabriel having access to even more realities, more opportunities to wreak havoc across the multiverse, was terrifying. He clenched his fists, trying to steady himself as waves of anxiety and determination washed over him.

If Gabriel has that kind of power, Drake thought, *we're in even more danger than we realized. But how? When did he get access to Justin's blood? And what does it mean for us... for all of reality?*

As the gravity of the situation settled over the room, Drake found himself searching the faces of his companions, looking for any sign of hope or understanding. The weight of their mission, the fate of countless realities, seemed to press down on him with renewed force.

45 - 46

Dr. Chen's eyes darted between Harrison and Drake, his expression a mix of fascination and uncertainty. "That's a good question," he admitted his voice tinged with a hint of frustration, "and one I am not quite knowledgeable on. Only time will tell, I suppose."

The words hung in the air, heavy with implication. Drake felt a surge of anger and impatience rise within him. *Time?* he thought bitterly. *We don't have time. Every second we waste, Gabriel gets closer to destroying everything.*

Without a word, Drake spun on his heel and stormed towards the door, his jaw clenched tight. He could feel the eyes of the others on his back, but he didn't care. The suffocating atmosphere of theories and uncertainties was too much to bear.

As he reached for the door handle, he heard quick footsteps behind him. Holly's voice cut through his tumultuous thoughts. "Drake, wait!"

He paused, hand on the door, torn between his desire to escape and his connection to Holly. He turned slightly, catching a glimpse of her determined face, her dark eyes filled with concern.

She doesn't understand, Drake thought. *None of them do. We're running out of time, and I can't just stand here listening to maybes and what-ifs.*

With a sharp exhale, Drake pushed through the door, his mind already racing ahead to what he needed to do next. He could hear Holly's footsteps following close behind, but he didn't slow down. The corridors of the facility blurred around him as he strode forward, driven by a desperate need for action.

47 - 48

Holly's voice cut through the tension, her words laced with a mixture of concern and frustration. "Where are you going?" she asked, matching Drake's hurried pace as they swept through the sterile corridors.

Drake's jaw clenched, his eyes fixed ahead. The fluorescent lights overhead cast harsh shadows across his face, accentuating the lines of worry etched there. *I can't just sit around theorizing anymore*, he thought, his mind racing. *We need answers, and we need them now.*

"To see a colleague," he replied tersely, his voice low and determined. He could feel Holly's questioning gaze on him, but he didn't elaborate further.

An Unexpected Loss

Red World – 2024

1 - 2

The flickering fluorescent lights cast long shadows across the polished marble floor as Drake and Holly stepped into the law firm's corridor. The air felt thick with unspoken tension, each breath a struggle against the oppressive silence. At the end of the hallway stood Richard Vega, his usually immaculate suit now rumpled and his eyes darting nervously between Drake and Holly.

Drake's fists clenched involuntarily as he locked eyes with Vega. The betrayal burned in his chest, threatening to consume him. How could someone he once trusted have led them into this nightmare?

"You!" Drake's voice echoed off the walls, sharp and accusing. "You're the one who tipped off Gabriel about that night. You betrayed us!"

Vega flinched at the words, his face a mask of conflicting emotions. Drake could see the guilt etched in the lines of his face, but there was something else there too—a desperate, cornered look that made Drake's skin crawl.

Holly tensed beside him, her hand hovering near her holstered weapon. Drake could sense her analytical mind working overtime, piecing together the implications of this revelation.

"Drake," Holly whispered, her voice low and urgent. "We need to stay focused. Remember why we're here."

He nodded, trying to rein in his anger. But the memory of that night, the chaos and terror that had unfolded because of Vega's betrayal, threatened to overwhelm him. Drake took a deep breath, the musty air of the corridor filling his lungs as he fought to maintain control.

"Why, Vega?" Drake demanded, his voice trembling with barely contained rage. "I trusted you. How could you do this to me?"

3 - 4

Vega's expression tightened, his eyes darting between Drake and Holly. The fluorescent lights flickered overhead, casting harsh shadows across his face. "Yes, I did," he admitted, his voice barely above a whisper. "But you have to understand, Drake. Gabriel is going to kill my family if I didn't cooperate. I had no choice."

Drake's fists clenched at his sides, his knuckles turning white with the effort of restraining himself. The anger that had been simmering beneath the surface now threatened to boil over. He could feel the weight of his grief, the loss of his own family, pressing down on him like a physical force.

"No choice?" Drake retorted, his voice dripping with contempt. Each word felt like it was being torn from his throat. "You always have a choice, Vega. You chose to betray us."

As he spoke, Drake's mind raced through the implications of Vega's admission. How many lives had been put at risk because of this betrayal? How many more would suffer if Gabriel's plans came to fruition? The thought made his stomach churn.

Holly's presence beside him was a steady anchor, reminding him of their mission. But even her calming influence couldn't fully quell the storm of emotions raging within him. Drake took a step forward, his eyes never leaving Vega's face.

"Do you have any idea what you've done?" Drake asked, his voice low and dangerous. "The lives you've put at risk? The damage you've caused?"

5 - 6

Holly stepped forward, her gaze unwavering as she positioned herself between Drake and Vega. The dim light of the corridor cast harsh shadows across her face, accentuating the determined set of her jaw. Her voice cut through the tension like a blade of ice.

"What do you know about Gabriel's plans?" she demanded, her tone cold and steely.

Drake watched Holly take control of the situation, grateful for her level-headedness. His own emotions were still roiling, threatening to overwhelm his judgment. He focused on Holly's steady presence, using it to ground himself.

Vega's eyes darted between Holly and Drake, his adam's apple bobbing as he swallowed hard. The man's earlier defiance seemed to crumble under Holly's piercing gaze. Drake could almost see the gears turning in Vega's head as he weighed his options.

After what felt like an eternity, Vega spoke, his voice barely above a whisper. "I know enough to know that he's planning something big," he admitted reluctantly. "Something that could destroy everything."

Drake's breath caught in his throat. The enormity of Vega's words hit him like a physical blow. His mind raced, trying to piece together what little information they had. What could Gabriel possibly be planning that could threaten not just their world, but everything?

"Destroy everything?" Drake echoed, his voice hoarse. "What does that mean, Vega? What exactly does Gabriel have planned?"

7 - 8

Drake's jaw tightened, the muscles in his face visibly clenching as he absorbed the gravity of Vega's words. A chill ran down his spine, and he felt his attorney's instincts kick in, pushing him to dig deeper, to uncover the truth hidden beneath Vega's vague admission.

"Where is he?" Drake demanded, his voice low and dangerous. The words came out as a near-growl, laced with a mixture of anger and urgency. His piercing gaze bore into Vega, silently challenging the man to withhold any more information.

Vega's shoulders slumped, the fight seemingly draining out of him. He shook his head, a look of resignation crossing his features. "The amusement park," he confessed, his voice barely above a whisper. "I can help you find him. I owe you that much."

Drake's mind raced, memories of that fateful night at the amusement park flooding back. The funhouse, the gunshot, the searing pain... He pushed the thoughts aside, forcing himself to focus on the present.

"The amusement park," Drake repeated, his tone skeptical. "Why there? What's Gabriel planning?"

As he waited for Vega's response, Drake's hand instinctively moved to his side, where the phantom pain of his old wound lingered. He couldn't shake the feeling that they were walking into another trap, but what choice did they have?

9 - 10

Drake's eyes flicked to Holly, catching her gaze. In that brief moment, a silent conversation passed between them. Holly's sharp features were set with determination, her eyes reflecting the same mix of wariness and resolve that Drake felt churning inside him.

He knew they were thinking the same thing: Vega was a liability, but also their only lead. The tightness in Drake's chest eased slightly, grateful for Holly's unwavering presence in this moment of uncertainty.

Running a hand through his hair, Drake turned back to Vega. "Fine," he conceded, his voice tight with reluctance. Every fiber of his being screamed against trusting this man, but the weight of Gabriel's threat loomed larger. "But if you betray us again, Vega, there will be consequences."

The words hung in the air, heavy with implication. Drake's mind raced, considering the possibilities that lay ahead. What if this was another setup? What if Gabriel was expecting them? The amusement park was already a place of nightmares for him – could he face those demons again?

"I understand," Vega nodded, his voice barely audible.

Drake's jaw clenched. "Do you?" he challenged, taking a step closer to Vega. "Because last time your understanding cost lives. It nearly cost everything."

11 - 12

Vega's eyes flickered with a mix of shame and determination. "I do," he said quietly, meeting Drake's intense gaze. "I'll do whatever it takes to make things right."

Drake's fists clenched at his sides, his knuckles white with tension. He wanted to believe Vega, but trust was a luxury he couldn't afford right now. "Let's move," he growled, turning towards the exit.

As they raced towards the amusement park, Drake's mind churned with memories and possibilities. The weight of his gun pressed against his side, a cold reminder of what might await them. Holly's steady presence beside him was both comforting and concerning – he couldn't bear the thought of losing anyone else.

"What's the plan when we get there?" Holly asked, her voice cutting through his thoughts.

Drake's jaw tightened. "We find Gabriel," he replied grimly. "And we end this, one way or another."

Meanwhile, across town in her sterile laboratory, Dr. Rachel Summers bent over her microscope, her brow furrowed in concentration. The vial of the virus sat ominously nearby, its contents potentially holding the key to saving – or destroying – countless lives across the multiverse.

With steady hands, Dr. Summers carefully extracted a sample of the virus, her heart racing with a mix of scientific curiosity and trepidation. As she placed it under the microscope, she couldn't help but marvel at the complexity of the pathogen that had brought so much devastation.

"Now," she murmured to herself, "let's see what Justin's blood can do."

13 - 14

The abandoned amusement park loomed before them, a twisted silhouette against the darkening sky. Drake's heart pounded as he and Holly approached the rusted gates, their footsteps echoing in the eerie silence.

"I never thought I'd be back here," Drake muttered, his eyes scanning the desolate landscape. The once-cheerful carnival rides now stood as grotesque monuments to happier times.

Holly's hand instinctively moved to her holster. "Stay alert. Gabriel could be anywhere."

As they stepped onto the main pathway, Drake's mind raced. How many realities had been torn apart by Gabriel's machinations? How many versions of himself had suffered losses he couldn't even imagine?

"Look," Holly whispered, pointing to a flicker of movement near the dilapidated carousel.

Drake nodded, his body tensing. "We'll approach from opposite sides. Be careful, Holly. This ends tonight, but not at the cost of more lives."

As they split up, Drake couldn't shake the feeling that they were walking into a trap. The shadows seemed to dance around him, every creaking board and rustling leaf setting his nerves on edge.

"I hope you're ready for the ride of your life, Drake," Gabriel's voice suddenly echoed through hidden speakers, chilling Drake to his core.

15 - 16

Drake's gaze snapped to the funhouse, its once-vibrant facade now a faded, peeling nightmare. The garish clown face that had once welcomed laughing families now leered at him with malevolent intent. His breath caught in his throat as memories flooded back, vivid and painful.

The crack of gunshots. His own desperate voice calling out for his son. The searing pain as a bullet tore through his flesh. The world spinning as he fell, darkness closing in...

Drake's fists clenched at his sides, his jaw tight as he fought to push the memories away. But the echoes of that night refused to fade, the phantom sounds of chaos and terror ringing in his ears.

A gentle touch on his shoulder startled him back to the present. Holly stood beside him, her eyes filled with concern. "Are you okay?" she asked softly, her voice barely above a whisper.

Drake swallowed hard, forcing himself to meet her gaze. "I... it's just..." He struggled to find the words, his usual eloquence deserting him.

Holly's grip on his shoulder tightened slightly. "We don't have to go in there if you're not ready," she offered, her tone understanding but firm.

Drake shook his head, steeling himself. "No, we have to end this. Gabriel's in there, I can feel it. I won't let my past hold me back from saving our future."

As they approached the funhouse entrance, Drake's mind raced. How many more lives would be destroyed if they failed? How many realities would crumble? The weight of their mission pressed down on him, but Holly's presence at his side gave him strength.

"Whatever happens in there," Drake said, his voice low and determined, "we face it together."

Holly nodded, her hand moving to her weapon. "Together," she echoed, as they stepped into the shadows of the funhouse.

17 - 18

Drake's fingers ghosted over the cold metal of the rusted gate as he pushed it open, the eerie creak echoing through the desolate amusement park. His heart thundered in his chest, each beat a reminder of the stakes at hand.

"It's too quiet," Holly whispered, her eyes darting from shadow to shadow. "Gabriel could be anywhere."

Drake nodded, his jaw clenched tight. "He wants us to find him. This is all part of his game."

As they made their way down the cracked and overgrown path, Drake's mind raced with possibilities. What if Gabriel had already succeeded in his plan? What if they were too late?

"Holly," he murmured, his voice barely audible, "if something happens to me in there—"

"Don't," she cut him off sharply. "We're both walking out of here, Drake. We have to."

He met her gaze, seeing the fierce determination that mirrored his own. "You're right," he agreed, forcing a grim smile. "We've come too far to fail now."

The looming silhouette of the funhouse grew closer, its once-cheerful facade now a grotesque mockery of joy. Drake's steps faltered for a moment as memories threatened to overwhelm him again.

"Focus on why we're here," Holly reminded him gently. "For your family, for all the realities at stake."

Drake nodded, drawing strength from her words. "For everything and everyone we're fighting to protect," he affirmed, his resolve hardening.

With a shared look of determination, they stepped through the entrance, the darkness of the funhouse swallowing them whole. Whatever lay ahead, they would face it together, united in their mission to stop Gabriel and save the multiverse from collapse.

19 - 20

The funhouse interior assaulted Drake's senses with a nauseating mix of stale popcorn and mildew. Distorted mirrors lined the narrow corridor, their warped reflections mimicking the twisted reality they now faced. As they rounded a corner, a gasp caught in Drake's throat.

"Meghan," he whispered, his heart pounding.

There she was, Meghan Johnson, bound to a weathered carnival chair. Her eyes, wide with terror, locked onto them as she struggled against her restraints.

Holly's voice was low and urgent. "I'll untie her. Watch our backs."

Drake nodded, scanning the shadows as Holly knelt beside Meghan. His fingers twitched, longing for a weapon. "It's okay, Meghan. We're here to help," he assured, trying to keep his voice steady.

As Holly worked on the knots, Drake's mind raced. This was too easy. Where was Gabriel? Why would he leave Meghan unguarded?

A creak echoed through the room, and Drake whirled around. His breath caught as a figure emerged from the darkness.

"Gabriel," Drake snarled, his fists clenching involuntarily.

The man's disfigured face twisted into a cruel smile. "Drake Miller. How kind of you to join our little party."

Drake's fury bubbled to the surface. This was the man responsible for so much pain, so much loss. He took a step forward, every muscle in his body tense.

"Why, Gabriel?" he demanded, his voice raw with emotion. "Why all of this?"

Gabriel's laugh was hollow, devoid of mirth. "Oh, Drake. You still don't see the bigger picture, do you?"

Drake's mind raced, trying to piece together Gabriel's cryptic words with everything they'd learned. What was he missing?

21 - 22

Drake's retort died in his throat as the dim light of the funhouse glinted off cold metal. Gabriel's hand emerged from the shadows, a gun firmly in his grasp. Drake's muscles coiled, every instinct screaming at him to lunge forward and disarm the threat. But he held back, acutely aware of Holly and Meghan behind him.

"One wrong move, Drake," Gabriel warned, his voice a silky whisper, "and this ends badly for everyone."

Drake's mind raced, calculating options. His voice came out measured, buying time. "You won't get away with this, Gabriel. Whatever you're planning, we'll stop you."

Gabriel's scarred face twisted into a sneer. "You don't even know what 'this' is, Drake. You're fumbling in the dark, as always."

A flicker of movement caught Drake's eye. Holly had silently risen, her own weapon drawn. Her voice cut through the tension, steady and determined.

"Drop the gun, Gabriel. It's over."

The funhouse fell deathly quiet. Drake's heart pounded in his ears as he watched Gabriel's finger tighten on the trigger. Time seemed to slow.

This is it, Drake thought. *One of us isn't walking out of here.*

The crack of a gunshot shattered the silence, echoing through the hollow chamber. Drake flinched, waiting for pain that didn't come.

Gabriel's eyes widened in shock, his scarred face contorting as the bullet found its mark. He staggered backward, the gun slipping from his grasp as he clutched his shoulder. His legs buckled, and he crumpled to the ground, body convulsing in agony.

Drake's breath caught in his throat. *Is it over?* he wondered, watching Gabriel's form go still.

"Holly, cover me," Drake commanded, his voice tight with urgency. He rushed to Meghan's side, fingers working frantically at her bonds. "It's okay, Meghan. We're getting you out of here."

Meghan's muffled whimpers tore at Drake's heart as he struggled with the knots. *Come on, come on,* he urged himself, acutely aware of every second ticking by.

A sudden movement caught his eye. Gabriel stirred, his hand inching towards the fallen gun.

"Drake!" Holly's warning came too late.

Gabriel's fingers closed around the weapon, his voice a raspy growl. "This time you'll stay dead."

Time slowed to a crawl. Drake saw Gabriel's finger tighten on the trigger, saw the muzzle flash. But the impact he braced for never came. Instead, a blur of motion crossed his vision, and Holly's cry of pain pierced the air.

"No!" Drake's anguished shout echoed through the funhouse as Holly crumpled before him, her body shielding his own.

25 - 26

Drake's world shattered as he watched Holly collapse. In an instant, he was at her side, his heart pounding with a fear he hadn't felt since the night he lost his family. Blood spread across Holly's chest, staining her shirt a deep crimson.

"No," he whispered, his voice thick with emotion. "Not again." His hands trembled as he pressed them against her wound, desperate to stem the flow of blood.

Holly's eyes, usually so sharp and determined, fluttered weakly. "Drake," she gasped, her voice barely audible. "I couldn't... let him... take you too."

Drake cradled her in his arms, his throat constricting with grief. "Stay with me, Holly. Please." He glanced frantically around the dilapidated funhouse, searching for something, anything that could help. But the abandoned attractions offered no salvation, only mocking shadows of a happier time.

This can't be happening, Drake thought, his mind reeling. *Not Holly. Not after everything we've been through.*

"It's okay," Holly murmured, her breaths coming in shallow gasps. "You... have to stop him. Save... the others."

Drake shook his head vehemently, tears stinging his eyes. "No, I'm not leaving you. We're in this together, remember?" His voice cracked, betraying the fear that gripped his heart.

But it was too late. Holly's eyes began to close, her strength fading rapidly. Drake held her tighter, his world narrowing to this moment, this loss that threatened to consume him once again.

"Holly, stay with me," he pleaded, his voice barely above a whisper. "I can't lose you too."

27 - 28

As Drake clung desperately to Holly, her body began to shimmer, becoming translucent before his eyes. Panic seized him, his heart pounding in his chest.

"No, no, no!" he cried out, his voice echoing through the empty funhouse. "Holly, what's happening?"

Her form flickered, like a faulty hologram. "Drake," she whispered, her voice fading along with her body. "Something's... pulling me away. I can't..."

Drake's mind raced, trying to comprehend the impossible scene unfolding before him. *This isn't real,* he thought frantically. *It can't be.*

"Fight it, Holly!" he urged, his grip tightening on her increasingly insubstantial form. "Stay with me, please!"

But Holly's body continued to fade, becoming more transparent with each passing second. Her eyes, filled with a mixture of fear and resignation, locked onto Drake's.

"Find the truth," she managed to say, her voice barely audible. "Don't let them win."

And then, in a final burst of ethereal light, Holly vanished completely. Drake was left grasping at empty air, his hands covered in her blood – the only tangible proof that she had ever been there.

"Holly!" he screamed, his voice raw with anguish and disbelief. The silence that followed was deafening, broken only by his ragged breathing and the distant, mocking laughter of Gabriel.

Awakening in Color

Nexus – Beyond Space and Time

1 - 2

Holly's eyes fluttered open, a kaleidoscope of shimmering colors dancing across her vision. The soft, ethereal glow that bathed her surroundings was unlike anything she had ever encountered in her years as a detective. Her analytical mind immediately began cataloging details, even as confusion fogged her thoughts.

"Where am I?" she murmured, her voice barely above a whisper. The words seemed to hang in the air, vibrating with an otherworldly resonance.

Pushing herself up, Holly's palms pressed against cold stone. The sudden, grounding sensation sent a jolt through her system, kickstarting her memory. Fragments of recent events began to coalesce—Justin, the Nexus, the end of her earthly existence. It felt like piecing together a surreal jigsaw puzzle.

She took a deep breath, willing her racing heart to slow. Years of facing high-pressure situations as a detective had honed her ability to remain calm, but this... this was beyond anything in her experience.

"Focus, Holly," she instructed herself firmly. "Assess the situation. Find the facts."

Despite the uncertainty that cloaked her like a heavy shroud, an unexpected sense of serenity began to settle over her. It was as if the very essence of this place—the Nexus, she recalled—exuded tranquility.

Holly's eyes scanned her surroundings, taking in the impossible architecture of light and shadow. Colors shifted and merged in patterns that defied logic, yet felt strangely familiar.

"Is this what it's like?" she wondered aloud. "To be beyond time and space?"

The detective in her couldn't help but marvel at the cosmic scale of this mystery. How many worlds converged here? How many lives intersected in this ethereal crossroads?

As her gaze swept across the shifting landscape, Holly felt a deep-seated resolve well up within her. Whatever challenges lay ahead in this new realm, she would face them with the same tenacity and courage that had defined her life on Earth.

"Alright, Nexus," Holly said, her voice gaining strength. "What secrets are you hiding? And more importantly, how do I unravel them?"

With a determined set to her jaw, Holly rose to her feet, ready to embark on the most extraordinary investigation of her existence—one that spanned not just a single reality, but the vast expanse of the multiverse itself.

3 - 4

Just as Holly was about to voice her myriad of questions, a figure materialized before her, cutting through the silence like a beacon in the night. Tall and imposing, yet exuding a sense of warmth and familiarity, it was Justin. Holly's heart skipped a beat as she recognized him, the memories flooding back like a torrent.

The countless conversations, the shared moments of laughter and contemplation—they all coalesced into a single point of clarity. This was not a dream or a figment of her imagination. This was real.

Holly's analytical mind raced, trying to process the impossibility of Justin's sudden appearance. Her instincts, honed by years of detective work, screamed that this defied all logic. Yet, her heart knew the truth.

"Justin?" she whispered, her voice barely above a breath. The name hung in the air, charged with a mixture of disbelief and hope.

Her eyes locked onto his familiar face, searching for answers. How many times had they sat across from each other, unraveling the mysteries of the multiverse? How often had his wisdom guided her through the labyrinth of alternate realities?

Holly's hand instinctively moved to her belt, reaching for a badge that was no longer there. Old habits died hard, even in a realm beyond time and space. She straightened her posture, drawing on the strength that had carried her through countless investigations.

"I have so many questions," she said, her voice stronger now. "But first, tell me—is this really happening? Are we truly in the Nexus?"

5 - 6

Justin's smile deepened, his eyes sparkling with an inner light that seemed to illuminate the ethereal space around them. "Welcome, Holly," he said, his voice resonating with a comforting cadence. "I'm glad to see you awake."

Holly felt a wave of relief wash over her at the sound of his familiar voice. It grounded her, even as the surreal landscape threatened to overwhelm her senses. She took a deep breath, steadying herself.

"It's real then," she murmured, more to herself than to Justin. Her detective's mind was already cataloging details, trying to make sense of the impossible. "But how...?"

She trailed off as her gaze swept across the vast expanse of the Nexus. Colors shifted and danced in patterns that defied logic, creating a mesmerizing kaleidoscope effect. The air hummed with an energy she could almost touch, vibrating with potential.

"It's... beautiful," Holly breathed, awe momentarily overriding her analytical instincts. "And terrifying."

Justin nodded, understanding etched in his features. "The Nexus often has that effect," he said softly.

Holly's eyes narrowed, her investigative nature reasserting itself. "You've been here before, haven't you? You know what this place is."

She took a step forward, her mind racing. The vastness stretched out in all directions, seemingly infinite. A sense of timelessness permeated the air, as if the very concept of hours and minutes had ceased to exist.

"It feels like we're standing on the edge of... everything," Holly mused, a mixture of excitement and apprehension coloring her voice. "Like all the rules I've known my entire life don't apply here."

7 - 8

Holly's detective instincts kicked in, her curiosity overriding her initial awe. She turned to Justin, her eyes narrowing with determination.

"I don't understand," Holly began, her voice tinged with uncertainty. "How did I get here? What is this place?"

As she spoke, she unconsciously shifted into an investigative stance, her body language reflecting years of interrogation experience. Her fingers twitched, longing for a notepad to jot down details.

Justin's smile widened, his eyes sparkling with an inner light that seemed to pulse in rhythm with the ambient glow of the Nexus. "The Nexus is a nexus, a convergence point of infinite possibilities," he explained, his words carrying a weight of wisdom born from eons of existence. "It exists beyond the confines of time and space, a realm where all things intersect and coalesce. You have been brought here for a purpose, Holly, a purpose that only you can fulfill."

Holly's mind raced, attempting to process Justin's words. A convergence point of infinite possibilities? It sounded like something out of a science fiction novel, yet here she was, standing in the midst of it. She closed her eyes briefly, focusing on the cool, smooth surface beneath her feet, using it to ground herself in this surreal reality.

"A purpose," she repeated, her analytical mind already dissecting the implications. "But why me? I'm just a detective from a small city. What could I possibly offer in a place like this?"

As she spoke, Holly's gaze darted around the vast expanse, taking in the ethereal beauty of the Nexus. The air shimmered with potential, and she could almost feel the weight of countless realities pressing in around her. It was exhilarating and terrifying all at once.

9 - 10

Holly's brow furrowed, her detective instincts kicking into high gear as she struggled to piece together this cosmic puzzle. "A purpose?" she echoed, her voice tinged with disbelief. Her eyes darted around the shimmering expanse of the Nexus, searching for answers in its ethereal glow. "What purpose could I possibly serve in a place like this?"

Justin's expression softened, his ancient eyes filled with a warmth that seemed to penetrate Holly's very soul. He took a step closer, his presence radiating a calming energy that contrasted sharply with the swirling chaos of the Nexus around them.

"You are a beacon of hope, Holly," he said, his voice resonating with quiet strength. "In a world beset by darkness and despair, your light shines bright. You have touched the lives of many, guiding them through the darkest of nights."

Holly's mind reeled, flashing back to the countless cases she'd solved, the people she'd helped. But those were just part of her job, weren't they? She'd never considered herself anything more than a dedicated detective doing her duty.

"But I'm just..." she began, her voice faltering.

"More than you realize," Justin interjected gently. "Now, it is time for you to embrace your destiny and become the harbinger of a new dawn."

Holly's heart raced, a mixture of awe and trepidation coursing through her veins. The weight of Justin's words settled on her shoulders, simultaneously thrilling and terrifying. She took a deep breath, steeling herself for whatever lay ahead.

"A new dawn," she whispered, more to herself than to Justin. "But how? What am I supposed to do?"

11 - 12

Holly's heart swelled, a potent mixture of trepidation and resolve coursing through her veins. The ethereal light of the Nexus seemed to pulse in sync with her racing thoughts. She clenched her fists, feeling the weight of destiny pressing down upon her.

"A beacon of hope," she murmured, her voice barely audible over the soft hum of energy surrounding them. "I've always believed in the power of hope, even when things seemed darkest. But this..."

She trailed off, her gaze sweeping across the vast, shimmering expanse of the Nexus. The enormity of what Justin was asking of her threatened to overwhelm her senses.

"It's daunting," Holly admitted, her eyes locking with Justin's. "But if I can truly make a difference, how can I turn away?"

A flicker of pride crossed Justin's face, but before he could respond, a sudden realization hit Holly like a thunderbolt. Her eyes widened, and she felt her heart constrict.

"But what about Drake?" she asked, her voice trembling with uncertainty. The image of the haunted lawyer flashed vividly in her mind – his determination, his pain, the bond they'd forged through shared adversity. "He needs me. I can't just abandon him."

Holly's hand unconsciously reached for the badge she no longer wore, a gesture born from years of grounding herself in moments of doubt. She found herself torn between the cosmic responsibility Justin had laid before her and the very human connection she'd formed with Drake Miller.

13 - 14

Justin's smile never wavered, his eyes holding a depth of understanding that transcended words. "Drake's journey is his own, Holly," he replied, his tone gentle yet resolute. "You have played your part in his story, but now it is time for him to find his own way. Trust in him, as he trusts in you. And remember, you are never truly alone, even in the darkest of times."

Holly's brow furrowed, her detective's mind racing to process Justin's words. She could feel the truth in them, but it didn't make the separation any easier. Her hand clenched at her side, remembering the countless times she and Drake had faced impossible odds together.

"It's just..." she began, her voice catching. "We've been through so much. The Red World, the virus, the hospital explosion. How can I leave him to face all that alone?"

Justin stepped closer, his presence radiating a calming energy that seemed to permeate the very air of the Nexus. "Drake Miller is stronger than you know," he said softly. "Your paths have intertwined for a reason, but they were never meant to run parallel forever."

Holly closed her eyes, letting out a slow breath. When she opened them again, there was a new resolve in her gaze. "You're right," she admitted. "Drake has his own strength, his own purpose. I have to trust in that."

With those words lingering in the air like a promise, Holly felt a sense of peace settle over her like a comforting blanket. The swirling energies of the Nexus seemed to respond, pulsing with a gentler rhythm that matched her newfound calm.

She knew that the road ahead would be fraught with challenges and uncertainty, but she also knew that she was not alone. With Justin by her side and the light of hope guiding her way, she would find the strength to face whatever lay ahead.

"So," Holly said, squaring her shoulders and meeting Justin's gaze with determination, "what's our next move?"

15 - 16

The ethereal light of the Nexus shimmered around Holly, casting dancing shadows across her face as her mind churned with conflicting emotions. Justin's words hung in the air, each syllable resonating with a weight that seemed to press down upon her very soul. She clenched her fists, feeling the enormity of her newfound role settle onto her shoulders like a heavy cloak.

"I understand what you're saying, Justin," Holly said, her voice low and tinged with uncertainty. "But this... this is so much bigger than anything I've ever faced before." She gestured at the vast, otherworldly expanse surrounding them. "I'm just a detective from Bridgewater. How can I possibly be the key to saving multiple realities?"

Justin's eyes held a depth of understanding that seemed to span millennia. "Your experiences have shaped you, Holly. Your tenacity, your empathy, your unwavering sense of justice – these are the qualities that make you uniquely suited for this role."

Holly's gaze dropped to her hands, her mind flashing back to countless crime scenes, late nights poring over case files, the faces of those she'd helped. Yet doubt still gnawed at the edges of her resolve.

"But what if I'm not ready?" she whispered, the words escaping her lips like a fragile prayer. Her eyes, usually so determined, now held a vulnerability rarely seen. "What if I can't live up to the expectations placed upon me?"

17 - 18

Justin's gaze softened, his eyes brimming with compassion as he reached out to gently grasp Holly's hand. The touch was warm, grounding her in the swirling ethereal landscape of the Nexus.

"You are stronger than you realize, Holly," he said, his voice a soothing balm to her troubled mind. "You have faced trials and tribulations that would break lesser souls, yet you have emerged unscathed, your spirit undimmed by the darkness that surrounds you."

Holly's mind flashed to the grueling cases she'd solved, the seemingly insurmountable obstacles she'd overcome. She felt the weight of her badge, a symbol of her unwavering commitment to justice, even if it was worlds away now.

Justin continued, his words resonating with profound certainty. "Trust in yourself, for within you lies the power to change the world."

As he spoke, Holly felt a surge of warmth flood her veins. It was as if his words had unlocked something deep within her, a wellspring of strength she hadn't known she possessed. She straightened her shoulders, lifted her chin.

"You're right," Holly said, her voice growing stronger with each word. "I've never backed down from a challenge before. I'm not about to start now, even if the stakes are higher than I could have ever imagined."

She looked out at the shimmering expanse of the Nexus, its swirling energies a testament to the infinite possibilities that lay before her. For a moment, she allowed herself to feel the full weight of her new role, but instead of crushing her, it fueled her determination.

"So," Holly said, turning back to Justin with a glint of her characteristic tenacity in her eyes, "where do we start?"

19 - 20

Holly's newfound resolve faltered as a pang of guilt pierced her heart. Her gaze dropped, and she bit her lower lip, a habit that always betrayed her inner turmoil.

"But what about Rebekah?" she asked, her voice trembling with unspoken fear. The image of Rebekah's warm smile and gentle eyes flashed through her mind, causing her chest to tighten. "What will become of her if I stay here?"

Holly's hands clenched into fists at her sides, her detective's mind racing through scenarios, desperately seeking a solution that would allow her to fulfill her destiny without abandoning the woman she loved.

Justin's expression softened, his eyes shimmering with understanding as he regarded Holly. The weight of countless lifetimes seemed to settle in the creases around his eyes, a reminder of the vast wisdom he carried.

"Rebekah will always hold a special place in your heart, Holly," he said, his words carrying a depth that seemed to resonate with the very fabric of the Nexus around them. "But you must trust that she will find her own path, just as you have found yours."

Holly's breath caught in her throat. She wanted to argue, to demand a way to ensure Rebekah's safety and happiness. But something in Justin's tone gave her pause.

He continued, "Love transcends time and space, binding souls together across the vast expanse of eternity."

As he spoke, the air around them seemed to shimmer, and for a brief moment, Holly could have sworn she saw fleeting images of herself and Rebekah across different timelines – laughing, embracing, supporting each other through countless challenges.

"You mean..." Holly started, her analytical mind grappling with the implications.

21 - 22

Holly's heart ached as she gazed into the swirling, iridescent mists of the Nexus. Memories of Rebekah's warm smile and gentle touch flooded her senses, threatening to overwhelm her resolve.

"I can't just leave her behind," Holly whispered, her voice thick with emotion. "How can I choose between destiny and love?"

Justin squeezed her hand reassuringly. "Sometimes, Holly, the bravest thing we can do is to trust in the invisible threads that connect us across time and space."

Holly's brow furrowed, her detective's instincts kicking in. "But what if I never see her again? What if she forgets me?"

"The bonds we forge are not so easily broken," Justin replied softly. "Your love for Rebekah will echo through the multiverse, guiding both of your paths even when you're apart."

Taking a deep breath, Holly straightened her shoulders. She'd faced countless dangers as a detective, but this leap of faith required a different kind of courage.

"I hope you're right," she murmured, taking a tentative step forward. The ethereal landscape of the Nexus seemed to respond to her movement, shimmering with newfound intensity.

As they walked, Holly's keen eyes noticed intricate patterns in the mist, like fragments of memories given form. "What are those?" she asked, pointing to a particularly vivid swirl of color.

Justin smiled. "Echoes of your past lives, Holly. The Nexus holds the essence of all possibilities."

Holly's mind reeled at the implications. How many versions of herself existed across the multiverse? Had any of them found a way to balance duty and love?

The air hummed with energy, a symphony of whispers that seemed to caress her very soul. For the first time since arriving in this surreal realm, Holly felt a profound sense of peace settling over her.

"It's beautiful," she breathed, her eyes wide with wonder.

"And you are now a part of it," Justin said, his voice filled with quiet pride. "Ready to shape the destiny of countless worlds."

Holly nodded, her resolve strengthening with each step. Though the ache of separation lingered, she knew that her love for Rebekah would be her anchor in the vast sea of possibilities that lay ahead.

23 - 24

In the distance, a shimmering veil of light beckoned, its radiant glow casting a warm embrace upon the world. Holly's heart quickened, her detective's instincts on high alert despite the serenity surrounding her. Justin's presence beside her was a comforting anchor amidst the swirling currents of uncertainty.

As they approached the luminous gateway, Holly's analytical mind raced. What lay beyond? Was this another piece of the complex puzzle she'd been trying to solve since stumbling into the multiverse? She'd faced down criminals and navigated treacherous situations before, but this... this was beyond anything in her experience.

"Where does it lead?" Holly asked, her voice barely more than a whisper. She gazed upon the shimmering threshold, her posture tense but ready, as if preparing to chase down a lead in one of her cases.

Justin turned to her, his expression serene yet tinged with an otherworldly wisdom. "It's a gateway, Holly. To what, exactly... well, that's part of the journey you're embarking on."

Holly's brow furrowed, her mind already dissecting his cryptic response. "You're not coming with me, are you?" she deduced, a hint of her usual directness creeping into her tone.

Justin shook his head. "This part of the path is yours alone to walk."

Holly took a deep breath, squaring her shoulders. She'd never backed down from a challenge before, and she wasn't about to start now. "Right," she said, more to herself than to Justin. "Into the unknown it is."

25 - 26

Justin's eyes gleamed with an otherworldly light as he continued, his voice resonating with quiet reverence. "To the next stage of your journey, Holly. Beyond this threshold lies a realm of infinite possibility, where time and space converge in a kaleidoscope of ever-shifting realities. It is a place of wonders and mysteries, where the boundaries of existence blur and the threads of fate intertwine."

Holly's heart quickened, her detective's instincts firing on all cylinders. She examined the shimmering portal before her, searching for any clue, any sign of what awaited on the other side. But this was no crime scene, no puzzle she could solve with deductive reasoning alone.

"A realm of infinite possibility," she echoed, her voice a mix of awe and determination. "That's quite the case file to tackle."

As she stood on the precipice of the unknown, Holly felt a familiar thrill course through her veins. It was the same sensation she experienced when piecing together a particularly challenging mystery, that moment when disparate clues suddenly aligned to reveal a hidden truth.

"I've spent my whole life searching for answers," Holly mused, her eyes never leaving the luminous gateway. "Uncovering truths, bringing justice to light. But this... this is something else entirely, isn't it?"

Justin nodded, a knowing smile playing at the corners of his mouth. "Indeed it is, Holly. You stand at the threshold of understanding far beyond the scope of any earthly investigation."

Holly took a deep breath, steeling herself for what lay ahead. Her fingers twitched, muscle memory from years of reaching for her detective's notebook. But she knew that where she was going, conventional methods wouldn't suffice.

"Well," she said, a hint of her characteristic determination creeping into her voice, "I've never been one to leave a mystery unsolved. Whatever truths are waiting out there, I'm ready to face them head-on."

27 - 28

As Holly's resolve crystallized, a pang of sorrow suddenly tugged at her heart, catching her off guard. The thrill of the unknown momentarily gave way to a wave of melancholy as faces flashed through her mind—Rebekah's warm smile, Drake's determined gaze, and countless others whose lives had intertwined with hers.

"Rebekah," she whispered, her voice barely audible. Her fingers instinctively reached for the locket around her neck, a gift from her partner on their last anniversary. "I didn't even get to say goodbye."

Holly's thoughts drifted to Drake, the tenacious lawyer whose path had crossed hers in ways she never could have anticipated. She remembered the fierce determination in his eyes as they worked together, unraveling the threads of a mystery that spanned across realities.

"And Drake," she murmured, her brow furrowing. "He's still out there, searching for answers. Will he ever understand what happened to me?"

The weight of her impending departure settled heavily on her shoulders. Holly turned to Justin, her eyes glistening with unshed tears. "Will they ever know what became of me?" she asked, her voice tinged with longing and a hint of fear. The question hung in the air, a testament to the bonds she was leaving behind and the uncertainty of what lay ahead.

29 - 30

Justin's hand settled on Holly's shoulder, warm and reassuring. The touch seemed to radiate a calming energy, easing the tension in her muscles. His eyes, filled with ancient wisdom, met hers with unwavering compassion.

"They will remember you, Holly," he said, his voice gentle yet firm. The words resonated in the ethereal space around them, carrying a weight of truth that Holly felt in her very core. "In their hearts, you will always be a beacon of light, guiding them through the darkness."

Holly's fingers tightened around the locket, drawing strength from the memory it held. She could almost hear Rebekah's laughter, see the sparkle in her eyes. "But will they understand?" she whispered, her voice catching.

Justin's expression softened. "Though they may never fully grasp the depths of your sacrifice, they will carry your memory with them. Your love, your courage—these are the legacies you leave behind. A testament to the power of the human spirit in the face of adversity."

Holly closed her eyes, letting Justin's words wash over her. In her mind, she saw Rebekah solving cases, Drake fighting for justice—both of them carrying a piece of her with them. A small smile tugged at her lips.

"You're right," she said, her voice growing stronger. "They'll keep fighting, just as I must."

With a deep breath, Holly squared her shoulders and faced the shimmering threshold before her. The ethereal light pulsed, as if beckoning her forward. She felt a surge of determination, mingled with a flutter of excitement in her stomach.

"Whatever's waiting for me on the other side," Holly said, her voice steady, "I'm ready to face it." She glanced at Justin, gratitude shining in her eyes. "Thank you for being here, for helping me understand."

Justin nodded, a proud smile playing on his lips. "You were always destined for greatness, Holly. Now, it's time to embrace it."

Holly closed her eyes, took one final, centering breath, and stepped forward. As the light enveloped her, she felt weightless, buoyed by hope and the strength of her convictions. Whatever trials lay ahead, she would meet them head-on, carrying with her the love of those she left behind and the unwavering support of those who believed in her.

31 - 31

The shimmering light engulfed Holly, its warmth seeping into her very being. As she vanished into its radiant embrace, a profound sense of peace washed over her. The Nexus dissolved around her, replaced by a kaleidoscope of swirling colors and fractured realities.

"This is... incredible," Holly whispered, her voice filled with awe.

She found herself suspended in a vast expanse, surrounded by shimmering threads of possibility. Each strand pulsed with potential futures, echoing with whispers of lives unlived. Holly reached out, her fingers brushing against a nearby thread. Instantly, a flood of images cascaded through her mind—glimpses of alternate realities, paths not taken.

As she floated in this sea of infinite possibilities, Holly's thoughts turned to those she'd left behind. "I hope they understand," she murmured, a tinge of melancholy in her voice. "That this is bigger than any of us."

Suddenly, a familiar presence materialized beside her. Justin's ethereal form shimmered into view, his smile reassuring.

"They will, in time," he said gently. "Your journey is just beginning, Holly. Are you ready to embrace your destiny?"

Holly took a deep breath, steeling herself. The enormity of what lay ahead was daunting, but she felt a surge of determination coursing through her veins. This was her purpose, her calling.

"I am," she replied, her voice firm and resolute. "Whatever challenges await, I'll face them. For Rebekah, for Drake, for all the worlds that need protecting."

As she spoke these words, Holly felt a shift within herself. The doubts and fears that had plagued her began to dissipate, replaced by an unwavering sense of purpose. She was no longer just Holly—she was a beacon of hope, a guardian of the multiverse.

"Then let us begin," Justin said, extending his hand. "There's much to learn, and countless worlds that need your light."

Holly nodded, taking his hand. As they moved forward through the cosmic tapestry, she couldn't help but marvel at the beauty and complexity of existence unfolding around her. Whatever destiny had in store, she was ready to embrace it, armed with love, courage, and an unshakable determination to make a difference across the vast expanse of the multiverse.

Nexus of Torment

The Nexus of Torment – Beyond Space and Time

1 - 2

As I step into the abyss of the Nexus of Torment, a bolt of lightning sears across the roiling sky, illuminating the nightmarish landscape before me. The crackling energy in the air raises the hair on my arms, a stark reminder that I've entered a realm beyond mortal comprehension.

"Welcome to your reckoning," a voice echoes from everywhere and nowhere, disfigured faces flashing in my mind.

I scan the horizon, searching for any sign of the enigmatic manipulator. "Show yourself, Lucian! I didn't come all this way to play hide and seek."

My words are swallowed by the swirling darkness above, the clouds merging and separating like a living, breathing entity. Another flash of lightning reveals strange, twisted structures in the distance – monuments to chaos and destruction.

As I take a tentative step forward, the ground beneath my feet crunches and shifts. I look down to see shards of what appear to be broken realities – fragments of worlds long destroyed. A chill runs down my spine as I contemplate the immensity of my plan.

"Do you truly comprehend what you've stumbled into?" Lucian's disembodied voice taunts me. "This is the culmination of years of meticulous planning across multiple realities."

I grit my teeth, fighting back the wave of nausea induced by the sickly-sweet stench of decay that permeates the air. "I understand enough to know that you need to be stopped," I retort, my voice steady despite the fear gnawing at my insides.

A low chuckle reverberates through the desolate wasteland. "Stop me? You can barely navigate this realm. How do you expect to challenge someone who has mastered it?"

I clench my fists, determination surging through me. Lucian may have the home-field advantage, but I've come too far to back down now. The fate of countless realities hangs in the balance, and I'm the only one standing between Lucian and his twisted ambitions.

"I'll find a way," I mutter, more to myself than to the dark prince "I always do."

As I trudge forward, the oppressive atmosphere seems to press down on me, a constant reminder of the impossible odds I face. But with each step, I steel my resolve. He may be a master manipulator, but I've got a few tricks up my sleeve too. And in this realm of infinite possibilities, anything can happen.

3 - 4

The jagged horizon looms before me, a twisted silhouette against the roiling sky. Each step sends shockwaves of agony through my body, the gunshot wound in my shoulder a constant, throbbing reminder of how close I came to death. Blood seeps through my fingers as I press my hand against the injury, staining my clothes a deeper crimson.

"Keep moving, Gabe," I mutter through gritted teeth, my detective's instincts kicking in despite the surreal surroundings. "One foot in front of the other."

As I press on, the landscape shifts and warps, defying logic and reason. Strange, chittering noises echo from the shadows, setting my nerves on edge. Suddenly, a grotesque creature emerges from behind a twisted spire of rock. Its body is a nightmarish fusion of insect and reptile, with too many limbs and eyes that glow with an otherworldly hunger.

"What in God's name?" I gasp, stumbling backward.

The creature lunges, its mandibles clicking furiously. I dodge, my wound screaming in protest as I roll across the cracked ground.

"Gabriel" my own voice cuts through the chaos. "Remember, this realm responds to thought and emotion. Your fear gives these entities power!"

I take a deep breath, forcing myself to focus. "Right," I call back, my voice steadier than I feel. "Mind over matter, even in this hellscape."

As I concentrate, visualizing a barrier between myself and the creature, it recoils, shrieking in frustration. The sound sends shivers down my spine, but I stand my ground.

"Is this what you had in mind when you talked about expanding our understanding of reality, Dr. Summers?" I ask, a hint of gallows humor in my voice.

Dr. Summer's response is tinged with both awe and trepidation. "I never imagined... the implications are staggering. We're witnessing the convergence of countless realities."

As we speak, more bizarre entities emerge from the twisted landscape. Some resemble distorted versions of familiar animals, while others defy description entirely. Their eyes burn with an insatiable hunger that chills me to the core.

"Stay close," I warn, my instincts to protect kicking in despite my own fear. "We need to find a way out of this nightmare."

5 - 6

The ground beneath my feet begins to undulate, rippling like waves on a stormy sea. I stumble, reaching out to steady myself against a nearby rock formation, only to watch in horror as it melts and twists into a grotesque sculpture of screaming faces.

"Dr. Summers!" I shout, my voice distorting as if underwater. "What's happening?"

The physicist's response comes from everywhere and nowhere at once. "The fabric of reality... it's destabilizing! The Nexus is reacting to your presence!"

I feel a sudden, violent tug at the core of my being. My vision blurs, colors bleeding into one another like a kaleidoscope gone mad. The pain in my shoulder intensifies, spreading through my body as if my very atoms are being torn apart.

"Focus, Gabriel!" Dr. Summer's voice cuts through the cacophony. "Remember who you are, why you're here!"

Gritting my teeth, I force myself to concentrate. "I don't know who I was before I became Gabriel" I mutter, clinging to my identity like a lifeline. "I'm here to set things right, to fix what was broken."

As I speak, memories flood my mind – the betrayal, the gunshot, the desperate journey through realities. Each recollection sends a jolt of determination through me, anchoring me against the chaotic storm.

"That's it!" Dr. Summers encourages. "Your will is stronger than this realm's chaos. Use it!"

I take a shuddering breath, pushing back against the forces threatening to tear me apart. "I won't let this place beat me," I growl, more to myself than anyone else. "There's too much at stake."

Slowly, agonizingly, the world around me begins to stabilize. The swirling colors coalesce into recognizable shapes, though still warped and alien. I can feel my body again, solid and whole despite the pain.

"Doctor," I call out, my voice hoarse. "Are you okay?"

There's a moment of silence before she responds, sounding shaken but alive. "I'm here, son. Your resilience is... remarkable."

I allow myself a grim smile. "Stubbornness has its uses. Now, let's find that key before this place decides to rearrange reality again."

With renewed determination, I press forward into the heart of the Nexus of torment, each step a defiance against the chaos surrounding us. Whatever trials lie ahead, I'm ready to face them. The path to redemption was never going to be easy, but I've come too far to turn back now.

7 - 8

As I venture deeper into the twisted depths of the Nexus, a chill runs down my spine. The air grows thick, oppressive, as if reality itself is congealing around me. Suddenly, a figure materializes from the shadows, his presence radiating malevolence.

"Welcome, Angel" the figure purrs, his crimson eyes boring into mine. "I've been expecting you."

I freeze, recognizing the entity before me. "Lucien," I breathe, my heart pounding.

He spreads his arms wide, a mockery of hospitality. "You've come so far, struggled so valiantly. And for what? To die alone in this forsaken realm?"

I clench my fists, steeling myself against his words. "I'm here for answers, Lucien. And justice."

A chilling laugh escapes his lips. "Justice? Oh, my dear boy, how naive you remain. Here, in the Nexus, I am judge, jury, and executioner. But perhaps... we can come to an arrangement."

His voice slithers around me, thick with promise. "Imagine the power you could wield, the wrongs you could right. All you need do is pledge your allegiance to me."

For a moment, I'm tempted. The weight of my past mistakes, the exhaustion of this journey – it all threatens to overwhelm me. But then I remember why I'm here, what's at stake.

"No," I declare, my voice stronger than I feel. "Your promises are poison, Lucien. I won't be another pawn in your game."

His eyes narrow, the crimson glow intensifying. "Then you've chosen your fate, kid. A pity. You could have been so much more."

As Lucien's words hang in the air, I brace myself for whatever comes next, knowing that the true battle for my soul – and for the fate of reality itself – has only just begun.

9 - 10

As Lucien steps closer, his form gradually materializes from the shadows. My breath catches in my throat as I finally get a clear view of this malevolent entity. His features, though shrouded, bear an unsettling resemblance to humanity – a cruel parody of the mortal form that sends an involuntary shiver down my spine.

"You think you're so righteous, don't you?" Lucien's voice drips with contempt. "But we're not so different, you and I."

I grit my teeth, fighting the urge to back away. "We're nothing alike."

A twisted grin spreads across his face, revealing rows of gleaming, razor-sharp teeth. "Oh, but we are. We both seek power, control. The only difference is, I embrace my nature."

As he draws nearer, I can see the hunger in his eyes – a primal, all-consuming desire to dominate and destroy. It's terrifying, yet somehow magnetic. I find myself transfixed, unable to look away.

"You've tasted power before," Lucien continues, his words a seductive whisper. "When you betrayed Justin. Tell me, didn't it feel exhilarating?"

The memory of that betrayal burns within me, a mix of shame and lingering excitement. I push the feeling down, desperate to maintain my resolve.

"That was different," I insist, more to myself than to him. "I was misguided, manipulated. I won't make that mistake again."

Lucien's laughter echoes through the twisted landscape of the Nexus. "Misguided? Perhaps. But the potential for greatness still lies within you. Why fight it?"

11 - 12

I clench my fists, steeling myself against the wave of temptation washing over me. Lucien's words are like poison, seeping into my mind, threatening to erode my resolve.

"No," I growl, meeting his gaze with defiance. "I've seen where that path leads. I won't be your pawn again."

Lucien's eyes narrow, a flicker of irritation crossing his features. "Such wasted potential," he hisses, circling me like a predator. "You could reshape realities, bend the very fabric of the multiverse to your will."

My heart races, a mix of fear and something dangerously close to excitement. I force myself to focus on the desolate landscape around us, a stark reminder of the consequences of unchecked power.

"At what cost?" I challenge, my voice stronger than I feel. "Look at this place, Lucien. Is this your idea of greatness?"

He stops, tilting his head in a mockery of consideration. "This?" he gestures to the twisted realm. "This is merely a canvas, waiting for a true artist to shape it."

I shake my head, fighting the allure of his words. "You're insane."

"Am I?" Lucien's voice drops to a whisper. "Or am I the only one who truly sees?"

As I stare into his eyes, I'm struck by an unsettling realization. Behind the malevolence, there's something... familiar. A reflection of my own ambition, twisted and magnified to horrifying proportions.

"What are you?" I ask, unable to mask the tremor in my voice.

Lucien's grin widens, a chilling sight. "I am what you could become," he says. "What you fear... and what you desire."

13 - 14

The air crackles with tension as Lucien's words hang between us. My mind races, grappling with the implications of his statement. I swallow hard, tasting the acrid remnants of my own bitter choices.

"You speak of potential," I say, my voice hoarse. "But you know nothing of the price I've already paid."

Lucien's eyes gleam with dark interest. "Oh? Do enlighten me, my ambitious friend."

I clench my fists, memories flooding back with painful clarity. "It was supposed to be simple," I begin, the words spilling out like poison. "A betrayal, yes, but one that would secure my place in the grand scheme of things."

As I speak, the desolate landscape of the Nexus seems to blur, giving way to vivid flashes of that fateful day. Justin's trusting face, the weight of my decision, the sickening twist in my gut as I made my choice.

"I did as I was asked," I admit bitterly, my voice tinged with resentment. "I handed Justin over to you, just as you commanded. But instead of receiving the reward I was promised, I was cast aside, banished to the past like some forgotten relic."

Lucien's laughter, a sound like breaking glass, echoes across the twisted realm. "And you expected what, exactly? A seat at the table of gods?"

I glare at him, anger flaring hot in my chest. "I expected justice! Recognition for my sacrifice!"

"Sacrifice?" Lucien sneers, his form seeming to grow larger, more imposing. "You sacrificed nothing but your integrity, and even that was given up eagerly enough."

His words cut deep, but I refuse to show how much they affect me. Instead, I focus on the rage building within me, using it as a shield against the crushing weight of my guilt.

"You used me," I spit out, taking a step towards him. "You manipulated me, dangled power in front of me like a carrot, only to snatch it away at the last moment."

Lucien's eyes narrow, a dangerous glint in their depths. "I offered you opportunity. It's not my fault you lacked the vision to seize it properly."

As we face off, the very fabric of the Nexus seems to pulse around us, responding to the intensity of our confrontation. I can feel the weight of my choices pressing down on me, but also a growing resolve. I may have made mistakes, but I refuse to be a pawn any longer.

"No more games, Lucien," I declare, my voice steady despite the turmoil within. "I'm done being your puppet. Whatever comes next, I choose my own path."

15 - 16

Lucien's twisted grin widens at my declaration, a cruel mockery of amusement dancing in his eyes. The scars on his disfigured face seem to writhe in the pulsing, ethereal light of the Nexus.

"Ah, yes," he muses, his voice dripping with malice. "I remember it well. You were so eager to please, so willing to do whatever it took to gain my favor. And yet, when the time came for your reward, you were left with nothing but betrayal and disappointment."

His words slice through me like shards of ice, reopening old wounds I had long sought to bury. I clench my fists, fighting to maintain my composure as memories of that fateful day flood my mind.

"You promised me power," I growl, my voice trembling with suppressed rage. "You said I would rule by your side!"

Lucien's laughter echoes through the surreal landscape, a chilling sound that sends shivers down my spine. "And you believed me? How delightfully naive."

I take a step back, my mind reeling. The charged atmosphere of the Nexus seems to intensify, mirroring the storm of emotions within me.

"The memory of that betrayal still haunts me," I admit, more to myself than to Lucien. "It's a constant reminder of the price I paid for my ambition."

As the words leave my lips, I realize the truth in them. But even as I dwell on the past, a part of me rebels against the crushing weight of regret.

"No," I say, straightening my spine and meeting Lucien's gaze. "Dwelling on regrets won't change my fate. I can't undo what's been done, but I can shape what comes next."

Lucien's eyes narrow, a flicker of something - surprise, perhaps? - crossing his face before it's quickly masked by his usual malevolent smirk.

17 - 18

I swallow hard, the bitter taste of my own failures lingering on my tongue. The air around us crackles with an unseen energy, the very fabric of reality seeming to warp and twist in response to our exchange.

"I thought I was destined for greatness," I confess, my voice laced with bitterness. My fingers brush against the rough fabric of my tattered clothing, a stark reminder of how far I've fallen. "I thought that by betraying Justin, I would secure my place at your side. But instead, I found myself cast adrift in a world that had no use for me. All I wanted was her love, and you promised me that."

As the words leave my lips, I can feel the weight of my choices pressing down on me, threatening to crush what little resolve I have left. The ghostly whisper of Justin's betrayed voice echoes in my mind, a constant reminder of my treachery.

Lucien's laughter suddenly pierces the air, a chilling sound that sends shivers down my spine. It reverberates through the vast emptiness of the Nexus, seeming to mock me from every direction. I instinctively tense, my body coiling like a spring ready to snap.

"Destined for greatness, you say?" he scoffs, his crimson eyes gleaming with cruel amusement. "Perhaps in another life. But here, in the Nexus of Torment, there is no room for ambition or aspiration. Here, only the strongest survive, and the weak are cast aside like so much refuse."

I feel my jaw clench, a surge of defiance rising within me despite the hopelessness of my situation. The faint hum of the Nexus seems to intensify, as if responding to the tension between us.

19 - 19

My fists clench at my sides, nails digging into my palms as I meet Lucien's malevolent gaze. The air around us crackles with an unseen energy, mirroring the storm of emotions raging within me.

"You're wrong," I snarl, my voice low and dangerous. "I am not weak, and I refuse to be discarded."

Lucien's eyebrow arches, a mixture of amusement and curiosity playing across his shadowy features. "Oh? And what makes you think you have any say in the matter?"

I take a step forward, ignoring the searing pain in my shoulder. "Because I've lost everything once before, and I clawed my way back. I won't let it happen again."

The memory of my wife flashes through my mind, her face a bittersweet reminder of all I've lost and all I'm fighting for. I feel a surge of determination course through my veins, drowning out the despair that had threatened to consume me.

"I may have made mistakes," I continue, my voice gaining strength, "but I'm not finished yet. This realm, these trials – they're just another courtroom, another case to win. And I've never lost a case I truly believed in."

Echoes in the Dark

1 - 2

Drake's footsteps echoed hollowly against the sterile corridors of the research facility, each step a leaden weight. The harsh fluorescent lights cast an eerie glow on the faces of his companions, their shadows stretching long and dark behind them. He could feel their eyes on him, probing, questioning, but he kept his gaze fixed ahead, unable to meet their concerned looks.

The silence was deafening, broken only by the rhythmic sound of their footfalls and the distant hum of machinery. Drake's mind raced, replaying the events that had led them to this moment. The weight of Holly's sacrifice pressed down on him, threatening to crush his resolve.

As they turned a corner, the familiar sight of the lab where their journey had begun came into view. Drake paused, his hand hovering over the keypad. He drew in a deep breath, steeling himself for what lay ahead.

"Dad?" Harrison's voice cut through the silence, laced with concern. "What's wrong? You look... different."

Drake's shoulders tensed, his son's perceptiveness both a comfort and a curse. He turned slowly, forcing himself to meet Harrison's gaze. The young man's eyes, so like his own, were filled with a mixture of worry and determination.

"I..." Drake began, his voice hoarse. He cleared his throat, buying time as he searched for the right words. How could he explain the enormity of what had transpired? The loss that threatened to tear him apart?

Harrison took a step closer, his brow furrowed. "Did something happen? Where's Holly?"

The name sent a jolt of pain through Drake's chest. He closed his eyes briefly, willing himself to maintain composure. When he opened them again, he saw the fear beginning to dawn on Harrison's face.

"There's been a... complication," Drake said, his lawyer's instinct for understatement kicking in despite the gravity of the situation. He glanced at the others, their expressions a mix of confusion and dread. "We should discuss this inside. There's a lot we need to go over."

As Drake turned back to the keypad, entering the access code with trembling fingers, he felt the weight of responsibility settling on his shoulders. How could he lead them forward when he felt so lost himself? The door slid open with a soft hiss, revealing the lab beyond – a stark reminder of how far they'd come and how much they'd lost along the way.

3 - 4

Drake's gaze flickered briefly to his son, his expression haunted by the memory of recent events. "It's... complicated," he replied quietly, his words heavy with emotion. The sterile white walls of the facility seemed to close in around him, amplifying the weight of his unspoken grief.

He swallowed hard, his throat constricting as he struggled to find the right words. How could he possibly explain the enormity of what had transpired? The sacrifice that had been made? Drake's mind raced, recalling the piercing light, the deafening silence that followed, and the gut-wrenching realization that Holly was gone.

Meghan, walking beside him, reached out a hand to squeeze his reassuringly. "Mr. Miller, you can tell them. We're all in this together," she urged, her voice soft but firm. Her touch anchored him, pulling him back from the edge of despair.

Drake took a deep breath, his lawyer's instincts kicking in as he organized his thoughts. "What happened... it's beyond anything we've encountered before," he began, his voice low and controlled. "We're dealing with forces that defy our understanding of reality itself."

As they walked, the rhythmic hum of the facility's machinery provided a stark contrast to the turmoil in Drake's mind. He glanced at the worried faces around him, feeling the weight of their expectations. How could he lead them through this when he felt so lost himself?

"Dad," Harrison pressed, his voice tinged with impatience and fear, "what aren't you telling us?"

Drake's steps faltered for a moment. He turned to face the group, his eyes meeting each of theirs in turn. "We've suffered a loss," he admitted, the words tasting bitter on his tongue. "But we've also gained crucial information. We need to regroup and strategize our next move carefully."

5 - 6

Drake drew in a deep breath, the sterile air of the facility doing little to calm his frayed nerves. His fingers tightened around the Ancient Codex he carried, its weathered leather a stark reminder of the weight of their mission.

"It's Holly," he began, his voice catching in his throat. The name hung in the air, heavy with unspoken grief. "She... she sacrificed herself to save me from Gabriel."

The words seemed to echo off the metallic walls, each repetition hammering home the cruel reality. Drake's mind raced, replaying the moment in vivid detail - Holly's determined face, the flash of otherworldly energy, and then... nothing.

A collective gasp rippled through the group. Drake watched as shock and disbelief washed over their faces, mirroring the turmoil he felt inside. Harrison's eyes widened, his young features contorting as he struggled to process the information.

"But... where is she now?" Harrison demanded, his voice rising with desperation. "What happened to Gabriel?" The questions tumbled out, each one laced with a mix of fear and confusion that tore at Drake's heart.

Drake's gaze met his son's, seeing not just the scared teenager before him, but the child he'd sworn to protect. How could he explain the inexplicable? The image of Holly vanishing into thin air played on repeat in his mind, a cruel reminder of their vulnerability in this multiversal chess game.

"I don't know, son," Drake admitted, the words tasting like ash in his mouth. "One moment they were there, and the next..." He trailed off, unable to voice the finality of what he'd witnessed.

7 - 8

Drake's gaze fell to the floor, unable to bear the weight of their questioning stares. The sterile white tiles blurred as he fought back tears, his voice barely audible as he continued, "They... they vanished. One moment they were there, and the next... they were gone."

The words hung in the air, heavy and oppressive. Drake's throat constricted, choking back the guilt that threatened to overwhelm him. He should have done more, should have been faster, smarter. Holly's face flashed in his mind - her determined expression moments before she...

A hand squeezed his shoulder, startling him from his spiraling thoughts. Meghan's touch was gentle but firm, grounding him in the present. "It's not your fault, Drake," she murmured, her voice thick with emotion.

He wanted to believe her, but the weight of responsibility pressed down on him. "I should have-" Drake began, but the words died on his lips as he looked up, finally meeting the eyes of his companions.

Instead of accusation, he saw shared grief and resolve etched on their faces. Harrison's jaw was set, tears glistening in his eyes but refusing to fall. "We'll find her, Dad," he said, his young voice steady with determination. "We have to."

The distant hum of machinery filled the silence that followed, punctuated only by Drake's ragged breathing. In that moment, surrounded by the cold, unfeeling technology of the research facility, he felt a spark of warmth ignite within his chest. They were united now, not just by loss, but by an unshakeable resolve to honor Holly's sacrifice and face whatever darkness lay ahead.

"She's gone son, Gabriel shot her in the chest. Theres no coming back from that" Drake managed, straightening his shoulders. "We owe it to Holly to finish what we started." He took a deep breath, steeling himself for the challenges to come. "Whatever it takes, we'll find a way to make this right."

9 - 9

Drake's hand hovered over the facility's exit panel, his fingers trembling slightly. The sterile corridor stretched behind them, a reminder of all they'd endured. He hesitated, his mind racing with the enormity of what lay ahead.

"What if we can't do this?" he whispered, more to himself than the others.

Dr. Summers stepped closer, her presence a comforting anchor. "We can, Drake. We have to."

He nodded, drawing strength from her words. With a determined press, the doors hissed open, revealing a world bathed in an eerie, muted twilight. The air outside felt thick, heavy with unseen possibilities.

Drake took a tentative step forward, his senses on high alert. "Stay close," he instructed, his lawyer's instinct for caution kicking in. "We don't know what we're walking into."

As they moved beyond the threshold, Drake's mind whirled with possibilities. The loss of Holly ached like a physical wound, but beneath the pain, a kernel of hope flickered. If there were multiple realities, perhaps there was still a chance... perhaps but stopping the virus from ever being released they can undo Holly's sacrifice.

"Dad," Harrison's voice cut through his thoughts. "Look."

Drake followed his son's gaze. In the distance, a faint, pulsing light pierced the gloom. It was barely perceptible, but unmistakably there – a beacon in the darkness. Light emitting from the glass vial of Justins blood.

"What do you think it means?" Harrison asked, his voice a mixture of apprehension and curiosity.

Drake squared his shoulders, feeling a surge of determination. "I don't know, son. But I intend to find out." He glanced at each of his companions in turn. "Whatever happens, we face it together. For Holly. For all of us."

With renewed purpose, they set off toward the mysterious light, ready to confront whatever challenges the multiverse might throw their way.

Blood Cure

Red World – 2024

1 - 2

The flickering television bathed the room in an eerie, pulsating glow, casting grotesque shadows across Drake's face as he leaned forward, his eyes locked on the screen. Images of chaos flashed before him: burning buildings, abandoned streets littered with debris, crowds of panicked people fleeing in terror. The familiar cityscape of the Red World had transformed into a nightmarish wasteland.

Drake's jaw clenched, his attorney's mind racing to process the unfolding catastrophe. He could almost taste the acrid smoke, hear the distant screams echoing through the desolate streets. This was no courtroom drama; this was the collapse of civilization itself.

"My God," he whispered, his voice barely audible over the frantic reports of news anchors struggling to maintain composure. "It's spreading faster than we thought."

Drake's companions sat in stunned silence, their faces etched with horror. He felt the weight of their shared burden pressing down on him, threatening to crush his resolve. But Drake Miller was not a man who surrendered easily, not in the courtroom and certainly not when the fate of multiple worlds hung in the balance.

His mind raced through possible strategies, analyzing and discarding options with the rapid-fire precision honed by years of legal battles. But this was no mere case to be won or lost; the stakes were infinitely higher.

"We have to do something," Drake declared, his voice cutting through the tension like a knife. He stood, pacing the room with restless energy. "We can't just sit here and watch everything fall apart."

3 - 4

Dr. Rachel Summers leaned forward, her sharp gaze fixed on the chaotic scenes unfolding on the television. The flickering images cast an eerie blue glow across her face, accentuating the deep furrows of concentration etched into her brow.

"Time is of the essence," she agreed, her voice steady despite the palpable tension in the room. Drake marveled at her composure, even as he felt his own heart racing. Dr. Summers' eyes darted between the screen and the ancient codex lying open on the table before her, its weathered pages covered in indecipherable symbols.

Is the key to stopping this madness hidden within those cryptic pages? Drake wondered, his mind reeling with the implications. The weight of responsibility pressed down on him, threatening to crush his resolve.

Before he could voice his thoughts, Dr. Maya Patal stepped forward, her lab coat rustling in the oppressive silence. Her eyes shone with fierce determination as she addressed the group.

"We need to act fast," she insisted, her voice ringing clear above the clamor of the television. "Every moment wasted is another life lost."

Drake nodded, feeling a surge of admiration for Dr. Patal's unwavering focus. He glanced at the others, noting the mix of fear and determination etched on their faces. We're all that stands between humanity and oblivion, he realized, the thought both terrifying and oddly empowering.

"Dr. Patal's right," Drake said, his voice growing stronger with each word. "What's our next move? How do we even begin to tackle something of this magnitude?"

5 - 6

Harrison's jaw tightened, his eyes reflecting a mix of fear and resolve as he met Drake's gaze. The flickering images on the television cast an eerie blue glow across his face, accentuating the determination in his features.

"We can't afford to wait," Harrison declared, his voice tinged with urgency. His fingers curled into fists at his sides, knuckles whitening. "We have to find a way to stop this virus before it's too late."

Drake nodded, feeling a chill run down his spine at Harrison's words. He watched as his son's eyes darted between the ancient codex and the chaos unfolding on the screen, his mind clearly racing with possibilities.

Is this how it ends? Drake wondered, a wave of dread washing over him. The weight of their task seemed insurmountable, yet he knew they had no choice but to try.

"You're right," Drake agreed, his voice low but steady. "his virus is unlike anything we've ever seen before."

As if in response, a particularly harrowing image flashed across the television – a hospital overwhelmed with patients, medical staff collapsing from exhaustion. The sight galvanized the group, a palpable shift in energy coursing through the room.

Drake felt it too, a steely resolve settling over him like armor. He looked around at his companions – Dr. Summers with her brilliant mind, Dr. Patal's unwavering focus, and Harrison's fierce determination. Together, they formed a formidable team.

"We start by pooling our knowledge," Drake said, straightening his shoulders. "Every piece of information, every theory, no matter how far-fetched. We leave no stone unturned."

7 - 8

Drake reached for the ancient codex, its weathered leather binding cool against his fingertips. He laid it on the table, the faded pages seeming to glow in the dim light of the research facility.

"Let's start here," he said, his voice barely above a whisper. "There has to be something we've missed."

Dr. Summers leaned in, her brow furrowed in concentration. "The symbols... they're shifting. I've never seen anything like this before."

As they watched, the cryptic markings on the page began to transform, rearranging themselves into patterns that seemed to pulse with an otherworldly energy.

Drake's heart raced. "Is this... normal?"

Dr. Patal shook her head, her eyes wide with a mixture of fear and fascination. "Definitely not. But if this text truly holds the key to stopping the virus, we need to decipher it now."

Harrison peered over their shoulders, his face a mask of determination. "What if it's not just a text? What if it's reacting to our presence, to our need?"

As Drake pondered Harrison's words, he felt a strange tingling sensation in his fingertips where they touched the page. The symbols seemed to dance faster, as if responding to his touch.

"I think... I think it's trying to tell us something," Drake murmured, his mind reeling with the implications. Could this ancient tome truly hold the key to saving their world?

9 - 10

Dr. Summers inhaled sharply, her finger hovering over a cluster of intricate symbols that seemed to pulse with an ethereal light. "It's here," she murmured, her voice tinged with awe as she traced her finger along the faded text. "The answer we've been searching for."

Drake leaned in closer, his heart thundering in his chest as he studied the cryptic markings. The ancient leather-bound codex seemed to hum with an otherworldly energy, its pages shimmering in the flickering light of the research facility. He could almost feel the weight of countless realities pressing in around them, the fate of the multiverse hanging in the balance.

"What does it say?" Drake asked, his voice barely above a whisper. He strained to make out the ancient words, his legal training urging him to dissect and analyze every detail. But this was far beyond any courtroom mystery he'd ever encountered.

Dr. Summers' eyes darted across the page, her lips moving silently as she attempted to decipher the text. "It's unlike anything I've ever seen," she murmured, her usual confident tone tinged with uncertainty. "The language seems to shift and change, almost as if it's alive."

Drake's mind raced, grappling with the implications. Could this truly be the key to halting the deadly virus that threatened to consume their world? He thought of the devastation they'd witnessed, the haunting images of abandoned cities and desolate landscapes across multiple realities. They had to find a way to stop it, no matter the cost.

"Maybe it's not meant to be read," Drake suggested, his legal mind searching for alternative explanations. "What if it's a code, or a map of some kind?"

11 - 12

Dr. Patal leaned in, her brow furrowed in concentration as she studied the cryptic symbols. Suddenly, her eyes widened, and she inhaled sharply. "It speaks of a cure," she interjected, her voice filled with a mixture of hope and apprehension. "A cure derived from your blood, Drake."

The words hit Drake like a physical blow. His breath caught in his throat, and he felt the room spin around him. His blood? How could that be possible? He gripped the edge of the table, steadying himself as he struggled to process this revelation.

"My blood?" he echoed, his voice tinged with disbelief. The implications raced through his mind, a whirlwind of questions and fears. Was this why he had been able to traverse the multiverse? Was there something unique about him that could save countless lives across realities?

Drake's gaze darted between Dr. Patal and Dr. Summers, searching their faces for any sign that this was some kind of mistake. But their expressions only confirmed the gravity of the situation. He swallowed hard, trying to find his voice.

"How... how is that even possible?" he managed to ask, his lawyer's instinct for clarity pushing through the shock. "I'm just a regular person. There's nothing special about my blood."

As he spoke, Drake couldn't help but think of his late wife and reunited son. Would they have been proud of him in this moment? Or terrified for what this might mean? The weight of responsibility settled on his shoulders, heavier than any case he'd ever taken on.

13 - 14

Dr. Summers leaned forward, her eyes alight with the fervor of discovery. "Yes, Drake," she confirmed, her voice carrying a mix of excitement and gravity. "Your blood contains the key to unlocking the cure. It's a genetic anomaly, a unique signature that can neutralize the virus and save countless lives."

Drake's mind reeled, struggling to grasp the enormity of what Dr. Summers was saying. He ran a hand through his hair, a nervous habit he'd picked up during countless late nights poring over legal briefs. "But how?" he asked, his voice barely above a whisper. "I've never been anything special."

As Dr. Summers opened her mouth to explain further, Harrison suddenly straightened, his eyes widening in realization. "So all we need to do is manufacture the cure and distribute it to those who are infected," he mused, his voice tinged with a note of cautious optimism.

Drake turned to Harrison, studying the young man's face. He saw a glimmer of hope there, a spark that ignited something within himself. For the first time since learning about his blood's unique properties, Drake felt a surge of determination.

"It can't be that simple, can it?" Drake asked, his gaze shifting between Harrison and Dr. Summers. He could feel his heart racing, the gravity of the situation settling over him like a heavy cloak. The fate of not just one world, but countless realities, potentially rested on his shoulders – or more accurately, in his veins.

15 - 16

Dr. Summers nodded, her gaze unwavering. "Exactly," she confirmed, her voice carrying the weight of their monumental task. "But we'll need to work quickly. Time is of the essence if we're going to stop this virus from spreading any further."

Drake felt a chill run down his spine. The urgency in Dr. Summers' voice was palpable, and he could almost see the virus creeping across the multiverse in his mind's eye. He clenched his fists, steeling himself for what lay ahead.

"What do you need from me?" Drake asked, his voice steadier than he felt.

Dr. Monroe stepped forward, his calm demeanor a stark contrast to the tension in the room. "We'll need to start with a series of blood draws," he explained, adjusting his wire-rimmed glasses. "Then we'll begin analyzing the unique properties of your blood to synthesize the cure."

As Dr. Monroe spoke, Drake's mind raced. How many lives hung in the balance? How many worlds teetered on the brink of collapse while they stood here talking? He took a deep breath, pushing aside his doubts and fears.

"Let's do it," Drake said, rolling up his sleeve. "Every second counts, right?"

With those words, a flurry of activity erupted around him. Dr. Patal rushed to prepare the necessary equipment, while Harrison began clearing space on a nearby workbench. Dr. Summers and Dr. Monroe huddled together, rapidly discussing the intricacies of isolating the crucial components in Drake's blood.

As Drake watched the team spring into action, a mix of awe and determination washed over him. These brilliant minds, working in perfect harmony, represented humanity's best hope. And somehow, inexplicably, he was at the center of it all.

"We can do this," Drake murmured to himself, his voice barely audible above the buzz of activity. "We have to."

Echoes in the Isolation Ward

Red World – 2024

1 - 2

Drake's footsteps echoed like gunshots in the eerie silence of the hospital corridor. The antiseptic smell burned his nostrils, a stark reminder of the sterile battleground he was entering. As he approached the isolation ward, memories of bustling emergency rooms and chattering nurses from his own world flashed through his mind, a jarring contrast to the emptiness surrounding him now.

He paused at the door, his hand hovering over the handle. "Get it together, Miller," he muttered to himself, drawing a deep breath. "Bird needs you."

With a determined push, Drake entered the ward. The harsh fluorescent lights assaulted his eyes, momentarily disorienting him. As his vision adjusted, he took in the rows of empty beds, their crisp white sheets untouched, waiting for patients that might never come.

The silence was oppressive, broken only by the faint hum of medical equipment. Drake's mind raced. How had it come to this? A virus that could jump between realities, leaving devastation in its wake. And now, his friend and ally lay somewhere in this room, fighting for his life.

"Franklin?" Drake called out, his voice sounding unnaturally loud in the quiet ward. He moved slowly between the beds, scanning for any sign of movement. "It's Drake. I'm here."

As he neared the far corner of the room, a familiar gruff voice responded, "Took you long enough, Miller."

Relief washed over Drake, quickly followed by concern as he caught sight of Detective Bird. The usually robust man looked pale and drawn, his stocky frame diminished against the stark hospital bed.

"How are you holding up?" Drake asked, approaching the bedside.

Franklin's sharp eyes fixed on him, a hint of his usual intensity still present despite his weakened state. "Been better," he rasped. "But I'm not out of the fight yet."

Drake nodded, a small smile tugging at his lips. Even facing down a multiversal plague, Franklin Bird remained as stubborn as ever. "That's what I like to hear," he said, pulling up a chair. "Because we've got work to do, and I need that detective brain of yours firing on all cylinders."

As he settled in, Drake couldn't shake the feeling that time was running out. The empty ward around them seemed to pulse with an ominous energy, a reminder of the devastation spreading across realities. But here, in this moment, he had a purpose. And as long as Franklin Bird drew breath, Drake knew they still had a chance to unravel the mystery that threatened not just their world, but all worlds.

3 - 4

Drake leaned in, his eyes scanning Franklin's face. The detective's usually ruddy complexion was now ashen, a sheen of sweat glistening on his brow. Each labored breath seemed to cost Franklin an immense effort, and Drake felt a pang of guilt for what he was about to ask.

"Franklin," Drake murmured, his voice barely above a whisper as he approached the bedside. "I'm here."

The detective's eyelids fluttered, struggling to focus on Drake. When they finally locked gazes, Drake saw a flicker of recognition in Franklin's weary eyes.

"Drake," Franklin wheezed, his voice a shadow of its usual commanding tone. "You shouldn't... be risking... exposure."

Drake's jaw clenched, his mind racing with the weight of their shared knowledge. The virus ravaging Franklin's body wasn't just any pathogen – it was a threat to the very fabric of the multiverse.

"I couldn't stay away," Drake admitted, his fingers curling around the edge of the hospital bed. "Not when we're so close to unraveling this thing."

Franklin attempted a weak nod, his eyes drifting closed for a moment before snapping open again with fierce determination. "What's... the plan?" he managed to ask.

Drake leaned in closer, his voice low and urgent. "We need your blood, Franklin. Dr. Summers thinks it might hold the key to understanding how the virus mutates across realities."

5 - 6

Drake's hand moved instinctively to clasp Franklin's, feeling the clammy weakness in his friend's grip. The gesture was both a comfort and a stark reminder of the dire situation they faced.

"I need to take a blood sample," Drake explained, his voice tight with determination. "It's for the greater good."

Franklin's eyes widened slightly, a mix of understanding and resignation flickering across his face. Drake could almost see the gears turning in the detective's mind, weighing the risks against the potential to save countless lives across multiple realities.

"You know the risks," Franklin rasped, his breath catching. "If Gabriel... finds out..."

Drake's jaw clenched, memories of their encounters with the ruthless temporal manipulator flashing through his mind. "We'll be careful," he assured Franklin, though doubt gnawed at the edges of his resolve. "The sample will be secure."

As he reached for the medical kit he'd brought, Drake's thoughts raced. Was he truly prepared for the consequences of this action? The weight of responsibility pressed down on him, heavier than ever before. But the image of his lost family, of worlds ravaged by the virus, steeled his resolve.

"Just... be quick," Franklin muttered, his eyes closing as he braced himself for the procedure.

Drake nodded, swallowing hard as he prepared the syringe. The fate of the multiverse, he realized, might very well hinge on what they discovered in this small vial of blood.

7 - 8

Detective Bird nodded weakly, his expression one of resigned acceptance. "Do what you have to do," he murmured, his voice barely audible over the hum of medical equipment that surrounded them.

Drake's hand trembled slightly as he reached for the syringe, the weight of the moment pressing down on him. He took a deep breath, steadying himself. "I'll make it quick, Franklin," he promised, his voice low and reassuring.

As he prepared to draw the blood, Drake's mind raced. How had it come to this? A successful attorney turned interdimensional traveler, now holding the potential key to saving countless realities in his hands. The absurdity of it all threatened to overwhelm him.

"You're doing the right thing," Franklin whispered, his eyes meeting Drake's with a mixture of pain and determination. "We can't let Gabriel win."

Drake nodded, carefully inserting the needle into Franklin's arm. "We won't," he affirmed, his voice tight with emotion. "I promise you that."

As the vial filled with crimson liquid, Drake couldn't help but marvel at its potential power. This small sample could be the difference between salvation and annihilation for entire worlds. The thought both exhilarated and terrified him.

"How will you get it back?" Franklin asked, his brow furrowed with concern.

Drake carefully sealed the vial, his movements precise despite the turmoil in his mind. "I have a plan," he replied, though uncertainty gnawed at him. "But the less you know, the safer you'll be."

He placed the vial in a secure container, acutely aware of the precious cargo he now carried. The weight of responsibility settled on his shoulders, a burden he had never anticipated bearing when he first stumbled into this multiversal conflict.

"Drake," Franklin called out as he turned to leave. "Be careful. And... thank you."

Drake paused, a lump forming in his throat. "Stay strong, old friend," he managed, before striding towards the door, the fate of countless realities now resting in his hands.

9 - 10

Dr. Rachel Summers leaned in close to the holographic display, her eyes narrowed as she studied the intricate patterns of DNA strands swirling before her. The soft blue glow illuminated her determined features, casting sharp shadows across the dimly lit lab.

"Anything yet, Dr. Summers?" asked one of her assistants, anxiety evident in his voice.

Rachel shook her head, not taking her eyes off the screen. "Not yet, but we're close. I can feel it." Her fingers danced across the control panel, adjusting parameters with practiced precision. The air in the lab felt electric, charged with a mixture of hope and desperation.

As she worked, Rachel's mind raced. This wasn't just about solving a scientific puzzle; it was about saving lives across multiple realities. The weight of that responsibility pressed down on her, fueling her relentless focus. She had taken Detective Bird's blood sample and isolated the DNA strands that were mutated with the virus and compared them to the sample of the virus that Holly has given her. The she examined a sample of the chosen ones blood and through exposure she injected the chosen ones blood sample with both samples of the virus. Her plan was to watch the virus react to the chosen ones blood and isolate a genome that had responded well to the blood and through precise chemistry she would take the strand and synthesize a cure. So far no such luck.

"Wait," she muttered, leaning in even closer. "There's something... different here." Her heart began to race as she isolated a particular segment of the genetic code.

The assistant rushed to her side. "What is it?"

Rachel's eyes widened as understanding dawned. "It's working," she announced, her voice ringing out with a note of triumph. "We've isolated the genetic anomaly."

She stood up straight, a surge of excitement coursing through her. "This is it," she thought, "the key to unlocking the multiverse and stopping the virus." For a moment, the enormity of their discovery overwhelmed her, and she allowed herself a small smile of satisfaction.

11 - 12

The lab erupted in cheers, researchers embracing and high-fiving each other. Dr. Summers felt a wave of relief wash over her, but she knew their work was far from over. She caught Drake's eye across the room, his usually stoic expression now alight with hope.

"We did it," Drake said, striding over to her. "But what's next?"

Rachel took a deep breath, her mind already racing ahead. "Now comes the hard part. We need to synthesize a cure based on this genetic anomaly, and fast."

Drake nodded, his jaw set with determination. "Wasn't the chosen ones blood meant for the machine though. The codex specifical says the machine will only work with his blood. The cure was meant to be constructed from my blood."

As the team bustled around them, preparing for the next phase, Rachel couldn't help but feel a spark of excitement beneath her professional exterior. "We're on the brink of something revolutionary, Drake. This could change everything."

"I don't think we are meant to use the chosen ones blood for the cure, the codex strictly stated..." Drake muttered, his thoughts clearly with Detective Bird and the countless others affected by the virus.

Rachel placed a reassuring hand on his arm. "What are you thinking Miller"

13 - 14

The dim fluorescent lights of the makeshift break room cast long shadows across Harrison's face as he studied Meghan from the corner of his eye. She sat perched on the edge of a worn leather couch, her fingers tracing absent patterns on the armrest. The air between them crackled with unspoken tension.

Harrison's heart raced as he struggled to find the right words. He'd faced interdimensional threats and navigated cosmic labyrinths, but this conversation felt infinitely more daunting. Finally, he cleared his throat.

"So," he began, his voice barely above a whisper. "What exactly did Gabriel want with you?"

The moment the words left his lips, Harrison winced inwardly. Smooth, he chided himself. Real smooth. But his curiosity burned too fiercely to be contained.

Meghan's hand stilled on the armrest, her gaze fixed on some distant point beyond the room's dingy walls. Harrison found himself mesmerized by the play of emotions across her face – fear, anger, and something else he couldn't quite place.

Is she reliving some trauma? he wondered. Or planning her escape? The silence stretched between them, thick and suffocating.

"I'm sorry," Harrison backpedaled, his words tumbling out in a rush. "That was too forward. You don't have to—"

"No," Meghan interrupted, her eyes snapping to meet his. "It's a fair question. I just... I'm not sure how to answer it."

Harrison nodded, forcing himself to remain still, to give her the space to continue. His mind raced with possibilities, each more fantastical than the last. Was she a fellow dimension-hopper? A Temporal Guardian in disguise? Or something else entirely?

"Gabriel," Meghan began, her voice barely audible, "he believes I'm... special. That I have some sort of future ahead of me that he wished to protect me from."

Harrison leaned forward, his curiosity piqued. "What kind of future?" Although he knew the answer. If the Meghan he met in the future was any indication of who she would become, Gabriel had sought to see her become the ruler of the wasteland. But why?

Meghan shook her head, a rueful smile playing at the corners of her mouth. "That's just it. I don't know. He never said, not really. It's all based on some ancient prophecy or text or... I don't even know anymore."

As she spoke, Harrison's gaze was drawn to her hands, now clenched tightly in her lap. He fought the urge to reach out and comfort her, unsure if the gesture would be welcome.

"But you don't believe it?" he prodded gently.

Meghan's laugh was sharp and bitter. "Would you? One day you're living a normal life, and the next, some maniac in a white robe is chasing you across realities, spouting nonsense about destiny and cosmic balance."

Harrison couldn't help but smile at that. "You'd be surprised at how relatable that sounds, actually."

Their eyes met, and for a moment, the tension in the room eased. Harrison felt a spark of connection, of shared experience, that transcended the strangeness of their circumstances.

15 - 16

Meghan's expression darkened, a shadow passing over her features as she continued. "He believed that I held the key to unlocking the secrets of this world," she explained, her voice tinged with bitterness. "He thought that by controlling me, he could control everything."

Harrison's mind raced, piecing together the implications of her words. He'd encountered Gabriel's manipulative tactics before, but this level of obsession was chilling. His hands clenched involuntarily at his sides, a surge of protective anger rising within him.

"Did he... hurt you?" Harrison asked, his voice low and strained.

Meghan shook her head, but her eyes betrayed a deeper pain. "Not physically. But the constant pursuit, the fear... it wears you down."

Harrison nodded, understanding all too well the toll of being hunted across realities. He studied Meghan's face, noting the strength beneath her vulnerability. This was a woman who had endured much and emerged unbroken.

"What makes you so special to him?" Harrison probed gently, his natural curiosity getting the better of him.

Meghan's laugh was hollow. "I wish I knew. Sometimes I think he's just delusional. Rambling like a lunatic filled with madness. Other times..." She trailed off, her gaze distant.

Harrison leaned forward, his voice soft but intense. "Other times?"

"Other times," Meghan continued, meeting his eyes, "I feel something... different. Like there's a current running through me, connecting me to... everything. Like maybe he's right. There felt like a spark of connection between us, like I've known him for twenty years."

As Harrison absorbed her words, he couldn't shake the feeling that Meghan was indeed pivotal to the cosmic chess game they found themselves in. The question was: what role would she play?

17 - 18

Meghan's piercing gaze shifted, her eyes locking onto Harrison's with an intensity that made him catch his breath. "And what about you?" she asked, her voice steady but laced with genuine curiosity. "What brings you here?"

Harrison felt a sudden tightness in his chest, the weight of his past and the uncertainty of his future pressing down on him. He ran a hand through his hair, buying time as he wrestled with how much to reveal. The flickering fluorescent lights of the research facility's break room cast dancing shadows across his face, mirroring the tumult of emotions within.

"I..." he began, then faltered. Harrison's fingers drummed an unconscious rhythm on the table between them as he gathered his thoughts. "I came here looking for answers," he admitted finally, his voice tinged with vulnerability. His eyes met Meghan's, and he saw not judgment, but understanding reflected back at him.

Taking a deep breath, Harrison continued, "But what I found was so much more than I ever could have imagined." As he spoke, memories flashed through his mind: the eerie silence of the Green World, the pulsing neon of the Red World, the haunting desolation of the Apocalypse World. Each reality had left its mark on him, shaping him in ways he was only beginning to understand.

"It's like..." Harrison struggled to find the right words, his brow furrowing in concentration. "It's like I've been given a glimpse into the vastness of existence, and now I can't unsee it. The multiverse, the Temporal Guardians, this virus that threatens everything – it's all so much bigger than me, than any of us."

He leaned back in his chair, a rueful smile tugging at the corners of his mouth. "And yet, here I am, somehow caught up in the middle of it all. Me, Harrison Miller, just a guy who used to think the biggest mystery in his life was what was happening on Lost."

19 - 20

A faint smile tugged at Meghan's lips as she regarded Harrison with a mixture of sympathy and understanding. "Sometimes, the answers we seek are found in the most unexpected places," she remarked cryptically, her words resonating with a depth of wisdom that belied her years.

Harrison's eyes widened slightly, struck by the profound simplicity of her statement. He leaned forward, elbows resting on his knees, his curiosity piqued. "What do you mean by that?"

Meghan's gaze drifted to the window, where the sterile white walls of the research facility contrasted sharply with the vibrant sunset beyond. "Think about it, Harrison. You came here searching for answers about your parents, about your place in all of this. But in doing so, you've stumbled upon something far greater – a multiverse in peril, a virus that threatens countless realities."

As she spoke, Harrison found himself captivated not just by her words, but by the quiet strength that emanated from her. He watched the play of emotions across her face, noting the determined set of her jaw, the glimmer of resolve in her eyes.

"I guess you're right," he admitted, running a hand through his hair. "It's just... overwhelming sometimes. To think that the fate of so many worlds might rest on our shoulders."

Meghan turned back to him, her expression softening. "That's the burden of knowledge, Harrison. But it's also a gift. We have the power to make a difference, to save lives across realities."

As the conversation flowed between them, Harrison found himself drawn to Meghan in ways he couldn't fully explain. There was a warmth and authenticity to her presence that filled him with a sense of comfort and ease, and he couldn't help but feel a growing connection to her with each passing moment. Was he falling in Love?

"You know," he said, a hint of wonder in his voice, "I never expected to find someone who could understand all of this. Someone who's been through it too."

Meghan's smile widened, genuine and warm. "Neither did I, Harrison. I think we've both found something unexpected here."

21 - 22

Harrison leaned forward, his elbows resting on his knees as he studied Meghan's face. The soft glow of the break room's fluorescent lights cast shadows that accentuated the determination etched in her features.

"You've been through so much," he said softly, his voice tinged with admiration. "How do you stay so... composed?"

Meghan's eyes flickered with a mix of emotions – pain, resolve, and something deeper that Harrison couldn't quite name. She took a deep breath before responding, her fingers absently tracing patterns on the table between them.

"Composure is sometimes just a mask," she admitted, her voice barely above a whisper. "But beneath it... it's a choice. To keep fighting, to believe that what we're doing matters."

Harrison nodded, understanding dawning in his eyes. He thought of his own struggles, the weight of his family's legacy, and felt a surge of kinship with the woman before him.

"I get that," he said. "It's like carrying an invisible burden that no one else can see."

Meghan's gaze met his, a spark of recognition passing between them. "Exactly. But Harrison, that burden... it's also what makes us uniquely capable of facing what's coming."

As she spoke, Harrison felt something shift within him. The curiosity that had always driven him seemed to deepen, transforming into a profound desire to unravel the enigma that was Meghan Johnson. He realized, with a jolt of clarity, that his feelings for her were evolving into something far more significant than he had anticipated.

Impulsively, he reached out and took her hand in his. The contact sent a surge of warmth through him, and he marveled at how right it felt.

"Meghan," he began, his voice thick with emotion, "I don't know what the future holds, but I do know that I want to face it with you by my side."

The words hung in the air between them, charged with possibility. Harrison's heart raced as he waited for her response, acutely aware that this moment could change everything.

Under the Microscope

Red World – 2024

1 - 2

The harsh fluorescent light cast a sickly glow over Dr. Rachel Summers' face as she leaned intently over the microscope. Her eyes narrowed, scrutinizing the blood sample Drake had just provided. The soft hum of equipment in the lab seemed to fade away as she lost herself in the microscopic world before her.

Drake stood rigid nearby, his jaw clenched tight. He watched Dr. Summers' every movement, searching for any hint of what she might be seeing. His heart thundered in his chest, each beat a painful reminder of what was at stake.

"Anything?" Drake finally asked, unable to bear the silence any longer.

Dr. Summers held up a hand, not looking away from the eyepiece. "Give me a moment," she murmured. "This isn't something to be rushed."

Drake nodded, though she couldn't see it. He ran a hand through his dark hair, his mind racing. If this doesn't work, what then? How many more chances do we have?

The seconds stretched into eternity as Dr. Summers continued her meticulous examination. Drake paced in a tight circle, his footsteps echoing in the sterile lab. He found himself staring at the Ancient Codex on a nearby table, its weathered leather cover seeming to mock him with its secrets.

"Dr. Summers," Drake began again, his voice tight with tension. "I know you need to be thorough, but-"

"Patience, Drake," she interrupted, finally straightening up from the microscope. Her sharp gaze met his, a mix of scientific detachment and empathy. "I understand the urgency, believe me. But we can't afford to miss anything. The fate of multiple realities hangs in the balance."

Drake nodded, forcing himself to take a deep breath. "You're right, of course. It's just... the waiting. It's killing me."

Dr. Summers' expression softened slightly. "I know. But remember, your blood you said so yourself could be the key to everything. The Blood of the Chosen One and yours– it's not just a myth. We have to approach this methodically."

As she turned back to the microscope, Drake's mind whirled with possibilities. Could his blood really be the salvation for countless worlds? The weight of that responsibility pressed down on him, threatening to crush his resolve. But he steeled himself, determined to see this through. For his lost family, for all the lives at stake across the multiverse.

He watched Dr. Summers work, her movements precise and focused. Whatever the outcome, Drake knew their next steps would shape the future of reality itself.

3 - 4

Dr. Summers straightened up abruptly, her normally composed features contorted in a mix of frustration and disbelief. The sterile lab seemed to hold its breath as she uttered the words Drake had been dreading.

"It's not working," she muttered, her voice tinged with disappointment.

Drake felt the ground lurch beneath him, his world tilting on its axis. The sinking feeling in his stomach threatened to pull him under completely. He gripped the edge of the lab bench, steadying himself as he struggled to process the implications.

"How... how can you be sure?" Drake managed, his voice barely above a whisper.

Dr. Summers ran a hand through her hair, a rare display of vulnerability. "The cellular response we were hoping for... it's just not there. Your blood isn't interacting with the virus sample the way we theorized it would."

Drake's mind raced, grasping for any shred of hope. "Could it be a problem with the equipment? Or maybe we need a different concentration?"

"I've triple-checked everything," Dr. Summers replied, shaking her head. "The Ancient Codex clearly indicated that the blood of someone in the Chosen One lineage would be the key. But something's missing. Something we're not seeing."

Drake closed his eyes, memories of the desolate Black World flashing through his mind. The haunting silence, the abandoned streets – a chilling preview of what awaited countless realities if they failed.

"We can't give up," he said, opening his eyes with renewed determination. "There has to be another way. The Codex wouldn't have led us this far if it was all for nothing."

Dr. Summers nodded, a spark of her usual tenacity returning. "You're right. We'll regroup, analyze the data. Perhaps there's a clue in the Codex we overlooked."

As they began to discuss their next steps, Drake couldn't shake the feeling that time was slipping away. Somewhere in the vast tapestry of the multiverse, the answer was waiting. They just had to find it before it was too late.

5 - 6

Drake ran a hand through his hair, his brow furrowing in that characteristic way it did when he was faced with a particularly vexing problem. "But how can that be?" he asked, his voice tinged with desperation. "We did everything right."

He paced the sterile lab, the soft hum of equipment a stark contrast to the turmoil in his mind. The muted green glow of the monitors cast an eerie pallor over Dr. Summers' face as she leaned against the workstation, her usual confidence wavering.

"I don't know," she admitted, her tone heavy with resignation. Dr. Summers removed her glasses, pinching the bridge of her nose. "It should have worked, but something's not right."

Drake's thoughts raced, images of the apocalyptic Black World flashing before his eyes. The haunting silence, the ruined buildings – a grim reminder of what was at stake. He clenched his fists, fighting back the wave of despair threatening to engulf him.

"Could we have misinterpreted the Codex?" he asked, grasping at straws. "Maybe there's a detail we overlooked, some hidden meaning in those symbols?"

Dr. Summers shook her head, her expression grave as she considered their predicament. "We've been over every inch of that manuscript. If there's a secret there, it's eluding us all."

The weight of their failure pressed down on Drake, making it hard to breathe in the lab's recycled air. He couldn't help but think of his lost family, of all the lives across the multiverse hanging in the balance. They had to find a solution – failure wasn't an option.

7 - 8

Drake paced the length of the lab, his footsteps echoing in the oppressive silence. The sterile equipment and blinking monitors seemed to mock their efforts, a stark reminder of how close they'd come, only to fall short.

"There has to be something we're missing," he muttered, more to himself than to Dr. Summers. His mind raced, desperately searching for a solution. "What if we tried combining my blood with he chosen ones blood?"

Dr. Summers sighed, her shoulders slumping. "Drake, we've pushed the boundaries of science further than I ever thought possible. But this virus... it's adapting faster than we can keep up."

The admission hit Drake like a physical blow. He braced himself against a nearby workstation, his knuckles turning white as he gripped the edge. For a moment, the enormity of their task threatened to overwhelm him.

But then, something inside Drake hardened. He straightened, his jaw set with determination. "No," he said, his voice low but firm. "I refuse to accept that this is the end. We've come too far, risked too much."

Dr. Summers looked up, surprise flickering across her face at the intensity in Drake's voice.

"We'll find a way," Drake continued, his eyes blazing with renewed purpose. "Even if we have to tear apart the fabric of reality itself. I won't let this virus claim another world, another family. We keep searching, we keep fighting – until we find the answer."

9 - 10

Drake's words hung in the air, charged with determination. The sterile laboratory, with its gleaming equipment and harsh fluorescent lights, seemed to pulse with newfound energy. He clenched his fist, feeling the weight of countless lives resting on their shoulders.

"We've faced impossible odds before," Drake continued, his voice steady despite the turmoil within. "Each time, we've found a way forward. This is no different."

Dr. Summers nodded slowly, a glimmer of hope rekindling in her tired eyes. "You're right, Drake. We can't give up now."

As they stood there, united in their resolve, Drake's mind raced through the possibilities. The multiverse stretched before him, a tapestry of infinite potential. Somewhere, in the vast expanse of realities, there had to be an answer.

"Maybe," Drake mused, his lawyer's mind dissecting the problem, "we're thinking too linearly. What if the solution isn't in any single world, but in the connections between them?"

Before Dr. Summers could respond, a tentative voice cut through the tension.

"I... I might have an idea," Harrison said, stepping forward from where he'd been observing silently.

All eyes in the room turned to the young man, a mixture of surprise and curiosity on their faces. Drake felt a surge of pride, tinged with concern, as he looked at his son.

"What is it, Harrison?" Drake asked, his tone encouraging despite the gravity of their situation.

Harrison took a deep breath, his expressive eyes reflecting a maturity beyond his years. "What if we use my blood? The Ancient Codex mentioned something about the 'Blood of the Chosen One.' Maybe... maybe that's in me?"

11 - 12

Dr. Summers regarded Harrison with a mixture of curiosity and skepticism, her brow furrowing as she weighed the potential risks and rewards of his proposal. "Are you sure about this?" she asked, her voice tinged with uncertainty. "We don't know what the consequences might be."

Harrison felt a chill run down his spine at her words, but he pushed the fear aside. The weight of countless lives across the multiverse pressed upon him, fueling his determination. He met Dr. Summers' gaze squarely, his expression resolute as he nodded.

"I'm sure," he replied with unwavering conviction. His hands trembled slightly, but he clenched them into fists to steady himself. "If there's even a chance that my blood could help, then I have to try. We can't afford to let fear hold us back when so much is at stake."

As he spoke, Harrison's mind raced with the possibilities. Would his blood truly be the key to unlocking the secrets of the multiverse? Could it somehow counteract the devastating effects of the virus that threatened to consume entire realities? The enormity of the situation threatened to overwhelm him, but he pushed through, drawing strength from the memory of all they had endured to reach this point.

"I understand the risks, Dr. Summers," Harrison continued, his voice growing stronger with each word. "But after everything you've seen – the Green World's isolation, the Red World's dystopia, the Blue World's desolation – how can I not at least try?"

13 - 14

Drake stepped forward, his eyes glistening with a mixture of pride and concern. He placed a reassuring hand on Harrison's shoulder, the warmth of his touch grounding Harrison in the moment.

"You're a brave young man, Harrison," Drake said, his voice thick with emotion. "I'm proud to call you my son."

Harrison felt a surge of gratitude wash over him, his father's words bolstering his resolve. He swallowed hard, fighting back the lump in his throat. "Thanks, Dad," he managed, his voice barely above a whisper.

With trembling fingers, Harrison began to roll up his sleeve, baring his arm. The sterile air of the lab felt cool against his skin, raising goosebumps. As he prepared himself, a thought flashed through his mind: What if this doesn't work? What if I'm not the key to saving everyone after all?

He pushed the doubt aside, focusing instead on the task at hand. "I'm ready," Harrison announced, his voice steadier than he felt. He looked around the room, taking in the anxious faces of Dr. Summers and the research team. "Whatever happens, we're in this together, right?"

Drake nodded, giving Harrison's shoulder a gentle squeeze. "Always, son. No matter what reality we find ourselves in."

As Dr. Summers approached with the necessary equipment, Harrison took a deep breath, steeling himself for what was to come. The weight of their collective hopes hung heavy in the air, but Harrison felt a strange sense of calm settling over him. This was his purpose, his chance to make a difference across the multiverse.

"Let's do this," he said, offering his arm. "For all the worlds out there counting on us."

15 - 16

Dr. Summers nodded solemnly, her expression one of grim resolve as she prepared to extract a sample of Harrison's blood. "Let's hope this works," she murmured, her words a silent prayer for salvation in the face of impending doom.

Harrison watched intently as Dr. Summers sterilized the area on his arm, the sharp scent of alcohol filling his nostrils. His heart raced, each beat a reminder of the precious fluid that might hold the key to saving countless lives across the multiverse.

"You might feel a slight pinch," Dr. Summers warned, her voice steady despite the tension in the air.

As the needle pierced his skin, Harrison gritted his teeth against the sting, his jaw clenched with determination. He focused on the syringe, watching as it slowly filled with his crimson blood.

"You okay?" Dr. Summers asked, her eyes darting between Harrison's face and the syringe.

Harrison nodded, swallowing hard. "Yeah, I'm fine. It's just... surreal, you know? To think that this," he gestured to the blood being drawn, "might be the difference between life and death for so many."

The weight of the moment pressed down on him, and Harrison's mind raced with possibilities. What if his blood really did hold the key to stopping the virus? What if it didn't? The fate of multiple worlds hung in the balance, and he was at the center of it all.

"Almost done," Dr. Summers said softly, her focus unwavering as she carefully extracted the last of the sample.

As she removed the needle, Harrison let out a breath he didn't realize he'd been holding. "So what now?" he asked, pressing a cotton swab to the tiny puncture mark.

Dr. Summers carefully labeled the vial of blood. "Now, we run tests. We analyze. And we hope," she said, her voice tinged with both determination and uncertainty.

Harrison nodded, a mix of emotions swirling within him. Fear, hope, and an overwhelming sense of responsibility. "Whatever happens," he said, his voice barely above a whisper, "we're not giving up, right? No matter what the results show?"

Dr. Summers placed a reassuring hand on his shoulder. "Absolutely not. This is just the beginning, Harrison. One way or another, we'll find a way to stop this virus and save the multiverse."

As Harrison watched Dr. Summers walk away with his blood sample, he couldn't shake the feeling that everything was about to change. For better or worse, their fate was now inextricably linked to that small vial of crimson liquid, a beacon of hope in the encroaching darkness.

17 - 18

Harrison's gaze followed the vial of his blood, its deep crimson hue seeming to pulse with an otherworldly energy. A wave of determination washed over him, steeling his resolve.

"I can feel it," he murmured, clenching his fist. "This isn't just about me anymore. It's about all of us, every world, every reality."

Dr. Summers glanced up from her work, her eyes softening with understanding. "That's a heavy burden, Harrison. How are you holding up?"

He took a deep breath, considering her question. "Scared," he admitted. "But also... ready. Like everything in my life has been leading to this moment."

As Dr. Summers carefully transferred the blood sample, Harrison's mind raced with possibilities. What if his blood really was the key? Could it truly bridge the gap between worlds, heal the fractures in reality itself?

"Dr. Summers," he said, his voice barely above a whisper, "do you think we have a real chance?"

She paused, her hands steady as she sealed the vial. "Science is about possibilities, Harrison. And right now, you've given us the greatest possibility we've had yet."

Harrison nodded, watching as each drop of his blood was meticulously preserved. He could almost feel the weight of countless lives resting on those tiny crimson droplets.

"Whatever happens," he said, his voice growing stronger, "we keep fighting. For every world, every person we can save."

Dr. Summers smiled, a glimmer of hope in her eyes. "That's the spirit. Now, let's see what your blood can tell us about saving the multiverse."

19 - 20

Dr. Summers turned swiftly, her lab coat swishing as she strode purposefully to her workstation. The soft glow of multiple monitors illuminated her determined face as her fingers flew across the keyboard, initiating a complex sequence of commands.

Harrison watched, transfixed, as the research facility seemed to awaken around them. Machines whirred to life, their rhythmic hum a stark reminder of the urgency that propelled their mission.

"What exactly are we looking for?" Harrison asked, his voice barely audible above the mechanical symphony.

Dr. Summers' eyes remained fixed on her screens as she replied, "Anomalies, patterns, anything that might indicate how your blood interacts with the virus on a multidimensional level." She paused, glancing at him. "It's like searching for a cosmic needle in a haystack of realities."

Harrison nodded, his throat tight. "And if we find it?"

"Then we might just have a chance at saving not just our world, but all of them," Dr. Summers said, her voice a mixture of hope and trepidation.

As the analysis began, Harrison couldn't help but feel the weight of expectation pressing down on him. His thoughts raced. What if his blood held the key? What if it didn't? The fate of countless lives across multiple realities hung in the balance, and he was at the center of it all.

"Dr. Summers," he began hesitantly, "what if-"

She cut him off gently, "No 'what ifs', Harrison. We focus on what we can do, right here, right now."

Harrison nodded, grateful for her steady presence. As they waited, the tension in the air grew thick, almost palpable. Each passing second felt like an eternity, the fate of humanity resting on the outcome of their desperate gambit.

21 - 22

The soft beep of the computer cut through the air like a knife, startling Harrison from his thoughts. His heart leapt into his throat as all eyes in the room turned to Dr. Summers. She leaned forward, her brow furrowed in concentration as she studied the readout with an intensity that made Harrison's palms sweat.

Dr. Patal broke the tense silence. "Rachel, what do you see?" Her usually calm voice held a tremor of anticipation.

Dr. Summers didn't respond immediately. Her lips pressed into a thin line as she scrolled through the data, her expression unreadable. Harrison's chest tightened with each passing second, his mind racing with possibilities.

"There's... something here," Dr. Summers finally murmured, her eyes never leaving the screen. "It's unlike anything I've encountered before."

Harrison stepped closer, his curiosity overcoming his anxiety. "Is that good or bad?" he asked, his voice barely above a whisper.

Dr. Summers glanced up at him, her expression a mixture of confusion and wonder. "I'm not sure yet. The data is... complex. It's as if your blood is interacting with the virus on multiple dimensional levels simultaneously."

The silence that followed was deafening. Harrison could hear his own heart pounding in his ears, each beat seeming to echo in the cavernous research facility. He thought to himself, 'Am I the key to saving everyone, or just another dead end?'

Dr. Monroe moved to Dr. Summers' side, peering at the screen. "Could this be the breakthrough we've been searching for?" he asked, his voice tinged with cautious hope.

Dr. Summers shook her head slightly, her brow still furrowed. "It's too early to say. We need more time to analyze these results. But..." she trailed off, her eyes widening slightly as she focused on a particular section of data.

"But what?" Harrison prompted, unable to contain his impatience.

Dr. Summers looked up, her gaze meeting Harrison's. "But I think we might be onto something here. Something big."

23 - 24

Dr. Summers' words hung in the air for a moment, heavy with possibility. Then, as if a switch had been flipped, she sprang into action, her fingers flying across the keyboard.

"It's working," she breathed, her voice tinged with disbelief and wonder. "The virus is responding to Harrison's blood. Much like it did to the chosen ones blood. It's... it's like nothing I've ever seen before."

Harrison's heart leapt into his throat. He glanced at Dr. Patal, whose eyes were wide behind her wire-rimmed glasses. 'Could this really be happening?' Harrison thought, hardly daring to hope.

"What exactly are you seeing, Rachel?" Dr. Patal asked, leaning in closer to the screen.

Dr. Summers shook her head in amazement. "The virus... it's not just being neutralized. It's almost as if Harrison's blood is rewriting its genetic code across multiple realities simultaneously. I've never seen anything like this before."

A collective sigh of relief swept through the room. Harrison felt his knees go weak, and he gripped the edge of the lab bench for support.

"So, does this mean we've found a cure?" he asked, his voice trembling slightly.

Dr. Summers looked up at him, her eyes shining with a mixture of excitement and caution. "It's too early to say for certain, but this is the most promising lead we've had. Your blood, Harrison... it might just be the key to saving countless lives across the multiverse."

For the first time in what felt like an eternity, Harrison allowed himself to smile. A glimmer of hope had emerged, a beacon guiding them through the storm of despair that had engulfed them for so long.

25 - 25

Harrison's heart raced as he rolled down his sleeve, his mind whirling with the implications of Dr. Summers' discovery. He clenched his fist, feeling the small pinprick where the needle had pierced his skin—a tiny wound that might just save countless lives across the multiverse.

"What's our next move?" he asked, his voice steadier than he felt.

Dr. Summers' fingers flew across the keyboard, her eyes never leaving the screen. "We need to synthesize more of the compound your blood is producing. It's not going to be easy, but it's our best shot."

Drake placed a hand on Harrison's shoulder, his touch grounding in the midst of the surreal situation. "You've given us hope, son. But this fight is far from over."

Harrison nodded, swallowing hard. "I know. Whatever it takes, I'm ready."

He glanced around the sterile lab, at the determined faces of Dr. Summers and his father. The weight of their collective purpose settled on his shoulders, heavy but not crushing. 'We're really doing this,' he thought. 'We're going to save the multiverse.'

"Dr. Summers," Drake said, his voice cutting through Harrison's thoughts, "how long until we can begin testing the synthesized compound?"

She looked up, her brow furrowed. "If we work around the clock, maybe 48 hours. But we'll need to move fast. The virus is still spreading across realities."

Harrison stepped forward, his resolve hardening. "Then let's get to work. We don't have a moment to lose."

Crimson Secrets

1 - 2

Drake's fingers trembled as he held the small vial up to the harsh fluorescent light, its contents shimmering with an otherworldly crimson glow. His mind raced, piecing together the fragments of information that had led him to this moment.

"Holly," he said, recalling a memory, his voice barely above a whisper, "you said Justin gave you this vial to bring to me across realities?"

Holly nodded, her sharp eyes studying Drake's face. "Yes, he was insistent. Said it was crucial you receive it. What's going on, Drake?"

Drake's legal mind kicked into overdrive, analyzing the implications. The chosen one's blood as a cure for the virus. This vial, crossing dimensions to reach him. It all made sense now.

"I think I know what I have to do," Drake said as the memory faded and present day reality settled in around him, his tone resolute. He uncapped the vial, the scent of copper filling his nostrils. His heart pounded in his chest as he raised it to his lips.

Dr. Summers's eyes widened. "Drake, wait! We don't know what that is or what it'll do to you! We need that for the machine."

But Drake had already made his selfish decision. With a swift motion, he tilted his head back and poured the contents into his mouth. The crimson liquid slid down his throat, leaving a trail of fire in its wake.

For a moment, nothing happened. Then, suddenly, a surge of power erupted within him. It coursed through his veins like lightning, igniting every fiber of his being. Drake gasped, overwhelmed by the sensation.

"Drake!" Rachel exclaimed, rushing to his side. "Are you alright?"

He turned to her, his eyes blazing with newfound intensity. "I'm more than alright, Summers. I feel... alive. Like I can take on the world – or worlds."

As the power settled within him, Drake's mind cleared. The fog of grief and despair that had clouded his thoughts since losing Linda and their son began to lift. In its place, a sense of purpose emerged, strong and unwavering.

"This is it, Holly," Drake said to himself, his inner voice filled with conviction. "This is how we fight the virus. How we save not just our world, but all worlds."

Dr. summers looked at him, a mix of concern and hope in her eyes. "What did you do?"

Drake clenched his fist, feeling the strength flowing through him. "The chosen one's blood – it's the key. And now, it's part of me. We can use my blood to create a cure. Not Harrisons"

As the words left his mouth, Drake felt the weight of his new purpose settle upon his shoulders. He was no longer just Drake Miller, grieving husband and father. He was now a beacon of hope in a multiverse ravaged by an unstoppable plague.

And he was ready to face whatever challenges lay ahead.

3 - 4

Drake's heightened senses overwhelmed him momentarily. The lab's fluorescent lights seemed to pulse with an otherworldly intensity, and he could hear the hum of equipment with startling clarity. He blinked rapidly, adjusting to his new perception.

"Holly," he said as if she was there with him, his voice carrying a new resonance, "I can see... everything. It's like the world has come into focus for the first time."

Hollys voice rang in his mind. "What else do you feel, Drake?"

He paused, searching within himself. "There's something else. Something... ancient. It's like I've tapped into a wellspring of power that's always been there, just beneath the surface."

As he spoke, Drake felt a surge of energy course through him. Instinctively, he reached out towards the beaker containing the virus. To his astonishment, it began to vibrate, then slowly lift off the table.

"My God," Dr. Summers whispered, her eyes wide.

Drake's mind raced, grappling with the implications. "This is more than just enhanced physical abilities. The chosen one's blood... it's awakened something in me. Something that defies the laws of our reality."

He turned to Rachel, his expression a mix of awe and determination. "We need to understand the full extent of these changes. And quickly. Time isn't on our side."

5 - 6

Drake's gaze swept across the laboratory, taking in every detail with newfound clarity. The soft glow of the lights seemed to pulse in rhythm with his heartbeat, each flicker a reminder of the monumental task that lay ahead.

"We have a cure to manufacture," Drake declared, his voice resonating with an authority he'd never possessed before. "And we will stop this virus before it has a chance to claim another innocent life."

Dr. summers's eyes widened, a mix of hope and apprehension crossing her face. "Drake, are you sure? The implications of this..."

He cut her off, his mind already racing with possibilities. "I've never been more certain of anything in my life. This power, this... gift, it's not just for me. It's for all of us, for every reality threatened by this plague."

As he spoke, Drake's fingers twitched involuntarily, and a nearby computer screen flickered to life, displaying complex molecular structures. He stared at it, mesmerized by his newfound abilities.

"We need to act fast," he continued, turning back to her. "Every moment we delay, more lives are at risk. I can feel it, Rachel. The weight of all those realities, all those lives... it's overwhelming."

Drake's thoughts drifted momentarily to Linda, to the life they'd shared before tragedy struck. 'I'll make this right,' he silently vowed. 'For you, for Harrison, for everyone.'

"What's our first step?" Summers asked, her voice pulling Drake back to the present.

He took a deep breath, centering himself. "We need to synthesize more of the blood. My blood. Then I'm going to go find my wife."

7 - 8

Drake's eyes swept across the laboratory, taking in the array of gleaming equipment with newfound clarity. "We'll need to use the centrifuge to isolate the components of my blood," he said, striding towards the machine with purpose. "Then we'll analyze its unique properties and begin replication trials."

As he moved, Drake felt a surge of energy coursing through his veins, each step infused with a strength he'd never known before. The weight of responsibility pressed down on him, but instead of crushing him, it seemed to fuel his determination.

"Harrison," Drake called out, his voice ringing with authority. "I need you to start prepping the sequencing equipment. We'll need to map out the genetic markers that make this blood... special."

His son nodded, a mixture of awe and concern etched on his features. "Dad, are you sure about this? We don't know what this could do to you long-term."

Drake paused, his hand resting on the centrifuge. He turned to face Harrison, his expression softening. "I understand your concern, son. But this is bigger than just me. It's about saving countless lives across multiple realities. The chosen one entrusted me with this gift. I will not let him or Holly down."

As he spoke, Drake's mind drifted to Linda. The thought of her face, her gentle smile, sent a pang of longing through his heart. 'Soon,' he thought. 'Soon we'll be together again. All of us.'

"Besides," Drake added, a hint of a smile tugging at his lips, "if you can cross worlds to be here, then bringing your mother back should be entirely possible. We just need to focus on the task at hand first."

Harrison's eyes widened at the mention of his mother, a flicker of hope igniting in their depths. "You really think we can bring her back?"

Fragmented Light

1 - 2

The white light consumed Drake, searing his retinas and penetrating to his very core. He felt his consciousness fragmenting, each shard of his being stretching across an infinite expanse. The sensation was both agonizing and exhilarating, as if every neuron in his brain was firing simultaneously.

"Is this... death?" Drake's thoughts echoed in the vastness. But no, this transcended mortality. He existed everywhere and nowhere, unbound by physical form.

In that timeless moment, Drake's analytical mind grasped at understanding. Years of legal training kicked in, desperately trying to make sense of the incomprehensible. But logic failed him here, in this realm beyond reason.

Memories flashed before him—arguing cases in court, holding his newborn son, kissing his wife goodbye on that fateful morning. "Linda... Harrison..." Their names were a prayer and a lifeline.

Then, as suddenly as it began, the light receded. Drake gasped, his lungs burning as if he'd been holding his breath for an eternity. He blinked rapidly, disoriented by the abrupt shift from blinding brilliance to the muted tones of his living room.

"I'm... home?" His voice sounded foreign to his own ears, raspy and uncertain.

Drake's eyes darted around the familiar space, taking in the leather sofa, the family photos on the mantle, the half-empty coffee mug on the side table. Everything was exactly as he remembered, yet fundamentally wrong.

An oppressive silence blanketed the room, broken only by the thunderous pounding of Drake's heart. The air felt thick, almost viscous, as if reality itself was holding its breath.

"Linda?" Drake called out, his tone a mixture of hope and trepidation. "Linda?"

Only silence answered.

Drake took a tentative step forward, his legs trembling. "Get it together, Miller," he muttered, falling back on the self-assurance that had served him well in the courtroom. "Analyze the situation. Find the facts."

But as he surveyed the eerily still room, Drake realized that all his years of legal training had not prepared him for this. He was in uncharted territory, facing a mystery that defied the laws of nature itself.

"What the hell is happening?" he whispered, a chill running down his spine as the weight of his solitude pressed in around him.

3 - 4

With each cautious step, Drake's heart rate accelerated. The familiar hallway of his home stretched before him, now an ominous gauntlet of closed doors and looming shadows. Every creak of the floorboards beneath his feet echoed like a gunshot in the oppressive silence.

"Linda?" he called again, his voice wavering. "Anyone?"

Drake's mind raced, analyzing every detail with the precision honed by years of legal practice. The family photos on the walls seemed to mock him with their frozen smiles, reminders of a life that now felt light-years away.

As he approached the master bedroom, Drake's hand trembled slightly, hovering over the doorknob. He hesitated, a wave of dread washing over him.

"Come on, Drake," he muttered to himself. "Whatever's on the other side of this door, you can handle it. You have to."

Taking a deep breath, he pushed the door open. The sight that greeted him sent a jolt of icy fear through his veins.

The bedroom lay in perfect order, undisturbed and immaculate. But it was empty. Devoid of life. The bed, still neatly made, stood as a silent accusation.

"No," Drake whispered, his voice barely audible. "This can't be happening."

He stumbled forward, running his hand over the cool, untouched bedspread. The scent of Linda's perfume lingered faintly in the air, a ghostly reminder of what was lost.

"Where are you?" he asked the empty room, desperation creeping into his voice. "What kind of sick game is this?"

5 - 6

Drake's heart plummeted as he surveyed the desolate space, his keen attorney's mind racing with a torrent of questions and doubts. The closet door stood ajar, revealing Linda's meticulously organized wardrobe, untouched and hauntingly pristine.

"Linda!" he called out, his voice cracking. "Please, if you're here, answer me!"

Silence was his only reply, mocking and oppressive.

Drake's thoughts spiraled as he paced the room. "Did she flee? Was she taken? Or is this some cruel trick of the multiverse?" He ran his fingers through his hair, fighting to maintain his composure. "Think, Drake. What would you tell a client in this situation?"

But this was no courtroom, and logic seemed to have abandoned him in this eerie, familiar-yet-wrong version of his home.

With trembling hands, Drake yanked open drawers, searching for any clue. "There has to be something," he muttered. "A note, a sign... anything."

As desperation clawed at his chest, Drake's methodical search became frantic. He tore through the study, upended the living room, and scoured the kitchen. His voice, once commanding in courtrooms, now echoed hollowly through empty halls.

"Linda! Linda! Can you hear me?"

The silence that greeted him was deafening, a stark reminder of the void that now loomed large in his life. Drake slumped against the wall, his breathing ragged.

"What if I've lost her forever?" he whispered, the weight of that possibility crushing down on him. "What if I'm trapped here alone?"

7 - 8

Drake slid down the wall, his legs giving way beneath him. He cradled his head in his hands, his fingers digging into his scalp. The cold, hard floor beneath him felt like the only solid thing in a world spinning out of control.

"No," he muttered, his voice barely audible. "I can't accept that. I won't."

With a deep breath, Drake lifted his head, his eyes blazing with renewed determination. He pushed himself to his feet, his lawyer's mind kicking into gear.

"Okay, Miller," he said aloud, his tone sharpening. "What are the facts? Linda's gone, but there's no sign of struggle. No note, no message. This isn't just our world - it's a parallel universe. Anything could have happened."

He began to pace, his footsteps echoing in the empty house. "If I found my way here, there must be a way to find her."

Drake's gaze fell on a framed photo of Linda and Harrison, their smiles frozen in time. He picked it up, his thumb tracing their faces.

"I swear," he whispered, his voice thick with emotion, "I will find you. No matter how many worlds I have to search, no matter what it costs me. I won't stop until we're together again."

Setting the photo down, Drake straightened his shoulders. The vast, unknowable expanse of the multiverse loomed before him, a daunting challenge to any ordinary man. But Drake Miller was far from ordinary.

"Where do I start?" he mused, his analytical mind already formulating plans. "The Nexus? Or should I try to retrace my steps through the other worlds?"

As he contemplated his next move, a flicker of hope ignited in his chest. In a reality where anything was possible, surely love could conquer even the barriers between worlds.

"Hold on, Linda," Drake said softly, his resolve burning bright. "I'm coming for you. Both of you. And nothing in this universe - or any other - will stop me."

9 - 9

Drake's fingers traced the edge of the photo frame, his eyes never leaving Linda's captured smile. The weight of the multiverse pressed down on his shoulders, but in that moment, he felt a surge of determination coursing through his veins.

"I'll find you," he whispered, his voice barely audible. "Even if I have to tear apart the fabric of reality itself."

He set the frame down gently, his attorney's mind already mapping out a strategy. Turning to face the empty room, Drake spoke aloud, his words a challenge to the universe itself.

"Alright, where do I start? The Green world? What other possibilities do I have?"

His eyes narrowed as he recalled visions of the surreal, kaleidoscopic realm that existed beyond time and space. The memory of it sent a shiver down his spine, but he pushed the feeling aside.

"It's the logical first step," he reasoned, pacing the room. "If anyone knows how to navigate the multiverse, it'll be Justin. I have to find him first."

Drake paused, a wry smile tugging at his lips. "Of course, getting there might be a challenge in itself. It's not like I can hail a cab to a realm beyond time."

He ran a hand through his dark hair, his mind racing. "Maybe there's a pattern to these... jumps. Something I can trigger."

As he spoke, Drake felt a familiar tingle at the base of his skull, a precursor to the dimensional shifts he'd experienced before. His heart raced with a mixture of anticipation and fear.

"Linda," he breathed, closing his eyes. "Guide me to you. Our love transcends space and time. It has to be enough."

Flash of Fate

1 - 2

A brilliant flash of white light consumed Drake Miller, his determined expression the last thing visible before he vanished entirely. Dr. Rachel Summers blinked away the afterimage, her heart racing with a mixture of hope and trepidation.

"He's gone," Harrison whispered, his voice barely audible over the hum of laboratory equipment. "Dad's really gone to find Mom."

Rachel placed a comforting hand on Harrison's shoulder, feeling the tension in his muscles. "Your father is resourceful. If anyone can navigate the multiverse to find Linda, it's him."

The sudden blare of a news alert drew their attention to the wall-mounted television. President Lockhart's stern visage filled the screen, the American flag a solemn backdrop behind him.

"My fellow Americans," the President began, his voice resonating with gravitas, "we face an unprecedented crisis."

Rachel's stomach clenched. The virus was spreading faster than they'd anticipated. She glanced at the vials of Drake's blood, their crimson contents a stark reminder of the stakes.

"Stay calm," she murmured, unsure if she was addressing Harrison or herself. "We need to focus."

As President Lockhart detailed the escalating pandemic, Rachel's mind raced. How much time did they have before the virus reached critical mass? Would Drake return with Linda before it was too late?

The President's words painted a grim picture: "Quarantine zones are being established in major cities. I urge all citizens to comply with emergency measures."

Harrison's fists clenched at his sides. "We can't just sit here and watch," he said, his father's determination evident in his voice. "There has to be something we can do."

Rachel nodded, her scientific mind already formulating possibilities. "You're right. We'll start analyzing your father's blood samples immediately. Every second counts."

As they moved towards the lab equipment, Rachel couldn't shake the feeling that they were standing on the precipice of something monumental.

3 - 4

Suddenly, President Lockhart's speech faltered. His eyes widened, a look of sheer terror flashing across his face. Rachel froze, her hand hovering over a vial of Drake's blood.

"Oh God," Harrison whispered, his voice thick with horror.

On the screen, the President's body began to convulse violently. His hands clawed at his throat, face contorting in agony. Rachel's scientific mind raced, recognizing the telltale signs of the virus's advanced stage.

"This can't be happening," she breathed, her heart pounding. "Not on national television."

Harrison grabbed her arm, his grip tight. "Dr. Summers, is this—"

Before he could finish, a collective gasp echoed through the room as President Lockhart's form began to dissolve. It started at his extremities, his fingers crumbling into a fine, crimson mist. The disintegration spread rapidly, consuming his body in seconds.

Rachel's mind reeled. The virus had mutated far beyond their worst predictions. She watched, transfixed, as the last vestiges of the President dissipated into a hovering cloud of scarlet particles.

"It's airborne now," she whispered, the implications hitting her like a physical blow. "And it's evolving faster than we ever imagined."

5 - 6

The studio erupted into chaos. Cameras toppled as technicians fled, their screams piercing through the television's speakers. The feed cut to a wide-eyed news anchor, her face ashen and hands visibly shaking.

"L-ladies and gentlemen," she stammered, "we… we're experiencing some technical difficulties. Please stand by as we—"

Her voice cracked, and she looked off-camera, terror etched across her features. "Oh God, it's here too. Run! Everyone run!"

Dr. Rachel Summers felt her blood run cold as the broadcast devolved into a cacophony of screams and static. She gripped the edge of the desk, her knuckles white, struggling to process the nightmarish scene they'd just witnessed.

"This is unprecedented," she murmured, more to herself than anyone else. "The rate of transmission, the speed of cellular degradation… it defies everything we know about viral pathology."

Harrison's voice cut through her thoughts, trembling but determined. "Dr. Summers, what does this mean for us? For everyone?"

Rachel turned to face him, her mind racing through calculations and possibilities. She saw the fear in his eyes, mirroring her own inner turmoil.

"It means," she said, choosing her words carefully, "that we're dealing with something far beyond a simple pandemic. This virus… it's almost as if it's been engineered to maximize devastation across multiple realities. Realities as we know it are colliding, collapsing in on themselves."

She paused, the weight of her realization settling heavily on her shoulders. "We're not just fighting to save our world anymore, Harrison. We're in a race against time to save the entire multiverse."

7 - 8

Dr. Rachel Summers took a deep breath, steadying herself against the overwhelming tide of implications. She turned to face her companions, her expression a mask of grim determination. The air in the room felt thick, charged with the gravity of the moment.

"It has begun," she whispered, her voice barely audible above the hum of equipment. "The worlds are colliding."

Dr. Jeremy Monroe stepped forward, his brow furrowed with concern. "Colliding? Rachel, what exactly do you mean?"

Rachel's eyes darted to the Ancient Codex lying open on a nearby table, its cryptic symbols seeming to pulse with an otherworldly energy. "The virus," she explained, her voice gaining strength. "It's not just spreading within our reality. It's breaching the barriers between dimensions, infecting multiple versions of our world simultaneously."

Harrison slumped into a chair, his face pale. "How is that even possible?"

"I don't know," Rachel admitted, running a hand through her hair. "But I fear it has something to do with the unique properties of the virus. It's almost as if it's… aware."

As her words hung in the air, a palpable sense of foreboding settled over the group. Rachel could feel the weight of their collective anxiety pressing down on her, threatening to crush her resolve. But she couldn't afford to falter, not now.

"We're standing at a crossroads," she continued, her gaze sweeping across the faces of her team. "Our actions here, in this lab, may well determine the fate of countless realities."

Dr. Monroe nodded solemnly. "Then we must redouble our efforts. Every second counts."

Rachel felt a surge of gratitude for her colleague's unwavering support. "You're right, Jeremy. We need to—"

She was cut off by a sudden tremor that shook the building, causing equipment to rattle ominously. The lights flickered, and for a moment, Rachel caught a glimpse of something impossible—a shimmering, translucent barrier rippling through the air, as if the very fabric of reality was tearing at the seams.

As quickly as it appeared, the phenomenon vanished, leaving them in stunned silence. Rachel's heart raced, her mind struggling to process what she'd just witnessed. She knew, with chilling certainty, that their greatest challenge had only just begun.

9 - 10

The television screen flickered, casting an eerie glow across the faces of Dr. Rachel Summers and her team. President Lockhart's disintegration replayed in a haunting loop, each iteration driving home the horrifying reality they now faced.

Rachel's fingers dug into the edge of the lab table, her knuckles white with tension. She forced herself to breathe, to think rationally despite the chaos unfolding before them.

"This isn't just a pandemic anymore," she murmured, her voice barely audible above the frantic chatter of news anchors. "It's a collision of realities on a scale we've never seen before."

Dr. Jeremy Monroe stepped closer, his normally calm demeanor visibly shaken. "Rachel, how is this possible? The barriers between worlds—"

"Are collapsing," she finished, meeting his worried gaze. "And with them, our understanding of what's possible."

Rachel's mind raced, piecing together fragments of information from the Ancient Codex, her own research, and the terrifying spectacle they'd just witnessed. The weight of responsibility pressed down on her, threatening to overwhelm her resolve.

"We need to act," she said, more to herself than the others. "But how do we fight something that defies the laws of our reality?"

As if in response to her question, another tremor shook the lab, stronger this time. Equipment rattled, and for a split second, Rachel swore she saw the air itself ripple, like heat haze on a scorching day.

"Time," she whispered, a cold realization settling in her gut. "We're running out of time."

11 - 12

Dr. Rachel Summers squared her shoulders, her piercing gaze sweeping across the faces of her colleagues. The air in the lab felt charged, thick with tension and the lingering echoes of President Lockhart's demise.

"We need to act fast," Dr. Summers declared, her voice tinged with urgency. Her fingers tapped a rapid rhythm on the sleek surface of a nearby console, betraying her inner turmoil. "If what we've witnessed is any indication, the virus is spreading rapidly, and we can't afford to wait for it to reach our doorstep."

The crimson mist that had enveloped the President flashed through her mind, a chilling reminder of the devastation they faced. Rachel's heart raced, her scientific mind already formulating potential strategies, discarding those too risky or improbable.

Harrison nodded in agreement, his expression grim. His eyes, so reminiscent of his father's, held a mix of determination and fear. "But what can we do?" he asked, running a hand through his hair in frustration. "We don't even know where to begin."

Rachel observed the young man, noting the tension in his lean frame, the way his hands clenched and unclenched at his sides. She felt a pang of sympathy, remembering her own first encounters with multiverse threats.

"We start with what we know," she replied, her tone softening slightly. "The virus adapts across realities, which means our approach must be equally flexible. If someone in one reality becomes infected, the virus mutates the individual's DNA spreading across multiple realities throughout the multiverse, finding every version of the known individual and contaminating them, destroying them from the insides. Once every known version is infected, they become connected throughout time and space and eventually collapse in on themselves as they merge together. What we witnessed is the beginning of the collapse of life as we know it." Her mind raced through possibilities, each more daunting than the last. How does one combat a threat that rewrites the rules of existence with each passing moment?

13 - 14

Rachel's gaze swept across the worried faces of her team, lingering on Harrison. The weight of their situation pressed down on her shoulders like a tangible force. She took a deep breath, steeling herself for what she knew she had to say.

"We better hope your father gets back in time and gives us his blood to manufacture this cure," she said, her voice steady despite the gravity of her words. "The only way to stop the spread is to contain it and isolate it. With a vaccine, if my theory is correct it'll work like the virus, instead curing an individual and spreading throughout the multiverse saving all variations of them."

The air in the room seemed to thicken, the tension palpable as the implications of her statement sank in. Rachel watched as Harrison's eyes widened, a mix of hope and trepidation flashing across his face. She could almost see the gears turning in his mind, processing the weight of responsibility that now rested on his father's shoulders.

Meghan Johnson, her usually composed demeanor cracking under the strain, spoke up. Her voice trembled slightly as she voiced the question that hung heavy in everyone's minds. "And if Drake doesn't return in time?"

The question hit Rachel like a physical blow. She closed her eyes for a moment, feeling the pressure of countless lives hanging in the balance. The image of President Lockhart dissolving into that horrifying crimson mist played on repeat in her mind, a grim reminder of what awaited them all if they failed.

When she opened her eyes again, Rachel found herself looking directly at Harrison. The young man stood straighter, as if bracing himself for what was to come. In that moment, she saw a glimpse of Drake in him – that same stubborn determination in the face of impossible odds.

15 - 15

Dr. Summers took a deep breath, her voice steady as she addressed Harrison. "Then you best hope you have enough blood in your body to save the entire world. Without your father, you're our only chance at salvation."

Harrison's face paled, his hands clenching into fists at his sides. The weight of Dr. Summers' words seemed to physically press down on his shoulders. He swallowed hard, his mind racing. Could he really be the key to saving not just this world, but countless others across the multiverse?

Dr. Summers stepped closer, her eyes softening with empathy. "I know it's a lot to take in, Harrison. But your blood, like your father's, carries a unique genetic marker. It's our best hope for developing a cure."

Harrison's gaze drifted to the ancient codex on the nearby table, its weathered pages seeming to mock him with their cryptic symbols. He thought of his father, vanished into that ball of white light, risking everything to find his mother. And now, here he was, potentially holding the fate of countless realities in his veins.

"What if it's not enough?" he asked, voicing his deepest fear. "What if I'm not enough?"

Dr. Summers placed a reassuring hand on his shoulder. "We won't know until we try. But Harrison, you've already shown incredible strength and resilience. You're more capable than you realize."

Harrison closed his eyes, taking a deep breath. When he opened them again, there was a newfound determination in his gaze. "Alright," he said, rolling up his sleeve. "Let's do this. For my dad, for all the worlds out there... I'm ready."

Echoes in the Station

Blue World – 2024

1 - 2

Drake's hand pushes open the heavy glass door of the police station, its surface smudged with countless fingerprints.

Drake's footsteps echoed through the empty lobby, each step punctuated by the crinkle of scattered papers beneath his feet. The air hung thick with an eerie stillness, a stark contrast to the usual bustle of law enforcement activity. His eyes scanned the deserted space, taking in overturned chairs and abandoned coffee cups, their contents long since gone cold.

What happened here? Drake thought, his lawyer's mind already cataloging the details, searching for clues. The silence pressed in on him, broken only by the steady hum of fluorescent lights flickering overhead.

As he made his way deeper into the station, Drake's hand instinctively reached for his cell phone, his fingers hovering over the keypad. Should he call for backup? But who would come in a world that seemed to be unraveling at the seams?

Rounding a corner, Drake's breath caught in his throat. There, amidst the chaos of strewn files and toppled filing cabinets, stood Chief Detective Franklin Bird. The older man's usually commanding presence seemed diminished, his shoulders slumped under an invisible weight.

"Chief Bird," Drake called out, his voice sounding unnaturally loud in the silence. "What's going on here?"

Bird turned slowly, his weathered face a mask of sorrow and resignation. "Drake," he acknowledged with a nod. "I wish I had answers for you, son. But the truth is, I'm as lost as you are."

Drake stepped closer, careful not to disturb the sea of papers at his feet. "Where is everyone? It looks like they left in a hurry."

"That's because they did," Bird replied, his voice gruff. "One minute it was business as usual, the next..." He gestured to the emptiness around them. "It's like this all over the city. People just... vanishing."

A chill ran down Drake's spine as he processed Bird's words. *Vanishing. Just like Linda.* The thought of his wife sent a fresh wave of determination coursing through him.

"Chief," Drake began, his tone shifting to the precise, measured cadence he used in the courtroom, "I need your help. Linda's missing, and I think it's connected to whatever's happening here."

Bird's eyes narrowed, a flicker of his old authority returning. "Connected how, Drake? What do you know?"

Drake hesitated, weighing how much to reveal. The multiverse, the alternate realities – it all sounded insane, even to him. But as he looked into Bird's tired eyes, he saw a man desperate for answers, just like himself.

"It's complicated, Chief," Drake said finally. "And you might not believe me. But I think we're dealing with something far beyond our normal understanding of reality."

3 - 4

Bird's expression hardened, his weathered face a map of worry lines. "Drake, I've known you for years. You're not one for wild theories. What's really going on?"

Drake ran his fingers through his hair, a telltale sign of his inner turmoil. "Chief Bird," he called out, his voice echoing in the silence of the station. "Have you seen Linda? Is she here?"

The desperation in Drake's tone hung in the air, mingling with the eerie stillness of the abandoned precinct. *Please*, he thought, *let her be here. Let this nightmare end*.

Bird turned to face Drake, his weary eyes reflecting the weight of the world upon his shoulders. For a moment, he seemed to age a decade before Drake's eyes. "I'm sorry, Drake," he replied somberly. "There's no one here. The place is deserted."

The words hit Drake like a physical blow. He staggered slightly, catching himself on a nearby desk. *Linda's not here. She's gone, just like everyone else*. The thought threatened to overwhelm him, but he forced it down, clinging to the last shreds of his determination.

"Chief," Drake said, his voice barely above a whisper, "what's happening to our world?"

Bird's gaze drifted to the window, where an unsettling green twilight had settled over the city. "I wish I knew, Drake. I wish I knew."

5 - 6

A pang of fear gripped Drake's heart, his chest tightening as he absorbed Bird's words. The eerie green twilight filtering through the windows cast long shadows across the cluttered desks, amplifying the desolation that surrounded them. Drake's mind raced, grasping for any thread of hope.

"What about Holly?" he pressed, desperation creeping into his voice. His fingers curled into fists at his sides, knuckles white with tension. "Did she mention anything about Linda?"

Drake's eyes searched Bird's face, silently pleading for any scrap of information. *Please, Holly, you must have found something. Anything.*

Bird shook his head regretfully, his weathered features etched with sorrow. "I'm afraid not, Drake," he replied, his voice heavy. "But she did call for an ambulance earlier. Said something about Linda being taken to another hospital outside of the city limits."

Drake's breath caught in his throat. *Outside the city? Why would they move her?* His mind conjured images of Linda, alone and vulnerable in some unknown facility. He took a step closer to Bird, his heart pounding.

"Which hospital?" Drake demanded, his tone urgent. "Did Holly say anything else?"

As he waited for Bird's response, Drake's gaze darted around the empty station, the silence pressing in on him from all sides. *This isn't right*, he thought. *None of this is right. What's happening to our world?*

7 - 8

Drake's stomach churned with apprehension, the mention of Linda's name sending a fresh wave of anguish through him. He swallowed hard, trying to maintain his composure. "Thank you, Chief," he murmured, his voice tinged with gratitude despite the turmoil roiling within.

He turned to leave, his mind already racing with possibilities. *Outside the city limits... I need to start searching, now.* But before he could take a step, Bird's voice cut through the eerie stillness of the abandoned station.

"Drake," the Chief said, his tone heavy with sorrow. "I need to tell you something."

Drake froze, his heart skipping a beat. He slowly pivoted back to face Bird, noting the grim set of the older man's jaw. *What now?* he thought, bracing himself for another blow. *How much more can I take?*

"What is it, Franklin?" Drake asked, his voice barely above a whisper. He searched the Chief's face, trying to glean some hint of what was coming. The weight of Bird's impending words seemed to press down on them both, amplifying the oppressive silence of the deserted precinct.

As he waited for Bird to speak, Drake's mind raced through a kaleidoscope of possibilities, each more terrifying than the last. *Linda... oh God, please let her be alright. I can't lose her again. I can't.*

9 - 10

Bird's weathered face contorted, his eyes reflecting a storm of emotions. He cleared his throat, the sound echoing in the desolate room. "The analysis of the blood left behind by Gabriel," he began, his voice low and strained. "It originally didn't match what Dr. Lee discovered."

Drake's brow furrowed, his mind struggling to process this new information. *What does this mean?* He leaned forward, hanging on Bird's every word.

"There were no signs of the three DNA strands," Bird continued, his gaze dropping to the floor. "There was only one. It belonged to Harrison, your son. We were flawed in our findings."

A chill ran down Drake's spine. *No. That can't be right.* He opened his mouth to speak, but Bird pressed on.

"Holly told me what you went through, how you knew about the bomb at the hospital." The Chief's eyes met Drake's, filled with a mixture of awe and concern.

Drake's heart raced, memories of that harrowing moment flooding back. *How could I have known? Was it just intuition, or something more?* He clenched his fists, trying to ground himself in the present.

Bird's voice softened. "I'm sorry, Drake. I hope you find your wife."

The sincerity in the Chief's tone hit Drake like a physical blow. He staggered back a step, overwhelmed by the implications of what he'd just heard. *Our findings were wrong. The DNA strands... Linda... What's really going on here?*

11 - 12

"And there's something else," Bird continued, his gaze haunted. The flickering fluorescent light cast deep shadows across his weathered face, accentuating the lines of worry etched into his skin. "This world... it's falling apart, Drake. We've run out of time."

Drake's heart hammered in his chest, a cold dread seeping into his bones. "What do you mean, Chief?" he asked, his lawyer's instinct for precision kicking in despite the surreal circumstances.

Bird's eyes darted around the empty station, as if searching for invisible threats. "Can't you feel it? The fabric of reality itself is unraveling. It's like... like the laws of physics are breaking down."

He's right, Drake realized with a start. The air felt charged, almost electric, and there was a strange shimmer at the edges of his vision. *But how is this possible?*

"We need to—" Drake began, but his words died in his throat as he watched Chief Bird reach for his holster with trembling hands.

Time seemed to slow as Bird drew his service weapon, the polished metal glinting under the harsh lights. Drake's mind raced, searching for the right words to defuse the situation. *This can't be happening. Not Bird. He's always been the steady one.*

"Chief, wait!" Drake called out, his voice cracking with desperation. "We can figure this out together. Just put the gun down and—"

But it was too late. With a look of grim determination, Bird pressed the barrel against his temple. Drake lunged forward, but he knew he'd never reach the Chief in time.

"I'm sorry, Drake," Bird whispered, his finger tightening on the trigger. "Find Linda. Save what's left."

The gunshot rang out, deafeningly loud in the empty station, and Drake's world shattered once again.

13 - 13

The thunderous echo of the gunshot reverberated through the empty halls, each repetition hammering home the finality of Bird's decision. Drake stood frozen, his ears ringing, as he watched the Chief's body crumple to the floor.

"No, no, no," Drake muttered, his legs finally propelling him forward. He knelt beside Bird, his hands hovering uselessly over the fallen man. The acrid smell of gunpowder mingled with the metallic tang of blood, turning Drake's stomach.

This can't be happening, he thought, his mind reeling. *First Holly, now this. How much more can I lose?*

As the shock began to ebb, a new urgency surged through Drake's veins. He rose to his feet, his piercing gaze sweeping the abandoned station. "Linda," he whispered, her name a talisman against the encroaching darkness.

Drake's attorney's mind kicked into high gear, analyzing the situation with cold precision. "Outside the city limits," he murmured, recalling Bird's final words. "But which hospital? And why would Holly take her there?"

He strode towards the exit, each step filled with renewed purpose. "I'll find you, Linda," Drake vowed, his voice echoing in the empty corridor. "Whatever it takes, whatever world I have to search, I'll bring you home."

As he pushed open the station doors, the sky above seemed to ripple and shift, as if reality itself was coming apart at the seams. Drake squared his shoulders, ready to face whatever challenges lay ahead.

"Hold on, Linda," he said softly. "I'm coming."

Mysteries of the Ancient Codex

1 - 2

The Ancient Codex lay open before Dr. Summers, its weathered pages glowing faintly in the dim light of the research facility. Harrison's eyes were drawn to the intricate patterns on its leather cover, which seemed to shift and dance as he watched. He couldn't shake the feeling that the book itself was alive, pulsing with otherworldly energy.

Dr. Summers hunched over the manuscript, her wire-rimmed glasses perched precariously on the edge of her nose. Her brow furrowed in concentration as her eyes darted across the page, deciphering symbols that defied conventional understanding.

Harrison's heart raced as he observed her. What secrets would she uncover? The fate of their world—of all worlds—hung in the balance. He ran a hand through his tousled hair, a nervous habit he'd never managed to shake.

"Anything?" he asked, unable to contain his impatience any longer.

Dr. Summers held up a hand, silencing him without taking her eyes off the page. "Give me a moment, Harrison. These translations are... complex."

Harrison nodded, chastened. He knew better than to rush her, but the weight of their mission pressed down on him like a physical force. He paced the length of the room, his footsteps echoing in the cavernous space.

What if we can't find the answer? he thought, doubt gnawing at him. What if I'm not the one who can save us after all?

He pushed the thoughts aside, focusing instead on Dr. Summers. Her lips moved silently as she worked, her fingers tracing the glowing symbols on the page. Despite the gravity of their situation, Harrison couldn't help but admire her dedication and brilliance.

"Dr. Summers," he began, his voice soft. "I just wanted to say—"

"Shh!" she interrupted, her eyes widening. "I think I've found something."

Harrison's pulse quickened as he rushed to her side, leaning in to examine the ancient text. The symbols swam before his eyes, to Dr. Summers, they held the key to saving their world—and perhaps countless others.

3 - 4

Dr. Summers' sharp intake of breath shattered the tense silence. Her eyes, wide with astonishment, locked onto Harrison's. "Harrison," she murmured, her voice barely above a whisper. "I think I've found it."

Harrison's heart leapt into his throat. Could this be it? The key to saving not just their world, but all the others teetering on the brink of destruction? He leaned in closer, his pulse quickening with each passing second.

"What is it, Doctor?" he asked, struggling to keep his voice steady. His fingers twitched at his sides, itching to reach out and touch the ancient codex, to see for himself the revelation hidden within its weathered pages.

Dr. Summers' eyes darted back to the text, her brow furrowing as she traced a line with her finger. The soft glow of the symbols cast an eerie light across her face, accentuating the deep lines of concentration etched there.

Is this really happening? Harrison thought, a mix of excitement and trepidation churning in his gut. After all we've been through, all the dead ends and false hopes, could we finally have found the answer?

He held his breath, waiting for Dr. Summers to speak, to confirm that their seemingly impossible mission might actually have a chance of success. The weight of countless lives—across multiple realities—pressed down on his shoulders, making each second of silence feel like an eternity.

5 - 6

Dr. Summers turned to face him, her expression grave. The light from the ancient codex cast deep shadows across her features, accentuating the weight of her words. "I'm afraid we can't use your blood after all," she said, her voice heavy with regret. "This world rests solely in the hands of Drake and his blood."

Harrison felt as if he'd been punched in the gut. The room seemed to spin around him as he struggled to process her words. No, this can't be right. We've come too far for this to be the answer. His mind raced, searching for an alternative explanation, anything that could prove Dr. Summers wrong.

"But why?" he demanded, his voice tinged with frustration. He clenched his fists at his sides, fighting against the growing sense of helplessness threatening to overwhelm him. "I thought my blood held the key to stopping the virus."

As he spoke, Harrison's gaze darted around the dimly lit research facility, taking in the complex machinery and scattered notes that represented days of tireless work. All of it now seemed futile in the face of this new revelation.

Dr. Summers sighed, her shoulders sagging slightly under the weight of her discovery. "I wish it were that simple, Harrison," she said, her tone softening. "But the codex is clear. The unique properties in Drake's blood are the only thing capable of neutralizing the Virus across all dimensions."

Harrison's mind whirled with implications. Drake? But he's not even here. How can we possibly...? He shook his head, trying to clear his thoughts. "There has to be another way," he insisted, more to himself than to Dr. Summers. "We can't just pin all our hopes on someone who doesn't even know about the danger we're facing."

7 - 8

Dr. Summers shook her head, her gaze unwavering. "It's not about the blood itself," she explained patiently, her fingers tracing the ancient symbols on the codex. "It's about the quantity. A single drop wouldn't be enough to manufacture the cure we need to save the world."

Harrison felt the floor tilt beneath him, his heart pounding in his ears. He gripped the edge of the research table, steadying himself as the implications of Dr. Summers' words sank in. The dim blue glow of the lab equipment cast eerie shadows across her face, emphasizing the gravity of her expression.

"How much?" he asked, his voice barely a whisper. "How much blood are we talking about?"

Dr. Summers hesitated, her eyes flickering with a mix of compassion and steely resolve. "More than any person could survive losing," she said softly.

The words hit Harrison like a physical blow. His mind raced, desperately seeking alternatives, loopholes, anything to avoid the unthinkable conclusion. But deep down, he knew. He knew what Dr. Summers was implying, and the thought of sacrificing his father for the greater good filled him with a sickening sense of dread and uncertainty.

"There has to be another way," Harrison insisted, his voice cracking. "We can't just... we can't..."

Dr. Summers reached out, placing a comforting hand on his shoulder. "I'm sorry, Harrison. I wish there was another solution. But the fate of not just our world, but countless others, hangs in the balance."

Harrison closed his eyes, memories of his father flooding his mind. Drake's laughter, his unwavering support, the strength that had carried their family through so much. How could he even consider sacrificing that? And yet, the weight of billions of lives pressed down on him, an impossible burden to bear.

"What do we do now?" he asked, opening his eyes to meet Dr. Summers' gaze, searching for guidance in the face of this overwhelming revelation.

9 - 10

Harrison's fingers gripped the edge of the research table, his knuckles turning white as he fought to steady himself. The whir and hum of machinery filled the air, a stark contrast to the deathly silence that had fallen between him and Dr. Summers.

"And what exactly do you propose we do?" he asked, his voice barely audible above the ambient noise. The words felt hollow in his mouth, as if by speaking them, he was somehow complicit in the unthinkable decision looming before them.

Dr. Summers' expression twisted with pain, her usual composure cracking under the weight of what she was about to say. She took a deep breath, steeling herself. "We need to extract all of Drake's blood," she said solemnly, each word measured and heavy. "And then we must use it to manufacture the cure. It seems that that was the way it was always meant to be. It's written all right here in the codex. Drake drinking the chosen one's blood, Drakes sacrifice, the virus, the multiversal collison. Every action, every consequence has been predetermined and written down throughout history years ago. All roads led to this outcome; this is manifest destiny."

Harrison's stomach lurched. He opened his mouth to protest, but Dr. Summers continued before he could speak.

"But in order for it to be effective, Drake must..." she faltered for a moment, her voice catching. "He must die."

The words hung in the air between them, sharp and devastating. Harrison's mind reeled, unable to fully process the implications. He thought of his father – strong, determined Drake – and tried to reconcile that image with the sacrifice Dr. Summers was proposing.

"There has to be another way," Harrison whispered, more to himself than to Dr. Summers. "We can't just... How could we even ask him to do this?"

Dr. Summers' eyes shimmered with unshed tears, her scientific detachment warring with her humanity. "I wish there was an alternative, Harrison. But the multiverse is at stake. Billions of lives across countless realities... they all depend on this."

Harrison closed his eyes, feeling the weight of worlds pressing down on his shoulders. How could they make this choice? How could they not?

11 - 12

The harsh fluorescent lights flickered overhead, casting stark shadows across Harrison's face as he struggled to breathe. The air felt thick, oppressive, as if the very fabric of reality was closing in around them.

"Drake... my father," Harrison choked out, his voice raw with emotion. "He's always been the hero, the one willing to sacrifice everything. But this..." He trailed off, unable to finish the thought.

Dr. Summers reached out, her hand trembling slightly as she placed it on Harrison's arm. "I know," she said softly, her eyes filled with a mixture of compassion and steely resolve. "But sometimes being a hero means making impossible choices."

Harrison's mind raced, images of his father flashing before his eyes – Drake teaching him to throw a baseball, comforting him after nightmares, standing tall against threats from other realities. How could they ask him to give up everything?

"What if we're wrong?" Harrison asked, his voice barely above a whisper. "What if there's another way we haven't considered?"

Dr. Summers shook her head, her grip on Harrison's arm tightening. "We've explored every possibility, run every simulation. This is the only way to stop the virus from consuming everything."

Harrison met her gaze, searching for any sign of doubt, any flicker of uncertainty. But all he saw was unwavering determination, a strength that both terrified and inspired him.

"How do we even begin to have this conversation with him?" Harrison asked, his voice cracking.

Dr. Summers took a deep breath, her expression softening for a moment. "With honesty, and with the understanding that we're asking for the ultimate sacrifice to save countless lives."

As Harrison looked at her, he realized that the weight of this decision wasn't his alone to bear. Dr. Summers carried it too, along with the responsibility of finding the cure. In that moment, he knew they had no choice but to move forward, no matter how much it tore him apart inside.

13 - 14

Dr. Summers' eyes darted to the holographic display on her wrist, its crimson glow casting an eerie light across her face. "We don't have much time," she said, her voice firm and resolute. "We need to act quickly if we're going to stop the virus from spreading any further."

Harrison felt his chest tighten, the gravity of their situation crushing down on him like a physical weight. He nodded, his mind a whirlwind of conflicting emotions. "How long?" he managed to ask, his voice barely above a whisper.

"Based on the latest projections, we have less than 48 hours before the virus reaches critical mass," Dr. Summers replied, her fingers dancing across the holographic interface. "After that, containment will be impossible."

Harrison's gaze fell to the ancient codex still lying open on the table, its weathered pages a stark reminder of the choice they faced. He ran a hand through his hair, trying to quell the rising panic in his chest. "And if we don't do this... if we don't use Drake's blood..."

Dr. Summers' expression softened for a moment, her eyes meeting Harrison's. "Then we lose everything. Not just this world, but every reality the virus can reach."

The weight of her words bore down on Harrison, threatening to crush him. He closed his eyes, memories of Drake flashing through his mind – shared laughter, quiet conversations, the unspoken bond between them. How could he reconcile those moments with the cold, harsh reality of what they needed to do?

"I understand the science," Harrison said, his voice hoarse. "But how do we live with ourselves after this? How do we justify sacrificing one life, even to save billions?"

Dr. Summers placed a hand on his shoulder, her touch both comforting and grounding. "We don't justify it, Harrison. We carry the weight of it, always. But we do what must be done to ensure there's a future at all."

15 - 16

Harrison's stomach churned as he wrestled with the impossible decision before them. He paced the dimly lit lab, the hum of machinery a discordant backdrop to his tumultuous thoughts.

"But how do we even begin to approach dad about this?" he wondered aloud, his voice tinged with uncertainty. He turned to face Dr. Summers, his eyes searching her face for answers. "How do we ask him to sacrifice himself for the greater good?"

The weight of the question hung heavy in the air between them. Harrison's mind raced, imagining Drake's reaction – shock, anger, fear? Would he understand? Or would he fight against a fate that seemed unimaginably cruel?

Dr. Summers stepped forward, closing the distance between them. Her touch was gentle as she placed a hand on Harrison's shoulder, a reassuring anchor in the sea of turmoil that surrounded them.

"We'll find a way," she said, her voice soft yet filled with unwavering determination. Her eyes, usually sharp with scientific focus, now held a compassionate warmth. "We'll make him understand that this is the only way to save our world."

Harrison felt a glimmer of hope at her words, but it was quickly overshadowed by the enormity of what lay ahead. He swallowed hard, his throat tight. "And if he refuses? If he can't bring himself to make that sacrifice?"

Dr. Summers' grip on his shoulder tightened slightly. "Then we'll face that challenge when we come to it. But Harrison, remember – Drake is part of this fight too. We have to trust in his strength, his courage."

17 - 18

Harrison drew a deep breath, feeling the weight of their impossible task settling on his shoulders. He met Dr. Summers' gaze, finding strength in her unwavering resolve. With a curt nod, he straightened his posture, squaring his shoulders as if preparing for battle.

"You're right," he said, his voice low but firm. "We can't falter now. Not when everything's at stake."

Dr. Summers gave a small, approving smile. "That's the spirit. Now, let's figure out our next move."

Harrison's mind raced as he paced the dimly lit lab, his footsteps echoing in the cavernous space. "We need to approach this carefully," he mused aloud. "Dad's not just a means to an end – he's a person, with fears and hopes of his own."

Dr. Summers nodded, her fingers flying across a holographic keyboard as she pulled up data on a nearby screen. "Agreed. We should present him with all the facts, let him see the full scope of what we're facing."

Harrison paused, a thought striking him. "What about showing him the infected areas? If he could see the devastation firsthand..."

"That could work," Dr. Summers replied, her eyes lighting up. "We have access to live feeds from the quarantine zones. It might help drive home the urgency of our situation."

As they spoke, Harrison felt a mix of determination and dread churning in his gut. He couldn't shake the image of Drake's face when they broke the news – would it be horror? Resignation? Or perhaps a noble acceptance that Harrison wasn't sure he himself could muster in the same situation.

"Once we've laid out the facts," Harrison continued, his voice tight with tension, "how do we... how do we actually ask him to do this?"

Dr. Summers' fingers stilled on the keyboard. She turned to face Harrison, her expression grave. "We tell him the truth, Harrison. That he has the power to save millions of lives. That without his sacrifice, our world – perhaps even the entire multiverse – will fall."

19 - 20

Harrison nodded slowly, his throat constricting. The weight of their plan pressed down on him, threatening to crush his resolve. He glanced at the ancient codex still lying open on the desk, its cryptic symbols a stark reminder of the cosmic forces at play.

"It's not just about our world, is it?" he murmured, his eyes tracing the intricate patterns on the weathered pages. "If this virus spreads across realities..."

Dr. Summers' voice was barely above a whisper. "The consequences would be unimaginable."

A heavy silence fell between them, broken only by the soft hum of equipment. Harrison's mind raced, grappling with the enormity of their task. He thought of Drake – his determination, his unwavering pursuit of justice. Would that same drive compel him to make the ultimate sacrifice?

"What if..." Harrison began, his voice hesitant. "What if we're wrong? What if there's another way?"

Dr. Summers placed a comforting hand on his shoulder. "We have to trust the codex, Harrison. It's led us this far."

He met her gaze, seeing his own conflicted emotions mirrored in her eyes. "I know," he said softly. "It's just... asking someone to die, even to save everything... it feels wrong."

"It does," she agreed, her voice steady despite the gravity of their conversation. "But sometimes, the right path isn't the easy one."

Harrison took a deep breath, steeling himself. "Alright," he said, his resolve strengthening. "Let's finish this plan. For Dad. For everyone."

As they turned back to their work, a faint shimmer caught Harrison's eye. He blinked, wondering if he'd imagined it, but there it was again – a subtle ripple in the air, like heat haze on a summer day. His heart quickened. Could it be a sign from the Nexus itself, an affirmation of their chosen path?

"Dr. Summers," he said, his voice low with wonder. "Look."

Haunted Hospital Run

Blue World – 2024

1 - 2

The flickering fluorescent lights cast an eerie green glow over the abandoned hospital corridor, mirroring the sickly pallor of Drake's face as he sprinted past empty gurneys and overturned medical carts. His heart pounded in his ears, drowning out the distant wail of sirens from the world outside.

"Linda!" Drake's voice echoed off the sterile walls, desperation clawing at his throat. "Linda, where are you?"

His mind raced, analyzing each room he passed with the precision honed from years of legal practice. Where would they have taken her? Intensive care? Emergency ward?

As he rounded a corner, Drake caught sight of a partially open door at the end of the hall. Something tugged at his consciousness, an inexplicable certainty that Linda was there.

Please, let her be okay, he thought, his typically composed demeanor crumbling under the weight of fear.

Drake burst into the room, his eyes immediately locking onto the still form on the hospital bed. "Linda," he breathed, rushing to her side.

His hands shook as he gently cradled her face, his fingers brushing against skin that felt too cool, too lifeless. "Linda, sweetheart, can you hear me?" Drake pleaded, searching for any sign of recognition in her closed eyes.

She's so pale, he thought, panic rising in his chest. What happened to her? What's wrong?

"Come on, Linda," Drake urged, his voice breaking. "Open your eyes. Look at me, please. I need you to come back to me."

He stroked her hair, willing her to respond, to give him any indication that she was still with him. "We've been through so much together," he whispered. "We can get through this too. Just... just wake up."

As the seconds ticked by with no response, Drake felt a cold dread settling in his stomach. This can't be happening, he thought. Not after everything we've survived. Not when I've just found her again.

"Linda," he tried once more, his lawyer's eloquence reduced to a single, desperate plea. "Please."

3 - 4

Drake's eyes frantically scanned Linda's motionless form, searching for any sign of life. Her chest barely moved with shallow breaths, each one seeming more fragile than the last. The silence in the room was deafening, broken only by the sound of his own ragged breathing.

"No, no, no," he muttered, his fingers pressed against her wrist, desperately seeking a pulse. "Come on, Linda. Fight. You've always been the stronger one."

His gaze darted to the various machines surrounding her bed, their screens dark and lifeless. The power must be out, he realized, another wave of panic washing over him.

As he leaned in closer, his eyes caught something on Linda's arm. At first, he thought it was a bruise, but as he gently turned her limb, his breath caught in his throat.

There, etched into her pale skin in stark, dark letters, were two words: "Buried alive."

Drake stumbled back, his mind reeling. "What the hell?" he whispered, his voice hoarse. "Linda, what happened to you?"

He traced the words with a trembling finger, feeling the slightly raised skin. These weren't just written; they were carved. The realization hit him like a physical blow.

"Who did this to you?" he demanded, anger mixing with his fear. "Linda, please, I need you to wake up. I need to understand."

But Linda remained silent, her face serene and unresponsive, oblivious to the horror that now gripped her husband.

Drake's mind raced, trying to make sense of the nightmarish situation. "Buried alive," he repeated, the words tasting like ash in his mouth. "What does it mean? Are you...are we...?"

He looked around the dim hospital room, suddenly feeling as if the walls were closing in. The emptiness, the silence, the words on Linda's arm – it all spoke of a reality far more terrifying than he could have imagined.

5 - 6

Drake's mind whirled, a tempest of questions threatening to overwhelm him. He gripped the edge of Linda's hospital bed, his knuckles turning white as he fought to steady himself.

"How?" he whispered, his voice cracking. "How did this happen to you, Linda?"

His eyes darted between her peaceful face and the chilling words on her arm. The stark contrast was almost too much to bear.

"Did you do this yourself?" he asked, knowing she couldn't answer. "Were you trying to tell me something?"

Drake's legal mind kicked in, analyzing the situation as if it were a complex case. But this was far more personal, far more terrifying than any courtroom drama.

"If you're buried alive somewhere," he said, his voice growing stronger with determination, "I'll find you. I swear it."

He closed his eyes, trying to make sense of the impossible. When he opened them again, a sudden realization hit him like a bolt of lightning.

"The other world," he breathed. "You're alive here, but there... Oh God, Linda."

The pieces began to fall into place, a horrifying picture forming in his mind. In this world, Linda lay before him, clinging to life. But in another reality, a world he had glimpsed, she was...

"No," Drake said firmly, squeezing Linda's hand. "I won't accept that. You're here, you're fighting. And I'm going to fight for you too."

He leaned in close, his lips nearly touching her ear. "I don't know how, but I'm going to save you, Linda. In this world, in every world. I promise."

As he pulled back, Drake's resolve hardened. The multiverse had thrown him into a nightmare, but he would navigate its twisted paths. For Linda, he would move heaven and earth – and even the boundaries of reality itself.

7 - 7

Drake's grip on Linda's hand tightened as he closed his eyes, his brow furrowing in concentration. The hospital room faded away, replaced by an image of Linda trapped, gasping for air in a claustrophobic darkness.

"I'm coming for you," he whispered, his voice barely audible.

He focused all his thoughts on that other world, on Linda's silent plea echoing across realities. The air around him began to crackle with an unseen energy, raising the hair on his arms.

"Drake?" A nurse's voice called from the doorway, startled. "What's happening?"

He couldn't answer, couldn't break his concentration. Linda's face filled his mind – not the pale, unconscious one before him, but the vibrant, loving woman he'd sworn to protect.

"I won't let you go," Drake said through gritted teeth. "Not in any world."

A blinding light erupted around him, engulfing his body. The nurse screamed, but her voice seemed distant, fading.

As the light intensified, Drake felt a violent tugging sensation. His last coherent thought was of Linda, of her warmth, her smile. Then, in a flash that seared his retinas even through closed eyelids, he vanished.

The light dissipated, leaving behind an empty space where Drake had stood moments before. His name hung in the air, a lingering whisper from those who'd witnessed his impossible departure.

Twilight Desperation

Green World – 2024

1 - 2

The air shimmered and crackled as Drake materialized in the Green World, his form coalescing amidst a swirling mist. He stumbled, disoriented by the teleportation, and steadied himself against a gnarled tree trunk. The perpetual twilight cast everything in an eerie green glow, shadows stretching unnaturally across the desolate landscape.

Drake's heart raced as he scanned his surroundings, searching for any sign of his wife. "Linda?" he called out, his voice echoing in the unsettling silence. No response came, save for the whisper of wind through lifeless branches.

He set off with determined strides, leaves crunching beneath his feet. The fog seemed to part before him, revealing a path he knew all too well. *I never thought I'd be back here,* Drake thought, a lump forming in his throat. *Not after burying her.*

As he approached the small clearing where Linda's grave lay, an icy dread gripped his chest. Something was wrong. The ground looked disturbed, freshly turned earth scattered about.

"No, no, no," Drake muttered, quickening his pace. He fell to his knees beside the grave, hands trembling as they scraped at the loose soil. "This can't be happening."

The hole gaped before him, an empty maw where Linda's body should have been. Drake's mind reeled, trying to make sense of the impossible. "Who would do this?" he shouted into the void, his voice cracking with anguish and confusion.

Think, Drake. Apply the same logic you'd use in court, he told himself, struggling to maintain composure. But this was no courtroom, and the rules of this world defied all reason.

"Linda!" he called out again, desperation creeping into his tone. "If you're out there, if you can hear me, please give me a sign!"

Only the eerie silence of the Green World answered him. Drake stood, brushing dirt from his hands, his eyes scanning the treeline for any movement. *I won't fail you again,* he vowed silently. *I'll find you, Linda. Whatever it takes.*

With one last look at the empty grave, Drake set off into the misty unknown, each step carrying him deeper into the heart of this isolating realm. The weight of uncertainty pressed down on him, but his determination burned brighter than ever. Somewhere in this twisted version of reality, Linda was waiting. And Drake would not rest until he brought her home.

3 - 4

Drake's footsteps echoed through the empty streets as he approached the familiar silhouette of their house. The perpetual twilight cast long shadows across the overgrown lawn, making the once-welcoming home seem alien and foreboding.

"Linda?" he called out, his voice trembling with a mixture of hope and dread. No response came.

Drake pushed open the front door, wincing at the ominous creak. The musty air inside hit him like a wall, carrying the scent of abandonment and decay. He moved through the dim interior, his lawyer's mind cataloging every detail, searching for clues.

As he entered the living room, his breath caught in his throat. There, on the faded couch, lay Linda's motionless form.

"Oh God, Linda!" Drake rushed to her side, his heart pounding. He gently cupped her face, noting the unnatural pallor of her skin. "Linda, can you hear me? Please, wake up!"

His fingers frantically searched for a pulse, finding only a faint, erratic flutter. *She's alive, but barely,* he thought, panic rising in his chest. *What do I do? How can I save her?*

"Come on, think!" he berated himself aloud. "There has to be a way."

Suddenly, a memory flashed in his mind - the strange power in his blood, the ability that had brought him here. Without hesitation, Drake pulled out a small pocket knife.

"I hope this works," he muttered, wincing as he made a small cut on his palm. "Linda, if you can hear me, I'm going to try something. Just hold on."

Drake pressed his bleeding hand to Linda's lips, watching with a mixture of fear and hope as droplets of his blood touched her pale skin. For a moment, nothing happened.

Then, a soft white glow began to emanate from Linda's body, growing brighter with each passing second. Drake shielded his eyes, his heart racing.

"Linda?" he whispered as the light faded. "Can you hear me?"

Slowly, miraculously, Linda's eyes fluttered open. She looked up at Drake, confusion and wonder mingling in her gaze.

"Drake?" she murmured, her voice weak but undeniably alive. "What... what happened? Where are we?"

Drake pulled her into a tight embrace, tears of relief streaming down his face. "You're back," he choked out. "You're really back."

5 - 6

As they held each other tightly, Drake's mind raced with the implications of what had just transpired. He pulled back slightly, cupping Linda's face in his hands, his eyes searching hers intently.

"Linda, I know this is going to sound impossible, but you can travel between worlds now, just like me," Drake said, his voice a mix of excitement and trepidation.

Linda's brow furrowed, confusion evident in her eyes. "What do you mean, travel between worlds? Drake, what's going on?"

Drake took a deep breath, struggling to find the right words. How could he possibly explain the enormity of what they'd both experienced? "It's complicated, but my blood... it has some kind of power. When I gave it to you, it didn't just save your life. It changed you, like it changed me."

He stood up, offering his hand to Linda. As she took it, he noticed a faint, silvery shimmer beneath her skin - a visual echo of the power now coursing through her veins.

"There's so much I need to tell you," Drake continued, his tone growing urgent. "About Harrison, about everything that's happened."

Linda's eyes widened at the mention of their son. "Harrison? Drake, what about Harrison? Is he okay?"

Drake nodded quickly, squeezing her hand reassuringly. "He's alive, Linda. He's okay, but he needs us. We have to go to him."

As he spoke, Drake felt a familiar pull in his chest - the call of another world. He knew they didn't have much time. "I know this is overwhelming, but I need you to trust me. I can take you to him, but we have to go now."

Linda looked around the room, taking in the familiar surroundings of their home with new eyes. "This isn't our world, is it?" she asked softly, realization dawning on her face.

Drake shook his head. "No, it's not. But I promise, I'll explain everything on the way. Are you ready?"

Linda took a deep breath, squaring her shoulders. Despite the fear and confusion evident in her eyes, there was also a spark of determination. "For Harrison? Always. Let's go."

As Drake prepared to guide them both through the fabric of reality, he couldn't help but marvel at Linda's strength. Whatever challenges lay ahead, he knew they would face them together.

7 - 8

The air shimmered and twisted, reality bending around them as Linda and Drake materialized in the heart of Bridgewater. The acrid scent of ozone filled Linda's nostrils, mingling with the ever-present metallic tang that seemed to permeate the Red World. Neon signs flickered overhead, casting an eerie crimson glow across rain-slicked streets.

Linda stumbled slightly, her hand gripping Drake's arm for support. "Is this... where Harrison is?" she asked, her voice barely above a whisper.

Drake nodded, his eyes scanning the towering facade of the Bridgewater Research Institute looming before them. "Yes, he's inside with Dr. Summers. Are you ready?"

Taking a deep breath, Linda steeled herself. "I've been ready since the moment I lost him."

As they entered the building, the stark contrast between the gritty exterior and the sleek, sterile interior was jarring. Dr. Summers greeted them in the lobby, her composed demeanor a steadying presence.

"Linda, Drake," she acknowledged with a nod. "Harrison's waiting upstairs. He's... eager to see you."

The elevator ride seemed interminable to Linda, her heart pounding in her chest. When the doors finally slid open, she caught sight of a young man pacing nervously at the far end of the hallway.

"Harrison?" Linda's voice cracked with emotion.

The young man turned, his eyes widening in disbelief. "Mom?"

In an instant, they crossed the distance between them, colliding in a fierce embrace. Linda's arms wrapped tightly around her son, tears streaming down her face as she held him close.

"I thought I'd lost you," Harrison choked out, his body shaking with sobs. "I thought... I thought..."

Linda pulled back slightly, cupping her son's face in her hands. "I'm here now," she whispered, her thumbs gently wiping away his tears. "I'm here, and I'm never letting you go again."

As mother and son clung to each other, their shared grief and joy palpable, Drake and Dr. Summers exchanged a knowing look. The road ahead would be fraught with challenges, but for now, this moment of reunion was all that mattered.

9 - 9

Dr. Summers cleared her throat softly, her eyes reflecting a mix of empathy and urgency. "I hate to interrupt," she said, her voice gentle but firm, "but there's something you all need to know."

Linda reluctantly loosened her grip on Harrison, though she kept an arm around his shoulders. Drake stepped closer, his brow furrowing with concern. The air in the room seemed to thicken with anticipation.

"What is it, Rachel?" Drake asked, his voice low and tense.

Dr. Summers took a deep breath, her composed demeanor faltering for just a moment. "I've been analyzing the data from all our encounters across the multiverse, and I've made a discovery that explains everything we've been experiencing."

Linda felt a chill run down her spine. What could possibly tie together all the chaos they'd endured? She glanced at Harrison, noting the worry etched on his young face.

"The virus, the dimensional shifts, even your unique abilities," Dr. Summers continued, her gaze sweeping across the group. "They're all connected to an ancient prophecy detailed in the Codex."

"It's very real," Dr. Summers replied, her voice dropping to barely above a whisper. "And according to its writings, the blood of the Chosen One had the ability to cure the virus, to bridge the gap in realities. It was meant as our salvation. But you drank it, giving you, like Holly, the ability to cross realities at will. You were never meant to drink it, you were supposed to sacrifice your wife to save humanity. Now the blood of the chosen one resides in you Drake – you are the key to either saving or destroying the entire multiverse."

Linda's grip on Harrison tightened involuntarily. She could feel her son trembling slightly beside her. Her mind raced, trying to process the weight of Dr. Summers' words.

"But... how?" Linda finally managed to ask, her voice shaky. "How can Drake's blood have that kind of power?"

Dr. Summers' expression softened with sympathy. "It's not just his blood, Linda. It's yours now, too. When Drake shared his blood with you in the Green World, he didn't just save your life. He made you part of a cosmic equation that's been unfolding for millennia."

The silence that followed was deafening. Linda felt as if the floor beneath her feet had suddenly become unstable. She looked at Drake, seeing the mixture of fear and determination in his eyes, and knew that their lives had just become infinitely more complicated.

Crimson Codex Secrets

Red World – 2024

1 - 2

The crimson mist swirled ominously behind the reinforced glass of the containment chamber, a stark reminder of the devastation wreaking havoc across multiple realities. Drake's eyes were fixed on the deadly pathogen, his jaw clenched as he struggled to process the weight of Dr. Summers' revelation.

"The codex was clear," Rachel said, her voice steady but tinged with urgency. "The blood of the chosen one is the cure to the virus. It was a trial, Drake. It wasn't you who was chosen—it was the blood in the vial you drank."

Drake's mind reeled, flashing back to the moment he'd consumed the mysterious liquid. He'd thought it was a simple act of desperation, but now he realized it had been so much more. His gaze shifted from the virus to his family, their faces a mixture of hope and fear.

"Then let's use my blood," Drake said, rolling up his sleeve with determination. "The chosen one's blood is part of me now. We can formulate a cure."

Dr. Summers' eyes widened, a spark of possibility igniting within them. "It's not that simple, Drake. The process of extracting and synthesizing a cure is fatal."

Drake's heart raced, but he steeled himself against the fear. If this was what it took to save his family, to save countless realities, he'd face it head-on. "I don't care about the risks," he said, his voice unwavering. "We have to try."

As he spoke, Drake couldn't help but think of all the lives hanging in the balance—not just in this world, but across the entire multiverse. The weight of responsibility settled on his shoulders like a physical burden.

Linda reached out, gripping Drake's hand. "Are you sure about this?" she asked, her voice barely above a whisper.

Drake squeezed her hand, drawing strength from her touch. "I have to be," he replied, his eyes meeting hers. "We may not get another chance."

Dr. Summers nodded, her professional demeanor momentarily softening. "If you're certain, Drake, we'll begin preparations immediately. But I must warn you—this won't be easy."

As the gravity of the situation settled over the room, Drake took a deep breath, steeling himself for what was to come. The swirling crimson mist behind the glass seemed to pulse with malevolent intent, a constant reminder of the stakes at hand.

"I'm ready," Drake said, his voice filled with resolve. "Whatever it takes to stop this thing, I'll do it."

3 - 4

Dr. Summers' expression grew grave as she stepped closer to Drake, her eyes reflecting a mix of fascination and concern. "Drake, there's something you need to understand about your... unique condition," she began, her voice low and measured.

Drake felt a chill run down his spine. "What is it?" he asked, bracing himself for the worst.

Dr. Summers took a deep breath. "The reason behind the collapse, the very fabric of reality tearing apart, it's... it's because of your inability to exist in different timelines simultaneously."

Drake's mind reeled. He'd known he was different, but this? "What do you mean?" he managed to choke out.

"Throughout history," Dr. Summers continued, her gaze intense, "there have been individuals like you. People whose existence creates... ripples in the multiverse. The great flood, the destruction of Pompeii - we believe these cataclysmic events were all caused by people who shared your ability."

Drake's heart pounded in his chest. He thought of the devastation he'd witnessed, the lives lost. Could he really be responsible for something on that scale? The thought made him sick to his stomach.

"But why?" he asked, his voice barely above a whisper. "Why can't I envision other universes like Harrison did?"

Dr. Summers' expression softened slightly. "Because, Drake... in those other universes, you're either dead or you never existed at all."

The words hit Drake like a physical blow. He staggered back, his mind struggling to process the information. Dead? Never existed? How was that possible?

As he grappled with the revelation, a terrible thought occurred to him. If his very existence was causing such devastation, what did that mean for the people he loved? For the world itself?

5 - 6

Drake's mind raced, piecing together the implications of Dr. Summers' words. The room seemed to tilt around him as the full weight of the revelation crashed down.

"So, I'm... what? Some kind of anchor being for these realities?" Drake asked, his voice strained. "Tethering these worlds together and tearing them apart at the same time?"

Dr. Summers nodded grimly. "Precisely. Your existence here is like a splinter in the fabric of reality, causing events to misalign across the affected universes. The collapse we're witnessing? It's a direct result of your presence as well as the virus."

Drake's stomach churned. He thought of Linda, of Harrison, of all the people suffering from the virus. "And the only way to stop it is if I..."

"Cease to exist," Dr. Summers finished, her eyes filled with a mix of sympathy and scientific fascination. "Gabriel clearly knew this would happen. The virus was a contingency plan to annihilate you. You are meant to die, that's always been the outcome. The virus starts the collision, your death ends the apocalypse."

The words hung in the air, heavy and suffocating. Drake's hands clenched into fists, his nails biting into his palms. He was meant to die, not his family. The cruel irony of it all threatened to overwhelm him.

Harrison stepped forward, his young face etched with concern. "Dad, there's something else you need to know," he said, his voice trembling slightly. "In the future I visited, I met a man named Jonathan Evans. He told me..."

Drake turned to his son, desperate for any shred of hope. "What did he tell you, Harrison?"

Harrison swallowed hard. "He said they developed a vaccine using your blood. But..." he trailed off, clearly struggling with the weight of his knowledge.

"But what?" Drake pressed, his heart racing.

"Most people never received it," Harrison continued. "And even some who did... they still succumbed to the collision of the multiverse. Just like the president we saw on TV."

Drake's mind whirled with the implications. Even if they found a way to use his blood for a cure, it might not be enough to save everyone. The enormity of the situation pressed down on him, threatening to crush him under its weight.

7 - 8

Drake paced the sterile lab, his footsteps echoing off the pristine white tiles. His mind raced, piecing together fragments of information like a complex legal case. Suddenly, he stopped, turning to face Dr. Summers and Harrison.

"What if we made the vaccine airborne?" Drake proposed, his voice steady despite the storm of emotions churning inside him. "Like the virus was. We could release it over major cities, let it spread rapidly like the virus did. That way, we might reach everyone."

Dr. Summers' eyebrows shot up, her analytical mind already dissecting the idea. "An airborne vaccine? That's... unprecedented, but theoretically possible."

Drake's heart quickened. "It could work, right? We have the technology, the resources. If we act fast—"

"Drake," Dr. Summers interrupted, her tone gentle but firm. She took a deep breath, steeling herself. "A vaccine of that magnitude... you must know it'll require everything."

"Everything?" Drake echoed, confusion etching his features. He didn't want to accept the outcome that everyone was forcing on him. History has to be able to be rewritten. If only he had used the blood for the machine and went back to stop Gabriel from spreading the virus in the first place. He could have went to the road the night of the accident and stopped Gabriel right there from starting this nightmare.

"Everything in your body," she clarified, her eyes meeting his with a mix of professional detachment and genuine sorrow. "The amount of blood needed, the cellular material... it would result in your sacrifice. Your death."

The words hit Drake like a physical blow. He stumbled back, gripping the edge of a nearby lab table for support. His mind reeled, grappling with the implications.

'My death,' he thought, a cold dread seeping into his bones. 'But if it means saving everyone else...'

"Dad?" Harrison's voice broke through his spiraling thoughts, filled with fear and concern.

Drake looked at his son, seeing the echo of his late wife in the boy's eyes. He straightened, drawing on the resolve that had carried him through countless courtroom battles.

"If that's what it takes," Drake said, his voice low but unwavering, "if my death means stopping this collision and saving countless lives... then so be it."

9 - 10

Linda's eyes widened in horror, her hand flying to her mouth. "No," she whispered, her voice trembling. "Drake, you can't—"

"There has to be another way," Harrison interjected, his young face set with determination. He stepped forward, rolling up his sleeve. "Use my blood. I've been to the future, I have the chosen one's blood in me too."

Linda nodded vigorously, her long hair swaying with the motion. "Yes, and I... I have Drake's blood now as well. We could both contribute, couldn't we?"

Drake felt a surge of love and pride for his family, even as his heart constricted at their willingness to sacrifice themselves. He glanced at Dr. Summers, who was shaking her head slowly.

"I'm sorry," the scientist said, her voice laced with genuine regret. "But it has to be Drake. The concentration of the chosen one's blood in his system, combined with his unique multiversal properties... it's the only way to ensure the vaccine's efficacy across all realities."

Drake took a deep breath, steeling himself. He turned to face his family, drinking in their features as if committing them to memory one last time. "Linda, Harrison," he began, his voice soft but resolute. "I love you both more than I can express. And that's why I have to do this."

He stepped closer, placing a hand on Harrison's shoulder and meeting Linda's tear-filled gaze. "If my death means you two can live, can be safe and together... then it's a price I'm willing to pay. It's what any father, any husband would do."

Drake's mind raced with memories—birthdays, holidays, quiet moments of joy and laughter. He pushed them aside, focusing on the present, on the weight of his decision.

"I've spent my life fighting for justice in courtrooms," he continued, a wry smile tugging at his lips. "But this... this is the most important case I'll ever take on. And I won't lose it. Not when the stakes are so high."

11 - 11

Drake turned back to Dr. Summers, his jaw set with determination. "I'll do it," he said, his voice unwavering. "But I have one condition."

Dr. Summers raised an eyebrow, her eyes filled with a mix of relief and curiosity. "What's that?"

Drake's gaze swept across the room, taking in the faces of his family and the research team. "We make a public announcement first. On live TV."

Linda stepped forward, her brow furrowed with concern. "Drake, are you sure that's wise? The panic it could cause—"

"People deserve to know the truth," Drake interrupted, his lawyer's instincts kicking in. "About the virus, about the multiverse, about... everything." He ran a hand through his hair, his mind racing with the implications. "If I'm going to sacrifice myself, I want it to mean something beyond just a cure. I want people to understand what we're facing."

Dr. Summers nodded slowly. "It's risky, but... you're right. Transparency might be our best ally in ensuring widespread acceptance of the vaccine."

Drake's thoughts drifted to the countless courtroom battles he'd fought, the importance of public opinion in swaying verdicts. This was no different, just on an unimaginably larger scale.

"We'll need to be strategic," he said, already formulating a plan. "Choose our words carefully, present the facts in a way that informs without inciting panic." He paused, a flicker of vulnerability crossing his face. "And... I want a chance to say goodbye. To everyone."

Harrison stepped closer, placing a hand on his father's arm. "Dad, are you absolutely certain about this?"

Drake met his son's gaze, seeing the mix of fear and admiration there. "I've never been more sure of anything in my life," he replied softly. "This is how I can protect you, how I can make things right."

Quantum Tension

1 - 2

Dr. Rachel Summers' hands trembled slightly as she made the final adjustments to the sleek, metallic machine before her. The lab buzzed with nervous energy as her team worked feverishly, their faces etched with determination and fear.

"Particle accelerator alignment complete," her assistant called out.

Rachel nodded, her mind racing. We're so close. But will it be enough?

A commotion near the lab's entrance drew her attention. Drake Miller strode in, his normally immaculate suit wrinkled and his eyes wild with a mix of resolve and desperation.

"Dr. Summers," he said, his voice hoarse. "It's time. I need to address the public."

Rachel's brow furrowed. "Drake, are you sure about this? Once you go on air, there's no turning back."

Drake's jaw clenched. "I have to. It's the only way."

As Drake stepped in front of the hastily set-up camera, Rachel couldn't help but wonder how they'd arrived at this moment. The weight of countless lives across multiple realities pressed down on her shoulders.

The red light blinked on, and Drake began to speak, his voice wavering slightly.

"My fellow citizens, of this world and countless others, I come before you today with a heavy heart and a terrible truth."

Rachel watched the monitor, her chest tightening as Drake continued.

"The virus that has ravaged our world and threatens to tear apart the very fabric of the multiverse... it's my fault."

Gasps echoed through the lab. Rachel's mind reeled. How could this be possible?

Drake's voice cracked as he pressed on. "In my desperate attempt to save my family, I inadvertently unleashed this plague upon us all. The collision of realities, the devastation you've witnessed – it stems from my actions."

Rachel's heart raced. The pieces were falling into place – Drake's unusual knowledge, his fervent drive to find a cure. It all made sense now.

As Drake continued his confession, detailing the events that led to this catastrophe, Rachel turned back to the machine. We have to make this work, she thought. Not just for our world, but for all of them.

The enormity of the situation threatened to overwhelm her, but Rachel steeled herself. There would be time for shock and anger later. Right now, they had a multiverse to save.

3 - 4

Drake's voice, filled with anguish, echoed through the lab as he continued his broadcast. "I stand before you now, not to ask for forgiveness, but to offer the only solution I can. My blood, my very life, holds the key to creating the cure that will save us all."

Rachel's eyes widened, her hands trembling slightly as she calibrated the machine. She hadn't known it would come to this. Drake's next words confirmed her fears.

"I will sacrifice myself to create an airborne antidote. If I had taken the time to understand, to look beyond my own family's needs, I could have prevented this suffering. For my shortsightedness, for my selfishness, I can only ask for your understanding."

As Drake's announcement concluded, Rachel felt a mix of admiration and sorrow. She watched him enter the lab, his eyes meeting hers with a resolute determination that belied the fear she knew he must be feeling.

"Are you sure about this, Drake?" Rachel asked, her voice barely above a whisper.

Drake nodded, his gaze never wavering. "It's the only way, Rachel. We both know it."

With a heavy heart, Rachel helped Drake into the machine, securing the straps around his arms and legs. Her fingers brushed against his skin, and she felt a surge of emotion she couldn't quite name.

"I'm going to administer the sedative now," she said, her professional demeanor masking the turmoil within. "You won't feel any pain."

Drake managed a small smile. "Thank you, Rachel. For everything."

As the sedative began to take effect, Drake's eyes started to close. "Tell my family... I love them," he murmured, his words becoming slurred. "And that I'm sorry..."

Rachel watched as Drake drifted off to sleep, the weight of his sacrifice settling over the room like a heavy blanket. She took a deep breath, steeling herself for what came next. The fate of the multiverse now rested in their hands.

5 - 5

The machine hummed to life, its intricate network of tubes and wires pulsing with an otherworldly energy. Rachel's hands trembled slightly as she initiated the blood extraction process, her eyes fixed on the monitors displaying Drake's vital signs.

"Extraction at 25%," she announced, her voice tight with tension. "Vitals stable."

Dr. Summers watched the crimson fluid flow through the translucent tubes, her mind racing. *This has to work. It's our only hope.*

As the extraction reached 75%, a low alarm sounded. Drake's heartbeat began to falter, its rhythm becoming erratic.

"No, no, no," Rachel muttered, her fingers flying across the control panel. "Stay with us, Drake."

The air in the lab grew thick with anticipation as the final drops of Drake's blood entered the machine. Suddenly, a blinding white light erupted from the center of the device, bathing the room in an otherworldly glow.

Rachel shielded her eyes, her heart pounding. "What's happening?" she shouted over the deafening hum of energy.

As the light intensified, she caught a glimpse of Drake's body. To her astonishment, it began to shimmer and fade, as if being erased from existence itself.

"Drake!" she cried out, reaching for him instinctively.

But it was too late. In a final burst of radiance, Drake's form vanished completely, leaving behind only an empty gurney. The monitor flatlined, its monotonous tone echoing through the now-silent lab.

Rachel stood frozen, her mind struggling to process what she had just witnessed. *Did we succeed? Or have we just lost everything?*

As the light faded, she noticed something unusual where Drake's body had been—a faint, shimmering residue that seemed to dance with possibilities.

Whispers of a Forgotten Fairground

Somewhere beyond the land of the living – where time and space don't not exist.

1 - 2

The rusted Ferris wheel loomed against the twilight sky, a skeletal reminder of happier times. Drake stumbled forward, his shoes crunching on broken glass and debris. The air hung thick with the scent of decay and forgotten dreams.

His heart raced as he took in the familiar, yet eerily distorted landscape of the abandoned amusement park. This was where it had all begun—where Gabriel had appeared like a specter and where the bullet had torn through Drake's flesh, sending him spiraling into this nightmare.

As he turned, his breath caught in his throat. There, amidst the twisted metal and crumbling structures, stood Linda. Her silhouette was bathed in an otherworldly glow, her hair flowing gently in a nonexistent breeze.

"Linda?" Drake's voice cracked, a mixture of disbelief and desperate hope. "How... how are you here?"

He stumbled toward her, his legs feeling like lead. Is this the afterlife? Did she follow me here? The questions swirled in his mind, but he pushed them aside, focused solely on reaching her.

"Drake," Linda's voice was soft, ethereal. "I've been waiting for you."

As he drew closer, Drake's hand trembled as he reached out to touch her. "I thought I'd lost you forever," he whispered, his eyes brimming with tears. "Our son... is he here too?"

Linda's expression flickered with an emotion Drake couldn't quite place. Was it sadness? Regret? Before he could decipher it, she spoke again, her words sending a chill down his spine.

"You shouldn't be here, Drake. It's not safe."

Drake's brow furrowed, confusion and fear warring within him. "What do you mean? Linda, please, I need answers. What happened to us? To our family?"

He took another step closer, his hand finally making contact with her arm. A jolt of energy passed between them, and for a moment, Drake felt as if he could see beyond this desolate park, beyond the boundaries of this world.

"Linda," he pleaded, his voice barely above a whisper. "Help me understand. Help me find a way back to you—to our son."

As he gazed into her eyes, searching for the warmth and love he remembered, Drake couldn't shake the feeling that something was terribly wrong. The park seemed to shift and waver around them, reality bending at the edges of his perception.

What is this place? he thought, a creeping dread settling in his gut. And what have I truly stumbled into?

3 - 4

Linda's eyes widened, a flicker of recognition passing through them. She stumbled back, her gaze darting around the ruins of the amusement park. The once-vibrant colors were now muted, swallowed by encroaching shadows that seemed to pulse with malevolent life.

"Drake?" she whispered, her voice trembling. "Is it really you?"

Drake's heart clenched at the fear in her voice. He took a tentative step forward, his hand outstretched. "It's me, Linda. I'm here."

As he moved, the twisted metal of a nearby roller coaster groaned ominously, sending a shiver down his spine. The air felt thick, oppressive, as if reality itself was struggling to maintain its form.

Linda's gaze locked onto something behind him, her face paling. "The Ferris wheel," she murmured. "Do you remember, Drake? How you and Harrison would ride it for hours, laughing and planning your next adventure?"

Drake turned, following her gaze. The once-majestic Ferris wheel now stood as a skeletal monument to happier times, its carriages dangling precariously in the otherworldly breeze.

"I remember," he said softly, his mind flooded with bittersweet memories. "But how are you here, Linda? What is this place?"

As he turned back to face her, Drake froze. Linda stood before him, but she was... different. An ethereal glow surrounded her, pulsing gently in sync with some unseen force. Her eyes, once a warm brown, now shimmered with an otherworldly light.

"What's happening to you?" Drake asked, his voice barely above a whisper. He reached out, his fingers brushing against the strange aura surrounding her. A jolt of energy surged through him, carrying with it a flood of fractured images – multiple realities, countless possibilities, all converging on this moment.

Linda's voice echoed strangely in the empty space around them. "We don't have much time, Drake. You need to listen carefully."

Drake's mind reeled, struggling to process the impossible scene before him. Is this real? Am I losing my mind? Or have I truly stumbled into something beyond my understanding?

5 - 6

"Linda," Drake said, his voice echoing through the darkness. "You shouldn't be here."

The words hung in the air, heavy with unspoken dread. Drake's eyes, still glowing with that otherworldly light, fixed on Linda with a mixture of concern and urgency. The rusted remains of the amusement park seemed to close in around them, shadows stretching impossibly long in the eerie twilight.

Linda tried to respond, but her voice caught in her throat. A wave of panic washed over her as she realized she couldn't make a sound. What's happening to me? she thought, her heart racing. She attempted to step towards Drake, but her body refused to cooperate.

She felt as if she were moving through molasses, her limbs heavy and sluggish as she struggled to make sense of what was happening. The world around her seemed to blur and shift, reality itself becoming as unstable as the crumbling structures surrounding them.

Drake watched her struggle, his brow furrowing with worry. "Linda, listen to me," he said, his voice carrying an authority she'd never heard before. "This place, it's not safe for you. You need to—"

But Linda couldn't focus on his words. Her mind was a whirlwind of confusion and fear. Why can't I move? Why can't I speak? This isn't right. None of this is right. She tried to call out to Drake, to reach for him, but her body remained frustratingly unresponsive.

The air around them seemed to thicken, pulsing with an energy that made Linda's skin tingle. She locked eyes with Drake, silently pleading for help, for answers, for anything that might make sense of this surreal nightmare.

7 - 8

Drake's eyes widened with sudden realization. Without hesitation, he reached out to Linda, his hand enveloped in an ethereal, pulsating light. As his fingers brushed her arm, a jolt of energy surged through him, and in that instant, he saw everything.

Images flashed through his mind: Linda, pale and motionless, trapped in a confined space. The suffocating darkness. The smell of earth and decay. The terrifying reality hit him like a physical blow. She's being buried alive.

"Oh God, Linda," Drake whispered, his voice thick with emotion. He struggled to maintain his composure, his legal training kicking in as he forced himself to focus on the immediate problem. Time was running out.

Linda stared at him, confusion and fear evident in her eyes. She tried to speak, but no words came out. What's happening, Drake? her eyes seemed to plead.

Drake grasped her shoulders, his touch gentle yet urgent. The ethereal glow from his hands intensified, casting eerie shadows across Linda's face. "Listen to me, Linda," he said, his voice low and intense. "You have to wake up. You're in danger."

Linda's brow furrowed. Wake up? But I'm already... Her thoughts trailed off as a creeping realization began to dawn on her.

"This isn't real," Drake continued, gesturing to the decaying amusement park around them. "It's a dream, a nightmare. But the danger is very real. You're..." He hesitated, not wanting to panic her further, but knowing the truth was crucial. "You're buried, Linda. You need to fight. Wake up and fight."

As he spoke, the world around them began to shimmer and fade. Linda felt a tugging sensation, as if something was trying to pull her away. No! she thought desperately. I don't understand. Drake, help me!

Drake saw the panic in her eyes and pulled her close, his voice urgent in her ear. "I know you're scared, but you're strong. Remember who you are, Linda. Remember our family. Use that love, that strength. Wake up and fight!"

The tugging grew stronger, and Linda began to fade from his grasp. Drake's heart raced, knowing their time was almost up. "I love you," he said fiercely. "Now wake up and live!"

9 - 9

As Linda's form dissipated like mist, Drake found himself alone in the ghostly remnants of the amusement park. The eerie silence pressed in on him, a stark contrast to the urgent exchange moments before. He stood motionless, his ethereal glow casting long shadows across the rusted remains of once-cheerful rides.

"No," Drake whispered, his voice echoing in the empty space. "I can't lose her too." He clenched his fists, the otherworldly light pulsing with his frustration and fear.

Closing his eyes, Drake tried to focus, to will himself back to Linda or to any place where he could help her. But the familiar sensation of traversing realities eluded him. He was stranded, cut off from both the living and the various worlds he had come to know.

"There has to be a way," he muttered, pacing frantically. His lawyer's mind raced, searching for a loophole, a way to bend the rules of this cosmic game. "Think, Drake. Think!"

But even as he struggled against his helplessness, Drake felt a familiar tingling sensation spreading through his body. The light emanating from him grew brighter, more intense.

"No, not now," he pleaded, fighting against the inevitable. "I'm not done. I can still-"

His words were cut short as the light engulfed him entirely. In a flash of brilliant radiance, Drake faded away, leaving behind only the hollow echoes of his desperation in the abandoned park.

Nightmare in Ashen Hell

The Nexus of Torment – outside space and time

1 - 2

The acrid stench of sulfur assaulted Drake's nostrils as he materialized in a nightmarish landscape. Screams of anguish echoed across a desolate plain, punctuated by geysers of flame erupting from fissures in the scorched earth. Ash rained from a blood-red sky, coating Drake's skin in a greasy film.

What fresh hell is this? Drake thought, his mind reeling. The scene before him defied comprehension, like something ripped from the pages of Dante's Inferno.

He stumbled forward on unsteady legs, the ground shifting beneath his feet. Skeletal figures writhed in agony, reaching out with gnarled fingers as he passed. Drake recoiled, his heart pounding. *Focus. I need to find a way out of here.*

As he trudged onward, Drake's thoughts turned to his family. Had his actions condemned them to this realm of suffering? The possibility made bile rise in his throat.

After what felt like hours of aimless wandering, a familiar figure came into view. Gabriel sat slumped against a boulder, clutching a bleeding wound in his side.

"So, the prodigal son returns," Gabriel wheezed, a mirthless grin twisting his disfigured features.

Drake's fists clenched at his sides. "What is this place? Another of your tricks?"

Gabriel's laughter dissolved into a hacking cough. "Oh no, Drake. This is all too real. Welcome to damnation."

"Why am I here?" Drake demanded, taking a menacing step forward.

Gabriel's eyes gleamed with malice. "You made your choice, didn't you? Used the blood for your own selfish ends."

Drake's mind raced, piecing together the implications. Had his attempt to save his family doomed the multiverse?

"It wasn't supposed to end like this," Drake muttered, more to himself than Gabriel.

"No," Gabriel agreed, his voice laced with bitterness. "It wasn't."

3 - 4

Drake's eyes widened as he took in the nightmarish landscape surrounding them. Twisted metal and shattered glass littered the ground, a hellish reflection of the intersection where his life had changed forever. The acrid smell of burning rubber assaulted his nostrils, mixing with the sulfurous stench that permeated the air.

"Doesn't this look familiar?" Gabriel's raspy voice cut through the cacophony of screams and wails. "This is where I took everything from you."

Drake's jaw clenched, his fists balling at his sides. The memories of that fateful night came flooding back – the screeching tires, the shattering glass, the agonizing silence that followed. He could almost hear the echoes of his own desperate cries.

"You bastard," Drake snarled, taking a menacing step towards Gabriel. "You orchestrated all of this?"

Gabriel's lips curled into a pained smirk. "I merely set the wheels in motion. You were always the architect of your own destruction, Drake."

Drake's mind raced, trying to reconcile the magnitude of Gabriel's actions with the hellscape before him. *How could one man's vendetta lead to this?* he wondered, his attorney's mind grasping for logic in a world gone mad.

"Why?" Drake demanded, his voice cracking with barely contained rage. "Why go to such lengths? What could possibly justify this?"

Gabriel's eyes gleamed with a mixture of pain and defiance. "You'll understand soon enough. We're all pawns in a much larger game, Drake. And the game isn't over yet."

5 - 6

Gabriel's disfigured face contorted with rage, his eyes blazing with a mixture of disappointment and disgust. "You squandered it all, Drake," he spat, his voice dripping with venom. "The blood of the Chosen One – the key to saving countless realities – and you used it for your own selfish desires!"

Drake felt a surge of anger course through him, but beneath it, a flicker of doubt. Had he made the wrong choice? The memory of his family's faces, alive and whole again, flashed through his mind. He pushed the doubt aside, steeling his resolve.

"My family wasn't just some casualty to be sacrificed for your grand plan," Drake retorted, his lawyer's instincts kicking in as he formulated his defense. "You talk about saving the universe, but you're the one who set all this in motion. Why, Gabriel? What possessed you to go back in time and destroy everything I held dear?"

As he spoke, Drake's eyes darted around the hellish landscape, taking in the twisted metal and charred earth that mirrored his worst nightmare. The screams of the damned echoed in his ears, a constant reminder of the stakes at play.

Gabriel's lips curled into a sneer. "You think you understand the complexities of time and space, Drake? You have no idea of the burden I carry, the choices I've had to make."

Drake took a step forward, his voice low and dangerous. "Then enlighten me, Gabriel. Why unleash a virus that brought about the apocalypse? What could possibly justify such wholesale destruction?"

7 - 8

Gabriel's disfigured face contorted, a mix of pain and fervor etched into his scarred features. "It was all for love and revenge, Drake," he hissed, his voice carrying an eerie calmness that sent chills down Drake's spine. "I thought surely you, of all people, would understand the Codex and set things right. The Chosen One's blood was meant to save humanity, not to be squandered on your selfish desires!"

Drake's mind reeled, grappling with the implications of Gabriel's words. The weight of the Ancient Codex's knowledge pressed upon him, its cryptic symbols dancing in his memory. He clenched his fists, the sulfurous air burning his lungs as he struggled to comprehend the magnitude of Gabriel's actions.

"Love and revenge?" Drake spat, his tone a mixture of disbelief and contempt. "You tore apart the fabric of reality for that?"

Gabriel's eyes gleamed with a manic light, his white robe billowing in the acrid breeze. "This time, it should have been different," he said, his voice dropping to a near-whisper. "I gave you the tools, the knowledge. You were supposed to be the one to fix it all."

Drake's thoughts raced, piecing together the fragments of this cosmic puzzle. The Temporal Guardians, the multiverse, the virus - it all swirled in his mind like a kaleidoscope of chaos. He found himself questioning every decision, every turn that had led him to this hellish version of his past.

"Different how?" Drake demanded, taking a step closer to Gabriel, the ground crunching beneath his feet. "You can't play god with people's lives and expect it all to work out perfectly!"

9 - 10

Gabriel's disfigured face contorted, a mixture of pain and desperation etching deeper lines into his scarred visage. He stumbled forward, his limp more pronounced as he closed the distance between them.

"Kill me, Drake," Gabriel pleaded, his voice cracking. "End this cycle of suffering. You have the power to finish what I started."

Drake's jaw clenched, his mind reeling from the audacity of Gabriel's request. The hellish landscape around them seemed to pulse with malevolent energy, mirroring the turmoil in his heart. For a moment, he was tempted

- to end it all, to silence the architect of his family's destruction. But as he looked into Gabriel's eyes, he saw something that stayed his hand: hope.

"No," Drake said firmly, his voice cutting through the cacophony of screams that seemed to emanate from the very air. "You don't get to escape that easily. You'll suffer here, just like me, just like all the people you've hurt across the multiverse."

Gabriel's face twisted in fury, his calm facade shattering. With a guttural roar, he lunged at Drake, his white robe billowing like wings of vengeance. Drake, caught off guard, stumbled backward, his legal training ill-preparing him for this primal assault.

They grappled, a desperate dance amidst the hellish backdrop. Drake's mind raced, analyzing Gabriel's movements like he would dissect an opponent's argument in court. He dodged a wild swing, feeling the rush of air as Gabriel's fist missed his face by inches.

"You fool!" Gabriel snarled, his limp forgotten in the heat of battle. "You could have been the savior of worlds!"

Drake's response was swift and decisive. He feinted left, then drove his right fist into Gabriel's solar plexus. The impact was more forceful than he'd intended, fueled by years of pent-up anger and grief. Gabriel's eyes widened in shock as he staggered backward, clutching his chest.

To Drake's horror, a dark stain began to spread across Gabriel's white robe. He hadn't realized he was holding a jagged piece of debris, now slick with blood. Gabriel collapsed to his knees, his breathing ragged.

"I... I never meant for it to end like this," Drake whispered, the reality of what he'd done crashing over him like a tidal wave.

11 - 12

Gabriel's eyes, once burning with rage, now dulled as he slumped to the ground. The sulfurous air seemed to thicken, closing in around them. Drake stood frozen, his hands trembling, the makeshift weapon clattering to the scorched earth.

With his last breath, Gabriel's gaze locked onto Drake's. His voice, barely a whisper, carried a desperate plea: "Father, please forgive my transgressions."

The words hit Drake like a physical blow. A maelstrom of emotions churned within him – confusion, anger, and an unexpected pang of pity. He clenched his fists, steadying himself against the onslaught of conflicting feelings.

"I'm not your father," Drake replied, his voice hoarse but firm. He swallowed hard, tasting ash and regret. "Save the forgiveness for the chosen one."

As he spoke, Drake's mind raced. Why would Gabriel call him 'father'? Was this another layer to the cosmic joke that his life had become? He felt the weight of countless realities pressing down on him, each decision branching into infinite possibilities.

Gabriel's eyes began to glaze over, his chest barely rising with shallow breaths. Drake stood over him, a mix of triumph and horror washing over him. He had won, but at what cost? And what new mysteries had this victory unveiled?

13 - 13

Drake watched as the last flicker of life faded from Gabriel's eyes. The disfigured face, once a mask of malice, now slack and empty. A chill ran down Drake's spine, not from the hellish landscape surrounding them, but from the finality of the moment.

"It's over," Drake muttered, more to himself than to his fallen adversary. He knelt beside Gabriel's body, his mind a whirlwind of conflicting thoughts.

Part of him wanted to feel victorious, to revel in the defeat of the man who had caused so much suffering. Yet, as he gazed at Gabriel's lifeless form, Drake felt only a hollow ache in his chest.

"Why?" he whispered, his voice barely audible over the distant wails echoing through this nightmarish realm. "Why did it have to come to this?"

Drake's hand hovered over Gabriel's face, hesitating before closing the man's eyelids. It was a gesture of respect he never thought he'd offer his tormentor, but something about Gabriel's final words had shaken him to his core.

As he stood, Drake's gaze swept across the hellish landscape, a twisted mirror of the place where his own journey had begun. The irony wasn't lost on him.

"What now?" he asked the desolate expanse around him. "Is this how it all ends? Or is this just another beginning?"

The silence that answered him was deafening, broken only by the crackle of distant fires and the howl of an otherworldly wind. Drake took a deep breath, steeling himself for whatever came next. Gabriel might be gone, but the mysteries of the multiverse remained, waiting to be unraveled.

A Gift or Judgement

The Nexus of Torment

1 - 2

Drake's fingers trembled as he closed Gabriel's lifeless eyes. The air around him shimmered with an otherworldly glow, casting eerie shadows across the ground that seemed to pulse with an unseen energy. A chill ran down his spine as he heard footsteps approaching from behind.

Turning slowly, Drake's breath caught in his throat. A figure loomed before him, tall and imposing, shrouded in a black robe that seemed to absorb the ethereal light around them. But it was the being's face that truly froze Drake in place.

The figure's features were unnervingly human-like, yet unmistakably otherworldly. Skin as pale as moonlight stretched taut over high cheekbones, contrasting sharply with eyes that burned like smoldering coals. A crooked smile played across lips that seemed both inviting and menacing.

"Who... what are you?" Drake managed to choke out, his legal training deserting him in the face of this impossible entity.

The figure's smile widened, revealing teeth that glinted like sharpened obsidian. "I am Lucian," it replied, its voice a sonorous whisper that seemed to reverberate through Drake's very bones. "And you, Drake Miller, have found yourself in the land known as the Nexus of Torment."

Drake's mind raced, trying to make sense of his surroundings and this bizarre encounter. The Nexus? Torment? None of it aligned with the rational world he knew as a lawyer. Yet the grief and confusion that had plagued him since losing his family now felt distant, overshadowed by a growing sense of cosmic significance.

"I don't understand," Drake said, struggling to maintain his composure. "How did I get here? What is this place?"

Lucian's eyes flickered with an unnatural light. "Understanding will come in time, Drake. For now, know that you stand at a crossroads of realities, where the choices you make will echo across countless worlds."

As Drake absorbed these words, he couldn't shake the feeling that he was being presented with a cosmic legal case, one where the stakes stretched far beyond anything he had ever encountered in a courtroom. Whatever came next, he knew his life would never be the same.

3 - 4

Lucian's gaze bore into Drake, his eyes like twin abysses. "You've proven yourself by vanquishing Gabriel," he said, his voice a silken caress. "Now, I offer you two paths."

Drake's heart raced, his lawyer's mind frantically analyzing the situation. "What kind of paths?" he asked, fighting to keep his voice steady.

"The first," Lucian continued, "leads you to the heart of the Nexus, where the Chosen One will pass judgment upon you." He paused, letting the weight of those words sink in. "The second... a gift. A world where your family lives, where the accident never happened. All the pain you've endured since that day... erased."

Drake's breath caught in his throat. His family alive? The agony of loss undone? It seemed too good to be true. "How is that possible?" he whispered, hope and suspicion warring within him.

Lucian's lips curled into a knowing smile. "The multiverse holds infinite possibilities, Drake. Your reality is but one among countless others."

As temptation flooded through him, Drake remembered his legal training. There had to be a catch. "And what's the price for this... gift?"

Lucian's eyes glimmered. "Perceptive. Should you choose to indulge your desires rather than face judgment, there will be... unforeseen consequences. The ripples of your choice will spread far beyond yourself."

Drake's mind raced. The prospect of seeing his family again was intoxicating, but at what cost? And what did "judgment" truly mean in this cosmic court?

"How am I supposed to make this choice?" Drake asked, his voice barely above a whisper.

5 - 6

Drake's heart pounded as two shimmering portals materialized before him, their edges rippling with otherworldly energy. The left portal pulsed with a deep, somber blue – the pathway to judgment. The right glowed with a warm, inviting golden light that seemed to whisper of home and family.

He took a tentative step forward, his mind a maelstrom of conflicting emotions. The attorney in him sought justice, demanded accountability for his actions. But the grieving husband and father ached for the chance to undo the tragedy that had shattered his world.

"My family..." Drake murmured, his voice thick with longing. He reached out, fingers trembling as they neared the golden light.

Suddenly, a desperate shout pierced the air behind him. "Drake, stop!"

He whirled around, startled by the familiar voice. Who could possibly be here, in this liminal space between realities? Drake's eyes darted between the portals and the direction of the voice, indecision gripping him.

"Who's there?" he called out, his lawyer's instincts kicking in, demanding more information before making a potentially irreversible choice. "Show yourself!"

Drake's mind raced. Could this be another trick? Or was it a lifeline, offering crucial information before he made his decision? The weight of consequences – both known and unforeseen – pressed down on him as he stood frozen between two destinies.

7 - 8

Drake's heart pounded in his chest as he made his decision. The promise of reuniting with his family, of undoing the tragedy that had torn his world apart, was too powerful to resist. With a deep breath, he turned back to the golden portal, its warm light beckoning him forward.

"I'm sorry," he whispered to the unseen voice behind him. "But I have to try."

He took a determined step towards the portal, his mind filled with images of his wife's smile and his son's laughter. The energy from the portal hummed, growing stronger as he approached.

"This is my chance to make things right," Drake thought, steeling his resolve. "To be the husband and father they deserved."

As he reached out to touch the shimmering surface, a flicker of movement caught his eye. Drake turned his head slightly, his breath catching in his throat at the impossible sight.

There, in the periphery of his vision, stood another version of himself. This doppelganger was haggard, eyes wild with desperation, and most alarmingly, pointing a gun directly at him.

"What the hell?" Drake gasped, his lawyer's mind struggling to process this new, inexplicable development.

The gun-wielding Drake opened his mouth as if to speak, but no words came. Instead, his expression conveyed a complex mix of anguish, determination, and something else... was it regret?

For a fraction of a second, Drake hesitated, his hand hovering just inches from the portal's surface. Was this a warning from his future self? Or another manipulation designed to sway his choice?

"No," Drake decided firmly, pushing aside his doubts. "I've come too far to turn back now."

With a final, decisive motion, he plunged his hand into the golden light, feeling its warmth envelop him as the world around him began to shift and blur.

9 - 9

The portal's energy surged through Drake's body, a tingling sensation that started at his fingertips and rapidly spread to encompass his entire being. The world around him dissolved into a kaleidoscope of swirling colors and fractured light, disorienting and mesmerizing in equal measure.

"Linda? Harrison?" Drake called out, his voice echoing strangely in the void between worlds. There was no response, only the rushing sound of reality bending around him.

As he tumbled through the dimensional rift, fragments of memories flashed before his eyes - his wife's smile, his son's laughter, the weight of the gun in his hand as he faced Gabriel. Each image burned with an intensity that made his heart ache.

"What have I done?" Drake thought, a creeping doubt gnawing at the edges of his resolve. "Did I make the right choice?"

The journey seemed to last an eternity and yet only a moment. Suddenly, the chaotic maelstrom of the portal gave way to solid ground beneath his feet. Drake stumbled forward, his senses overwhelmed by the abrupt transition.

As his vision cleared, he found himself standing in a familiar place, but one that felt subtly wrong. The air smelled different, the light cast unfamiliar shadows. Drake's heart raced as he tried to process his surroundings.

"Drake?" a voice called out, achingly familiar yet tinged with confusion. "Honey, are you alright?"

He turned, his breath catching in his throat as he saw her. Linda stood there, alive and whole, concern etched on her beautiful face. Behind her, Harrison peered around the doorway, his curious eyes fixed on his father.

"I... I'm fine," Drake managed, his voice thick with emotion. "Just felt a little dizzy for a moment."

As Linda approached, reaching out to touch his arm, Drake's mind raced. He had made his choice, but at what cost? And what were those unforeseen consequences Lucian had warned about? But suddenly as he appeared in this world so to did his memories of past events begin to fade. Eventually he could no longer remember the events that transpired in the Green, Blue and Red world. All he was left with was the warm fading embrace of the Grey World.

The Sound of Silence

Red World – 2024

1 - 2

Throughout the streets, people were suddenly enveloped in brilliant white light. Some collapsed to their knees, gasping as if drowning in memories. Others stood stock-still; eyes wide with wonder.

A woman's voice rang out, filled with joy: "I remember! Oh God, I remember everything!"

Lucian's lips curled into a bitter smile. How naive they were, celebrating this forced enlightenment. Didn't they realize the price of such knowledge?

As he watched, a man stumbled from his house, coughing violently. The telltale crimson mist of the Virus billowed from his mouth. He took two more steps before crumpling to the ground, his body dissolving into a red haze.

"Not everyone gets their happy ending," Lucian mused, adjusting a dial on the bomb. The lives lost were regrettable, but necessary sacrifices for the greater plan.

He closed his eyes, allowing himself a moment to recall the countless realities he'd traversed, the myriad versions of himself he'd encountered. Each one had led him here, to this pivotal moment.

"Soon," he whispered to the device, "soon we'll tear it all down and build anew."

The sound of approaching sirens pierced the air. Lucian's eyes snapped open, cold determination settling over his features. Time was running short. He had to act now, before the so-called guardians of reality could intervene.

With practiced movements, he began the final preparations. The multiverse would never be the same after tonight. And neither, he knew, would he.

3 - 4

Meghan Johnson raced through the eerily quiet streets, her heart pounding in her chest. The world around her seemed to flicker and warp, reality itself struggling to maintain coherence. As she rounded the corner onto her street, she saw her childhood home – a beacon of normalcy in a world gone mad.

"Mom! Dad!" she cried out, bursting through the front door.

Her parents emerged from the living room, their faces a mixture of relief and confusion. "Meghan? What's happening?" her mother asked, voice trembling.

Meghan rushed towards them; arms outstretched. "I don't know, but I'm so glad you're okay. I was so worried-"

As their bodies collided in an embrace, Meghan felt a sudden, sickening lurch. Her parents' forms began to shimmer and distort, as if viewed through a kaleidoscope.

"Meghan, we feel... strange," her father whispered, his voice echoing unnaturally.

Horror dawned on Meghan as she realized what was happening. "No, no, no! Hold on, please!"

But it was too late. With a sound like reality tearing apart, her parents' bodies imploded. Meghan stumbled back; a scream caught in her throat as she found herself drenched in warm, viscous liquid.

She stood there, frozen in shock, her mind reeling. *This can't be real, * she thought, staring at her blood-soaked hands. *This has to be another nightmare, another twisted reality. *

But the metallic scent of blood, the wet warmth soaking through her clothes, the aching void where her parents had stood moments ago – it was all horrifyingly real.

Meghan sank to her knees, a primal wail of anguish finally escaping her lips. "Why?" she screamed at the uncaring universe. "Why them and not me?"

As her cries echoed through the empty house, the world outside continued to unravel, indifferent to her loss and pain.

5 - 5

Meghan's anguished cries slowly subsided, replaced by a cold, seething rage that bubbled up from the depths of her soul. She clenched her fists, blood dripping between her fingers, as her mind raced with dark thoughts.

"The Temporal Guardians," she hissed through gritted teeth. "Drake's family. The so-called 'chosen one.' They did this. They're responsible."

She stood up abruptly, her eyes blazing with determination. "I won't let them get away with this," she muttered, pacing the room. "I'll make them pay. All of them."

Meghan's gaze fell on a family photo on the mantel, her parents' smiling faces now a cruel reminder of what she'd lost. She picked it up, her bloodied fingers leaving smears on the glass.

"I promise you," she whispered to the image, "I'll find a way to bring you back. To make this right."

A memory stirred in her mind – whispered conversations she'd overheard, rumors of an ancient artifact. "The Codex," she breathed. "That's the key."

Meghan set the photo down gently, her resolve hardening. "I'll steal it. I'll rewrite history. I'll erase the Temporal Guardians from existence if I have to."

She turned towards the door, a new purpose driving her. "They think they can play God with our lives? Well, two can play at that game. And I've got nothing left to lose."

As Meghan stepped out into the chaos-stricken world, her heart was ice, her mind aflame with vengeance. The multiverse had taken everything from her – now, she would take everything from it.

Mushroom Cloud Awakening

Red World – 2024

1 - 2

The world shattered with a blinding flash and deafening roar. Dr. Rachel Summers instinctively shielded her eyes, her heart pounding as the bunker trembled around them. Through the tiny reinforced window, she glimpsed a mushroom cloud blooming on the horizon, its deadly beauty a stark contrast to the chaos unfolding below.

"My God," Linda whispered, her voice trembling. "They've actually done it."

Rachel's mind raced, processing the implications. "China's made the first move. The U.S. won't be far behind."

As if on cue, alarms blared throughout the Bridgewater Research Institute's underground facility. Screens flickered to life, displaying a barrage of missile launches across the globe. Rachel watched in horror as years of delicate international relations crumbled in mere minutes.

Harrison paced the room, his youthful energy barely contained. "We can't just sit here! There has to be something we can do!"

Rachel closed her eyes, centering herself. The weight of responsibility settled heavily on her shoulders. Drake's work, his sacrifice – it couldn't be for nothing. She turned to face her team, her voice steady despite the tremors that continued to rock the bunker.

"We may not be able to stop this immediate carnage," she began, her tone infused with the calm authority that had guided them through countless crises, "but we can work towards preventing it from ever happening."

Linda looked up, hope kindling in her eyes. "You mean..."

Rachel nodded. "Drake's research. The multiversal mapping. We have the foundation – now we need to build upon it."

As she spoke, Rachel's mind whirred with possibilities. The virus, the collapsing timelines, and now this global conflagration – they were all connected, she was sure of it. If they could just find the right thread to pull...

"We're going to need a name," Harrison interjected, his earlier restlessness replaced by a focused determination. "Something that reflects our mission."

Rachel allowed herself a small smile. Even in the face of Armageddon, Harrison's spirit remained unbroken. "What did you have in mind?"

"The Temporal Guardians," he said without hesitation. "Keepers of the Multiverse."

The name settled over the room, carrying with it a sense of purpose and destiny. Rachel nodded, feeling a spark of hope ignite within her chest.

"And a symbol," Linda added softly. "Something to identify ourselves, to unite us."

Rachel pondered for a moment; her brow furrowed in concentration. "Any ideas?"

Harrison's eyes lit up. "It's been in front of us the whole time," he exclaimed. "The green dragon!"

As understanding dawned on their faces, Rachel felt a surge of emotion. Drake's legacy, their shared history – it all coalesced in that moment.

"The green dragon it is," she declared, her voice steady and resolute. "From this day forward, we are the Temporal Guardians. Our mission: to mend the broken timelines and prevent this destruction from ever occurring."

As the world above them descended into madness, a new hope was born in the depths of the Bridgewater bunker. Rachel looked at her team – no, her fellow Guardians – and saw in their eyes the same determination that burned within her.

"Let's get to work," she said, rolling up her sleeves. "We have a multiverse to save."

Desolation of Bridgewater

20 years later – the future made present – the worlds have collided and now there is but one reality

1 - 2

The scorched landscape stretched endlessly, a testament to the devastation wrought by the collision of universes two decades ago. Gabriel limped along the cracked asphalt, his scarred face twisted in a grimace as he surveyed the desolation around him. Having abandoned Harrison in this world to fight for his own survival. Skeletal remains of buildings jutted from the earth like broken teeth, while the acrid smell of decay hung heavy in the air.

As he approached a makeshift settlement on the outskirts of what was once a thriving city, Gabriel's sharp eyes caught sight of a familiar white-robed figure. A Temporal Guardian. His lips curled into a sneer.

"Greetings, citizen," the Guardian called out, her voice carrying a forced cheerfulness that grated on Gabriel's nerves. "What brings you to our humble community?"

Gabriel considered his response carefully. These self-appointed peacekeepers were a nuisance, but they could also be useful. "Just passing through," he replied, his tone carefully neutral. "Looking for supplies, perhaps some information."

The Guardian's eyes narrowed slightly. "Information about what, exactly?"

Gabriel limped closer, his mind racing. How much should he reveal? These fools believed they could turn back time, undo the apocalypse. Little did they know, he had set those events in motion for a reason.

"I've heard whispers," he said, letting a hint of desperation creep into his voice, "of a way to reverse all this. To go back to before... before everything fell apart."

The Guardian's posture relaxed slightly, sympathy softening her features. "Ah, I see. You're not the first to come seeking such knowledge. We Temporal Guardians are working tirelessly to find a solution, to restore balance to the multiverse."

Gabriel nodded, feigning interest while inwardly scoffing at their naivety. If only they knew the true nature of the cosmic equilibrium they sought to maintain.

"Perhaps you'd like to stay a while?" the Guardian offered. "We have food, shelter, and the protection of our order. It's dangerous out there for lone wanderers."

For a moment, Gabriel was tempted to refuse. His mission required secrecy, and lingering too long in one place was risky. But the allure of gathering more intelligence on the Guardians' plans was too strong to resist.

"That would be... most appreciated," he said, forcing a grateful smile onto his scarred face.

As the Guardian led him into the settlement, Gabriel's mind whirled with possibilities. These fools, with their dreams of restoring a flawed past, were playing right into his hands. Little did they know, the true chosen one walked among them, ready to shape the future according to his grand design.

3 - 4

The Bridgewater Research Institute loomed before Gabriel, a monolithic structure of reinforced concrete and gleaming steel, its imposing facade a stark contrast to the desolate wasteland surrounding it. Armed guards patrolled the perimeter, their vigilant eyes scanning the horizon for any signs of threat.

Gabriel approached the main entrance, his heart racing beneath his tattered cloak. *This is it,* he thought. *The culmination of years of planning. The key to reshaping reality itself.*

As he drew closer, a shrill alarm pierced the air. Red lights flashed along the building's exterior, and guards materialized from hidden alcoves, their weapons trained on him.

"Halt!" barked a burly guard, his face obscured by a tactical helmet. "Identify yourself immediately!"

Gabriel raised his hands slowly, careful not to make any sudden movements. "I mean no harm," he called out, his voice steady despite the adrenaline coursing through his veins. "I've come seeking knowledge, nothing more."

A female guard stepped forward, her eyes narrowing suspiciously. "Knowledge? This isn't a public library, stranger. Turn back now, or we'll be forced to take action."

If only they knew the power I possess, Gabriel mused, a wry smile tugging at his lips. Aloud, he said, "Please, I've traveled so far. Surely there's someone here who can help me understand what happened to our world?"

The guards exchanged glances, their weapons still raised. Gabriel could sense their uncertainty, the conflict between their duty and the remnants of human compassion that still lingered in this harsh new reality.

"I know about the scientists here," Gabriel pressed, gesturing towards the building. "The ones in white robes with the green dragon emblem. They're working to fix things, aren't they? To make the world right again?"

The female guard's eyes widened slightly. "How do you know about that?" she demanded.

Gabriel shrugged, feigning innocence. "Word travels, even in a broken world. I just want to understand. To help, if I can."

As he spoke, the main doors of the institute slid open with a hydraulic hiss. Two figures emerged, their white robes billowing in the dusty wind, the green dragon emblems on their chests catching the fading light.

Perfect, Gabriel thought, suppressing a triumphant grin. *Now, the real game begins.*

Before they could introduce themselves there was a blinding white light and suddenly Gabriel was gone as quickly as he came.

5 - 6

As if time stood still right where Gabriel stood was now a cloaked figure dressed in white.

Dr. Rachel Summers strode forward, her eyes narrowing as she took in the scene before her. The cloaked figure stood at the center of a ring of armed guards, an island of calm amid a sea of tension. Linda Miller followed close behind, her gentle presence a stark contrast to the hostility in the air.

"What's the meaning of this intrusion?" Dr. Summers demanded, her voice sharp and authoritative. She glanced at the guards, then back to the mysterious visitor. "Who goes there, and what do you want?"

The cloaked figure chuckled softly, a sound that sent a warmth down Linda's spine. With deliberate slowness, he reached up and pulled back his hood, revealing a face that radiated confidence and charm.

"Who am I?" he repeated, his eyes twinkling with amusement. "Why, I'm the one you've been searching for all this time. The chosen one, as some might say." He paused, savoring the stunned silence that followed his declaration. "But please," he added with a casual wave of his hand, "call me Justin."

Dr. Summers felt her heart race, a mixture of excitement and skepticism coursing through her veins. *Could it be true?* she wondered. *After all this time, has the prophecy finally come to pass?* Aloud, she said, "That's quite a claim, Justin. What makes you so certain you're the one we've been looking for?"

Justin's smile widened, a spiritual gleam in his eyes. "Oh, I have my ways, Doctor. Let's just say I've seen things... experienced things that would make your scientific mind question everything."

Linda stepped forward, her voice soft but steady. "If you truly are who you claim to be, then you must understand the gravity of the situation. Our world... all worlds... hang in the balance."

Justin's gaze softened as it fell on Linda. "Oh, I understand more than you know, my dear. The question is, are you ready for the answers I bring?"

Epilogue – The Grey World

1 - 1

The cracked asphalt stretched ahead like a dark ribbon, winding through the twilight. Drake's hands gripped the steering wheel, his knuckles white as he navigated the treacherous curves.

"This road is a lawsuit waiting to happen," Drake muttered, his eyes flicking to the rearview mirror. "I'm going to petition the city council next week. It's criminally negligent to leave it like this."

Linda turned to him, her elegant evening dress a stark contrast to the dilapidated surroundings. "You're right, dear. It's a miracle there haven't been more accidents."

Drake nodded, a familiar fire kindling in his chest. He lived for these moments – the chance to right wrongs, to bring order to chaos. "I'll draft the proposal tomorrow. We can't let bureaucratic red tape endanger lives."

Harrison piped up from the backseat, his voice tinged with pride. "Dad's going to save the day again!"

A warm smile tugged at Drake's lips, but it quickly faded as headlights suddenly flooded the car's interior. A black sedan roared up behind them, horn blaring.

Drake's pulse quickened. "What the hell?"

The sedan lurched closer, its grille filling the rearview mirror. Drake's grip tightened on the wheel as they approached a sharp bend. To their right, the ground fell away into a steep embankment, a silvery stream glinting far below. No guardrail stood between them and disaster.

A chill ran down Drake's spine. This felt hauntingly familiar – the aggressive driver, the dangerous road, his family in peril. For a heartbeat, he was paralyzed by an overwhelming sense of déjà vu.

"Drake?" Linda's voice was taut with fear.

He shook off the strange sensation. "It's okay. I'm pulling over."

But before he could, the sedan abruptly swerved around them, engine roaring as it sped into the night.

A collective sigh of relief filled the car. Drake's shoulders sagged, the tension draining from his body.

"What a jerk," Harrison muttered.

Linda reached over, squeezing Drake's arm. "You handled that perfectly, honey."

Drake nodded, but couldn't shake the lingering unease. Why had that moment felt so familiar? So... inevitable?

He pushed the thought aside, focusing on the warm glow of the restaurant's lights appearing in the distance. "So, who's ready for some overpriced seafood?"

As his family's laughter filled the car, Drake allowed himself to relax. But a part of him remained on edge, as if waiting for the other shoe to drop in a cosmic game he didn't understand.

To Be Continued...

Stay tuned for Book 3 of the Drake Miller Saga: The Grey World.

<u>Other Books in the Drake Miller Saga:</u>
Worlds Apart: A world so cold novel

<u>Other Books by this Author:</u>
Vicious Circle (Screenplay)
World So Cold: A collection of short stories

| Page

www.ingramcontent.com/pod-product-compliance
Lightning Source LLC
Chambersburg PA
CBHW082122180726
48291CB00011B/2806